Books by David Gurr

Troika

A Woman Called Scylla

An American Spy Story

The Action of the Tiger

On The Endangered List

The Ring Master

The Voice of the Crane

Arcadia We$t

www.davidgurr.ca

The
Charlatan
Variations
A Novel Autobiography

David Gurr

QUARRY PRESS

Cataloging in publication data is available.

ISBN 978-1-55082-376-9

Text design by Paul Dalcanale and updated for this revision by Susan Hannah.
Interior illustrations by Julie McIntyre © CARCC 2008.
Cover design by Susan Hannah featuring a photo by Diane Tolomeo.
Set in Garamond No 12.
Published by Quarry Press Inc., PO Box 1061, Kingston, ON K7L 4Y5
www.quarrypress.com

www.davidgurr.ca

For **D***iane, who made our trip to Forli possible ...*
and for **T***eddy, who rests there ...*

ACKNOWLEDGEMENTS

I am most grateful to the following for permission to reprint copyrighted material:

Faber and Faber for lines from *The Love Song of J. Alfred Prufrock,* by T.S. Eliot, and especially to A.J., who suggested that I use them.

The *Victoria Times-Colonist* for the D-Day article.

Marion Freeman Wakeman, for the illustration on page 120, from the frontispiece to *The Curious Lobster's Island,* published by Jonathan Cape, 1942 edition.

Quotations from *A Hundred Years in The Highlands,* written by my Great Great Great Uncle Osgood Hanbury MacKenzie of Inverewe (who also created his magnificent garden there, starting at the stripling's age of twenty, then waiting an equal number of years for windbreak trees to grow!), from the Edward Arnold, London, 1922 edition.

Thanks to the Writers' Trust of Canada through the Woodcock Fund for their financial and psychological support at a difficult moment while writing this book.

VARIATIONS

Childhood memories

DAVID GURR

Sixty-five years ago, on the sixth day of this sixth month, U.S. Rangers scaled the cliffs at Omaha Beach, in Normandy. I think I must be the last person still alive who watched them rehearse it. I was eight, living in a villa on top of a cliff in Dorset. (The villa looked like the hotel in *Fawlty Towers*.) The closest village was a mile away. Behind our house the fields were mined, guarded by barbed wire and scarlet signs with death's heads on them. On the beach below the house a searchlight battery was manned by a mini-platoon of soldiers in khaki battledress and

FAMILY PHOTO
Eight-year-old David Gurr in the replica British army battledress created by his mother in 1944.

tin helmets, who smoked cigarettes by day and stabbed the sky every night. Occasionally they stabbed a German bomber. Sometimes they let me sit in the seat and turn the handle that kept the beam on target. It was a lot of fun, but serious too. I had my own battledress and tin hat. The battledress was made by my mother.

I was the only male in a house full of women. My mother, her two guardians (a pair of maiden "Aunts" in their late sixties), my baby sister and a nanny: Doreen, a young girl from the village. There was a second villa next to ours, but it was empty for the Duration. The first exciting surprise was coming home from my day school in Bridport to find the empty villa full of American soldiers with black paint on their faces. There was also a tank at the bottom of the hill of Cliff Road leading to our house. The tank was to stop cars but as I had a bicycle the tank driver let me through.

The second surprise was an Army officer talking to my mother, the Aunts, and Doreen. He was standing in the sunroom, which had a super

of the Longest Day

view out over the English Channel. The officer said that something Very Special was going to happen. It would take about ten days. We could stay and watch it but we couldn't use the telephone, or write letters, or go to the village. When the Aunts said, "What about shopping?" the officer told them that the Army would do it. He also said that if we did use the telephone or write letters, the Army would know, and we would have to leave the house and be taken somewhere else until the Very Special thing was over. The Aunts said of course they would Do their Duty. (They used to stand to attention when the wireless played *God Save the King* or the *Hallelujah Chorus*.) My mother — who had an American GI boyfriend while the man I thought was my father was away in Ceylon with the Royal Marines — was cross, and Doreen was frightened because her family wouldn't know why she didn't come back to them on her Saturday afternoon off, but the officer said the Army would explain that.

It was difficult to sleep because of the excitement of having a ten day Special Holiday. The next morning I got up early and crawled out along my favourite ledge of the crumbling sandstone cliff to try and find an egg in the burrows of the puffins who nested there. The U.S. Rangers arrived at that moment. They came out of the sea in an amphibious half-tank, called a DUKW. Then they fired rockets with ropes which went right past my ledge. The ropes had anchors on the ends that dug into the turf on the top of the cliff. Then the Rangers climbed up the ropes. (Forty years later I watched them do it again. You can too if you get a video of John Wayne winning the War in *The Longest Day*. The footage used in the film was actually shot on my beach. If the camera was a little to the left you could see me on the ledge.)

At the end of the ten days all the American soldiers in the next door villa, and their DUKWs, went away. I cried a lot because one of the soldiers had a Russian name and sang me songs like *The Volga Boatmen*. Some of the soldiers used to take out photos of their own children and look at them. Then thousands of gliders flew over the minefields behind our house. We heard gunfire all day long. That night there was a

Childhood D-Day memories, cont'd

big storm. A carrier pigeon landed on the ledge of my nursery window. The pigeon had a band on its leg. The same Army officer came back the next day and thanked us all for not Disobeying the Rules, and took away the pigeon. He said it was Very Special too.

This year, in May, I went to see the other side of the English Channel. The side where they truly did do something special. I also went to the furthest southern tip of Sicily, and up through Italy, to a War Cemetery at Forli, where the man, whom my mother later said almost certainly was my real father, lies buried.

FAMILY PHOTO
David Gurr stands on one of the Normandy invasion beaches, May 23rd. As a boy he watched from his home as U.S. soldiers prepared for their bloody assault on Omaha Beach.

But all that, and the utter solemnity of the American Cemetery above Omaha Beach — where I had no way of telling how many of those soldiers next door, with their painted black faces, who looked at photos of their children, or sang to me, became names now inscribed in white stone — all that is part of an adult story.

After various Blitz, Evacuation, and D-Day boyhood adventures, David Gurr immigrated to Victoria, British Columbia, in 1948. He served in the Royal Canadian Navy for seventeen years, then designed and built West Coast houses before deciding to write novels.

11

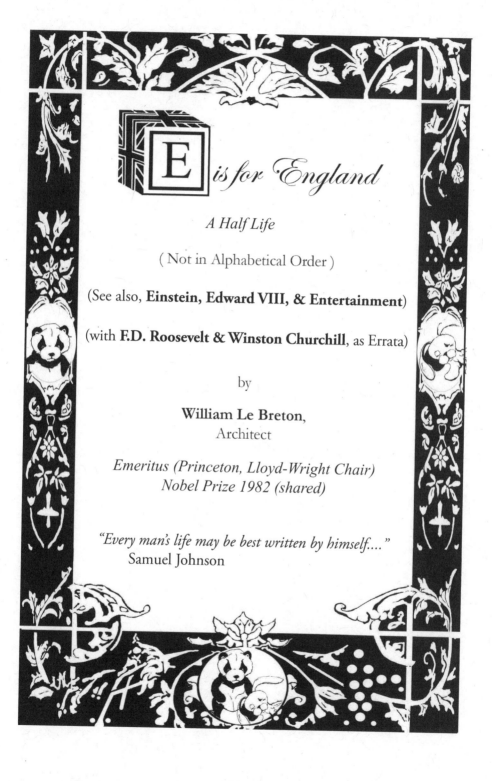

E is for England

A Half Life

(Not in Alphabetical Order)

(See also, **Einstein, Edward VIII, & Entertainment**)

(with **F.D. Roosevelt & Winston Churchill**, as Errata)

by

William Le Breton,
Architect

Emeritus (Princeton, Lloyd-Wright Chair)
Nobel Prize 1982 (shared)

"Every man's life may be best written by himself...."
Samuel Johnson

England

Preface

It is true I am a god — Einstein always called me his little *Marktschreier*, a charlatan — but who can agree with the humble opinion of a man who made the first letter of his own name equal the unleashed power of the sun?

$E = mc^2$! Humility may stand highest in the Christian graces of Ralph Waldo Emerson but Sherlock Holmes is a truer judge. "Mediocrity knows nothing higher than itself, but talent instantly recognizes genius."

I offer that direct extraction from Sir Arthur Conan-Doyle's *Valley of Fear* because it was the last thought but one to enter my mind as I fought to regain control of my plunging Avenger fighter aircraft before we both struck that New Guinea volcano. . . .

And now I write these words aboard a ship, the *MV Southern Cross*, bearing me (and six-hundred far more illustrious fellow-citizens of Contentment Cay than I) on an Association Cruise — by the extra-ordinary co-incidence I am more than ever convinced is the random Hand which guides our fate — which will, in two short weeks, re-unite me with that Lost Island World of savage worshippers from fifty years ago, to greet together the Third Millennium.

I said, a last thought but one . . .

A thought we now know (through analysis of Japanese Naval Radio traffic) that I shared with my Kamikazi brethren of the air as they prepared for their Final Plunge. The last word from their lips into the Eternal Ether.

A pure Flame to whom I dedicate this Work:
Mother . . . !

Us in Hyde Park

DAVID GURR

May-Day Lunch

Vancouver Island,
May 1st, 19-ish

Charlie : *(aka, Mother, at 75-ish, discussing Mount St. Helens, while toying with Poached Salmon.)*

"Talking about volcanoes, of
course you do know that your
father — Jim — wasn't really your
father? I suppose it doesn't matter
too much now that you're fiftyish.
After all, you weren't really you
then, either — you were born as
somebody else, I used to call you my
Darling Willum. I've explained in a
rather longish letter. You'll have to
excuse the spelling."

Christmas
Glen Lake.

Dearest David.

If you are reading this it will mean that death or a physical disaster overtook me. I hope I will have talked with you but the years at time of writing have not been kind for you and yours. I cannot predict how you will feel as you read on. Sometimes I think you must know or have wondered and I never knew how much the nurse in Dr L's office said to you, for I think James talked a lot to him. I speak of James because he was never 'Jim' till latterly —

Anyway I keep waiting for securer times to prevail but must be realistic at 73. So just in case I'm snatched before I'm ready to go it is important I get substance on paper. What I'm working up to & which may not be a shock to you is that James is your adopted Father.

I wanted you to know from an early age but Jim's fragile ego would never agree. He was afraid 'you would love him less' if you knew. He really loved and wanted you but we know now that his personality was in no way equipped to handle the traumers of parent hood or family life —

It is quite difficult to get ages-dates exact but at the age of 19 or 20 I had cast the trammels of the darling Aunts (Dorothea and Elspie) and was living in London. Sister Nan too was there but she was 5 yrs my senior & all our girlhood we had no common ground, after our parents both died. Nan was above & beyond me — strict, judgemental, disapproving. (This might hurt her but it's how she seemed to me then). We were poles apart & never saw one another.

I was quite wild, I have to say, men & I were Bees & honey I had a marvellous time discovering that I wasn't just a fat plain little girl in a grey sweater & skirt in winter and a brown holland dress in summer. Dorothea and Elspie never complimented on appearance — clothing was

of the best but not to attract. Sex to the Aunts
was 'Close your eyes & think of England!'

I shared an apartment flat with a french girl
friend, Pauline. Two paralell streets faced each
other and a railed-off garden ran up the middle,
about as wide as Douglas Street in Victoria.
These were Oxford and Cambridge Terrace. The
houses were old & converted to flats — occupied
by struggling actors — one of whom was later to
take me for evenings of 'chat' and not much to
drink to his friends' apartment.

The friends were struggling at the Old Vic
in a Midsummer Night's Dream — their names,
Olivier, Richardson, Gielgud and Redgrave — we
were all poor but no one felt deprived or hard
done by — it was a lot less 'gimme' society than
now. And then at a party I met a young man and it
wasn't long before we were inseperable and madly
in Love. In these days we would have just moved
in together. Life then was not so simple.

Edward Brisbane-Le Breton (Teddy) lived at
home in the suburb of Watford (or was it Hendon)
no Watford I'm sure. He lived with his father, an
authoritative bitter Vice Admiral — this was a
period of restraint for the Royal Navy and he had
been axed and bore a huge grudge. Anyway he ruled
Teddy & older brother with a cruel tonge and
rigid house rules. In the 30's young men accepted
a way of life they would never tolerate now.

Teddy worked in some office capacity as a
junior thanks to 'Daddy's connections' for W.H.
Wills Tobacco (I think they became Players, not
sure). He was on the Wills cricket team and a
Rugby team and so when matches were played or
practised — he didn't go home. By hook or crook
we managed lots of weekends & whatever the
excuses old Admiral Dad bought it.

We were the same age and to tell the truth
I don't think we ever looked at the idea of
marrying — we concentrated on having a marvellous
time. After cricket & Rugby games there were
always parties or meeting in the local pub. To
Cambridge for May Week and Ascot for the Derby,

always on the cheap and with a group. Teddy had a
beat up old Morris two-seater with a rumble seat
and we'd somehow pile in and off. In the summer
often to the sea, Brighton, Tennis at Wimbledon—
   He was handsome in a regular English way
— medium height & build, light brown short
hair, blue grey eyes a flush of colour on his
cheekbones. Looked good in browns. Even tempered,
easy going conservative, not very ambitious a
'Nanky Poo' sort of young man with a background
and upbringing much like mine. His mother had
died when he was about 16 —
   Anyway my love — this man who I dearly, dearly
loved fathered you. We must (and were) have been
incredibly ignorant and naive. I don't recall
that it occurred to either of us that we might
have a child, we were totally carefree and you
my love were the result, but as the country folk
would say 'he were a love child.'
   How will you re-act? 'Out of wedlock' is
almost prestige in 1980's day and age. Your
generation long ago moved away from the attitudes
of the 30's. In an era of fullest knowledge
and matter of fact protection it must seem
extraordinary to have gone our blissful way.
Of course we were terrified when we knew via Dr
that I was pregnant and we talked about getting
married but we had no savings & Teddy as a
junior-junior had few 'prospects'.
   Finally he talked with his brother who talked
to God ('dear old Dad!') and the heavans crashed
around us! 'Disinherit!' 'Without a penny!'
'Leave this house!' and on & on. The man wielded
power, he called the shots. Teddy on pain of
'being cast out' was forbidden to see me —
   'Daddy' talked to his lawyers who talked to
me — unsophisticated, sheltered me. Now I would
have fought them tooth & nail by God.
   How Victorian and feeble we must both seem to
you — Ready cash was a very real factor & young
men did obey in those days — there were no kindly
social work ladies to strew rose petals along the
rocky path!!

DAVID GURR

I was lucky that I remained extremely well
& 'didn't show' so I could go on working till
birth day. I was on call for two or three french
fashion houses in Chelsea — Funny things you
remember. I travelled of course by bus (few of
the young had cars) & I ran and jumped on as
always. Sometimes if the conductor didn't catch
my arm I wanted to say 'don't you know I'm having
a baby?' I thought I should receive the respect
due my interesting condition. It was possibly in
Dec or Jan that my roomate Pauline panicked and
spilled the beans to Nan.

It must have been a huge shock to 'school-
teacher, straight laced Nan'. But sister rose
to the occasion and never scolded or preached as
we planned and replanned the future. We decided
quite firmly that you would be adopted — prior to
birth it was pretty easy to be dispassionate — as
the best and only solution.

Teddy would make time we could be together
but Daddy the Admiral's shadow was over us and we
couldn't see a future.

Nan & I had a gruesome day (funny in
retrospect) when the Aunts wrote that they were
coming up to London from Whitchurch and would
we lunch at their club in Cavendish Square. God
knows how we got through the day — I know I had
a Jeagur Top Coat 3/4 length and loose in large
check tweed — I guess I kept it on all thro'
the meal. Anyway the visit was happy & the old
darlings went happily off to the Albert Hall.

Time was flying and we had to decide where
I was going to live before and following your
birth. Pauline, a good R.C., knew some Nuns who
had a House of Retreat and always room for 3 or 4
young mothers. This proved an excellent solution.
The Nuns were kindness itself with a great
sense of fun — no preaching — rather Aunt Elspie
people.

In the late afternoon of Feb 4th labour began.
After an hour or two the Sisters put on their
capes and matter of factly said we would walk to
the hospital — they assured me that walking was

the finest exercise for me at this point. So in
the clear, frosty very cold London evening, a
Sister comfortably on each side of me we walked.
Twenty, twenty-five minutes — I don't know. I do
know I was totally unprepared & ignorant of what
to expect thro'out the birthing process.

Anyway love you made your way into this world
around 6.30 a.m Feb. 5 1936 in Queen Charlottes
Hospital. Marylebone — London.

They didn't put babies in seperate rooms
then — little bassinettes hung at the foot of
each bed — if you stretched with your toe you
could rock the cradle if your baby cried. We were
all hospitalised for two weeks — you were breast
fed and I realised that I could never let you go
for Adoption.

When I broke that news to Nan she was very
good & never tried to persuade me otherwise tho'
I imagine she was worried sick how we'd make out.
She arranged for me to stay with her best friend
Kita Corbett in Surrey while we sorted things out.

You were duly christened William Brisbane
Le Breton Harvey. I wanted to Register you
without my Maiden name but the old Clerks were
very intimidating as to legalities, 'No hyphen
with Brisbane!' — and dire punishment to use
the father's name last unless you were married.
Nowadays of course one would demand 'one's
rights'.

I have thought you should use William Brisbane
Le Breton as a nom de plume — it's legally
yours — or just William Le Breton sounds good to
me. ('A Proper writer's name for a Proper Novel,'
Dorothea would say. I've often wanted to do a
Harlequin myself.)

At this distance plans get fuzzy. But Kita
had a friend Ann Crowe who had a nursery (like
the Aunts), she would have you while I looked for
a job & a flat. Now you remember the link. Ann
Crowe was the lady at 'the White House' down at
Reigate in Surrey where you stayed when you were
evacuated from London Bombing.

I found an apartment near Marble Arch on

Cambridge Terrace (no blacks were acceptable I
believe it's now overrun.) A Scottish widow lady
'Auntie Rita' owned the big old house. She lived
in the basement. A dignified frenchman, Monsieur
Laurillard (funny the things that are recalled
clearly) a part-time something to do with Freud,
was on the main, he used to call you 'mon
petit Guillaume'. He was a Warden in the Blitz.
Upstairs Dorothea Clayton a violinist and teacher
(a 'Brown Owl' type) — I had known her for some
time & she was your Godmother.

Next there was you & me and up in the very
top an aspiring young Shakespearian actor — Teddy
Bach, who would introduce me to the Old Vic (tho'
I never liked Shakespear) & his friends. The old
portable H.M.V record player you used to play
endlessly was Redgrave's. Michael asked me to
house it when he went on tour as his landlady
wanted it in lieu of unpaid rent.

Our flat had very good high windows and a
small balcony big enough for plants and a nine
inch railing, there's a story!

One day I was tidying the mantlepiece and
looked into the mirror. In it I saw you outside
the window settling down in the tiny balcony.
I've never moved so fast before or since &
without a word snatched you back. When Monsieur
L returned from whatever he did by way of real
work Auntie Rita had him nail the bottom of the
windows firmly shut.

It was a companionable house and the tenants
welcomed & loved you. It didn't cost much to
live quite adequately. I had an odd variety of
jobs — modelling again — cashier in an Odeon — I
don't remember.

Granny Monk was a prop & stay. She lived in a
tiny, cluttered little house in a lane that ran at
the back. She was neat as a pin & short & plump.
She loved you. I have a picture of walking in one
afternoon — you were bare naked leaping up & down
on her sofa while she rocked in her chair and
knitted. 'Carnt do nuffin' with him mum' she said
placidly.

We walked lots, Dorothea Clayton me & you in
the pram into Hyde Park, beside the Serpentine to
feed the ducks, and play by the Peter Pan Statue.
We sat on the benches comparing notes with other
young Mothers — and uniformed nannys who offered
firm advice to us silly young things.

And then Teddy began to drop by.

He had got our address from Pauline. He was
fascinated by you and the idea of having a child
but frightened of the implied responsibilities of
this. It's probably hard for you to believe that
we did love one another so much yet he couldn't
go against his father. We didn't waste time on
post mortems or talk of marraige. We three walked
in the park or into the country in his same
rattle trap little Morris —

Now on a side street near Granny Monk there
was a small restaurant in a house run by two
sisters. Home cooking, it was always packed.
Medical students from St Marys Hospital and
the assortment of us who lived nearby — people
squeezed onto a chair and sometimes shared one.
And so on occasion we shared a table with a man
who was quite different in dress & deportment
from most of the regulars. The owner ladies
fussed over him 'dear Mr Gauer' he left large
tips on the table, most of us left pennies
(sixpence was a lot). Debonair & sophisticated
best describe him. He wore good suits starched
white shirts & was immaculate obviously a man
about town — tho' Nan loathed, and called him a
'lounge lizard' because of his Brylcreem hair.

He had a good new car, a Vauxhall, and took me
to concerts. (I was bored with some.) The Music
Hall became a regular Saturday date. We listened
to the speakers in Hyde Park on Sundays — he paid
you a great deal of attention — played games &
bought presents. He lived near us where Oxford &
Cambridge Terraces became Sussex Gardens which
had slightly larger flats and Professional people
as tenants and felt itself superior.

He loved to take you around with him & I
suspect even then he introduced you as his son —

Brylcreem Lounge Lizard

and later when he came to the idea of marrying
I believe he wanted a son much more than a wife.
(Looking back that is.)

He had been married twice. The first at about
18 to a woman nearly double his age — Mickie.
It didn't last long & she divorced him and
married an Australian — it seems to have been
a Mother / son affair & they parted I believe
amicably. Then he married a concert singer
Gladys Knight — that was very unhappy — two
temperemental people and he divorced Gladys. She
had fallen for a rich business man who offered
Jim several thousand pounds if James would let
Gladys bring the divorce. Jim in his odd way
refused to accept such a deal — and told me he
felt at the time 'two divorces as "the guilty
party" ' might give any other woman cause to
pause if he ever wanted to marry again.

He was just coming up for air about the time
we met and certainly we never talked marraige.
He gradually assumed more & more of my time — was
immensely jealous of Teddy & couldn't countenance
any continuing contact between Teddy you or I.

He encouraged me to quit working and we took
the flat on Boundary Road, in Hampstead, near
the Heath. It was a good time — plenty of Jim's
friends — parties — a nice garden for you to
play in. It is hard to sort out time spaces over
that period. War was creeping up on us. We were
desparately ashamed of not going to Austria's
help and when Hitler went into Poland there was
only a huge feeling of relief when at last we
acted. It's interesting to see, looking back how
one got emotionally ready to go to war

When Jim did begin to talk of marraige it
seemed like a marvellous thing for you & I
thought I loved him — never like I loved Teddy
(most of Jim was I think the glamour of new
experiences & Man about Town bit.) His friends
begged us not to — said they'd give us a year or
less.

I was no judge of character and knew nothing
of neurosies, psychosis etc. etc. There was an

episode only once in the period before we married
but I couldn't read the signal. One evening on
no pretext he flew into an ungovernable rage,
threw things and then didn't speak for two days.
I had never seen such behavior but it carried no
message to me — no danger signals waved.
     Ah me what if I had taken you and run —
     In this period Teddy phoned and asked to
meet. We did and he seriously asked me to marry.
With all my heart I wanted to but I was afraid
he might fail me that in the crunch 'Daddy' the
Admiral would once again prevail.
     Jim seemed to offer the best security for us —
he certainly loved us, you particularly — who
could guess at the underlying shattered ego?
the need for everyone connected with him to be
perfect! He wanted so much to be his own ideal:
a generous, sensitive loving parent and husband.
Luckily for him he believes he has achieved this.
     Anyway I made my choice and let Teddy go
out of our lives. I'm sure he joined up right
away — R.N. perhaps because of his father, but
I suspect it was a Commando Unit or Air Combat.
I never knew if he survived the war — he was
the sort of young Englishman who died in their
thousands.
     He hoped in the face of all our problems
something would work out for him, you, and me.
But Jim couldn't share, it was too threatening,
not even to keep pictures, like Us in Hyde Park
which I barely managed to save — and he has
always been dead against you knowing he adopted
you — as I say, fearing you would 'love him
less'.
     Adoption in England was a simple and straight
forward affair — no investigations, no social
worker report. We went with you before a little
old Judge in the local Marylebone Court. He asked
a few questions, we were in & out in ten minutes
& you were re-registered with names of Jim's
choice — I would have liked to keep my Darling
Willum at least, but no.
     We must have been married before that (the

certificate is in the safety deposit in Langford
Commerce Bank) — I can't set the year but know
it was Jim's birthday, June 20. in Marylebone
Registry Office. (All the theatre stars got
married there because of course they'd all been
divorced and Churches wouldn't marry you at that
time.) Nan was there and Jessie Franks the buyer
from Paris you liked, she taught you French. And
Marjorie & Timmy Vaughan — a charmer who elected
himself your Godfather, died in one of the
Bombing raids.

And now you begin to see the pattern —
Evacuated out of the blitz to your old friend,
Ann Crowe at Reigate, and then when Jim was
called into the Royal Marines the Aunts suggested
we go up to them, near Monmouth — until then they
had not met you or James. You know how much they
loved you but they never really accepted Jim.
His ways were quite foreign, his world a strange
one to them. In their old fashioned way they had
always the feeling I had married 'into trade'
'beneath me'.

They were good solid years with the Aunts
— then Bunna was born before Jim was posted
overseas. The Aunts sold Barton-Olivers 1 at
Whitchurch and bought B.O.2 in Burton Bradstock
to be near their sisters Margery & Rhoda in
Dorset. During the move you & Bun went to Ann
Crowe again while everything settled in — and we
stayed with the Aunts till it was the time (by
English standards) for you to go to prep school at
Sherbourne.

I cannot predict
Don't feel belittled — you had an awful lot
of loving people around you, most of all probably
Nan, who gave you your favourite books -- Just
William and the Curious Lobster. But Dorothea
as well, reading you Don Quixote or Pilgrims
Progress and Dickens Bleak thing — rather rich at
six. Even Great Aunt Kythe — how furious she got
when Jim called her Old Trout! — who filled you
up with all that Hundred Years in the Highlands
rubbish about being descended from Kings of

David Gurr

Scotland on our Gairloch MacKenzie side, tho'
you did look simply adorable in your Hunting
Tartan kilt. And your stuffed animals — Panda and
Rabbit.
   'P&R' as you called them.*
   Of course I have wondered what our lives
would have been had we been with Teddy — a very
conservative English pattern of upper middle
class, predictable and happy because we were
both pretty equable temperaments. Living with
Jim — well you know his oddities & problems but
that's not to say I haven't had a happy and
satisfying life.
   I've loved Canada — after Duncan, on the farm,
where you saved all our lives from the stove
gas and shot Bun with the arrow! I enjoyed the
childhood & growing years at the Lake, being a
parent, my work, good friends — the many loved
real animals — the outdoors of us riding together
up the Old Pipeline Trail and latterly Nan as a
friend, a great Joy.
   Apart from Jim — who I did love in the early
days, but I think the gap of war service, as with
so many families was too great to cement our
marraige firmly — there was all the adjustment
for him of coming back not to almost babies, but
children with minds of their own! He was always
at his best if we were all totally dependent.
   I have always liked & attracted men three
stand out in my life as lovers Teddy my one &
only true love as the stories go. Dickie B, an
American wartime fun fairy tale but painful too.
And latterly Arthur, in Qualicum Beach — the
world is exactly right for us when we are
together but Arthur loves his money & in B.C.
if he seperated he could be taken for half his
worldly goods! — the fishing tackle shop — and
love me as he protests, no woman could be worth
that sacrifice to Artie.
   I have been blessed with excellent health and
all in all the balance of the years weight out on
the positive end. This go around I have loved,
and as I am a firm believer in re-incarnation
I am very ready & interested in the next Turn
of the Wheel — what indeed will our roles
be? — there will be the feeling of familiarity

tho' we won't know how we have met before.

No Aunts' Version of the prayer book, please. Just Memorial Society cremation and my ashes in a flower bed (it's all paid for) but maybe, and depending if you intend to share this — I'd love to see the kids expressions when they learn what a wild one I was!

We've not been very demonstrative — our actions more than words, but you have been my very dear son. God bless. Your

loving Mother.

* PS: To end on a lighter note — whatever happened to P&R? They aren't in the Toy Cupboard.

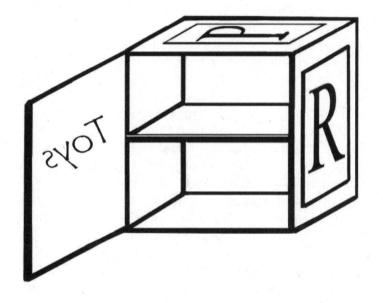

Come out, come out, wherever you are!

The lunatic lightness of that loving post script... 'whatever happened to P&R?' ... begins a descent into fragments of something too close to madness for Dearest David to handle on his own. After Mother's May Day Lunch drops on the plate, *I* is no longer our own first person. *Darling Willum* holds that unique place in her heart. D.D. finds himself shouting in the dark to an imaginary pair of stuffed animals.

...BEFORE MY MOTHER'S MAY DAY LUNCH I KNEW WHO I WAS.

"And who was that?"

Thank God I'm not Jim's!

A trick-question-and-answer exchange of such simplicity can only be delivered by the professional guile of a fully trained Shrink. The Letter drove us to one — *and because DD has no memory whatsoever of anything before the age of five* — but before we attempt to provide the next thrill-a-fifty-minute-installment, the sequence of events leading from Lunch to Couch needs to be explained.

The Lunch came out of the blue, and two weeks before the Letter.

The Lunch's casual "You do know Jim isn't your father" was an immediate maternal hit below the belt. The Letter's Harlequin Romantic attempt at an excuse for waiting half a century to tell us the good news was melodramatically further delayed because Charlie didn't have it with her. "I left it with Nan for safekeeping in her Deposit box at the bank and she's away for a fortnight, visiting a friend."

After fifty years of silent deception another fourteen days of hide-and-seek Father is child's play. The next nursery game seems obvious:

Let's Find Teddy.

The Provincial Archives, beneath the volcanic ice-cream shadow of Mount Baker, reveal a glimmer of Charlie half-truth buried in old Royal Navy Lists. Brisbane-Le Bretons have indeed served at His Majesty's pleasure, circa 1934, but as half-paid Commanders. No Admirals.

No signs of Panda and Rabbit either. The cupboard at Glen Lake where they used to rest holds only a Dinky Toy London Cab and a dog-eared *Scarlet Pimpernel* as survivors of the Mount St Helen's blast that hurled a New Daddy in our path.

We seek him here,
We seek him there,
Damned volcanoes, everywhere!

We leave the *Pimpernel* but take the Dinky Cab to join a rusted, four-inch incendiary bomb-casing — still with its silvery phosphorous inner circle: hard evidence of Hitler's war on Willum. The bomb fragment, recovered by Charlie during one Blitz night of hell in Hampstead, sits on a shelf above D.D.'s ghostly laptop, beside a Dickensian sterling ink-well, itself a tangible reminder now of what our loving Mother dismisses in her Curious Lobster Letter as that Bleak House Thing:

Illegitimacy at the Heart of England.

"You were saying you knew who you were?"

I'm a bastard.

As, in our beginner's opinion, is our first full-time prying psycho-analyst, who wormed the admission out of us. Dr.S. — shorthand for a barely five-foot South African Jewish refugee hiding in the shadows with a loaded question mark at the end of every simple statement made even more Bar Sinister by the snake sibilance of a South African Jewish accent. Like *thiss*. Also one glass eye, gold-rimmed specs, and a Doctor Strangelove limp.

But continuing our first baby steps towards the light of understanding how Charlie could have kept us as her Dirty Little Secret for so long:

The morning of the second day after Lunch brings a cheering-up maternal phone call: "It's about your Old School trunk." Painted black metal, with two hasps and handles, the tin box not only went to Sherbourne: a faded Canadian Pacific label with a picture of a three-funnelled ocean liner, *Empress of Canada*, above DESTINATION: HALIFAX NOVA SCOTIA, proves that it crossed the Atlantic. Now the trunk lies forgotten under a saddle blanket in the Glen Lake stable, where Charlie-at-75ish still keeps and rides a perverse mare called Folly. In a fit of equine inspiration or terminal boredom, Folly had kicked the hasps. The lid flew open. "You'll never guess who's inside! If you want to come and get them, Panda seems the same but Rabbit's lost an eye."

Thirty-Fifth Reunions are always bittersweet . . . in P&R's case, by the Maytime perfection of Glen Lake's rhododendron blossoms. Rabbit's missing blue-glass eye is only a ragged hole with cotton wadding sticking out beside his nose. Panda's brown-button pair are in place, but dusty, and they jiggle. Then there's the matter of the missing fur.

Panda : (*grumpily*)
"Missing fur? He's a fine one to talk!"

Rabbit : *(squinting in astonishment)*
    "Whatever's happened to His hair?"
Owner : *(huffily)*
    "Going bald early is a sign of
    virility."

"You acted out playlets with your toy animals?"

More psychoanalytic brilliance. We assume the mention of glass eyes put him onto it — wait till Dr. S-for-Strangelove finds out that our pet stuffed Eeyore had a limp — but Charlie's Poached Salmon Confession gave a clear hint. Since our earliest Toy Cupboard days the above Trio (Panda, Rabbit & Owner) have indeed addressed each other in Quixotic moments of nursery stress like the May Day Lunch and London Blitz, via Laurel & Hardy dialogue and stage directions.

After a preliminary vacuum-cleaning, the Pair are restored to their Owner's D.D. life: sitting on the shelf above the laptop, between Hitler's incendiary, and Dickens's inkwell. Balancing like Monsieur Laurillard's petit Guillaume on the third-floor Hampstead balcony.

"Have you always shifted into Present Tense to avoid the past?"

Avoiding our past is the first dodge against madness. Talking to stuffed animals comes next, but looking at Panda on the shelf helps us see things in black and white.

"And the switching to first-person plural?"

Is more of the blindingly obvious. The use of We (or neutral Owner) in our nursery playlet completes the charmed circle of self-protection. It also allows Dearest David to duck the second-most bleak question stirred up from Mother's Monsieur Laurillard Lunch stew:

Did Rabbit originally belong to Darling Willum?

"So you knew who you were?"

We only **knew** we were as curious as Mr. Lobster about our lifetime of loathing the mere idea of Jim calling himself Our Father. . . . but working ass-backwards by decades from the corner of the present Toybox madhouse into which we have been shrunk reduces us to the following Case History: a monogram on a psychiatric file at fifty; ghost-writer at forty; designer and builder of houses at thirty; commissioned naval officer at twenty.

"Lobsters propel themselves 'ass-backwards' — but before thiss?"

A child actor playing Puck in *A Midsummer Night's Dream* and hero-worshipping Olivier. *Different ships, different cap tallies.* Or, on our Prep School flannel hair-shirt name tapes, D.H.C.G., woven in red. Like paternity, changing careers with the decades was never questioned. D.H.C.G. was offered up to West End barbers as the only son begotten by James Hugh Courtney Gauer and Jim had been in Lingerie, before Gentleman-Farming, Sawmilling, and Real Estate. Switching jobs on a dime was all-in-the-Swiss-family-Gauer tradition.

"You served in several warships — but the 'different cap tallies'?"

A simple sailor's expression for Darwinian adaptation to changed circumstances: no more significant than the Gauer Family's spur-of-the-moment leap from Monsieur Laurillard's blitzed heart of London to Vancouver Island on the Nature Channel's *Rim of Fire*.

"Thisss name of Laurillard comes up frequently. Do you really blame a French analyst for the inferno of Hitler's Blitz?"

We blame him for nailing our balcony window shut, thus preventing us from watching an organ grinder and his monkey passing every day in the street below. Besides which, until a lot of recent legwork — *and because, to repeat, DD has no memory whatsoever of anything before the age of five* — we didn't know for certain that a psychoanalyst called Laurillard really existed as anything more than a figment of Charlie's fictive imagination.

"Henri Laurillard came to London to work with Freud after helping him escape from Vienna, and at the time of this Balcony episode you would only have been three when the organ grinder went by with his monkey, but what about your family's leaping to 'The Rim of Fire'?"

Seven days on a North Atlantic ocean liner, seven more on a transcontinental steam train, in the last half of December, seemed more like Dr. Zhivago's frozen Siberian exile — but once the immigrants have landed: for relative reassurance of Life in Canada we have a sister Anthea (who — which should be whom but we're being conversational — Jim calls Bunna), six years younger; an Aunt Nan (who Jim calls Goosegog), five years older than *her* sister, our mother, Charlotte (who Jim calls Charlie), a self-made social-worker, climbing to Supervisor of Adoptions — until she decided to call herself "Gotchie" (to ward off Grannie), when her first grandchild arrived.

"Your mother became a Supervisor of Adoptions, and you never asked questions about the name changes either?"

Anyone for tennisss? . . . isn't the irrelevant change of subject it appears. Charlie's Romance mentioned Teddy playing centre court at Wimbledon.

"How did you finally get your mother's letter?"

As we were about to do a midnight flit out of Vancouver, bound for Gatwick on a ghostwriting jaunt. Nan returned in the nick of flight-departure with the key to the Safety Deposit Box at the Langford Bank. Eighteen hand-written-yellow-foolscap-pages, Legal-sized, of a Harlequinned dream . . . *dropped on our lap-table as we fly over Greenland's icy mountains in the light of a midnight sun.*

"You write ghost stories?"

We can hardly expect a one-eyed South African Strangelove to grasp every nuance, but the art of writing someone else's rubbish life story seems pretty bloody straightforward. The ghosted rubbish in this case is Lord What's-His-Name's — a newly-made Peer who sold his Canadian citizenship in order to buy up Fleet Street. Charlie knew we would be going back to the UK for the Launch Parties and as a sideline entertainment, check out why she and Jim could never agree if their Wedding Anniversary was silver or gold.

"In your mother's letter, she mentions what she calls this nonsense of an old Aunt telling you of being descended from ancient Scottish Kings. Your mother also said that she didn't believe this 'ghost-writing' was being a quote, Proper Writer. Is it so surprising that having to be a 'ghost' for a new Lord What's-His-Name would make you this hostile?"

Thisssss repeated thrice makes us think of a South African snake coiled in a leather recliner immediately behind our right shoulder. What makes us *hostile* is everybody else's parents knowing exactly when they were locked into marriage, and the precise length of the Life Sentence. Charlie and Jim are obviously lying about their Anniversaries but we had always assumed it was just to hide the fact of Dearest David being born out of wedlock.

"Not that Jim wasn't your real father?"

It all happened before we were five. Anyway, between Lord What's His Launch Parties, the legal entity known as *I-D.G.* takes a trip back in time to Dickens's London, still alive and well in the cellars beneath the Probate Division of Somerset House. Lord Chancellor's procedures for the examination of a Last Will & Testament haven't changed since the first Bleak Jarndyce versused Jarndyce; documents still pass via hand-to-hand transmission. For trivial amounts of petty cash (a separate 10p for each petty request) massive Ledgers can still be consulted; a Name still discerned, an ancient, bent Clerk still summoned, a Bell still rung . . . a creaking-dumb-waiter Lift sent to unseen depths where unseen Niebelungs toil in mines of words and wishes from those who departed as far away as five centuries ago — or yesterday afternoon.

For either span, a long, long pause . . .

"Do you think your mother would call such a long description 'proper writing'?"

Mind your own beeswax candles. The main desk at Somerset House still has one, 'In case of Power Failure'. Another bell! The creaking lift ascends. The ancient Clerk returns bearing a document bound with Lord Chancellor's red ribbon. I, Edward Le Breton, being of sound mind . . . Edward in copperplate script is surely longhand for Teddy.

Panda : *(always black-and-white)*
> "You mean Daddy! But tell us how exactly you found him?"

Rabbit : *(always Feeling)*
> "And what you *felt?*"

Owner : *(squeezing a legal brief into exactly one sentence)*
> "We found him, Panda, by following those Royal Navy Lists of Le Bretons at sea since 1850. What we *felt*, Rabbit — "

"Talking to your stuffed animals is therapy of a kind, but have you ever tried to express these feelings about your search for a missing father to another human being?"

Our first inclination is to say *Stuff you!* to Strangelove. The lawyers who advised us to try the Wills at Somerset House would make it perfectly clear that any exchange between an Owner and his Toys falls under the rubric of privileged communication. i.e., and to wit, still private, handwritten in our Journal.

JULY 4th . . . . . . Saturday 1987
INDEPENDENT DAY (USA)

Nat West Bank's lawyers will forward a letter.

> "We regret however, that as a matter of confidence, the Bank cannot disclose a customer's last known address."

Writing to a man who may or may not be my father, who may or may not be dead . . . to say the least a curious letter to compose; the strangest in my life.

"Thisss word 'curious' again?"

Forgetting as we write that, when God's still in the nursery, all thoughts are wide-open: no prayers or secret letters can be hidden from a pair of know-it-alls like P&R peering over our shoulder. Or from Hopalong Dr. S. falling back on the tried and true cross-examination for the meaninglessness of existence.

"What are you thinking?"

About a letter from Graham Greene. Two lines long of proper writing. And stuff them up your jumper cable!

La Résidence des Fleurs
Avenue Pasteur
06600 Antibes

```
17 June 1980
Dear Mr Gauer,
Many thanks for your letter. As for my
Mr Le Breton, who knows?


                Yours sincerely,
                Graham Greene
```

"Two lines from Graham Greene, at least it must have pleased your mother for you to get recognition from a 'proper writer'. Who is this 'my Mr. Le Breton' he mentions?"

For serious enquirers — like Panda and Rabbit, not snoop shrinks hiding their boredom behind people's backs: in his autobiographical *Ways of Escape*, Greene, the great deceiver, had reported a charlatan Other: an imposter called Le Breton trading on Greene's copyrighted name in Paris. The old pro's droll two-line comeback from Antibes was in reply to our rank amateur ghost's offering — composed seven years *before* Charlie dropped her bombshell that his charlatan's name, "Le Breton," had also been our own:

```
                              Victoria, B.C
                              May 27, 1980

Dear Mr. Greene:
I rather suspect that I met your "Other" Mr.
Le Breton: not in Paris, but a bush High
School outside Victoria. I immigrated to
this part of the world when I was twelve. A
few years earlier, I attended Sherbourne.
```

Panda : *(remembering being disgruntled)*
    "We didn't attend. You said we
    couldn't."
Owner : *(remembering Dorothea: "Patience is a Virtue")*
    "The school said it. Sherbourne
    wasn't Brideshead. Stuffed Toys
    weren't allowed —"

"Being able to talk with your stuffed animals would have been a comfort to a little boy at Boarding School. This Dorothea — one of your mother's guardians, I think — did she often tell you to be patient?"

She told us to mind our P's and Q's and stop reading our favourite 'Just William' stories. But Aunt Dorothea's not the point. What we were trying to explain to Panda, before we were so crudely interrupted, is just think of the rest of our letter to Greene like more Once upon a time ...

    . . . A substitute teacher, an
Englishman, showed up in the Glen Lake
bush and announced that he too had
been at Sherbourne — as a master — and
laid on a heavy exercise in grammar to
punish an essay he claimed, "let down
the Old School side." Next morning,
"Mr Le Breton" was arrested by Canadian
immigration, charged with false
entry and impersonation (of doctors,
professors — no writers) and deported.
Two years later a Reuters item from
Australia relayed that our namesake had
been nailed Down Under as a General.
        Yours sincerely

PS: Victoria was founded by a con-man.

"A curious postscript ending. And these 'Just William' stories you so much enjoyed describe the adventures of a very rebellious little boy. You think of this ghost-writing perhaps also as a 'con'. Not 'proper grown-up writing'?"

We *think* this reveals a total lack of understanding what anyone except a shrink half-asleep at the wheel would possess as common knowledge: to wit, *all* Proper Writers think of themselves as charlatans, but half of them are too scared of the dark and/or Reviewers to admit it. We think of our Postscript about Victoria's founding father as a historical footnote: *I-Amor-de-Cosmos, Lover of the Universe* — born as somebody-William-Smith; a lobster-fishing Nova Scotian Nostromo from the Sacramento gold rush who photographed claim-jumpers, before governing Vancouver's Island, still with an apostrophe. Full stop.

"Lobsters again. And 'fishing' for them. Your letter to Greene had no other purpose?"

Ask Panda and Rabbit. Our one-sided exchange with a Big Name about Con Artists did produce an aborted daydream of Owner writing a First Novel that Dorothea could have been proud of. A Proper Entertainment Adventure for grownups, hiding sex with religion like Greene.

"More changes of names and hiding secrets. Before your daydream of a first novel was 'aborted', did it have a title?"

The C-for-Charlatan Scenario. Unsaleable, but this is at the time of The Hitler Diaries so it seemed logical. A Con writer rips off publishers by floating "Great Man" memoirs — God knows, we've Vanity-ghosted enough of them! — complete with Edwardian Bordered title-pages of Errata, Professional Associations, & Meaningful Verse; the superfluous Preface to heighten non-existent suspense, before the inevitable Big Name Dropping, and "accidentally-included" edit-notes from Gay or Widowed secretaries in love with their Author.

"Perhaps love for a Charlatan Writer who could not get it from his mother because she promiscuously loved the Universe instead?"

Charlie loved us. She just couldn't show it. And there's a lot more to the damn book than frustrated secretaries. It's meant to be a bunch of Boy's Own adventures in grownup exotic locales. Each time the Charlatan gets caught, he escapes and plays for higher stakes — and for bullshit reviewers we can throw in a musical puzzle connecting phoney lives.

"You say there's a lot more to the book. Is this 'daydream' perhaps still actually being written?"

Being attempted. A first draft. No wonder Greene's reply was droll. The definition of Amateur Memoirs is Pompous when they aren't Dull. A fraud Tell-All in a novel would have to be just bad enough to be readable. The old pro in Antibes would have known we were trying an impossible balancing act.

"Like your mother showing love for a bastard child she had secret thoughts of aborting perhaps?"

She said *adopting*, and bugger you Strangelove! When Charlie told us she used to call me her Darling Willum, for a split second the hair stood up on the back of my neck. The only other time that happened was hearing the soundtrack bombers in a movie of Eric Maria Remarque's 'A Time to Love and a Time to Die'. Anyway, David was five when Willum vanished and nobody has a fucking clue to what makes a writer write for Churchill's autograph. Or a bloody Writer's Block.

"Or perhaps the blocks in a Toy Cupboard. And you are blocked by this 'Churchillian' enigma?"

Like E-for-Edward Elgar. *Just close your eyes, and think of Eliot.* Also known as S-for-Sex sells better.

> *There will be time, there will be time*
> *To prepare a face to meet the faces that you meet;*
> *There will be time to murder and create,*
> *And time for all the works and days of hands*
> *That lift and drop a question on your plate....*

> T.S. Eliot, *The Love Song of J. Alfred Prufrock*

5th November, 1947.

Dear David,

On behalf of Mr. Churchill, I am writing to acknowledge your letter of October, 1947.

Unfortunately, Mr. Churchill receives so many requests for his autograph that he has had to make it a general rule to refuse, unless the circumstances are most exceptional.

He is very sorry not to be able to make an exception in your favour.

Yours faithfully,

Spencer Loch

Honorary Secretary.

Master David G___,
30, Ferme Park Road,
London, N. 4.

England
One

M Y FIRST MEMORY OF SPATIAL RELATIONSHIPS IS THE cottage . . . triangulated by the Bumble-Bee, my mother, and a hollyhock with a stammering man behind it. His mouth opened and closed, *"Um um um um L-L-ottie . . ."* in rhythm with the hum of the bee's wings. The bee's legs were furred with golden pollen. The hollyhock was deep pink, matching the man's face.

"L-l-ady L-L-ottie, I l-l-ove you!"

As the daughter of a Marquis my mother of course had her own title, Lady Charlotte. "David," she said, with that throaty laugh which so entranced her male friends, before she closed my nursery door. "Your imitation of the Duke of York is quite priceless — but we really shouldn't make fun of your unfortunate brother's impediment, Sir, not in front of Teddy."

The next time I saw my mother speak to the man called David she addressed him as "Your Majesty," at a small lunch with Wallis Simpson before his Coronation. ("Abandoned," said my father, "because of thrice-divorced Mrs S's motto: *Felicity through fellatio.*") But when my mother poured him tea between sittings for his portrait in the privacy of her studio at the Cottage, Edward the Eighth was still only a Prince of Wales.

The bumble bee stung my knee, which is why I remember. Late summer, 1929, aged two-and-a-half: my faculty for recall has always been phenomenal. While my father was away, delivering his newest paper on Inner Orbit Binding Levels at a Quantum Symposium in Berlin, my eye discovered the third dimension we call Architecture.

The Cottage was outside the village of Swyre, in Dorset, set in one of those bowl-shaped, wooded valleys which West Country folk still call a combe — but "cottage" is hardly the word to describe our house. It had a thatched roof and leaded window panes, but its half-timbered walls extended in all directions to encompass a space large enough for a hamlet!

My father had his laboratory in one wing, at the south end, facing the stream. My mother's studio naturally was in the north wing, for the light. From this happy separation you will deduce that my parents' was that closest of marriages: Science and Art.

My mother's second name, Diana, made her goddess of the moon to all male visitors (few of whom knew, or would have cared for, that name's other Roman connotation: patroness of unmarried girls, and chastity — and childbirth.) In our Cottage life my father was always the central sun. As you will know from his Nobel Prize, he too was plain William Le Breton but confusion was avoided on a first-name basis. Where I have been a life-long "Teddy" (inseparable from my nursery Bear), my father was always "Bill" to close friends.

His wider circle was eclectic. (Like his choice of clubs: the Athenaeum, of course, but also one on Albemarle Street, whose high-colonic membership had massaged-policemen from Scotland Yard rubbing shoulders with the Music Hall Artiste-demimonde.) He was anything but a snob. It is a matter of derision nowadays for a man to be heroic. Qualities such as patriotism, courage, gallantry and manners are seldom acknowledged as singular: combined with brain power of the highest order their possessor would be regarded as a laughing stock, a throwback to a time of inequality and unearned privilege.

Although his Christian and surname came to Britain from Normandy with the Conqueror, my father earned all his privileges. My mother's origins are an amalgam of Celtic Romance (MacKenzie Earls of Gairloch) and Nordic, that doubtless provided the richness in her water-coloured art. Also in certain of my own post-war works (The Niarchos and Onassis Garden Terraces, Hampstead) adjudged "Dead pink flamingos on a blasted Heath!" by a later leery Prince of Wales.

Besides the Albemarle Club, Le Breton family creativity was bolstered by our annual holidays in Greece. At that time — the twenties and thirties — making such a visit on a yearly basis was more of an expedition than vacation. After Southampton to Cherbourg by ferry and *wagon-lit* across France, it required a three-day steamer trip from Marseilles to Athens. Once there, you stayed put. It was unusual for us to be back at the Cottage so soon (for the first Prince of Wales's cup of tea) but my father had cut our Greek holiday short in order to dispose of various stocks and shares which he held on the London and New York markets, before continuing without us (but with James, a touring younger friend and cabaret pianist from his Albemarle set) to Berlin.

His market actions were regarded as lunacy by his brokers (and his friend Maynard Keynes, who was still buying metals) but as always the subsequent headlines proved him right. Our family life was untouched by Depression.

Greece was still in ruins; or at least that part of the Peloponnese Peninsula where we had our small villa. The great earthquake of 1928 had levelled Corinth, and portions of the Cut's wall partially blocked the ship canal across the isthmus. We went the rest of the way by a mule wearing a red blanket with a gold border. The earthquake did more harm to the temple pillars of Apollo at Corinth than the preceding two thousand years, but our villa was undamaged.

We used it not so much for its proximity to the silver sand and azure sea as for a jumping-off spot for expeditions into the heart of the Peloponnese: rural and still-hidden Arcadia. My father's disciplines, as you know, were those studies of physics and mathematics which would lead him through cloud chamber tracks to the nuclear heart of the atom. His own heart — his off-duty passion! — lay in finding living traces of the original golden Greeks who would lead him to King Midas. In Athens and Delphi those gilt-haired male specimens were only to be found in museums: in the narrow streets were the inheritors: sloe-eyed boys, dark-visaged and black-headed, barbaric leftovers from Turkish and earlier Bulgarian invasions.

But once, in Arcadia . . . as far as I ever saw in those childhood years, were only more of the same — bent dark peasants in darker stone hutches — but on his solitary searches my father was convinced that around the next hairpin bend on the remotest mountain track he would find blond Ulysses striding with flashing spear and burnished shield towards Midas's Hill of Gold. The romantic in his nature, not the fraudulent pseudo-science of Freud (my mother captured that charlatan in her *Sigmund at Hampstead, 1939*) was obviously what bound him so strongly to my mother.

During his solo pursuits of Ulysses she remained at our villa and painted the romance of Greece into her pictures. Bronzed modern Apollos, posing nude for her, or diving for coins in the Aegean. Aquamarine doors and the unbearable whiteness of walls at noon with dark green, scrotal figs ripening under a still-Apollonian sun.

She captured them in oils — and capture them she did, as current prices for her Greek works show — but before Freud she never exhibited her male nudes. Indeed, not until after my father's tragic death. (Under mysterious circumstances in a Lisbon hotel, in 1941. The State ban on the documents which might reveal so much was recently extended by the British Government for a further 30 years.) Her status as a minor

Royal Academician rested principally on the Prince of Wales's Cottage visit and her Dorset water colours.

In summer 1932, when I was five, the Le Bretons abandoned Ancient Greece for Princeton, where I first fell in love with sky-scraping America, and met Einstein.

I knew nothing of physics beyond the bedtime games my father employed to introduce such concepts as mass, inertia, and momentum. (My first advanced differential equation, for example, for the vortex generated by a Christening spoon stirring my nursery "goodnight" hot chocolate cup.) Quantum levels were above me; so too was German. I could ask for fresh bread and goat's cheese in coarse Arcadian Greek but there were no Arcadians at Princeton.

One must not be too hard on the place. It is always a surprise to visitors to find natural beauty in New Jersey. It exists, even today, betwixt slums and Super Fund toxic dumps. Now, as then, there is the river and the ivy. (Neither has been "raped on campus," in my opinion, by its reflection in the "glassy, yet starkly definitive" Le Breton Tower.) Now, as then, there is a meld of juvenile and adult thought, an influx of foreign talent. Now, as then, the influx is Jewish. At that time, of course, they were from Germany, fleeing Hitler. Today, as I write aboard the *Southern Cross*, they flee a possible successor, through financial turmoil, in a barely-capitalized Russia.

The excitement for me was not Hitler but the *Queen Mary*. Her funnels alone seemed the size of the Athens steamer! The blasts from her sirens shook the teak decks and rattled silver on the Captain's Table.

> *The stately ship is seen no more,*
> *The fragile skiff attains the shore;*
> *And while the great and wise decry,*
> *And all their trophies pass away,*
> *Some sudden thought, some careless rhyme*
> *Still floats above the rocks of Time.*

The fragile skiff was Einstein's — the interrupting verse, Lecky's "Reflections on an Old Song" — but the careless rhyme that ruined my concentration comes from a second-rate piano player in the Solaris

Lounge, relaying his Nightingale from Berkeley Square without a by-your-leave, to my present-day cabin aboard the *Southern Cross*.

My first Einstein encounter did not occur in the ivied brickwork of Princeton but at another cottage, one he had rented or been loaned for the summer at Peconic, on Long Island, by the beach beyond the town.

My father drove us out there in a single-seater Packard with its spare wheel mounted on the passenger's side running board. I was sitting on my mother's knee so that the wheel was right in front of me. I could see my face and my mother's in the bevelled side mirror. "Genuine Corning Safety Glass," True life is in the details.

My father had first become acquainted with the genius behind relativity at a symposium on the subject in Berlin. Their reunion on this occasion was delayed because we got lost. The Long Island villages had Indian names and my father could not read his own writing. It was only when we arrived in Cutchogue, on the north shore, that my mother deciphered his scrawl —

"It looks like Patchogue," she said, taking a map from the Packard's glove box. "That's on the south shore. You should never have tried to be a doctor!"

My father always blamed his impossible writing on his first post-graduate degree, in medicine. "Combined with the use of Latin, to prevent patients forging their own prescriptions. The dual precaution is sound."

"We need Long Island Sound." She laughed and kissed him. In Peconic she put away his prescribed instructions and asked a passing newspaper delivery boy instead. "Do you know where Professor Einstein lives?"

"Sure. Everybody does. At Doc Moore's. Four boxes past the drug store, maam."

As my father let out the clutch, the boy added, "But the prof ain't home right now. He's out in his sail boat."

With the floating carelessness of Time, I cannot swear that I recall the dialogue. I shall never forget the boat. It was a dinghy called the *Seagull*, and the genius in command met us with his trouser legs rolled up.

He looked as ancient as a wizard to me — the celebrated wild hair even more out-in-all-directions after tacking in the wind — but he was twenty years younger than I am now. A man in his fifties. A famous man. Something of a ladies' man.

We walked across the lawn. He pulled the Seagull up on the beach.

"Herr Le Breton. Guten tag."

I am sure I remember those words to my father, because he looked at my mother as he said them, bowing to her in a formal German way, but with the same hidden message in his slightly protuberant brown eyes as the laughing Prince of Wales'. It is only now that I think, Ah ha! Of course. They both had German backgrounds!

I cannot say what else he said. After the formal introduction to my mother — a Teutonic kissing of hands — he dismissed me with a slight smile and spent the next hour deep in science with my father on the seaside cottage porch. My mother painted the *Seagull*. That picture came to me twenty-five years later, after Einstein's death. I have it above me now. A genteel water colour of a dinghy and a man with his pant-legs rolled up. A singlet undervest below the tea-strainer moustache. A little boy watches . . .

"Guten tag, mein Marktschreier."

That is artistic license.

I was not in the picture. In real life, Einstein gave my father some notes on his Unified Field hypothesis to study (in German) and then, because the breeze was chill, suggested to my mother that she should paint him and the *Seagull* on a more sheltered beach in an adjacent cove, shielded from view.

They were away for two hours. I built a magnificent sandcastle. (The child's crudely blocked-out spatial relationships matured as the "economically spare, ergonomically generous" Le Breton Community for Young Offenders, in Toronto.) A languid young man with buck teeth and Brylcreemed dark hair strolled past in a form-fitting, knitted woollen bathing suit and complimented me on the castle — at which point my father came out carrying the Field equations. He stared for a moment at the back of the retreating Brylcreemed youth with an abstracted air, "He rather resembles James, but without those pianist's expressive hands" . . . and then the *Seagull* returned around the point with my wind-flushed mother and her captured Genius.

On the cottage porch, while my mother washed her hands and then prepared tea, the two academicians discussed the Nature of Matter. After the Science, a coral and black-spotted ladybird landed on the notorious moustache.

When my mother presented the painting to him, Einstein touched the ladybird with his forefinger absentmindedly and gave her back the Prince of Wales Look with a Teutonic reverence for rank:

"Danke, Gräfin Charlotte."

In the Packard, driving home to Princeton, we passed the Bryl-creemed figure in the knitted bathing suit who looked like the piano friend from the Albemarle Club. My father's brow creased in a frown.

"A penny for your thoughts, darling?" my mother said.

"Nothing."

"It must be something."

"Just his Unified Field. I admire him enormously, but it is childish to the point of absurdity to believe that the ultimate secret of matter must have a neat and tidy solution. I told him, God knows human interactions are small enough in the scheme of things, and yet even they are infinitely complex!"

"And what did he say?"

"Nothing. Just gave that damn smile of the meek inheriting the earth. But I hear he's hell to live with. He wants us to come back when I've revised my gravitational equations."

Bumble Bees and Ladybirds on knees and moustaches: gravity and magnetism in a unified field. Who can truly recall more than a handful of scraps from a lifetime?

DAVID GURR

Dear Maestro Le Breton:

Here are the first "Cottage" and "Seagull" pages. The "ladybug on the moustache" makes everything so real but I agree, it must be very difficult to remember exactly what was said and done so long ago. A few small things may help the "Rocks of Time" chapter fit on one 5 inch diskette:

1.Repetition of "of course." My new KayPro portable computer (I am just learning Version 4) suggests eliminating some of these. And I know I use too many !!! marks myself! — but would you like me to edit out a few of yours? Also, "Betwixt." The Perfect Writer SpelChek tried to change this to "bewitched" and when I ran the WordStar GramMar it came up with Archaic. Do you want to try something else for New Jersey?

2.I am enjoying your Mother's story very much. Especially her secret affair with the Prince. (Of course you do not admit she had one out of loyalty — especially after Mrs Simpson's "Felicity"! — but even in a Scholarly Work people with Romantic Hearts can "read between the lines.")

3.I agree it all seems nonsense about Sigmund Freud. Surely even Academics will appreciate a Genius* coming after a Prince of Wales!
Sincerely,

        Mavis Monk (Mrs)

*And your mother alone on the beach! (My late husband was also an Albert.) Most sincerely,
M.M.

England
Two

THE LE BRETON SUMMER AFTER EINSTEIN WAS ARCADIAN AGAIN (following a brief German delay, because of the elections, in Berlin). We had made the detour to Berlin to visit the Schliemann collection of Trojan relics and further my father's pursuit of the King Midas Myth.

He now decided that the roots of the legend came not from Phrygia, as commonly supposed, nor from Mycenae, whose great walls lie on the north-western edge of the golden Argolids' Peninsula. After the Berlin visit he was convinced that the legend stretched farther back in time and location: that Midas had been an Aryan, not Arcadian, Chieftain.

From the universally known first version of the Midas Legend — Dionysus granting wishes turning everything to gold — through the second (in which Midas is a mere judge at a musical competition) my father pursued his quarry to the Well of Lousoi, below Nonakris, backed by the Aroanian Mountains. From Pausanius, he traced the legend to Midea, in the Argolid, and the internecine murder by Hippodameia's sons, Attreus and Thyestes, of their half-brother Chrysippos, Pelops's unfortunate bastard. Thence southward . . .

Neither I nor the rest of the world have been able to follow my father through this thicket of mythological illegitimacy, but he died convinced that Midas was buried not in a lost cave at Nonakris, but in an Aryan Tumulus on a lost island deep in Southern Oceania; and that one of the limestone peaks above it — the last thing Aryan Midas's hand touched — had a core of solid gold.

(In his defence I must add that his acumen in picking mining shares bordered on the magical. And Maynard Keynes believed in Midas.)

In September of 1933 — the eleventh, my final day of freedom before being sent away to Prep School — after our return from the visit to Princeton, Lord Rutherford, as Director of the Cavendish Laboratory (at Cambridge, in those days before Los Alamos, the shrine of atomic physics) spoke to the British Association for the Advancement of Science. My father took me to the lecture for a parting treat.

As reported by the Times, Rutherford ended with these words: "Anyone looking for a source of power in the transformation of the atom is talking moonshine."

As observed by me, he stared directly at my father and hissed —
All The Things You Are . . .

Another interruption above my head from the music-hall-turn's latest unasked-for serving of nostalgia — being roundly applauded by my post-prandial fellow alumni consuming A Promised Breath of Springtime and drinks-with-parasols in the Solaris Lounge!

My father's Albemarle Club pianistic entertainments with buck-toothed James were mere Brylcreem diversions. Serious music was present constantly in the Le Breton family. My mother played the viola; Father the 'cello — as an amateur, but occasionally in duet with professionals like Gerald Moore (at the Connaught, my father was a High Mason). And, in the same peripheral manner that literature brushed the Dorset roots of our family tree (through my maternal grandmother's intimate association "on the poetic level" with Thomas Hardy), my father was a close friend of Sir Edward Elgar. The day of Rutherford's Atomic Moonshine lecture was capped by our attendance at Elgar's last public performance: the *Enigma Variations*, at the Albert Hall.

It is common knowledge that by this time Elgar was crushed by the death of his wife and embittered by the public's love for the Pomp and Circumstance of "Hope and Glory". It is not, I think, well known that my father's name holds one of the clues to the letter "E" of the *Enigma*.

The surface meaning of the six letters, "Dedicated to my friends pictured within" on the original score, has long been understood. (Not always correctly. W.H. Reed, Elgar's memoirist, violinist, and orchestral Leader, claimed in 1936 that Enigma was composed "at Craeg Lea, an anagram compounded of C.A.E. and Elgar". In fact, the Variations were written at *Forli*, Elgar's first Malvern home.) Hidden at a deeper level, however, is a "mysterious, unheard theme".

This musical-mathematical mystery was uncovered by my father. He provided his explanation to Elgar in a sealed — but not before showing it to me! — envelope, sent by afternoon registered post.

The composer summoned him to Marl Bank, his cottage in the Cotswolds, that same evening and admitted the truth of the solution, adding with a rueful smile, "I had hoped to puzzle the world a little longer, Bill."

"In that case, Edward, so you shall."

My father took the envelope containing his solution and cast it into the coal fire burning on the cottage hearth. The evening concluded with my father playing the final movement of the 'Cello Concerto in homage to its composer. Elgar died the following year.

The Enigma's deeper secret has not since been revealed. . . .

"We are not bleedin' savages in the South Seas, Master Le B. Boxin' is the ticket!"

A red-letter, Le Breton day: May 5, 1935, the Silver Jubilee of George the Fifth. I was seven: My advisor, Dizzy Dixon, was the prep school's physical training and drill instructor, a former army sergeant-major. Today, most parents would be appalled at the thought of their gifted progeny's brain being scrambled in its shell. Fortunately, my reflexes were always one punch quicker than my ring opponent's. (Had they not been, I should have had an entirely different first rendezvous with my Papuan volcano!)

My return Volcanic face-to-face, now lies only one day's steaming . . .

Dizzy, besides his preoccupation with South Seas' savages, had only one eye and an intriguing quirk of behavior. Before demonstrating any routine — vaulting the box horse — he would first come rigidly to attention and address himself:

"Hands down sides of trousers, thus. Sergeant-Major Dixon, Go!"

This was apparently a trace element from his days in the South Staffordshires. I used to imagine them, a thin red line poised at the top of their trench at the Somme . . . waiting for that last few seconds, amidst unremitting machine-gun fire, as they pressed their hands down their trouser seams and called out their names in alphabetical order . . . *thus* contributing with statistical inevitability to the appalling Allied losses on the Western Front.

Dizzy's missing eye was replaced by a patch. As with Admiral Nelson after the Battle of Copenhagen, this arrangement allowed the sergeant-major considerable flexibility. If he felt that a match could proceed to the desirable goal of a knockout — though the school rules required a standing count — he would simply leave the black patch turned towards the action long enough for Natural Selection's survival-of-the-fittest to run its bloody course. The patch performed with equal facility in his home life. Mrs. Dixon — "Auntie Rita, my dears" to those boys fortunate enough to be invited to share her Scotch drop scones — was formidably Hibernian. (A few years later, now sadly as the Widow Dixon, Auntie Rita opened and ran a small restaurant in London, with her sister, through the Blitz.)

Dizzy took his Darwinianism with utmost seriousness. Between home bouts with Auntie Rita, and in term breaks, his one good eye pored laboriously over a leather-bound, and much-stained copy of *The Origin of Species*, which had been with him at Gallipoli. Pressed by an inquiring mind, the sergeant major could show physical proof of the Great Theory:

"This 'ere 'ole in the cover, young Master Le B, is where the wolume fervored the aufor's cause — which means the total triumph of our British Empire, we are not bleedin' savages — by stoppin' a nine-mill Jerry bullet!"

Germans were increasingly a Le Breton topic of conversation after Hitler's assumption of the Reich Chancellery. My mother was quicker to see him as a threat than my father. She had talked to Einstein about more than atomic critical mass on their secluded Long Island beach.

"He will have to be stopped," she said in the summer I left Prep School — 1936, during Hitler's Re-Militarization of the Rhineland — to move on to Sherbourne Upper and greater things.

"A strong Germany is the key to a sound Europe, Lady Charlotte," the Prep's head master advised her at Speech Day prize-giving. "We are all most proud of your gifted boy. The Javelin and a working sketch for Restoration of the Chapel Roof! Our architectural loss is Upper School's gain, but do not let them go at things too hard. Remembering my Ovid, '*Fit cito per multaspraeda petita manus*' — how's that, young Le Breton?"

" 'The booty sought by many hands is quickly plundered', sir."

"Just so. But, as for Hitler, let me leave you with another. '*Fit scelus indulgens per nubila saecula virtus*' — In overcast times the virtue of tenderness becomes a crime."

"That sort of damned Classic twaddle is why the educational system in this country needs a complete overhaul," said my father, on the drive home to Swyre. "I still have my doubts about Sherbourne but it has managed to produce Turing and his new Thinking Machine. It can't be all bad."

Sherbourne, sitting approximately at the half-way mark in the British Public School Top Ten, by most parental standards would have been considered middle-class nirvana. My father, however, had gone to Eton, as had his father. My mother broke the daisy chain. Sherbourne was Dorset, a short distance from Swyre.

What so many loathed of School, I loved: its special mellow stone, light golden-brown, its ancient Abbey next door, the timbered town with its narrow cobbled streets and gingerbread railway station, the adjacent ruined Castle brooding on its hill: the whole surrounded by delightful country walks.

Only recently, reading a Life of Alan Turing, *The Man behind Enigma*, I discovered that his unique insight into computer theory (the sequential use of binary instructions) came to him as he tore off the petals of a daisy, playing that most familiar of schoolboy games:

He loves me, he loves me not. . . .

I was not bothered by that cliché of British public-schoolhood: homosexuality — but I should perhaps add a detail of Sherbourne's private life. As a consequence of the First War's manpower shortage, a handful of women had been taken on as temporary teachers. At war's end, a smaller number remained. In our male bastion, one such was Miss Frost.

In an obscure token gesture to the revolution of Freudian thought, she was assigned as Games Mistress to the youngest boys in the First Form. This resulted in two curious anomalies:

Nude Swimming, and Shower Supervision.

Boys of all ages swam nude in the school's large pool, located out of doors, behind an enclosing wall. Only Miss Frost wore a bathing suit. There was also a slide at the deep end, next to the spring diving board. Miss Frost would invite — command is perhaps the better word — the youngest, pre-pubescent boys to ride naked on her back as she went, headfirst, on her stomach down the slide. This had the frequent effect of simultaneously presenting a maturely-large-and-hairy adolescent male groin standing on the opposite side of the pool, directly in line with the end of her nose.

These juxtapositions had apparently cultivated in her — as with Freud's friend Fleiss — a pronounced nasal-genital fixation. This was demonstrated a week after my arrival when I heard my name called sharply, during shower supervision:

"Le Breton! Come here!"

"Yes, Miss Frost?"

I presented myself nakedly in front of her. I reached for my towel on an adjacent peg. (I was still not used to riding nude on her back.)

"There's no point in false modesty now. What were you doing in the shower just then, after picking your nose?"

"Doing, Miss Frost? Washing, I suppose."

"You suppose? You were urinating in public. Revolting habit."

"But I wasn't, Miss Frost."

And if I had — how could she know? How alert her gaze must have been . . . over twenty boys, as the water from twenty showers drenched and dripped from twenty pre-pubertal, wee cocks. To detect among foaming white suds the telltale yellow stain, gone in a flash down the floor drain . . .

In an architectural footnote: I was not only privileged to see the chapel roof restored from my infantile "Javelin" drawing, but also the fully-matured Le Breton Annexe. (Described on another Speech Day by my same Regal Expert at Large, as "a Mock Stalinist Excrescence!" A simplicity of expression fitting both building and critic.)

Nude swimming and urinary episodes aside, my privileged years at Sherbourne were as golden as its stone. A lower Jurassic lime, it came from the quarry at Ham Hill, in use for more than a thousand years, still located thirteen miles westward from the town. An extract from the Journal of the Dorset Archaeological Association — I have the honour to be a Special Member — records "a slightly coarse grain formed from seashells crushed by strong currents in a shallow sea, and stained a rich yellow-brown by iron."

And in less than a week, on the other side of the globe, we shall encounter it again. . . .

But before leaving Sherbourne, mention of the chapel brings one last vignette to mind. In the way of all emotionally overheated, closed communities, the episode was both inconsequential, yet slightly sinister. Sherlock Holmes might have solved it. Doctor Watson would have called it, "The Curious Case of the Curate and the Cat."

The "curate" was not in fact ordained, but only the twenty-seven year-old Junior Biology Master, who had an interest in theology usually at odds with Darwin's branch of science. His name was Thornethwaite-Barqhuar (MA, Cantab) and he "stood in" for the Chaplain on such occasions as influenza epidemics, or supervising God Swot (evening bible-study prep).

On a beautiful May evening, as barn swallows were making their last swoops of the day, the God-Swotter was discovered by Dizzy Dixon in the chapel, before the altar, preparing it seemed, "To bleedin' sacrifice old Whiskers!" the Headmaster's Cat.

"He didn't have no bayonet, Master Le B, but he had old Whisk's knackers strapped to the cross good and proper, I can tell you!"

This clue to a sexual motive would doubtless have been glossed over by Dr Watson. There was no disguising the other physical evidence: *The Criminal Prosecution and Capital Punishment of Animals*, by E.P. Evans, Heinemann edition, London, 1906.

"Your God Swotter was only at the bleedin' Trial stage when I jumped him in the trenches," Dizzy recounted to his enthralled audience. "Rantin' something fierce about the Head and 'Fornication with the Beast!' 'What else would you flippin' expect?' I asked 'im. 'When old Whiskers is a tom?'"

"And what happened next, Dizzy?"

"The Head 'ad me order up an Hire motor. 'Back to Canterbury, is it, Sir?' I said. 'No, Sergeant Dixon,' says the Head. 'Mr. Thornethwaite-Barqhuar will be furthering his theological enquiries at Dorchester.' Meanin', Master Le B — discreet-like — in the Loonie Bin."

The Le Breton family's first atomic approach to the centres of power on both sides of the Atlantic came in the golden Indian Summer of 1939. While other British children were being separated from their parents and evacuated from the London heart of Empire to far America, or deep in England's pastorale, as usual, I travelled between both with my parents, from Swyre to Princeton, First Class, on Cunard.

"This time I do believe we shall win the Blue Ribband!" my mother cried. We were only ten hours away from Ribband success, aboard the *Queen Elizabeth*, when a U-Boat alert sounded and spoilt the fun. It was a false alarm — it was the Phoney War — but a necessary "sub-dodging" detour in course denied us the Trans-Atlantic prize.

We met Roosevelt at his country seat, Hyde Park. He was vacationing there with his wife. Eleanor Roosevelt had purchased one of my mother's Long Island beach paintings of Einstein.

"You have done the impossible with genius, Lady Charlotte. You have captured its eyes!"

Mrs. Roosevelt's own, slightly thyroid eyes were fastened on my mother throughout our visit. On their walks together Eleanor had a gaiety towards her which seemed to me somehow misplaced. Too extreme and clinging for such a short acquaintance. It was years later — in New Guinea, I had fallen in love myself — before I realized *(nor had I yet met my next-door Cay neighbor on Contentment, Margaret, Lady T —)* I had been witnessing a middle-aged schoolgirl's crush.

Did it go further in the Hyde Park Summerhouse? The two ladies at one point retired there. When they emerged, Eleanor's cheeks were a heightened pink and wisps of hair had escaped from her bun. And the formal, "Lady Charlotte" had softened to "Darling Lottie." But as we have seen from the Einstein-Beach episode one cannot judge my mother from the outward appearance of others: she herself was never *en déshabille* after such situations, with either sex.

Franklin Roosevelt and my father got on as famously as natural athletes invariably do. The President could of course no longer play football as he had at Yale, but he played water polo with great vigor in the outdoor swimming pool.

"I don't mind telling you, Bill," he boomed, lobbing a pass over the steel leg-braces resting beside his basket wheel chair, "it would be my hide on the barn wall for a third term if the damned Press ever got a shot of me like this!"

My mother painted him like that — a bull walrus's strength in the torso; desiccated-insect legs — with jaunty grin and cigarette holder under a straw hat, and an extra-long gin-and-tonic at hand.

His eyes rested on my mother at least as keenly as his wife's, but this was a look I was used to since the bumble-bee Prince of Wales. It was the look all men — except certain "theatrical" male friends, *viz* John Gielgud — sent her. A look my father never liked.

"Roosevelt reminds me of one of those bloody satyrs at Corinth," he told her that night. "I thought he was going to pull you into the pool and do it like Poseidon taking Demeter underwater."

"Shhh, darling. Teddy will hear us!"

I heard her giggle. And shortly afterwards a different sound. And after that, before the silence of sleep at Hyde Park, my father groaned.

In the morning, he had coffee alone with the President. "To do my damnedest as 'the middle man' for that clown Szillard," he told my mother beforehand.

"Clown" may have been too strong a word for Leo Szillard — a scientific dabbler, and somewhat of a showman, who nonetheless had certain useful insights into the nature of atomic fission: It was certainly the most momentous breakfast cup of coffee my father ever drank!

Szillard, in his flamboyant way, had dreamed up a madcap Hungarian scheme to have Einstein write a letter to Roosevelt, urging him "To build the Bomb before Hitler does It!" Einstein was too proud to go cap in hand to any politician. An Anglo-Saxon intermediary with impeccable trans-Atlantic atomic credentials was required.

Quod erat demonstrandum, William "Bill" Le Breton.

Roosevelt was never at his best at breakfast. I suspect that on waking up, each day brought him freshly to the harsh physical imprisonment of his illness. My mother did not want me too close to him — at that time infantile paralysis was regarded with the dread now accorded to AIDS: the previous afternoon she had been reluctant to have me even swim in the same pool — yet when he caught sight of me and boomed out, "Young Teddy! Let the ladies have their morning stroll alone. You come here and join us fellahs. Steward, fresh orange juice for Master Le Breton, that's the ticket!"

She allowed it. Eleanor took "Darling Lottie's" elbow and drifted once more towards the Summerhouse. We fellahs sat at a glass-topped, wrought-iron circular table, beneath a blue-and-white striped umbrella awning. My mother was wearing a pleated chiffon dress to match. The pleats accentuated the sway of her hips. The colours (and perhaps the movement) reminded the President of his days at sea.

"And what days those were, Young Teddy! The sea stretching away to every horizon. Nothing there but God, and the odd porpoise."

"I know, sir. We saw porpoises this time on the Q. E. And a whale."

"Did you, by golly? But I'm not talking about ocean liners, young fellah. Destroyers! Join the navy and see the world at thirty knots from just above the wave tops like a flying fish! That's the ticket. Now Bill, what's this atom nonsense of Einstein's you want to bore me to death about? 'A single bomb? Carried by boat? Destroy a whole port?' This sounds like H.G. Wells and that movie actor fellah, Orson What's-his-name. 'E equals MC squared', indeed! Young Teddy-my-lad, drink up your orange juice and don't believe a word of it!"

That was Franklin Delano Roosevelt's laughing, booming reaction to the celebrated Einstein breakfast letter. It took my father the rest of the day, in tactful five-minute bites out of the Presidential vacation, to impress upon his host the seriousness of the atomic threat.

" 'A whole port'!" Franklin Roosevelt stared thoughtfully at the backs of his wife and my mother, emerging arm-in-arm from the

Summerhouse, above a low boxwood hedge bordering a herbaceous flowerbed heavy with chrysanthemums and dahlias and Michaelmas daisies. "A handsome woman, your wife. Nice painter. Better than Churchill. D'you reckon your mother would paint these Fall flowers of mine, Young Teddy?"

If you have visited Hyde Park you will know that she did. They hang beside the reverentially preserved Desk in the Presidential Study. One languorous afternoon during my obligatory rest while my father and Eleanor were otherwise engaged judging the Hyde Park Quilting Society (Eleanor's current New Deal good work) in the village, my mother even overcame her phobia about paralysis and swam with the President in his pool. I heard the phrase, "Poseidon taking Demeter underwater!" repeated, followed by a bull-walrus splash and FDR roar of laughter.

And you know that the breakfast Bomb letter worked: eventually, in accordance with bureaucratic Army time, not Hungarian Leo Szilard's darting-dragonfly measure of it.

The breakfast accomplished one more thing. Roosevelt was also a born salesman: his Boy's Own nautical pitch by the pool actually managed to divert my eleven-year-old eyes from their narrow focus on the shadows cast by earth-bound Architecture . . . to a sunlit vision of myself in *Wings Above The Sea* — as a flying fish!

DAVID GURR

Dear Maestro:

1.In spite of your kind Supper offer (my
Tuna Casserole on Tuesday, when you said
"Academe abhors Romance, Mrs. M" about
New Jersey) I cannot bring myself to use
"just 'Dear plain Le B' ," but herewith
Miss Frost's* and Freud's mischief at
Hyde Park pages. Sexual Abuse is The
Modern Curse! (on this week's cover of
Time) — but it is funny how some things
remind us of others which don't seem to
connect at all like her nude swimming
with young schoolboys and President
Roosevelt in his pool.

2."Eleanor" has always been one of my
heroes (I have a passion for quilts!) so
it almost takes my breath away that she
walked "arm-in-arm" with your mother!

3.This is very personal because I know
how you feel about Mrs Simpson and your
Mother is not in the same league for that
kind of behavior! — but you will have to
swallow your Scholar's Pride and accept
that after "Love in the President's
Swimming Pool" you are giving the
Academic world a Romantic Best Seller!

Truly Most Sincerely,
Mavis
(Your Plain "Mrs. M")

* The FBI's On-Line LawChek, through
a friend in the Sheriff's Office at
Ogdensburg, asked: Re British Libel, Is
this her real name? (When it also wanted
a Call ID, as I am a nobody I gave it
Guess Who's Who for a Reference!)

England
Three

CHURCHILL WAS SEATED IN AN ARTIST'S FOLDING CANVAS chair by his Chartwell lake. His back was turned towards us (and Clemmie, his wife: a family tiff). Only his hunched shoulders, even more shapeless in an artist's smock, were visible beneath a broad-brimmed, straw artist's hat. In case there was any doubt as to his occupation, an easel, palette, and box of squished-tube oil paints confirmed it.

"A beginner," my mother said, as we stood at the top of the lawn, looking down to the black swans and deep-pink water lilies floating at the foot of it, "but of course he does love any fancy dress."

"I can't say the boiler suits are very fancy," said my father. "But I'd rather have them on a prime minister than Anthony Eden in his corset."

"Isn't Mr Chamberlain still Prime Minister?" I asked. "Did something change while we were in America?"

There was a moment of silence. My parents looked at each other . . . as a deep voice rumbled from beneath the straw hat,

"Nothing has changed, young man. And nothing will until I get America up to bat."

The hat swung around and the bulldog face was exactly as you have seen it in ten-thousand-lesser newsprint versions of the Karsh portrait. The chin, the scowl (at Clementine), the Cigar. But not the Boiler Suit. Below his abbreviated smock, the artist was stark naked!

"Professor Le Breton. Pray tell me, before your charming lady wife passes judgement on these blasted lilies, what did the President say about the Bomb?"

"Not too promising, I'm afraid, Winston."

Pretending that the Emperor was fully clothed, we approached the cigar more closely. The black swans glided in a circle. A tiny, bright green frog leaped onto a lily leaf. The pink blossom swayed above a gulping Japanese carp.

"Pure Monet," sighed my mother.

"I trust not, Lady Charlotte." This was followed by a Churchillian grunt at her and Clementine. "As I too-frequently have to remind my own spouse: in England swans are swans. France's abstraction is the modern curse. Professor, is your 'not promising' the official reaction of Roosevelt's War Department?"

"The Department of Terrestrial Magnetism," said my father. "Szillard, the Hungarian, hopes to get it pushed harder by Lindbergh."

"Good God! The man's in Hitler's pocket. Euripedes should be modified from 'put not your faith in any Greek' to a blanket ban on all Hungarians! *Terrestrial magnetism!* You advised me that Einstein's scribble would give us the unleashed power of the sun!"

"And so it will," my father replied. "I at least convinced the Americans to buy up all the Belgian Congo pitchblende. In the meantime, with our access to Canada's, we must just keep —"

"Canada, Professor, may I remind you, rests in the pocket of a man who corresponds daily with his dead mother and a dog. William — Lyon — MacKenzie — King!"

As each name of the Canadian prime minister was pronounced it was accompanied by a viciously Churchillian jab of colour, with a Number 6 camel-hair brush. Each jab jerked the smock a notch higher. Following the last, its wearer gave my mother an impish grin. No room here for Prince of Wales Looks. This Chartwell nudist's clash of temperament and sex was a duel to the death about Art.

"So, My Lady Impressionist! What do you think of Monet now?"

The swans and lilies were vaguely perceptible on the canvas through a splodge of yellow-and-green dots. "Look!" I whispered to my mother. "He's also got them on his Willie."

"If you have so much artistic energy to burn over Mr King and his dog," my mother smiled back at him, "perhaps instead of a brush, dear Winston, you could try the palette knife. Just be careful how you wipe it on your smock."

Two Red Admiral butterflies danced over the ruffled head of one of the male black swans. Churchill scowled at the idyllic scene.

"Terrestrial magnetism and MacKenzie King's mother against the *Nahzi* war machine! With Chamberlain dancing around the edges like those damned insects. Worse! They at least contribute something to the eye during their brief existence." He swung around and stared at my parents with a glance which seemed to take in all of Kent. The heart of England. "This war will not be brief. It will go on and on and on. There will be no surrender. You, boy, are you training? Do you have a toy gun?"

Forces a child could not fathom were at work here. Emotions too. No fleeting Churchillian family tiffs. Patriotism, the scoundrel's final refuge. It is fashionable now to sneer but,

When cowards mock the patriot's fate,
Who hangs his head for shame?

I did not then know Ingram's Irish query. (From The Memory of the Dead: nor that I was hearing Churchillian words that would soon be shaped into Immortal English.) In answer to his training question I shook my head.

"No toy gun? What is Britain coming to! And if the brute heel lands, what shall defend her, but blood and sweat, and mother's tears."

"Instead of being an architect, sir, I shall join the navy. In destroyers, like a flying fish. President Roosevelt suggested it."

"The Senior Service. Did he, by Jove? But not destroyers, boy." He took a crumb of bread from a cigar box, flicked it at the closest carp, and added with an oddly sardonic note, "If you wish to join the Immortals, better to leave a riddle in the sands of time for history's bottom feeders, than a tourist-class enigma like the Sphinx. Meanwhile, Lift your sights *up!*"

He stabbed the camel brush at the sky. His long-suffering wife rolled her eyes and spoke for the first time.

"Winston," said Clementine. "The smock!"

Had risen to his navel. But above the butterflies and swans a Spitfire barrel-rolled against the blue.

"*That* element is where this war will be decided. When you go to sea, be a flying fish! Join the Fleet Air as a torpedo pilot — and if any damn deskbound Admiralty fool objects, say Winston sent you!"

So . . . between a crippled presidential Poseidon . . . and the paint-spattered Monet penis of a Prime Minister-in-waiting . . . and two dancing Red Admirals . . .

My first volcanic rendezvous with Destiny was sealed.

May-Day for P&R . . . !

And their fragmented laptop owner. While we were searching our hard-drive's entrails to find any unconscious pluperfect Maternal *What & Whens & with Whoms?* that might give a fucking clue, or even hint at the Paternal Truth behind our conception in E-for-England . . . we were brought to a grinding System Default by old-fashioned crossed phone wires from Glen Lake.

"Folly's found the Black Book you asked for. But there aren't any Birthday Party pictures of Teddy because Jim made me burn them all."

WE didn't ask for any of this, Mama.

From Elation to Depression: Dorothea introduced us at six to Pilgrim's Slough of Despond. Churchill's Black Dog. We should have let Charlie's past-tense Darling-Willum Story stay in the toy cupboard with our Marktschreier Einstein abortion where both Harlequin Scenarios belong.

"Your mother telephones you with this name, 'Folly', and a 'slough of despond' stops work on the novel?"

Thisss accented intrusion by Dr. S-for-Strangelove opens another productive fifty minute session of wondering why it requires four years of a Bachelor of Science, about the same for an M.D., ditto to become a Trick Cyclist, and seven more of personal angst to get your name listed in the Johannesburg Yellow Pages under Psycho-Analyst merely to restate — for the umpteenth time of not being asked — the mundanely obvious.

"So you aborted the first draft of the Charlatan novel because your mother told you about this 'Black Book' of photographs which you had said you wanted her to find. Black like Winston Churchill's depressive illness, perhaps?"

Black because that's what the leatherette cover of any common-or-garden 1940's photo album looks like. And *perhaps* we'd be a lot better off just psycho-babbling to ourselves about birthday parties in the dark.

Panda : *(Birthday Party squeak means overexcitement)*
```
    "We're in the Black Book, Rabbit!
     The picture of us on the summer-
     house bench, after He sicked
     up from Whooping Cough and you
     had your Tummy Operation. Aunt
```

Dorothea read us Little Pliny's
Mount Vesuvius with our pumice
stone in the bath."

Rabbit : *(Ears drooped, means hurt feelings)*
"That was when He shaved you,
Panda. After Mother had Half-
Sister. It wasn't fair, when I was
his favourite Lop-Ears, giving her
one too. Especially not calling it
'Proper Bunny'! "

Panda : *(huffy; birthday parties always end in tears)*
"You never worried about being
Proper before Half-Sister arrived
and He shot her with the arrow."

Owner : *(bringing in Dorothea again to referee)*
" 'Little birds in their nests
agree.' "

"You shot your half-sister with an arrow because of this toy rabbit?"

Accidental near misses happen to the best regulated families. The Arrow Incident had nothing to do with Proper Bunny, who was only called that because it was made of real fur from an old coat. And our William Tell episode on the farm in Duncan was as accidental as the unregulated Gauers all being gassed with carbon monoxide from the cottage stove, the first week we arrived. It was only thanks to Dearest David having a pellet gun hole in a bedroom window pane that Charlie got woken up in time to get help and drag everyone out instead of being an Immigrant Family Suicide headline in the local rag.

"Saving your family's lives seems more significant than suicide and sibling rivalry — however, this toy bunny rabbit is called 'proper', and in our first session you said that your step-father called your half-sister 'Bunna' instead of her real name, Anthea?"

Until this brilliant observation, we thought we were a whole brother. At least *Suicide vs. Sibling Rivalry* gives Strangelove's South African sibilance a fifty-minute marathon for its money — and Owner only operated on Rabbit (in 1942, when Pliny the Younger gave Panda his pumice-from-Pompeii nightmares after a Luftwaffe bombing run) to try and see where Baby Bunny Half-Sisters came from.

"This mention of Mount Vesuvius, the birth process can seem a violent eruption, and the pubes of expectant mothers are often shaved.

Your half-sister was born in a bombing raid. This violence by the Luftwaffe against your mother might have had something to do with the
'operation' you performed on your stuffed toy perhaps?"

Share-and-share alike: our nosy little bastard trimmed *both* pets
using Jim's safety razor. The strop for which Jim later employed on
our pre-pubescent Hollow Buttocks in retribution for the William Tell
Arrow — which actually missed sister's eye by a carefully calculated
half inch while playing a scene from our favourite Arthur Ransome
yarn, *Swallows and Amazons.*

"Another 'Just William Tell non-accident' which might have
severely injured your half-sister, like the balcony episode in Hampstead
which might have done the same to you: this does seem, if not
repeating an infantile death wish, certainly a compulsion to get parental
attention, and what is this association between Jim and your 'hollow
buttocks'? — but I am afraid our time for today is up."

With which close shave we take a leaf out of Monsieur Laurillard's
Freudian commonplace notebook and bid a fond au revoir to Petit
Guillaume's death-wish and any Repetition Compulsion by Dearest
David for destroying Proper Bunnys with poison arrows. Or describing
Jim's keen observations of our Hollowed Buttocks.

Until next time.

Jim's primary displacement mechanism after losing one ball (for pure
Laurillardians, in Grimsby, we'll get there) was infantile nicknames;
his secondary, a more obscure and lifelong adult aversion to wet bread.

His primal displacement of Darling Willum is from Dickens, this
time via Pickwick, not Dorothea's Bleak House: a post-nasal threatening,
*"Someone's looking for **Mr. Snodgrass?**"* Cockney slang for nose, or
something worse. *"Who wants to play our Crane Game with the towel,* **Mr.
Snodgrass** —?"* and "chug-chug" noises-off as he hoists a-son-of-his-own
naked and dripping (pretending the Wicked Crane may drop us at any
minute!) from the bath. Then *"Night-night **Snod**"* as he kisses the prize catch
with his soppy-wet-bread lips and bristling Hitler moustache — before
the *"Bye-bye **Dai-Dai**"* (rhymes with Day-Day) maudlin Welsh farewell
for David's "Phoney War" Evacuation to — quoting from Charlie's
Letter — "our old friend Ann Crowe" in the White House at Reigate (for
our third time of *not* asking for Maternal separation!), before dragging us in
front of the Kindly Judge who finally solves the Darling Willum Problem.

After which judicial Name (Blitzed Willum's) Annihilation, Jim's enthusiasm for promoting the golden-curled merits of a Hollow-Buttocked Son-of-My-Own to his West End barber and tailor appears to decline co-equally with Burning the Teddy-Daddy Photos of a Real Father figure — which Charlie writes she went along with because "I knew nothing about neurosies[sic], psychosis etc. etc."

"This mention again of your 'hollow buttocks', the 'wet bread' aversion, there seems little doubt that your step-father was neurotic — but there is also this reference to being evacuated against your will. 'Evacuation' that equals 'expelled', as in the birth process, to a White House, after which rebellious Just William is 'reborn' as David, who 'forgets'. Your first attempt at a 'proper' novel of an idealised promiscuous mother and famous men was aborted, as you put it, shortly after the fictional mother's involvement in a swimming pool with President Roosevelt, who also lived in a White House."

In Washington D.C., and we were writing about Hyde Park —

"Which is near this Boundary Road, and the Balcony."

Bugger the bloody Balcony and 'birth process'! Screw Jim's nickname tics and those "fictional" glimpses of shrunken heads in E-for-England's lava flow of references to a Brylcreemed, piano-playing "James" mixing it up with brawny policemen at the Albemarle Artistes Club, and a Widow "Auntie Rita" running a back-lane restaurant in London with the "Celtic Romance" of MacKenzie Earls from Gairloch.

*They **were** my names!*

"References in novels may be creatively-constructed — or seen as co-incidences because they are too painful — by the unconscious."

We don't need Strangelove to tell us that. In a world that runs on Synchronicity — unlike Charlie's Letter where "now you begin to see the pattern," there are no such things as co-incidences. Before our Dickensian descent into the Blitz cellars of Somerset House, D.D. checked the Record of Births and Adoptions. Volume upon volume of the same perfect copperplate script, each with a human value that no computer printout will ever attain. But that same sense of an absolute event in Vol 1a, p678 — *Born, February 5th, 1936, William Brisbane Le Breton Harvey* — makes the seismic shock of its deletion as #66984 Vol 134, even greater.

Changed by Adoption, David Hugh Courtney Gauer, October 2nd, 1940.

Leaving only a white blank for the rest of our Willum half-lifetime . . . like a page of an Unperson in Stalin's Soviet Encyclopaedia.

But is our fictional Teddy, Charlie's Teddy —?

"What are you sinking?" murmurs M. Laurillard on the balcony.

We're drowning in Archetypes. Freud or Jung, take your pick. Zurich is no more help than Vienna in sorting the Guillaume out of Dai-Dai's dreams. Not a trace comes back from those first five years.

"Not even from this Black Book?"

With its two-and-a-half-inch-square black-and-white-glimpses of Panda-and-Rabbit-on-the-Summerhouse-Bench (with Donald Duck Gas Mask) . . . plus Elie-the-Elephant (knitted-grey-jacket-and-scarlet-tie), and Penguin (orange-webbed-feet-and-beak), and Hippo (washed-out-blue-polka-dots), and Eeyore (missing a leg, hence the afore-mentioned Limp) . . . and Charlie circa 1941 (brunette-beauty-with-male-figures-in-uniform "like a bee to honey") . . . and Jim circa '38 (Brylcreemed white-tie-and-tails-at-a-Steinway-grand; he could be the twin of Young Horowitz — except for the Noël Coward repertoire), and *Empress of Canada* postcard, "Signed by the Captain!" . . .

The Black Book pictures all show only our Life as David.

A sepia handful, on tattered grey torn-out pages, show Willum's in Hyde Park, and By the Serpentine, as Archetypal Paradise permanently lost.

> **Rabbit :** *(smugly, still one ear down from Whooping Cough puke)*
> "I remember the Donald Duck mask. It didn't fit."
>
> **Panda :** *(witheringly, keeping one up)*
> "That's because ducks don't have ears. They have beaks. I remember them on the Serpentine."
>
> **Owner :** *(firmly, keeping track of reality for Laurillard)*
> "You remember a photograph. The mask was useless. When gas actually mattered, in Duncan what saved us was a BB pellet hole in the window of my bedroom."

"Can you recall more of this gassing event?"

Just off the kitchen, right next to the stove. Like Hansel and Gretel and the oven. Somehow I woke up and found my mother. My sister and Jim were out cold for the count. And it was cold! January, next morning I remember Steller's blue jays and pheasants against the snow. This was after midnight. I managed to get Charlie awake and say I felt sick and she managed to stagger up the path through the orchard to the main house and they all came back and dragged the other two outside.

I used to compose headlines: Immigrant Family Dies in New World. It would have been totally absurd to croak from monoxide after surviving the Blitz.

Going back to the Black Book, after Jim's death, the glamorous Horowitz look-alike Portrait from the West End has gone as well. Ripped out in some Lear's whim of Aztec fury at the ruin of Age . . . together with his Signed-by-Fellow-Artistes' glossies "Best from Hutch," and "Your pal, Turner Layton" (two black, velvet-piano/vocalist immortals), and "Love from Playmate Arthur! —" fey comedian, "I'm a Bizzy Bee!" — Askey. And "What a simply marvellous party! Love, Noël."

The party's over. As is Coward.

All that remains to compound our volcanic confusion of how a lifetime run started between Charlie & Jimmy, is the following:

SINGER & KEYES.

NEXT WEEK

We have a very attractive novelty for the Pavilion, that is, the appearance of **Frakson**, the Spanish man of mystery, who does amazing things with cards and coins and who is simply miraculous with his lighted cigarettes. Where he gets them from, Frakson only knows, but if he gets coupons with them he must have furnished a row of houses by this time. I have witnessed his act in three Capitals—London, Berlin, and Paris, and in each case he has left the audience bewildered, so come next week and see how it's done.

Singer & Keyes also join the company. These boys are newcomers to Aberdeen, where they are certain to emulate the great success they have had in the South with their excellent pianoisms and vocal selections. They will put the seal on one of the strongest programmes we have ever had and as the season is reaching its height, early booking is advised.

Will the lady who left a kid glove in the hall last Wednesday, 2nd house, please call with the other one as they just fit one of the Tillers.

Which steers us into . . .

The Rye-and-Ginger Sessions

The fragile skiff of Jim's life is long overdue for a firm hand on its tiller. He was eighty-four, and already frail, when Mr. Snodgrass returned from Dickens' London determined to take off the kid gloves and emulate the Amazing Frakson by straightening things out — re Charlie (Letter) vs. Charlie (Thomas) — from Jim's side of the Singer & Keyes stage-horse's mouth, to find where the rest of the cast stand in his affections. We ghost-record our pre-cooked questions for the prosecution in the Glen Lake kitchen. Jim's sometimes half-baked responses take their own stage-directions for "Noises Off" self-defence.

(Dai-Dai never has to make our Oedipal stalking-horse drink.)

Get us another Rye-and-Ginger! We'll need a good stiff one for my parents, I don't mind telling you! He was Harry Augustus Gauer, she was Nancy Amelia. "NAG and HAG" on their gown-sample trunks. Everyone thought they were a vaudeville turn. Half their time in Liverpool, half in London. He was one of seventeen children! Gauers. She was one of eighteen or nineteen, Belhams, in Brighton. "A spewing childmaker!" On Montpelier Terrace off the Western Road behind the Grand Hotel, in a basement. My mother's father was a Frog. They might have been Jewish. When we rode on the tram all together as a family — Brother Reg, "the blue-eyed boy," Sister Nina, and me — people used to point at our noses and say, "They are." One of her sisters, Alice, married the Eau de Cologne factory on Guernsey. Came to Liverpool for the war. She said, "Mind this bag." It had fifty thousand pounds in it! Kept it under the bed. She was in Liverpool all through the war. Never gave Nag a nickel! **What happened to the bloody rye? Too much ginger. I can't**

even taste the poison! They lived in Lord Street over Hope Bros. Hag worked with Martin & Newman on Conduit Street next to Morney's on Regent Street, they were the perfumiers. Nag did the Hope orders. Hag bought too much hosiery at top price and went broke from investing in a tram-light indicator. Played organ in many churches. Trained choirs. Nag sang a soprano. They fought like bloody cat and dog. She had a wedding ring with a diamond in it the size of a rock. She used to slap me across the face with the back of her hand. The men on both sides were alcoholics. Fourteen out of the sixteen died. My father was given six months. He took the Pledge and the Seventh Day Adventists bled him dry. Every bloody copper! He got it in Brighton. The fucking religion. **This rye is more like it!** Education in Liverpool was a "penny-a-week" school. Off Penny Lane where the Beatles' song comes from. Stanborough Park College was more Seventh Days. They ran a farm, Watford, outside London. On the other farm at Mold — my parents packed me off, I was twelve — in Wales, I knew more than the village teacher so I taught kids my own age. "Hughie-bach." I was always Hugh, then. The Courtney was a friend of Hag's. I added James later. J.H.C. Three initials looked better. Names matter. In London, at 11 a.m. all the Commercial Travellers in top hats would stop along Cheapside for a twopenny beer. Free bread and cheese and pickles! Every week Hag would send me to get the money from Martin & Newman. Ten gold coins in a flannel bellyband pouch around my waist. On Fridays. I ran like merry hell! In Liverpool — the Philharmonic Hall — the Syncopated Singers, some very talented niggers. A drummer, Buddy, would go around all the members of the orchestra clipping their hair with his sticks. A month later a ship foundered in the Atlantic. All lost. That was the end of the Syncopated Orchestra. In London, we used to go to Collins Music Hall in Islington, near the Angel Pub. "Flotsam and Jetsam" couldn't stand the smell and the hurled lemons. Father substituted. The crowd booed, then sang. All the women were in shawls. Front row stalls sixpence. They were the acid test!! Then there were Messiahs in Swindon and Bedford. **Not so much bloody ginger in the next one!** Moisevitch — the pianist, he knew my father — smoked Russian cigars. He would practice on a dummy box of three octaves and stamp the cigar on the carpet. It was choking the contralto. Gladys Knight was the contralto — She was my second wife. **What's your mother looking at? A face like a bull's arse! "I'm just a Poor Weak Dog," having a little ginger with his Seagram's.** Moisevitch sent for a programme from a page boy. "I've forgotten what I was to play!" He played in the De Montfort Hall in Leicester — a small Albert Hall. He closed his eyes for fifty minutes of playing! Opened them at the end and wanted a ride to London from my father. Hag refused because of the insurance claims. As a boy I lived in the London Palladium. Sixpenny seats upstairs to catch the First House, then run like merry hell a mile and a half for the second in the threepenny seats at the Empire. I saved all the programmes. When we were coming to Canada I threw them away. I used to drop in at the real Albert Hall, at rehearsals, on Mondays, to catch old Henry

Wood conducting. Just in his shirtsleeves.
Marvellous musician but a voice as common
as muck. "Nah then, cellists! Sawin' away
regardless!" In selling it made a
tremendous difference how you sounded. Like
dear old Coxedge: Bob made the most
beautiful belts! "At my new awfice, James,
in East Cawstle Street." Simply too
frightfully-frightfully bloody la-di-da!
Can't the boy see the glass is empty? Hag
and Nag were always on the road, I was just
in their way. Hag got me a job through
another Seventh Day, Mr Pym, President of
the Banana Company, up on Primrose
Hill — the Liverpool one, not London — he
could look through his telescope to see
ships coming in. The job was a cabin boy on
a nigger whaler. The Chief Steward and the
Captain were both black as your hat. They
would have screwed you before the boat was
out of the Mersey! No one came to see me
off. One foot away from the jetty I jumped
ship. When I got home I got merry hell from
Nag and Hag for disappointing Mr Pym!
Religion came first for my parents. Work
second. They had their bloody Bible. **What
does your mother mean, I never said before
the Captain was black? Thank God for rye!
Seagram's *is* special.** Miss Peebles, the
buyer at Val Smith's, on Church Street in
Liverpool, said, "Your lines are no good to
me but I know Rossi & Co in London. You're
a first class salesman. They should give you
the agency." Rossi — an Italian in a
bowler; his house was the gown factory
— said, "You're too young!" I was only
sixteen but Mrs Hipparch — his partner
— took a shine. "We'll send you a range of
gowns — and five pounds a week." Hag had
been giving me ten shillings! But selling

wasn't my fortier. It should have been
music. In London I joined the Albemarle
Street Club on Jermyn Street near Scotland
Yard, with the 'High Colonic Massage'
advertisements. The Albemarle owner had a
monocle. "The Major." Every walk of life.
The Western Brothers. Flotsam & Jetsam.
One-and-sixpence got lunch. Wonderful food.
I belonged to the Connaught Artists Association. You auditioned for membership. At
the Connaught Rooms, in Holborn — like a
hotel for Masons — doing my patter and "All
The Things You Are" I could get twenty
guineas, three times a night. Gerald Moore,
a marvellous accompanist, but no patter,
only got fifteen once. As for the women
— **Ignore your mother, we'll switch to
sherry** — I screwed myself to death under
Renault's guidance. The brother of the car
manufacturer, he was the biggest in
handmade lingerie. When I was with Wolsey's
I went to France with Renault. Vineyards by
the bloody mile! — **the Kelowna. A bottle a
day. Nice and sweet** — On the way up to
Paris he went into the villages, left a
roll of material with a family. Got a
receipt. Rang a bell. People came out.
"Good with their needle" he said. On the
way back to Calais he'd ring a different
bell. Different peasants came out with
material embroidered. He paid in cash from a
bloody great roll of francs. One woman who
worked for him had four tits. She was a 42
and a 40! He found her in a tent in a
circus. He employed her for the rest of her
life. Making brassieres. "She's invaluable,"
Renault said, "Saves endless time." She
didn't give a damn. I was scared shitless.
Complete lack of safety in their cars! The
French police just waved us on. Beautiful

trains. Much cleaner than English trains. Paris had more lights, it was gayer than London. You walk into the Follies Bergère — all these cubicles — a stark bollocked naked woman! Some cross their legs so you don't see too much pubic hair — others don't care. God help you if you touch! The VD Museum at Blackpool. Brother Reg took me, he was nineteen. Scared the bloody hell out of us. When I was twelve I saw the first Zeppelin crash in flames on top of a men's toilet, killing everyone. Inside the Follies, the show itself, they could really dance. Whatever you call them, they were no old tarts. More glamorous than anything you would see in London. Except Dietrich. She just died the other day.... **Thanks, Dai-Dai, old boy. Let your mother get her own damn sherry if she's going to turn her nose up at Kelowna.** Charlie and I were in Marlene's Knights without Armour, by Sir Alexander Korda. Two of "1000 soldier extras," at Elstree — Charlie Thomas, this is, the "Thank you, Mr. Singer" in our "Singer & Keyes" act. He was a dresser, did a beautiful window, for Hollingsworth's. I did the piano. "Thank you, Mr. Keyes!," in white-tie-and-tails. We were also in For Valour. I was a barman, along with Tom Walls. He had to shove a pea up his nose to look like a thug. It kept falling out. In Without Armour, Marlene threw off her swimsuit at a pool in the woods. **"Darling" she said to Korda, "you know I can't stand it between my legs."**

Block your nursery eyes and ears, P&R!

By now. . . we've spent enough hours on the Couch replaying Crane Games in the Bath for it to sink in that the Brylcreem Man on the other end of the towel from Mr. Snodgrass is definitely Latent, if not yet proven Bi — which Owner intends to project toot sweet to our Monsieur Laurillard surrogate in another snatch of Sigmundian fragmentation prompted by Dr. S.'s Waiting Room *Time*-cover head-line:

Is Freud Dead?

"When did you decide to record these 'Rye' interviews with Jim?"

As soon as we returned from Somerset House with proof of Willum's existence. Charlie hadn't just been lying about their wedding anniversaries. I needed to get Jim's side of what she said in the letter. E-for-England brought a lot of clues out of the closet.

"For example?"

Jim had buck-teeth before his false ones. And although I never knew it consciously when I started my first go at the novel, both Solaris Lounge-lizards have the High Masonic Connaught and Albemarle Club's 'All The Things You Are' in common. Plus his 'high-colonic massage' advertisements with Charlie Thomas and Bizzy B Askey are obviously anal compulsion.

> **Rabbit :** *(predictably getting wrong end of the stick)*
> ```
> "In the Promiscuous Mother Story,
> was that the dancing penis
> bit about Winston Churchill's
> butterflies?"
> ```
> **Panda :** *(predictably belabouring the pointed end)*
> ```
> "He said sex should be for
> grownups. It was supposed to be a
> Mummy f***ing King Midas story,
> not flying fish and Granny Monk."
> ```
> **Owner :** *(predictably put off)*
> ```
> "Thank you Mr. Singer! If you want
> adult sex, take Jim's late tiger-
> lily, Marlene!"
> ```

We found him with her last night. Korda Classics was rerunning *Knights Without Armour* at one in the morning on CBC — which we discovered by accident while trying to avoid Owner's Blitz dreams about Charlie murdering naked Willum, as placid Maternal stand-in Granny Monk rocks and knits like Madame Defarge murmuring her "Carn't do nuffin' with him mum" to prevent our routine guillotine act of leaping up and down towards the balcony . . .

"You were drowsing in front of the television and yet you're quite sure your stepfather was in this film?"

Strangelove point taken. Picking one Extra out of an epic Cast of Thousands had indeed almost rocked us back to sleep — when the Mob began to tear Dietrich's diaphanous scarves off and there Nan's Lounge Lizard was.

A Black Book picture of Brylcreemed Jim in Turtleneck & Jodhpurs (building a henhouse for the Aunts) is a dead ringer for the Revolutionary slimeball-moustache now frozen on our VCR. Plus a custom soundtrack dubbed from 1914 marching songs of O What a Lovely War.

Gassed last night,
And gassed the night before —
We don't care if
We never go home any more!

When we left England on the *Empress of Canada*, the Captain let us visit the bridge and blow the ship's whistle off Newfoundland.

"The Captain who signed the postcard for you."

Jim wanted the damn autographs not us.

"And so now you 'blow the whistle' on your parents?"

Ignoring that bit of Strangelove. . . Panda is right about the Granny F***ing. Our Mavis Monk insertions of widowed-secretaries-in-love pall as quickly as "Big-Hearted" Playmate Arthur's autograph.

"The name of your mother's present 'out of wedlock' lover?"

We mean Jim's playmate Arthur Askey, not Charlie's Artie — the fishing-tackle-shop owner spincasting his lures while terrified of losing half his worldly goods in Qualicum Beach.

"You're still jealous of your mother's 'playmates'?"

Sticks and stones may break our bones: Nanky-Poo nursery names have long since lost their power to destroy and *'out-of-wedlock is almost prestige in this day and age.'* But for any Pure Kleinians still remaining in the CBC's dwindling audience-share, and awake enough to wonder at the strength of our Late Show vituperation of No-thanks to Mr. Keyes:

If that soppy-wet-breaded "Dai-Dai" of Jim's which followed his hoisted "Snod" out of our Hampstead bath is given its properly lethal

Welsh pronunciation, it becomes **Die Die**...

"This is thinking of the death wish again?"

Au contraire , Monsieur Laurillard!

What we are sinking is Jim's soppy wet-bread kissing Crane Game in the bath. It made us mad enough to launch a second crack at a novel.

"Another building block from the toy cupboard?"

Just close your eyes and think of Nelson.

Kiss me Hardy.

Playmate Arthur

Canadian Pacific 'EMPRESS OF CANADA' 20,000 tons

Signed by the Captain!

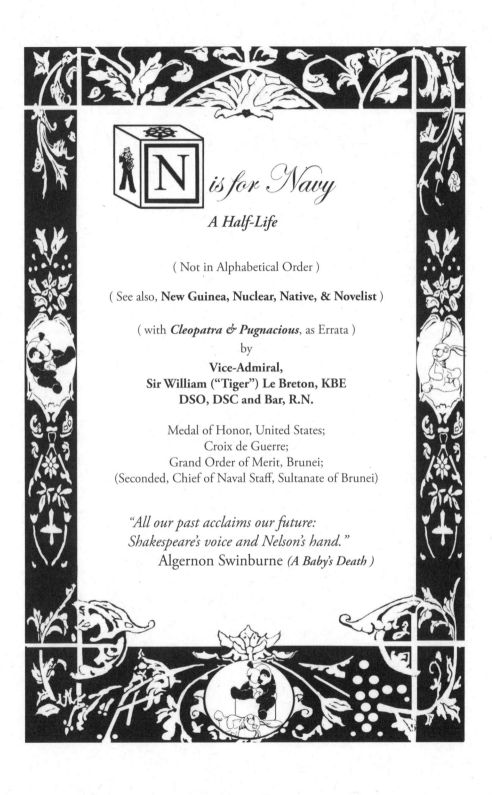

N is for Navy

A Half-Life

(Not in Alphabetical Order)

(See also, **New Guinea, Nuclear, Native, & Novelist**)

(with *Cleopatra & Pugnacious*, as Errata)

by

**Vice-Admiral,
Sir William ("Tiger") Le Breton, KBE
DSO, DSC and Bar, R.N.**

Medal of Honor, United States;
Croix de Guerre;
Grand Order of Merit, Brunei;
(Seconded, Chief of Naval Staff, Sultanate of Brunei)

*"All our past acclaims our future:
Shakespeare's voice and Nelson's hand."*
Algernon Swinburne *(A Baby's Death)*

Navy
Preface from the Fo'c'sle

It is true I am a god — Dickie Mountbatten always called me "a top-fidded bloody charlatan" — but who can agree with the humble opinion of a Commanding Officer who made himself Viceroy of the Jewel in the Crown in order to smash the damn thing after he lost his own ship?

All India! Humility may stand highest in the Christian graces of Ralph Waldo Emerson but Sherlock Holmes is a truer judge. "Mediocrity knows nothing higher than itself, but talent instantly recognizes genius."

I offer that direct extraction from Sir Arthur Conan-Doyle's *Valley of Fear* because it was the last thought but one to enter my mind as I fought to regain control of my plunging Avenger fighter aircraft before we both struck that New Guinea volcano. . . .

And now I write these words aboard a very different sort of ship! The *MV Southern Cross*, bearing me (and five-hundred far sharper Contentment Cay brains than mine!) on an Alumni Association Cruise — by the undeserved award to an all-too-ordinary seaman of an Honorary Doctorate — which will, in two short weeks, re-unite me with that Lost Island World of savage worshippers I so narrowly missed in *Pugnacious* the first time round.

I said, a last thought but one . . .

A thought we now know (through recent release of Empire Naval Radio traffic) that I shared with my father as he prepared for his Final Plunge beneath the bounding wave. A perpetual Flame of Duty and Courage, to whom, Sir, as your still Humble & Obedient servant, I have the Honour to dedicate this Work in the last words from your lips:

God save the King . . . !

Navy
One

T HE FIRST MEMORY OF MY FATHER GOES WITH LIFE AT SEA: Splicing the Mainbrace with Pusser's rum on the holystoned teak deck of the Flag Officer's Yacht moored in Trincomalee Harbour, in Ceylon. Today, of course, it is Sri-Lanka, and a vicious civil war, but then it was still the Pearl of the Pacific. If not the ultimate jewel in the crown of our Empire, at least a special bauble.

As the Flag Officer's only son, I was another.

At two I had a sailor suit from his uniform tailors, Messrs Gieves, 22 The Hard, Portsmouth; and my own cox'n (coxswain, for landlubbers) — in photographs, looking just like the murdered young Tzarevitch in pre-Bolshevik Russia — to carry me down the companionways, or take me ashore in the Admiral's Barge to be reunited with my mother.

"What ship?"

"Flag. Cleopatra."

I can still hear the shrilling of the bosun's calls — the whistles, or "pipes," modulated with the little finger — as passing boats hailed each other or were challenged at the gangway. *HMS Cleopatra* was my father's yacht. Indeed, between the ages of three and five I believed it was his, and not the property of their Lordships at the Admiralty on the far side of the world.

The world as I knew it was red because the shortest nautical distance between any two points on the globe had red land masses at either end on the Mercator's Projection that hung in the Midshipmen's Gunroom (or wherever people needed to see where they were going), presided over by an unlucky sub-lieutenant called the Snotties' Nurse.

In 1932, maps and globes were still defined by the British Empire. All the lands outside it (colored green, brown, or yellow) were of no consequence. All that mattered were those Great Circle routes curving up or down towards the Arctic and Antarctic Oceans. Where distances were not long enough, or nearby land was too confining — the Indian Ocean or Malacca Straits — courses were set by Rhumb Lines, straight ones cutting off the tops of the navigational arcs.

Empire distance was measured in nautical miles: two-thousand yards. Naval distance was measured in cables — one-tenth that amount, two-hundred yards — and fathoms: six feet. Metrification played no part in delineating the boundaries of the British World.

From the start, my life was destined to protect or extend it.

At birth — "A boy, thank God!" — I was named and enrolled at Dartmouth Naval College in accordance with my grandfather's — I was going to say, wishes: Executive fiat would be better. "Like Captain's Orders, boy!"

My grandfather was a dinosaur. One of the Cannon-Ball Term, like Beatty (the Lion of the Dogger Bank) who reached the second-highest Flag Rank — to sport the one-broad-and-three-thin gold stripes of Full Admiral — by polishing the muzzles of eighteen-inch guns.

"Battleships!" and "Line of Battle!" were the four principal words (apart from oaths) they used. The name of Billy Mitchell never passed their lips. His news-reel grandstand act of sinking an anchored dreadnaught with a single airborne bomb was dismissed with another oath, "Bloody American!"

Don't blame only British wardroom prejudice. America's own admirals were equally appalled when they visited my father in Ceylon.

"Mitchell bombed her like a tethered goat, with no teeth to fire back! But you know those Army bastards, Tiger. What else would you expect?"

Tiger Le Breton. The nickname wasn't from hunting in the Ceylon jungle, but the U.S. football field. In an unusual move for the day, my father served on exchange at Annapolis, the American Dartmouth, where he introduced a new mess-dinner game: a mix of rugger and Yankee football played in full mess kit, with no padding, and drinks — "Tiger Balls," striped layers of crème de cacao and yellow anise — at each ten-yard line. (It was a great success at the time but couldn't survive the post-war increase in tailors' bills.)

I inherited the nickname when I was discovered by my cox'n, Leading Seaman "Dixie" Dixon, as he reported to my father, "Sittin' in the gunlayer's seat, Sir, of the after-starboard Four-inch. Callin' out, 'Fire!' like a proper bleedin' little Wale Island tiger!"

The lethal weapon in question wasn't aboard *Cleopatra* — yachts don't carry four-inch guns — but arming the suitably named *Pugnacious*, a heavy cruiser, flagship of the Pacific Station. (A decade later, to the day, she was sunk when Mitchell's news-reel "dreadnaught" stunt came true: one bomb down the funnel, off Singapore, escorting the battleship *Prince of Wales*.)

Between the wars, however, she led a charmed life. The 1936 newspapers were full of reports of *HMS Pugnacious* visiting Shanghai or Tokyo, Sidney or British Columbia. As the Victoria *Daily Colonist's* social reporter put it,

> The Royal Navy's flag can seldom have been shown to better advantage than under Admiral W. "Tiger" Le Breton, VC, DSO, R.N. At a banquet or "Mess Dinner" in his spacious quarters aboard *HMS Pugnacious*, with His Honour the Lieutenant Governor, His Worship the Mayor, and their Ladies in attendance (as well as the Senior Canadian Officer Afloat on our West Coast, in *HMCS Rainbow*), the flowers on the tables amidst the blued steel of enormous guns made guests feel quite as though they had stepped back into the age of Nelson!
> This was partly due to the Admiral's dashing eye-patch, covering a wound acquired during his famous engagement against three German light cruisers in his destroyer, the *Rameses*, off Le Havre. He would blush to read it, but this is the first Flag in the Pacific to have won the Victoria Cross. Perhaps to lessen the severity of this image the Admiral has with him his young son. (Already another "Tiger" to the crew and destined to be another gunnery officer, no doubt!) Little William quite won the hearts of all when he sang "Hearts of Oak" as the Royal Marine band played the Sunset Ceremony, and the shadows of Douglas Firs and Fisgard Light were cast across the gleaming stillness of Esquimalt Harbour. . . .

The *Colonist's* reporter didn't mar the scene with an account from the other end of Victoria's social scale. Three suitably *Pugnacious* ratings and five loggers, brawling over a girl named Betty, dancing naked on a table in a hamlet marked on the charts as Captain Langford's Station.

(Which curiously resembles the Cabaret act in the Solaris Lounge on the deck below me now — "Swinger and Keyes" — with the modest addition of a G-String and a grand piano lid for the table!)

As for Little William . . . I broke the family mould: "Tiger-Minor" didn't become a gunner like father and grandfather. Nor, to their astonishment, did I go to Dartmouth. But that comes later. My first education was held aboard a variety of capital ships. In those days all cruisers and above carried "schoolies," officer-schoolmasters who wore pale blue between the gold of their stripes. Lieutenant-Commander L.C. Thornethwaite-Barqhuar (MA, Cantab) RN, my initial tutor, had two-and-a-half.

Inevitably, a name like that became "Elsie Barker" to the "Hairy-Feelers": an assortment of unlikely scholars — "Skates, Shags, and Ordinary Seamen!" — flotsam-and-jetsam of the Fleet scooped from the lower deck to qualify for promotion in trades requiring basic maths, a neat hand, and minimal spelling; i.e., Captain's Coxswains requiring drivers licences, Paymasters, and Chief Stewards. (The stewards for Seating Plans and menus at Mess Dinners.) Vital naval knowledge, like astral navigation and ballistics, was passed on by specialists in those subjects.

"It is a tragedy waiting to happen, Le Breton Minor. But a day will come, mark my words, when education will be seen as too important to be left to the sextant-and-cuff-hanky crowd and those rifle-bored blockheads of the Gunnery School at Wale Island. Officers will attend proper universities and get proper degrees, like myself. Only when that day happens will we prevent fiascos such as the last Entrance Exam for Greenwich. I still cannot believe that in 1935, when we are learning how to split the atom, officers qualifying for command rank are being asked how to strike the fidded topmast on the *Royal Sovereign* when passing beneath the Firth of Forth bridge!"

Alas, poor Elsie: as late as 1971 (when I presided over both a Hydrogen Bomb Test on Christmas Island, and the Commonwealth Fleet Command Board in Plymouth), qualifying officers still were.

Lacking any hope of mastering Top-fidded seamanship, Elsie was forced to fall back on what he'd absorbed as an Old Cantabrian: Epicharmus and Tacitus in their original tongues, Latin and Greek.

"Be sober and remember to distrust: these are the very mainsprings of understanding."

Not in the Royal Navy — though more so in Brunei. On occasion, serving the Sultan (and Sultana) I had cause to reflect on Elsie's imparted Epicharmus. Less so, until now, his Tacitus:

" '*Mediocres poetas nemo novit; bonus pauci,*' Le Breton Minor. 'Third-rate poets no one knows; and but few know those who are good'."

I can see him, declaiming what might have been his epitaph, as he rode down Signal Hill at Hong Kong, full speed ahead through the coolie dockyard mateys, black gown flying, barely avoiding getting caught in the spokes of his woman's bicycle, although its wheels were protected by string skirt-guards. Costume was his first undoing.

On a formal visit to Yokosuka, Elsie had the luck to be greeted by a "wanky-wanky" Tokyo bar girl wearing only a bunch of purple grapes.

We are all hostages to pubic fortune. Schoolmaster Lieutenant-Commander Thornethwaite-Barqhuar was in his tropical whites. When the wanky-wanky girl sat in his lap the Dionysian result was visible to all the passengers while he sang Glory Glory Hallelujah for a thirty mile train ride. ("Bugger the Battle Hymn of the Republic!" the Captain of the Court Martial reported informally to my father. "Your poor sod of a schoolie looked less the grapes of wrath than being rogered full-astern by bloody Mount Fuji!")

As this was at a time when great efforts were being made to impress the Rising Sun with the power of an Empire on which it never set, Elsie's mishap was seen as an excess of noblesse oblige. He was stripped of his thinnest pale-blue stripes and reverted to Lieutenant; a punishment severe enough, without the additional torture of becoming the Fleet's Senior Snottie's Nurse. He wasn't sent home in disgrace (to Canterbury where he subsequently took holy Orders) until the second shoe dropped over the Fleet Chaplain's Concupiscence business with Bollox, the Ship's Cat.

Navy
Two

S EX IN THE BIBLE WAS A VERY REAL HELP TO ALL NAVAL FAMILY members troubled by the lack of a good word of their own for special occasions. Every signal bridge and Captain's cabin had a Concordance, heavily thumbed. Clewed-up Chief Yeomen would anticipate the quote required in response to another ship's flag hoist or message flashed by Morse light, and have it buttoned on the halyards ready to go before their commander could say,

"Chief Yeoman! What's that bloody thing about fingering father's loins?"

"First Kings, sir. Twelve and Ten. 'My little finger shall be thicker than my father's loins'. Or if he's being a clever dick, sir, you could use Second Chronicles. Ten and Ten. Same wording. I have both bent on."

Mess bills were run up higher than the signal flags as ships competed to be first off the mark in looking up the quote and snapping back an appropriate reply.

I've always had a soft spot for Esther — *"And the king loved her above all the women, and she obtained grace and favor in his sight more than all the virgins . . . "* — which is only natural from a boy to his mother.

Charlotte Esther Winifred Mellon-Du Pont was her full maiden name; Freddie to my father, and love at first sight. They met on a tennis court at Annapolis and, yes, she was American and, yes, those are the Mellons and Du Ponts who split the ownership of America with the Rockefellers and Morgans. She was from a branch far enough down the tree to avoid the responsibility of bearing the full weight of the Family. Her father had been an amateur archaeologist whose small claim to fame in Who's Who was the possible discovery of the Fifty-Cubit-high gallows on which a king of Israel hanged Haman at Esther's instigation. My own father always took this as a warning not to take my mother's wishes lightly. Her father — "Granpa Du Pont" — went on from Haman's execution to King Midas, whose every touch was solid gold.

"Those Midas Expeditions cost a fortune!" my mother would laughingly tell luncheon guests. "It was a good thing he had one. It meant selling the cottage at Newport, with its thirty rooms, so I grew up either in a tent in the desert or an ordinary house."

The final bee in my maternal grandfather's Midas bonnet somehow managed to put the King's Golden Mountain on a mythical desert island, West-nor-west of Java — and Admiral's House in Trincomalee wasn't ordinary by today's suburban standards! The view over Koddiyar Bay surpassed description. The Indian Ocean has always been my favorite, even more than the South Pacific. Its colors shift through all the range of blues from lightest azure to deepest royal and back again in just the time it takes for a Tamil servant to bring out a green-speckled, four-minute egg in a knitted woollen cosy.

Speaking navigationally, Ceylon is bounded by a Sea, the Laccadive, and the world's largest Bay, of Bengal, but the Indian Ocean controls the movement of the Sub-Continent's waters, and all who venture on them.

My mother didn't. She would have liked to sail in *Pugnacious* around both capes, the Horn and Good Hope; to her continual chagrin, her maritime excursions were confined to *Cleopatra*, and yachting picnics in exquisite Ceylonese coves. These disputes over a woman's place at sea were the only times I ever heard my parents quarrel.

"Why not?" my mother demanded. "The Island *might* be there, and in 'Moby Dick' all the whaling captains had their wives with them."

"Good God, Freddie! Since James Cook we've charted every scrub-coral strand between Ceylon and Surabaya — and even an American suffragette can't equate a Bedford whaler with a Far East flagship of the R.N. There's something damned unhealthy in Melville. Aboriginal harpooners sleeping with young men and a weapon between them in the bed."

"I'm surprised the RN knows so much about Sigmund Freud's psychology."

"Freud is now in London. That may be the reason for an Admiralty medical bulletin suggesting Melville be removed from ships' libraries. And you know perfectly well why a woman can't go to sea. Apart from the Lower Deck's superstition about females and disaster, it simply isn't fair to the men that you and I should be able to enjoy each other in bed every night, when all they can get is ten minutes ashore with a native girl for half a dollar in the Boola Tallee Club —"

He broke off at that interesting point as I came into the room.

Hence, on those trans-Pacific voyages to British Columbia and Polynesia, I went without my mother. But there was so much to do and see that I scarcely missed her. And while cruises took three or four months, I still saw far more of her in my early years than most British children whose parents were stationed in the East. The normal thing was to be shipped Home for schooling like Rudyard Kipling, and not enjoy one's family for years on end. In many cases, no doubt a blessing.

In mine, I continued an education with naval schoolmasters as private tutors until my thirteenth birthday when it was time for me to go to Dartmouth. By which time I had been initiated into the two greatest of life's mysteries.

Both happened in Samoa.

The year was 1939, the month, June, the longest day and start of summer in the Northern Hemisphere; the shortest, and winter in the Southern. In the tropics the sun rose and fell with its unchanging equatorial regularity as *Pugnacious* ploughed through sapphire seas. Flying Fish skimmed the crests with silver-laced wings.

This land-locked descriptive flight of fancy took off from a mid-commission refit in Singapore to install a launching ramp and catapult adjacent to the quarter-deck of the cruiser. The idea of seaborne planes wasn't brand new; the first primitive carrier had been converted from a merchant vessel at the end of the Great War, but an aircraft flying from a conventional warship was still an infrequent sight, and a risky business for the pilot. Launching off was bad enough; recovery could only be effected by landing alongside and being hauled aboard by a crane. In sea states more than One or Two, even a light chop —

I took one look and knew I wanted to do it.

"He can't!" my mother insisted to my father in Singapore. "Not at sea, Tiger darling. Promise me you won't let him."

To my mortification he acceded to her request. Ten days out of refit, steaming south, I had given up all hope . . .

A runner summoned me to the Flag Officer's Bridge.

Except for death in battle, the Flag Bridge of a British heavy cruiser in those days was as close as a male mortal could get to the grace of God.

One deck lower, the approaching aura of heaven on earth was reflected from the ship's brass bell with the name, *Pugnacious*, engraved and polished so hard that it gleamed like gold. The white webbing on the Royal Marine sentries was snowy as the marble of the Taj Mahal. Civilians' first reaction on arriving at the Command bridge was always, "Something's missing! Where's the wheel?"

In ocean liners the helm could be out in the open. On a battle cruiser it was six decks down, behind two feet of steel armour-plating. Orders were passed through an echoing voice pipe.

"Full speed ahead, all engines."

"All engines full speed ahead. Aye, aye, sir."

I heard that command, and the quartermaster's response, as I made my way through the enclosed Command, with its glass windows, and up to the Elysian atmosphere of the Admiral's Bridge. My father stood smoking his pipe in a remote corner. I knew immediately what was happening. The signal flag F for Fox, or Flight Operations, snapped on the mainmast halyard. Full speed increased the wind across the deck. Standing on tiptoe, squinting into a gale-force thirty knots, I saw an island on the horizon.

"Still want to do it?" my father asked between puffs.

I didn't think twice. "Yes!"

"Good boy. I'm not breaking my word to your mother. You'll be landing in Pango Pango harbour. Wear your life jacket and do everything Lieutenant Vaughan tells you."

The plane was a two-seater. That was all that could be said in its favor. A sea-going variant of the Sopwith Camel, it was one of the most lethal flying machines ever invented — for its pilot. In certain (unfortunately always random) conditions of heavy air and temperature inversions, the single-engined craft had the unnerving habit of dropping its nose and plummeting to earth. Or in this case, water.

The pilot on *Pugnacious* was happily without imagination. Lieutenant Timmy Vaughan took life as it came with the cheerful sangfroid that earned him the G&S nickname "Nanky Poo" from the *Mikado*: a figure who lived in the constant shadow of Imperial execution. He was already waiting in the dual cockpit. A leading seaman delegated as ground crew helped me into my life jacket.

"You won't be wearing a chute, sir. Not going high enough today to pull the cord."

"Sir" to a thirteen-year-old blocked out No Parachute. I put on a leather helmet and goggles to look like Lindbergh. The leading seaman helped me up the ladder. I stepped over the hatch coaming. He strapped on my shoulder harnesses in the seat behind the pilot. Nanky Poo turned his goggled head, grinned, gave an interrogative thumbs-up? and mouthed, "Are we on?"

I gulped and raised a juvenile thumb. Ahead, to the left, another sailor stood, white-bellbottom trouser legs wide apart, holding two red and green semaphore flags. The red was high above his head. *Pugnacious* heeled to starboard, making a turn of twenty degrees into the wind. The red flag streamed straight back towards us. Air howled past the Plexiglas. Nanky Poo raised both thumbs a second time. The cruiser steadied. The red flag dropped. The green went up. The catapult fired. Something struck the small of my back.

Gravity.

I was in the air.

Flight is such a commonplace today . . . but I shall remember the feeling of that first airborne morning until I die — although there was really nothing to look at close-to except the leather back of Nanky Poo's helmet, and outside the cockpit just endless blue. The only hint of anything more interesting was a faint triangular wisp to the southwest.

I tapped Nanky's shoulder, pointed at the wisp, and shouted over the slipstream, "It could be Granpa Du Pont's Golden Island! Can we go and have a look?"

He shook his head and shouted back, "There's nothing on the chart between here and New Guinea. And if I took you even a cable off our flight plan, your father would have my guts for new catapult garters!"

The flight plan was only seven miles, but at the Bay of Pago Pago Lieutenant Vaughan did give me a mini grand tour, banking in a steady curve to let me look down at the fifty different denominations of Christian churches strung along the beach to bring the once-pagan natives of American Samoa ever closer to God. Then we glided down onto the turquoise-mirror surface of the bay and waited for *Pugnacious* to catch up to us.

Her anchor let go with a great roar as the cable rattled through the hawse. Nanky Poo taxied alongside. The crane hook lowered.

"Button us on, Tiger Minor."

Vaughan gave a final lazy grin. I snapped the hook into a steel eye behind my seat. We were hoisted inboard. High above me the figure of my father stared down, still puffing on his pipe. Still in his exalted position. But he never looked quite the same again. I had been closer to heaven than a Flag Officer's Bridge.

So near and yet so far . . .

Nanky Poo routinely dismissed my Golden Wisp of *Boys' Own* imagination in his Sopwith flight log as mere, "Clouds: Normal cumulous for Tropical-Convergence."

Navy
Three

SAMOA AND SEX PROBABLY SEEM SYNONYMOUS TO THOSE PEOPLE who've never found themselves on a South Pacific Island — the majority of humanity — but this state of mind was particularly heightened in the Fleet Chaplain; a man whose on-the-job clerical training (as a vicar in Cheltenham, attending its celebrated finishing school for young ladies to give them sermons on Sundays) wouldn't at first glance have appeared a plausible seedbed for his virulence against all aspects of weakness in the flesh.

He had come to sea because he had lost his wife: not to the Grim Reaper, but a Games Mistress at Cheltenham. A domestic loss which, to borrow from my mother's favorite, Oscar Wilde, smacked more of carelessness than grief. He had another personal cross to bear. We've already seen how the close confinement of Naval Family life has a unique facility for bringing together inapposite names and professions. As my former schoolmaster, Thornethwaite-B, became "Elsie Barker," so Fleet Chaplain Spittlehouse was inevitably Christened by the Far East hammock decks, "Holy Gob."

Hammocks also confront that other issue of the forced intimacy of naval life alluded to by my father's glancing remark about Melville's harpooner. Unlike the Guards Regiments protecting Buckingham Palace, there was no pride in being "gay" in one of His Majesty's warships. Hidden under the Kings Regulations euphemism, "A Disposition of Unnatural Offence," buggery — like an officer consulting psychiatry — was grounds for instant dismissal with disgrace from the Service.

Which brings us full circle to concupiscence and Bollux the cat.

Returning from my first memorable flight . . . I made my way from the recovered Sopwith Camel up to the Flag Bridge to report to my father. I found him in group conference with Toughie, the Captain of *Pugnacious* (from half a twisted jaw, shot away at Jutland), holding a copy of the cruiser's Standing Orders, and Holy Gob waving a Book of

Common Prayer in a High Church state of agitation.

"Tomorrow is not only Trinity Sunday, sir," Spittlehouse insisted, as I came into earshot, "it is also the Nativity of Saint John the Baptist, Easter having fallen at its latest this year. This is a day of special Abstinence in the Church year. Under such circumstances, granting leave tonight surely runs the risk, if not the direct promotion, of venality on a prodigious scale. To say nothing of the health problem. I have spoken to the Fleet Surgeon. Then too, there is the theologically distasteful matter of Thornethwaite-Barqhuar's charge of blasphemy against the cat and —"

"Damn and blast your bloody eyes!" roared Captain Toughie, smashing the Orders with a Jutland iron fist. "The Ship's Cat is the responsibility of the Chief Quartermaster. Bollux's job is to catch bilge rats before they fall into the Grog barrels. Yours is to protect my crew's immortal blasted souls. The Malayan Rubber Company will take care of their pox-shrivelled cocks and balls!"

I observed the twitch of a smile at my father's mouth. His outward concern was the disciplined chaos caused by the arrival and anchoring around us of a squadron of six destroyers. He gestured with his pipe at the innumerable churches on the shoreline. "With so much local inspiration for devotion, Fleet Chaplain, I'm sure you'll find the spiritual words for your sermon with no difficulty." His pipe pointed next at Toughie's Standing Orders. "Standard Service discipline can cope with the cat and the schoolmaster."

"But excess of devotion, sir, is the problem." Spittlehouse flapped a page of his prayer book. *A Table concerning the Regulation of Services when Two Feasts or Holy Days fall upon the Same Date.* As destroyer sirens screamed and salutes fired, he began to read aloud: "Then, ordinarily the days set out in the column to the left of the table following shall be held to take precedence of those in the column to the right and the services appointed for the days set out in the column to the right shall either be transferred as therein directed, or be altogether pretermitted for —"

"Good God Almighty!" Toughie swore, and saluted my father. "The Fleet *pretermitting*, sir, I have to make Rounds."

By now there were boats everywhere, hailing and replying as anchors splashed and ensigns unfurled. One approaching craft bore the flag of the American Governor of their part of Samoa. My father nodded at Toughie: "I think the regular rules for short leave, Captain, but in view of the Kava Bowl hospitality in this part of the world perhaps double up on the Shore Patrol." And then to Holy Gob: "The choice of sermon texts is entirely at your discretion, Padre — but not too long for the Tropics. And steer clear of the cat."

I couldn't wait any longer to recite my first flying adventure and ask, "When can I go up again?"

"You've obviously caught the bug," said my father. "I'll talk to Vaughan after the destroyers finish. Now I have to meet the Governor."

The berthing of the six destroyers was a nautical work of art. The senior ship, driven by its Squadron's Captain D, went alongside a primitive jetty next to a sand beach. Once that was accomplished two more destroyers secured outboard. Then came the tricky bit. The fourth vessel swung around so that its stern was to the beach, at right angles to the other group, dropped an anchor, reversed her engines, and heaved a line ashore from the stern. The final pair of destroyers took up position on either side. My father watched, with his good eye to the telescope, nodding in approval.

"A perfect Mediterranean Moor. Chief Yeoman, send them Baker Zebra."

Nautical abbreviation for Well Done!

The American Governor left his calling card. Then it was my father's turn. His Admiral's Barge drew alongside the companionway. "Not as much fun as flying but you may as well see how it's done," he said to me.

The Barge Coxswain was Dixie — now Petty Officer — Dixon, my naval nurse when I still had to be carried onto *Cleopatra*, in Ceylon. When we were alone Dixie still addressed me as "Master Tiger, sir" in a rich Devon burr. His Barge was painted emerald green in the highest gloss enamel. The cheesed rope work lay in perfect whitened coils. Bronze dolphins stood on their heads and tails to frame the cabin hatch. My father stood on his feet to inspect the Squadron. As we passed, each destroyer in turn piped their bosun's call while the Officer of the Deck saluted. Meanwhile the guns of *Pugnacious* offered their own roar: not to the Governor's person — a rotund little man, who once sold shirts in Poughkeepsie — but to the emerging might of America on the far side of the Pacific.

Their eastern portion of the Samoan Island Group contained only a handful of Caucasian Americans. The female half had skins of yellow leather from too much tropical sun and gin. The Admiral's Barge secured alongside a set of rickety steps, crusted with coral and slippery with weed. My father made an agile leap. I followed. Dixie and his bowman performed an elaborate saluting drill with their boat hooks.

Then protocol began to fall apart. The Governor's car, a 1930 Packard, broke down. His Mansion was at the top of a small hill, perhaps five hundred yards.

My father said, "We'll walk."

It isn't every day that a British admiral in his dress whites, a single purple ribbon on his right chest (his Victoria Cross) and the other ribbons and orders of Empire knighthood around his neck, strides the dusty shores of Pango Pango. As we left the beach, a small crowd cheered us up the hill. The Barge crew did a final bit of boathooking — somewhat sloppily . . . as a young woman moved out from behind a frangipani plant with nothing to obscure her perfect breasts.

"The missionaries don't seem to have killed human nature completely," my father said dryly. We had already passed three churches, which left another forty-seven. Government House was only a large bungalow and dull. I was introduced, given lemonade, and then a wink by my father that let me off the leash.

I strolled back alone through my first tropical paradise, down the hill towards the Barge. In a blinding sizzle of lightning and simultaneous deafening thunder, Nature chose that moment for her daily cloudburst.

A palm tree split open. I got soaked to the skin, but rain and air were the same temperature: 80 Fahrenheit. Wearing sodden white shorts, knee socks, and an open-necked shirt, I approached the Barge. There was no sign of its crew. I heard a moan behind the palm tree. Fearing a human injury from the lightning strike, I turned —

In one of those indelible moments of life's evolution my eyes took in the form of the Cox'n, standing. The eight-buttoned fly of Dixie's white bellbottoms was unflapped. A masculine organ as stiff (almost as long!) as his boathook, and the color of my father's VC, protruded from the opening. Then, seconds later, impaled and supported by it was the young Samoan woman. Her legs wrapped Dixie's waist, her arms his neck.

A bellow that combined a Devon, "Aargh!" and "Ahoy!" issued from his throat. The Samoan girl screamed. For the first time I realized that sound could be one of feminine pleasure, as well as terror.

She threw back her head. Her black hair cascaded below her buttocks, hiding their purple central support. I felt my own body performing inside my wet shorts — but my veins held more than primitive instinct. Generations of naval officer's training. This lower deck scene was not one the Wardroom had been meant to observe.

I withdrew uphill to whistle *Hearts of Oak*. Loudly.

After allowing some time for whatever had to happen . . . I returned to the head of the steps with a certain trepidation. The purple impaler had vanished. The white bellbottoms were buttoned up. The Samoan girl sauntered, giggling, into the frangipani flowers. Dixie saluted professionally. I detected a slight anxiety.

"It's all right," I said; "I won't tell."

"That be very good of you, Master Tiger, sir. Very good."

His junior bowman grinned, sliding a hand up and down his (wooden) boathook — and got a clip across the ear. When my father returned by Packard from Government House, his Barge was shipshape.

Navy

Four

NEXT MORNING, SUNDAY, AFTER THE MARINE BAND ON THE quarter-deck of *Pugnacious* had played both anthems — *The King* and *Star Spangled Banner* — I accompanied my father again in his Barge: this time to the church service on board the senior destroyer berthed alongside the decrepit jetty, closest to the land. The Royal Marine musicians preceded us to boost the hymns. Perched on a gun hatch, Fleet Chaplain Spittlehouse droned through the Collect for the Day; then the Lesson, read by my father in Tropical short order. Despite his Jutland jaw, Captain Toughie managed the Naval Prayer at the double:

O Eternal Lord God, who alone spreadest out the heavens, and rulest the raging of the sea; who hast compassed the waters with bounds until day and night come to an end: Be pleased to receive into thy Almighty and most gracious protection the persons of us thy servants, and the Fleet in which we serve . . .

"We will now sing hymn number 278," Holy Gob dropped the service back to Slow Ahead. " 'Sow the seed beside all waters' . . . "

Not a popular number. A ragged choir launched into it.

" *'Sow the seed beside all waters,*
North and south and east and west,
That our toiling sons and daughters
In the harvest may be blest.' "

"On this most special day of Abstinence," Spittlehouse continued, as the voices trailed to a weak Amen, "when Venality is foremost in our Christian minds, as we look around this broad expanse we see monuments to God — not Church of England — but no less valiant in their fight to keep Lust and Concupiscence at bay . . . "

Holy Gob allowed a dramatic pause from his gun-hatch pulpit. I thought of last night's purple episode.

"One wonders what else he's 'pretermitted' for this interminable occasion," my father murmured under his breath to Toughie.

At which moment, in the curious way the God of Battles manoeuvres to perform His wonders on the deep . . . a sound, also now familiar from Dixie's "boathook" encounter, issued from aft of the forward six-inch turret. A yowling screech!

"I am reminded of two poems — " Spittlehouse raised his voice above it — "the first by Byron Rufus Newton. And as we are in this part of Samoa, suitably he is an American. He wrote these words about New York; however, one cannot help but feel amidst this too-ripe foliage of the pagan jungle —" an even louder howl from the six-inch — "that his words are just as appropriate for Pago Pago. Indeed, taking poetic license, I have made small changes to reflect our locale. I will not begin with the first line. 'Overdressed' hardly seems the word to describe —"

A flurry of ginger fur. And, to the bored congregation's delight, the feline image of Tom Bollux perpetuating his Royal Naval lineage with a local female tabby on a teak grating! The Fleet Chaplain, like Queen Victoria, was not amused — but nor was Holy Gob deterred from his single-minded pursuit of poesy in the jungle.

" 'Heartless, Godless, hell's delight,
Rude by day and lewd by night.
Raving rotting, money-mad;
A squirming herd in Mammon's mesh' — "

"God's flaming teeth!" an outraged Toughie swore. "Mammon! The lower deck don't have a spare bloody sixpence. Chief Quarter-master — do something about those fucking cats!"

" 'A wilderness of human flesh;
Crazed with avarice, lust and rum,
Samoa, thy name's Delirium'."

"The fucking cats. Aye aye, Sir!"

With a true sense of Awe, I watched the inexorable workings of the Lord of Hosts continue to unfold behind the Chaplain's back. As the Chief Quartermaster cautiously approached the six-inch turret from its Starboard side . . . a wild-eyed Elsie Barker, waving aloft a schoolmaster's tome bound in antique leather, appeared to Port . . . and to complete this Pago-Pagan Trinity —

Dixie's bare-breasted former companion appeared out of the too-ripe Samoan foliage and strolled onto the beach. Fifty feet behind the Chaplain she removed her sarong, stood stark naked under a perforated Palm Oil can in a tree, yanked on a hemp string, and while she showered . . . and casually scratched . . . 1200 pairs of male eyes swivelled as one to the focus of her itch.

Except Spittlehouse (declaiming), "My other poetic thought for this morning, is by A.E. Houseman, one of our own. *'Thinking of Home'* —"

And the Chief Quartermaster (to Bollux and Tabby, murmuring), "There's a Good Pussy —"

And Elsie (hissing at Toughie), *"Get Thee behind me Satan —!."*

And Gob (still bleating), " 'A Shropshire Lad', like many of you. 'If the heats of hate and lust, In the house of flesh are strong' —"

And Elsie, *"He that hath in his possession a fornicating Stenchy Beast —!"*

And Gob, " 'Let me mind the house of dust, Where my sojourn shall be long' — "

And Elsie, *"King Mode warns us, Be not ensnared by that Beauteous Maiden —"*

Dixie's Samoan companion continued her ablutions.

"I urge you to consider those words — " Holy Gob, still oblivious of the beach scene, now concentrated on outpointing his demented theological rival. "Recalling our Lord's admonition that the body is a Temple, whose portals of procreation are not to be defiled —"

The Samoan Temple spread wide her portals to examine and cleanse herself.

"For her true animal likeness is as a foul harlot! And he that owns it shall be judged — !"

The Chief Quartermaster booted Bollux and his tabby lover apart with a final feline screech, while Cleric and Academic continued their mad duet:

"How that defilement arrives is now too awfully apparent through the workings of medical science — "

"I adjure thee, Creature Witch — "

"Master at Arms!" bellowed Toughie. "Put Mr. Thornethwaite-Barqhuar under arrest!"

"A spirochete even now in the blood of those among us who have lapsed," Spittlehouse counter-tenored, "may be crawling its way upwards to — "

"Arrest the Schoolmaster! Aye aye, Sir!"

It had become the most memorable church sermon any man Jack present would ever attend, but Elsie and Bollux's part in it was already forgotten. The 1200 pairs of eyes followed the smallest feminine movement of the Samoan Temple's fingertips, and every bead of water coursing down the Samoan Temple's thighs.

"Let us conclude with, 278. verse 3: 'Where our brothers, sowing, reaping, Delving for the hidden ore' — "

Elsie shifted targets and hurled his leather book at the local tabby. *"Beware of Circe — !"*

The tome missed the tabby. Elsie hurled himself at Holy Gob.

"I again adjure thee —!"

" 'Tell of Jesus, Jesus only, Who alone can save and bless'."

"Thou voice of the Serpent —!"

"That's enough of that, sir."

Elsie's screeching counter-delirium came to a gurgling end as the Master at Arms crushed him in a full Nelson.

"Thanks be to God," declared the winner of this hollow victory. "And now, in the name of the Father, the Son, and the Holy —"

"AMEN!"

Roared 1200 throats. The naked Temple slipped on her sarong and sauntered back into the devil's vegetation. Elsie was carried below in a strait-jacket. My father accepted Captain D's invitation to lunch. I stayed on the destroyer's quarterdeck, trapped by the object of my infatuation . . . Nanky Poo's aircraft, secured to the boom alongside *Pugnacious*.

"Excuse me, Master Tiger, sir." It was Dixie. "One good turn deserves another, if you don't mind my sayin'. Come along of me."

I followed him down the ladder into the Admiral's Barge. We proceeded a hundred yards along the coast of Pango Pango Bay, around a small promontory. Two gumwood logs lashed together formed a landing place. Dixie brought the barge alongside. We were hidden from the destroyers. A particularly glorious Bougainvillea vine twined itself around a grass-thatched hut.

"Find something rather special for the occasion inside, Master Tiger, sir, if you wouldn't mind collectin' her."

My heart beat fast. I stepped out of the barge onto the gumwood logs, onto the silver beach, over the scalding sand, up to the door of the darkened hut. Now a temple. The Samoan girl of the Palm Oil can shower stood inside.

Droplets of water still on her dark skin. A white blossom, waxed and more fragrant than any perfume from Paris, in the jet hair behind her ear.

Thirteen-and-a-half years old, with no clue what to do next . . .

She had.

Gravity and Puberty. The greatest forces in our lives.

Navy
Five

I F I HAD BEEN THE ONLY ONE WITH STINGING URINE, THE COXSWAIN of the Admiral's Barge wouldn't have lost his Good Conduct stripes. When I visited the sickbay for the inevitable diagnosis — followed by the inevitable post mortem from my father — I took the path of honour as a future officer and young gentleman by refusing to divulge the identity of my venereal benefactor. But once the Admiral's Cox'n was struck down by the same cruel agony, the chain binding us both to the girl with the waxen flower was all too obvious.

Dixie took his lost stripes with Lower Deck philosophy. "Easy come, easy go. Bain't the first time, sir, and won't be the last I reckon. If old Mother Nature puts pleasure in a man's or old Tom Bollux's way, he's bound to do his duty, like Admiral Nelson says, and grab her bum with both hands. Stripes be two-a-penny. Get us a good smoky old war goin' with this Hitler, I'll have 'un back on my sleeve afore the First Dog Watch. Young Master Tiger, sir, just don't you fret."

Easier said than done!

Yet though the mills of God may grind exceeding slow — as the visit of Chaplain Spittlehouse to the brothel in Victoria, British Columbia (on the very day Dixie's smoky old war was declared!) so hilariously revealed — there is a Higher Justice always laughing up its sleeve at how...

DAVID GURR

The Mounties Always Get Their Man . . . !

Jim's been nabbed. Gotchie's "gotcha!"call comes as Panda & Rabbit's ex-naval Owner is patting all three of us on the back for that clever-dick honey-pot trapping of Little Tiger in the far-away morality of 1939 Samoa. Fifty years later, Mr. Keyes has finally been nailed by the local RCMP Sergeant for pocketing bar-coded cans of lobster from the corner grocery at Glen Lake.

"Thisss is not the first time your step-father had shop-lifted?"

Strangelovian interruptions for queries bordering on ludicrous are beginning to really piss off our negative transference. *The Curious Case of the Lobster* was just the lifted tip of an iceberg, hoist on its own petard. The other nine-tenths below the waterline explains the constant over-supply of pens, wallets and watches which Jim generously offered to share with visitors over the years. Also, the four Gold Goblets that miraculously appeared last week under the Rye-and-Ginger counter in the kitchen — which treasure the magpie was barely prevented from returning to the robbed drugstore owner "for credit on my Visa," when the aggrieved thief discovered his gilt prize was only plastic!

I will feed them wormwood, and water them with gall . . .

"The prophet Jeremiah served goblets of wine to a family of abstainers. What was your mother's view of Jim's kleptomaniac jokes?"

Naturally Charlie-Mother has been in on the magpie act from the start — or at least since she took over as understudy from window-dressing Charlie Thomas, to be the straight man of Messrs Singer & Keyes. But let her speak for herself:

"I suppose the first sign was when we'd temporarily borrowed the shillings from the gas meter at Hampstead, and then the meter man came to make the collection. We heard the knock on the bathroom door. The sound of doom. Although we laughed afterwards it was pretty awful at the time. You can imagine what Jim felt when he saw the cruiser lights flashing in his rear mirror for the lobster. I've told him flatly I won't appear in court."

If to Starboard, Red appear —
'Tis your duty to keep clear!

"This preoccupation with the shoplifting — which perhaps is fear of plagiarising — means you have stopped writing again?"

Rabbit : *(still clutching wrong end of nautical big stick)*
"In the Bollux Story, was the
Cox'n's purple penis in Samoa or
Delirium?"
Panda : *(still belabouring the pointedly obvious)*
"It isn't fair to call beasts
Stenchy and I didn't understand
anything about King Mode."
Owner : *(still equally at sea)*
"It was based on a true
story. Which doesn't mean
plagiarising — and don't ask Mr.
Snodgrass what makes Chaplains pick
their goddamn sermons."

"Sermons against abortions perhaps — 'Red' for danger? And an iceberg is a frozen block. It isn't surprising this would stop your novel of an idealised Father. Excuse me, I have to remove a piece of celery."

Which, to our utter disbelief he does! Limping from leather recliner to a small washbasin, fully equipped with dental flossssss for just such purpose — the Celery Extraction is mercifully just out of our line of sight — then hopalonging back to his chair to tongue-test a molar, before adding, "That's better. I'm sorry. Where were we?"

Struck dumb for a moment! But not blocked. The previously quoted Rule of the Road only means we decided to navigate with caution by ghost-chatting with Charlie in a Motherly replay triggered by [typically-out-of-sequence] pictures in the Black Book and/or discrepancies in her Dearest David Letter. Any maternal revisions can then be set in context with Jim's Rye Sessions to round off the Happy Gauer Family view of their Tolstoyan joint history when [her words again] **"the sticky-fingered old bugger gets out of jail!"**

Red to Red, Green to Green —
Perfect safety. Go between . . .

"The go-between your parents — this is how you see yourself?"

We see our self off to a slow start. Charlie's first Sessional consideration of her sticky-fingered time with Jim gets side-tracked by a small grey volume [soft-covered, about twice the width of a Beatrix Potter] which falls out of the Black Book. A collection of postcards, entitled "All Saints Nursery College, Harrogate." Handwritten by Nan underneath, *"1913, a great many alterations since this date. Electric Light,*

118

Central Heating." A loose card inside has Inland & Foreign Postage, One Penny. The front picture shows A View from the Window of Pastoral Yorkshire. The area for text on the back has a printed verse from Blake's *Jerusalem*, "In England's green and pleasant land."

Charlie's eye is caught by

The Drawing Room

Brass warming pans on the walls, Turkey rug on the floor, five-globed gaslight on the ceiling; pictures, piano, bric-a-brac — six vases of daffodils or narcissus (four on the mantelpiece alone). Two women in Florence Nightingale costumes; the Small One (Elspie) sews, the Large One (Dorothea) writes.

```
Who exactly were "The Aunts."..? Well they
weren't really, not blood relations. There
were two groups of three sisters — or
three groups of two — at school together
in Scotland, at New Abbey near Loch
Kindar, South of Dumfries. On our side,
MacKenzies, were my mother, Kythe — who
Jim called Old Trout, my real Aunt,
your Great — and Marjorie. Then there
was Elspie and her sister Rhoda — the
Harrisons. And Dorothea and her sister,
another Marjory — the Hodgesons. It sounds
```

awfully confusing but when my mother died,
Kythe couldn't do anything because she was
out in India or somewhere with Lord Haldane
as his private secretary, and Daddy was
in the Army in France, and Dorothea and
Elspie — the Misses Harrison and Hodgeson,
both daughters of Bishops — but that was
such a mouthful they were always called
simply, "The Aunts" — had this nursery
college, All Saints, outside Harrogate
where they trained children's nurses to be
nannies. And of course they needed children
to look after.

Babies in the Garden

*Granite wall against the Yorkshire wind; flowering trees outside, ivy in; four
Ultimately-Edwardian perambulators; three large wicker (Utterly Victorian) rocker-
bassinettes. Six Uniformed Nannies — also looking like (young) Nightingales.*

That's funny. Only one pram actually has
babies — twins. Anyway, after Mummy and
Daddy died the Aunts became Nan's and my
Legal Guardians. Nan hated All Saints,
they gave her a very hard time, especially
Dorothea. **[Sidetracked back to the Black**

Book by White Egret Feathers] This one in
the silver helmet is Uncle Christopher, a
Knight of Windsor, like Uncle Billy who
used to chase me. Of course the "Uncles"
weren't really proper, either. Christopher
was Dorothea's beloved youngest brother, a
great cricketer, everything always had to
be perfect when he was coming to visit. He
made passes at Nan but "uncles" in those
days all did — except Uncle John who was
a saint. The Aunts slept together all
their lives in a brass double bed — but I
cannot believe in that day and age they
even knew what lesbian meant! **[Sidetracked
by Typical-Edwardian-Male elegance]** "Uncle
John" was a Master at Hethendon, a very
exclusive boys school. A quite beautiful
pianist. He had silver-white hair and
wore a brown velvet jacket for dinner at
night. He was a bachelor. I suppose it was
peculiar but it didn't seem at the time.
He died before the Aunts sold the College
and had his funeral on the farmer's cart
next door. I always remember the cart
and the big horses. It was completely in
the country, Yorkshire, lovely fields all
around. Mr Melia was the farmer next door.
Oh look, the snowdrops! **[Stopped Cold by
White Flowers]** Doodlie — Elspie's pet name
for Dorothea — had been saving all the
snowdrops for Uncle Christopher's arrival
but you didn't realize. You picked every
one in the garden and gave them to her in
a bunch. The major crime of your life!
**[Middle-aged Woman smiling down at Smiling
Charlie-at-29 holding David (not smiling,
almost 6); Winter, 1941]** There's snow on
the roses... Dorothea didn't mean to be
cruel. I'll always remember her pushing
me away when I ran up to her after being
late playing in the village, and then she
was appalled — by her pushing away — and

burst into tears when she saw what she'd
just done. With the snowdrops, I was open-
mouthed in the doorway at her reaction but
I don't think you cared. Very much. You
slipped off somewhere. **[David with Panda
& Rabbit in Summer House]** In spite of the
snowdrops episode Dorothea loved you. She
still called you William when we arrived
at Barton-Olivers One, in Whitchurch,
Hereford, on the Monmouth border. She used
to read Pilgrim's Progress to you for
hours in the Library, and Bleak House. You
loved the Just William books. Dorothea
didn't approve, she thought they were a bad
influence. **[Sidetracked by Yorkshire Picnic]**
Aunt Elspie always made little cakes at
the annual Haying Party. They were heavy as
lead. Aunt Dorothea called them her "kill-
me-quicks." I suppose it is a bit strange
that you never remembered being a William.

A Morning Drive

*Slightly moth-eaten Donkey, one ear forward; two-wheeled "dog cart" with six
unsmiling, slightly startled faces, ages 3 to 5; one Nanny. The boys wear sailor-suits.
One little girl has ribbons.*

Good Lord, that must be me! The donkey is
Josephine. She used to lie down in the
road when she got tired. There were two
groups of us kids — three, counting the
babies. Outside the Nursery, there were
Other children — from Higher-Ups in the
Civil Service who had gone to China and
India doing things in the Empire. They
were either too young for boarding school
or spending holidays with the Aunts. Our
Inside group were the adopted ones. Nan,
but she left to go to boarding school much
sooner, being five years older, and me,
and Kiff — who was an awful thief. I've
often wondered whether he was Elspie's
child. Or Uncle Christopher's. **[Typical-
Adolescent-Kiff]** Gaunt and weedy. Nan's
contemporaries were Jack and Mowbray,
sons of the Earl of Effingham. I was with
Prince Phillip of Serbia — he was the
child the Archduchess was pregnant with at
Sarajevo. Mowbray had an incident with a
rifle. A shot hit a rock, then his brother
Jack, in the leg. Blood, screams. A tiny
wound. I absolutely hated Mowbray. **[4
Typical Boy-Earls & Princes, 2 Aunts in
beads and sunhats, 1 Delicate Girl, all
eating breakfast outdoors at a chequered
tablecloth]** Anthony — Bun's Godfather — he
married well, Lord Hope's daughter. I
think he divorced her after he came back
from the War. Kiff again — who we couldn't
stand! He used to twist Josephine's tail
to make her get up. And Lefroy, always
frail, my dearest friend. **[And a Typical-
Oddball (out of sequence) one of Jim's
Lovely Bunch of Coconuts collection marked
"Monkey's Palm-Tree in Ceylon"]**

The Tennis Court

*Four Nightingales with catgut rackets on a grass court; three large elms;
a high wooden fence, of sharpened uprights,
like the posts of a frontier stockade.*

```
Priscilla was the daughter of "The Gay
Divorcée" who lived in a tiny Doll's House
in Harrogate. She ate sweets and had
men friends. Then she went to Australia.
We all hated Edna. Like a white mouse.
Her brother was in a camp later — like
Auschwitz — with his arm stamped. There
were a variety of ones not as strong
as Priscilla and me within the circle.
Darling Lefroy was youngest. No one went
after her. We protected her from Nurse
Dixon who was a dragon. A real sergeant-
major! We all stood to attention for her.
```

The Cubicles
*Wooden ceiling, row of central gas lights, wooden dividers (vertical
boards, head high, like the tennis court stockade). Brass bedsteads,
dressers, swinging facial mirrors, wind-up alarm clocks. Gabardine
curtains, drawn back, on steel pipes.*

We went on Expeditions or played Doctor
and Nurse games in a dungeon. One stood
on guard. I remember us all lying down in
the drawing room and Kiff saying "Let's
fuck." I can't imagine where on earth he
heard it. The Aunts would have had an
absolute fit! Kiff used to put his hands up
the housemaids' skirts. They all squealed,
"Oh don't, Mr Christopher!" When he pushed
a stick up Babette's bum she screamed.
We none of us felt sorry for her. That's
what's so terrible when you think about
it. She was low man on the totem pole, I
guess. On our Expeditions Elspie did the
driving. Dorothea just sat in her cloak.
Elspie called the cars special names:
"Come on Trojie!" — the first was a Trojan
with solid tires and no clutch. **[Tiny
Elspie at wheel of Huge (1916, army tank-
like) Open Car]** Once we were going along
this narrow country lane and there was a
mad woman standing in the middle. Hands
over her head. Holding the most enormous
rock! It barely missed the side of the
car. Elspie dodged, and just said, "Oh
poor dear." Another time we took Nan to
Liverpool. The solid tires got stuck in
the tram tracks. We had to go all the
way to the depot and be lifted out. I've
no idea how it actually worked — the
Trojan — with no clutch.

Dinner Time

Eight little faces at a ten-foot-long table (child height), white cloth. Six starched Nannies. Bare linoleum floor, winter sunlight through (open) windows at a low angle. One Toy Elephant on wheels.

That's me, at the end, with the curls. At Christmas the Aunts had to get a present for everyone in the College. They arrived in two black tin trunks. I got a paint box and a pen knife. And the Pantomime Trip to Leeds. I had never been anywhere except Harrogate by pony and trap. Before the Trojan the Aunts ordered a Daimler taxi for Leeds. It was a considerable distance and real Expedition. We saved our church collections — one penny got a single cigarette in a wrapping. Of course we weren't allowed to smoke! **[Sidetracked by Puffing-Billy Locomotive]** The train. The engine driver would take us down the valley for free standing on his footplate. We scrounged rides back. **[Sidetracked by Forbidding Old Woman]** Our Harvey Grandmother was still alive, somewhere in Ireland — an old-old woman in black — but

absolutely no contact with me and Nan.
Only a postal order at Christmas. Granny
Harvey died when I was nine or ten. After
Daddy. **[Sidetracked by Explorers (1880) in
North American Bush]** One of Aunt Elspie's
grandfathers was the first to climb — or
perhaps it was survey — Mount Baker. The
volcano near Vancouver. **[Sidetracked by
Typical Village Shop]** And "Soft Willie"
the village idiot who was two bricks short
of a load! His mother had a grey beard
and ran the sweet shop. We used to shout
at him in a circle, "Have a fit, Willie!
Have a fit!" And he would. Nowadays people
would be appalled. And we stole — eggs
from the farmer next door. **[Sidetracked by
Aunt Dolly's Ears]** Aunt Dolly had heavy
earrings. Her lobes had been dragged
right down like a blood hound — but her
earrings would all be good. I mean real
stones, not paste. **[Sidetracked by Who-
Knows-What?]** Lefroy's oldest sister,
Helen, became an Oxford Don, quite
brilliant. Then after vacation she met a
farm yokel, Archie — and married him, to
utter consternation! They lived on a farm
near us at Barton-Olivers Two, in Dorset,
between Burton Bradstock and Swyre, where
Marjorie and Rhoda lived with Great-Aunt
Hetty and the parrot. Helen never washed-
up a dish until every single other thing
in the house was dirty. **[Typical Adorable
Dorset Thatched Cottage]** I babysat for
Helen and Archie once on a holiday. No
dishes. I asked a landgirl, "Where are the
dishes?" I had to wash them all before
we could eat. Helen's father was Rector
of Stowe-on-the-Wold church. And a real
sleazy bundle of rubbish he was! "Uncle
Rex." He had a very wandering eye and
hands. I shudder to think what his little
girl got up to in the choir with him.

[Typical Pastoral Anglican Vicar] There was some monkey-business about a mad young curate with the Vicarage cat! You know these things are really embarrassing even now, but that All Saints business of Kiff poking the stick up Babette's bum — when we were first together Jim wanted to do it that way. I let him know in no uncertain terms, absolutely not! **[Sidetracked by Female Figure (face hidden) in 1920's Cloche Hat]** Rex's wife, Aunt Ruth, Lefroy's mother, was the kindest woman, always. **[Garden-Gate of Mock-Lutyens-Manor: "Barton Olivers"]**

A lovely garden with the Summer House and Kingcups by the pond, and croquet lawn, where you first played cricket. The house names always confused people but it was quite simple. "Barton" was the name of Dorothea's father's Vicarage — before he was made a Bishop — and the "Olivers" was the same for Elspie's father — another Bishop, they sat in the House of Lords. When the Aunts sold the

College they bought Barton-Olivers-One at
Whitchurch, in the Wye Valley — where we
went first, from London, in the bombing.
B-O Two **[Edwardian, brick 3-storey,
Cliffside Villa]** was Burton Bradstock,
near Bridport, down in Dorset. Bridport
is the second school picture of you — the
Headmistress was a pleasant woman **[David-
at-7 in Rabbit Suit]** with the Doctor's
Stethoscope round your neck. My first
school was meant to be tremendously
special. A "New Wave" approach like
Montessori. Called P.N.E.U. — Parents
Natural Education Union, or something
like. Quite small, girls only, about
forty. At Ambleside, in the Lake District.
The top of Lake Windermere. We took long
walks through dales and hills, past
Conniston Water, to where John Peel
used to have his tea. The Inn put out
food and drink for us. It really was a
lovely place. After a little while we
had a beautiful threesome. We ran the
school. The head-mistress, what was her
name? — Miss Devonshire! — was reputed to
wear a wig and only take it off at night
when she hung it on a chair. We used to
look through her keyhole.

The Night Nursery
*Central gaslight, globes hooded with dark cloth; ceiling blackened by
smoke; metal-barred cribs around the walls. Bare, wide-planked floor.*

The Ghost episode with this poor girl
we didn't like. We rigged it up in a
sheet with a Girl Guide belt we could
pull across our three beds. It made a
terrifying clanking sound. My dear! She
went into hysteria! That was the final
breaking point. I was the ringleader. Miss
Thing wrote to the Aunts. So then they
sent me to a very classy Queen Margarets,

in Scarborough — it has links to the one
here in Victoria. Fashionable and large.
It was all right, but not my type of
school and as I didn't want to work hard
or do well I just never liked it. Thank
heaven for the French holidays! **[Derailed
by France]** Marseilles — "Marsales" if
you didn't speak French — with a huge
open air market. Flowers, little cafés.
Tall glasses of chocolate with whipped
cream. Fantastic! Once, in the train —
Priscilla was rather pretty, I was rather
fat — a man had hold of Priscilla! The
Aunts rushed out, cloaks flapping! Some
passionate Frenchman was being "Uncley."

Egret feathers and medals means Knight of Windsor.
Good Lord, it's Uncle Christopher again! How did
he get here? Continental Uncles were worse! They
were rather naughty old men under the guise of
uncle-ism. We stayed at a hotel for a night in
Marseilles. Four of us kids got in a revolving
door, going round and round. A screaming woman
pushed a button. The door collapsed. We were all
trapped! Then on to Hyères. A tiny little boat took
us from there to the island.

DAVID GURR

Oh look! The fort, with its tremendous
guns. And the French flag on top. Seeing
the flag, you knew then how close you
were getting. "Deaf-and-Dumber" was
charming and very handsome — he drove the
boat — like Errol Flynn, in faded denim
and singlet. **[Steam Launch, Le Cormoran,
docking]** A little wooden jetty. Eucalyptus
trees. Old men would sit around the Place
drinking coffee in the Bistro. We went to
the Bakery every morning for croissants
and bread. We taught the baker's wife
backwards English. Whenever we walked in
she said brightly, "Goodbye." Margery and
Rhoda's house was called Miramar. The
Aunts' next-door was Villa du Vierge.
[Grotto Statue of the Virgin] Lemon
trees — with lemons! — orange trees. We
went to bed early. You could hear the
old men singing and talking. We used to
wish we could be with them. And the rich
Madame Fournier, kneeling on the floor in
her silk dress and white gloves — and in
no time she emptied our stove of old coals
and had it going again. Monsieur Fournier
had a little beard. And there were huge
fir cones. Also cocoons of caterpillars,
bigger than our heads. They would fall
on the path and go in a circle, round and
round. We used to stamp on them of course.
And grey rocks covered with a sea of

Portulaca. Beautiful swimming. The ladies wore big straw hats to do it. **[Hatted Ladies, Doing It]** I only paddled. When I was about sixteen I had an experience where I nearly drowned at Rugby. Two very handsome young masters rescued me. I had simply jumped in at the deep end, convinced I could do it and I couldn't. Of course on Porquerolles the French never swam either. They thought all the English were mad. **[Beached "Doodlie" in a Cape]** Dorothea was always mortified if one of us showed any emotion — after I almost broke my ankle falling off a wall! We were playing a game called "cockie-ockie." As soon as you tagged someone you called it out. **[French Picnic]** Food was of the simplest, at a long wooden table. Fruit and fresh bread. I never had a formal supper till after I went to boarding school. At twelve. Then you had gone a notch up and had "Supper with the Aunts." Often just an egg and bread and butter. **[Typical Bishop, in Gaiters]** When we visited at "Olivers" Aunt Elspie's father, the Bishop, had prayers every morning. Coulson the chauffeur — where do these names come from? — and the other servants around the dining room table. **[Typical Bishop's Servants, in front of Fireplace]** And the heat in the French train! There weren't any other whites — I mean not Island people. We children never did the shopping, ever. There were paraffin lamps. Disgusting stuff. The forts were built up in 1938-39. The Aunts finally sold the Virgin's villa to the Army just before the War. **[Typical Fox Hunt]** At fifteen or sixteen I went to the three Bowen-Colhursts — Zoe, Maxwell and one other — her father was another Earl, in Colchester. Then at sixteen or seventeen to Devon. He was

Master of Harriers near Totness. I helped
look after the hunters. There were two or
three girls helping with the horses. The
wife fell in a hunt and broke her pelvis.
She had a slow recuperation. One evening
we girls were grumbling in the Totness
kitchen. The Master's wife arrived in the
doorway, having overheard. "If that's the
way you feel you can go — no! Not you."
The "you" was one girl that was probably
a lesbian — she wore men's suits and so
on. We thought he might have been trying
to have an affair with her. The Aunts
simply wouldn't believe that I hadn't done
anything to warrant having to leave. Then
I went to Uncle Billy, **[Another Typical
Bishop]** the Bishop of Newbury, with Aunt
Grace who had a clay pipe and a parrot.
White-ish, it could really talk. Every
time he went out it used to call him back,
"Billy! Are you going to Nottingham?
Billy!" That dreadful odious greasy old man
with his ugly red hair! He made a pass and
Aunt Grace sent me back to the Aunts. In
between I stayed again at Colchester — it
had the Army Camp — with Aunt Ruth, who
I really loved. Oliver Cromwell stayed
there once. He sent a thank you note, over
the fireplace. **[Typical Cromwell & Bishop,
over Fireplace]** Aunt Grace used to call
me "Her wicked Charlotte." Her husband was
always "The Bishop." The Aunts bought me
a motorcycle when I was at the Bishop's
house — "Olivers," isn't that odd? I never
thought before, the name could have been
from Cromwell — and I used to ride it
into the Camp. The officers never gave me
any trouble. I always got on with boys.
[Charlie-at-16, on BSA (250cc) Bike] I
suppose the Aunts giving it was a bit
strange but they were like that. They
trusted you. But at this point they decided

I must have something like a career and
sent me back to Harrogate — All Saints,
which they still owned. I trained for at
least a year. They had children, infants,
in their care for us to train on as
practicums.

The Baby Nursery

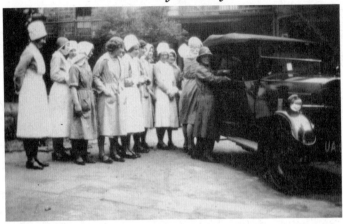

*Rocking wooden cribs, and wicker bassinettes. Six Starched Nannies,
Six Babies on laps (babies in floor-length lace-edged gowns). Wooden
floor, stockade wooden wainscoting, with windows inset.*

This isn't the Nursery it's the Trojan, with
Elspie and all the servants, the first day it
arrived at All Saints. I don't know why Jim
keeps shuffling the photos. I really could
kill him! When I was trained I went first to
a couple in Rugby, at the school. He was a
master, they were middle-aged, and out of
the blue she had a baby at fifty! They were
besotted about each other. It was ludicrous.
I can't remember all the lovey-dovey names
they called each other but I had never seen
anything like it. Through them I met the two
young masters who saved me from drowning
in the pool. One called something Inge, I
think became a writer. There was no sex.
When we went to Cambridge for May Week we
stayed in separate rooms. Lots of kissing

and petting — but even in Colchester, with the motorbike and the Army, if you said No, they didn't push. **[Charlie-at-18, in Spoke-Wheeled MG]** Then I went as a nanny for Lady Barbara Gore. I realised this kind of job just wasn't for me. I began a succession, first as a model in a Chelsea dress shop, then Woolworths in what was then a brand-new idea: a Cafeteria! Shortly after arriving in London I met up with Nan again **[Typical Nan]** who introduced me through her friends the Corbetts — John and Kita — to John's friend. He was a stock-broker, probably in his mid-forties, very well dressed. We would go out to dinners. It was my first sexual experience. **[Typical Stockbroker]** The stockbroker thing didn't go on. When I was twenty, twenty-one I had several male friends but only two or three were sexual. And then Teddy ...
[Naive-Nineteen: No Pictures]

Memory Lane

Owner-at-54; our antique Word Processor (a Xerox 850, the size and weight of a washing machine); Charlie-at-80's first Chat Transcript vs. her Dearest David Letter; Two Stuffed Animals (P&R, ageless innocents); the Black Book of Happy Family photographs —

Plus more unresolved bloody sacrificial questions from the Bench than Dickens started with in Jarndyce versus Jarndyce! And don't expect any further Strangelovian Idealised Father bullshit from sibilant Dr. S. because after the Celery Flossssssing episode we've sssssacked him.
Here endeth the Session.

Consider us Cured.

> **Panda :** *(dubious)*
> "Were we really in the Summer House
> in winter?"
> **Rabbit :** *(nervous)*
> "Who suggested picking the
> snowdrops?"
> **Owner :** *(venomous)*
> "The fault, Dear Brutes, lay not in
> the picking —"

WE didn't pick any part of this journey from a Mad Woman in the middle of the road to our present position with stars in our eyes on the verge of Eruption after lying too long on the Couch! Every step of the way from those back paths in Yorkshire through the May Day bedrooms and Green Rooms of Southern England . . . from Brighton-thru-Cambridge and most of London, the problem has lain with Charlie.

> Unsophisticated sheltered me . . . I met
> a young man and it wasn't long before we were
> inseperable [sic] and madly in love . . . In
> this day of fullest knowledge and matter of fact
> protection it seems extraordinary to have gone
> our blissful way . . .

Extraordinary? She met blissful *old* men. The Stockbroker Thing. And if anything on this earth can be described as matter-of-fact it must be a Typical (circa 1936) Bowler Hat & Brollie & Sheik Prophylactic riding up in the Brighton-to-London morning train for a bit of Birth-Controlled City-Lunchtime Slap & Tickle below the Stockbroker Belt. Even a clapped-out naval dinosaur like Little Tiger's Captain Toughie knows about the Malayan Rubber Company's protection.

David Gurr

Was Teddy Daddy?

...IT COULD BE HALF THE OLD VIC CREW OF HMS PUGNACIOUS!

And yet . . . as we pre-process material for a third fictional fuckup of a Half-Assed Life, finding it even more unfit for Panda and Rabbit's consumption of Midsummer Night wet dreams, *their names Olivier, Richardson, Redgrave* . . . a different backstage picture-postcard title drifts from M-is-for-Memory Lane.

Not Charlie's questionable new facts of what the peepshow butler saw of Anglican high life — "The Mad Curate and the Cat with sleazy old Uncle Rex" — or "real Sergeant-Major" nurses and coxswains and boxing instructors called Dixon, or being groped by a Bishop in a house called Olivers, with a Puritan's thank you note from the Great Pretender. This is only a whisper of a trace "of something in the air" as Sexy-Rex Harrison said of his Fair Lady.

A scent of perfume of Camellias. A bedtime vision of Mummy going out for an Evening on the Town so long ago and far away that the Goodnight Darling kiss on David's brow must have been for Willum. A matinee understudy's vision of dark hair piled up in a Victory roll, and a flower behind her ear. The same footlight vision that would be seen by the eyes of a lover for an incendiary night in the Blitz . . .

"Do not be afraid, mon petit Guillaume," murmurs our part-time Air Raid Warden patrolling the nightingales of Barclay Square as we play it on our Redgrave's windup gramophone. "Mama is what she is. The Girl in Samoa. Relax and enjoy her singing Brahms' Lullaby."

On a British Isle of the Damned.

The Monkey's Palm Tree in Ceylon

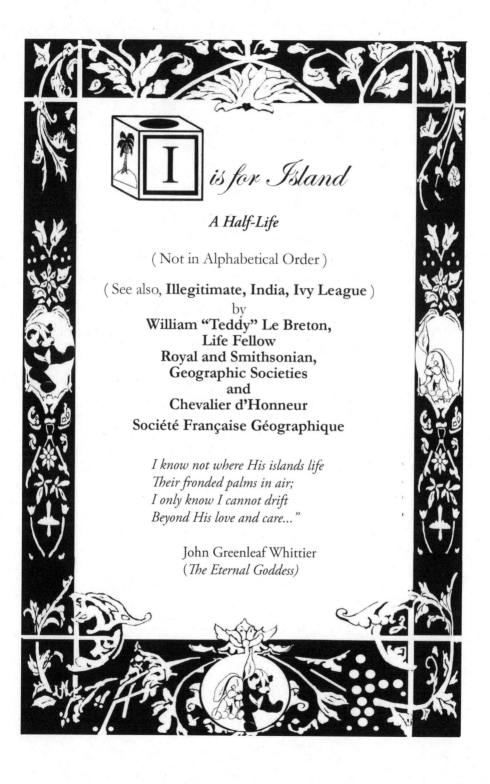

I is for Island

A Half-Life

(Not in Alphabetical Order)

(See also, **Illegitimate, India, Ivy League**)
by
**William "Teddy" Le Breton,
Life Fellow
Royal and Smithsonian,
Geographic Societies
and
Chevalier d'Honneur
Société Française Géographique**

*I know not where His islands life
Their fronded palms in air;
I only know I cannot drift
Beyond His love and care..."*

John Greenleaf Whittier
(*The Eternal Goddess*)

Island
Preface

It is true I am a god — Amelia Earhart called me "My Darling Charla-tan!" — and who can disagree with the charming conceit of a woman who made herself a Heroine forever, to those few of us who still remem-ber?

Alone across the Pacific! Humility may stand highest in the Christian graces of Ralph Waldo Emerson but Sherlock Holmes is a truer judge. "Mediocrity knows nothing higher than itself, but talent instantly recognizes genius."

I offer that direct extraction from Sir Arthur Conan-Doyle's *Valley of Fear* because it was the last thought but one to enter my mind as I fought to regain control of my plunging Avenger fighter aircraft before we both struck that New Guinea volcano. . . .

And now I write these words aboard ship, the *MV Southern Cross*, bearing me (and six-hundred far more heavyweight contenders from Contentment Cay than I) on an Association Cruise — by the extraordinary co-incidence called Luck of the Draw — in two short weeks to be re-united with that Lost Island World of Olie's from fifty years ago. To greet together the Third Millennium.

I said, a last thought but one . . .

Madagascar!

Island
One

THE INTRA-UTERINE EXPERIENCE IS FORMATIVE ACCORDING to the shrinking minds of quacks like Melanie Klein. My mother knew her and believed it. I only know that I've loved chameleons and Ring-Tailed Lemurs since before I set eyes on them. My mental emergency strip always resembles Madagascar because it saved my mother's life when she crash-landed on her first Trans-African solo flight — solo within the strict limits of the International Cockpit Rules, she was six months pregnant with me at the time.

What I actually remember as my first visual impression outside the womb is my goggle-eyed mother and Amelia Earhart kissing passionately behind the Owl and the Pussycat: a biplane with red-striped wings in a hangar at Croydon.

I was in a bassinet made from a Sopwith Camel engine housing. Of course, at that time — aged nine months — I didn't know it was Amelia, or a biplane, or passion. I did know my mother's eyes. Huge, and a blue so deep that it seemed violet. A colour I've only seen in one other woman, Elizabeth (Taylor), on the set of *Cleopatra* when I was acting as a technical advisor. Unobtrusively: the chameleon's ability to blend.

We got away from Madagascar with the aid of a Latvian engineer who happened to have missed a ship taking him to Mombassa. My mother never told me his precise contribution to our getting airborne. With a nod to Melanie, I've never liked Latvia.

Mom's second Trans-African, however, ended in triumph and my being born on American soil. In Los Angeles — Santa Monica, precisely, a tiny beachfront cottage behind wrought iron gates on Arcadia Lane, *"Installed in 1911;"* you can still see it next to the garish Loew's Hotel. As a happy consequence I have dual American and British citizenship, but no father on my birth certificate where my mother simply wrote "various" — which scandalized recording clerks on both sides of the Atlantic but entranced Amelia Earhart.

This frank display of affection didn't endear her or my mother to officialdom either. The Hollywood Family was in the firm male grip of the Hayes Office. Women kissing each other or married men came under the heading of Moral Turpitude. As Charlie Chaplin used to say when we visited in Switzerland, "It was another thirty years until Lenny Bruce could make a joke in America about the transitive verb, 'to come' — and look how long he lasted!" Mother and I left Hollywood under a rare cumulous nimbus cloud with Amelia promising to raise the ante for a two-woman race around the world.

I spent the next eleven years chasing this maternal shadow from hangar to hangar. The money was always on-again, off-again depending on the current condition of things like lust and the Gold Standard. The Great Depression itself wasn't a problem. The reverse; as Louis Mayer and Stalin proved, in revolutionary times the masses need entertainment more than ever to keep them quiet. Bob Hope once told me that he and Bing actually got *Road to the Gulag* into pre-production with a Soviet advance. As Bob said about this vehicle — he was still writing his own gags then — "It crashed before takeoff in front of Joe McCarthy's Un-American Activities Committee."

Name dropping isn't something I do out of Melanie's insecurity. Alec Guiness may have been tormented all his life by not knowing who his father was. I found illegitimacy totally liberating. The first screenplay of my life was called *A Proper Bastard — and Proud of It!* Peter Sellers loved it. If he hadn't been sidetracked by his third coronary and Blake Edwards' *Pink Panther . . .*

But that lies far ahead. Back in 1939 Amelia had been lost in the Pacific for two years and we were in Croydon again to raise cash for another Earhart Rescue Mission. At that time Croydon was London's main airport and the hub of my mother's racing schemes and love affairs. Consequently we needed a local base of operations. We found it in a bed-sitting-room over a corner grocer's shop. The week before, we had the run of Blenheim Palace with Winston (Churchill)'s brother. Dukes and Grocers. My mother's life was like that.

TYLER'S
Comestibles & Essentials
For Home & Trade

I can see the sign as though it were yesterday. The only other things I remember are Kit Kat chocolate wrapped in silver paper (aluminum foil for America), Heinz 57 Tomato Soup red labels, and Mags, the toffee-nosed grocer's daughter. Of course if I had known then that she was going to become a toffee-nosed Prime Minister — the point is, I know now. And our friendship is solid enough that I can be honest about childish first impressions. My God! She put me up for a knighthood on her last Honors List.

When war came to Croydon the first Nazi bomb destroyed the Racing Piper 112 that my mother was modifying for her latest long-range search for Amelia in the South Pacific. The second bomb took out our bed-sitting-room at the grocer's, but left the Comestibles & Essentials intact below it.

After the Fall of France and a minor fling with both halves of a window-dressing Armed Forces Entertainment act called Singer & Keyes — "With only three balls between them, who kept on with *I've Lost My Little Yo-Yo* and *Smoke Gets in Your Eyes* as our barrack-room rendezvous was blown up by a visiting Messerschmidt 109!" — my mother, denied the publicity from another rescue attempt for Amelia, at Winston Churchill's request joined the Special Operations Executive instead, and was parachuted into Occupied Europe to become a Heroine.

Before she left on her first mission to suffer heroically (but stoically) at the vile hands of the Gestapo she sent me to America to do the same at Choate Academy. Her parting words to me were:

"Tell the Headmaster to let you keep up your flying, Darling Teddy, mind your Yo-Yo, and be happy. They show Tarzan films on Sunday evenings."

Four years later, when I got my wings as a US Naval aviator in Pensacola, Florida, she followed up with a postcard sent mysteriously from "Somewhere in England" between Gestapo missions:

"Congratulations, Teddy darling. If you get a chance between bagging Japs in the South Pacific keep trying for Amelia. The Ouija people at Special Ops swear to me she's still on the Board. Near New Guinea."

I won't bore you with the Yo-Yo-Years Between of Johnny Weiss-muller. Go and see Streisand and Redford in *The Way We Were*.

(To add a personal footnote on the ravages caused by Adolf Hitler, Mr. Tyler moved the stock down into the cellar, claimed maximum losses, and sold the Kit Kats and Heinz tomato soups on the black market at ever-increasing profit throughout the balance of the war. Mags moved her accent up-market towards the West End and became Margaret-the-budding-biologist — but still kept her hair in the conservative Croydon-school-girl bob she used until she remade herself into the fabulous Brazen Boadicea we know and love.)

To combat the ravages of Hirohito . . . we sailed to sea from Colombo in an aircraft carrier leaking like a sieve and a crew that was pea-green from seasickness and inexperience.

Instead of the Edward Lear nonsense verses my mother used to hum to both of us in those intrauterine flights of the Owl and the Pussycat, the *USS Catharsis* — Enemy Ears are listening: no real names allowed — offered Swinger & Beans, a pair of ex-music hall Royal Marine comics, plus a piano for Allied entertainment.

"How do you tell the difference between a fart and a hurricane, Mr. Swinger?"

"I don't know. You tell me, Mr. Beans."

"The hurricane is the one with a propeller up its arse!"

Followed by a fart in unison with a rousing chorus from all hands of *The Girl I Left Behind Me.*

The real swinging got done by a tame monkey who leaped through the audience, swiping the Captain's watch. Cheers all round. Beans was the one with the Groucho moustache, and the last punch line for *Catharsis.*

"Let's have one more of 'Smoke before your Eyes' — or Death before Disaster — as the Nurse said to her date from the Shortarm parade. 'Just what the Doctor ordered!' "

The carrier got zapped by a kamikaze, in mid performance, three days later. But by then I had left her.

Island

Two

FLYING OVER THE SOUTH PACIFIC IS AN INTRODUCTION TO ETERNITY. Blue sea and sky forever-and-ever Amen. Otherwise known as Combat Air Dawn Patrol. After a month of endlessly doing it en route from Pearl Harbor as a workup to our undisclosed Theatre of Operations . . . human nature being what it is, when Lieutenant (Junior Grade) Teddy Le Breton, U.S. Navy, first saw land below him — I longed for the previous emptiness of space.

The land was shooting at me. Wee puffs of black soot popping off in a symmetrical pattern at all main points of the compass around my Avenger. It was only a matter of a very small amount of time until the puffs zeroed in on the armored-steel seat under my flight-suit pants. Also, "land" in the South Pacific is not the solid comfort which the word usually brings to a mind embedded with objects on the map the size of the continents of Europe and North America.

From twenty thousand feet the green atoll beneath the Avenger was scarcely larger than the black puffs too close to the squared tips of my wings. (At an altitude we had been assured at Pensacola the Japanese AA guns could not reach!) It is not for nothing that the Avenger's Fleet nickname was the Turkey. On takeoff or landing I couldn't see over its vast snub nose. In flight, it rose with all the graceful speed of an overstuffed centrepiece from a Thanksgiving table. At the other end of the scale, when a pilot — me — wanted to make a small but subtle correction in altitude to avoid complete disintegration of body and soul . . . the brute plummeted like a stone.

The atoll came up to me at a heart-stopping rate.

The gunners below me anticipated it. The vitamin deficiencies in the Japanese diet (which all USN pilots had also been assured at Pensacola buggered slit-eyes by day or night) failed to do their bit in America's war effort. The black puffs stuck to my wings as tight as the scales on a flying fish's anus.

Then tighter.

The starboard tip vanished in a shower of alloy fragments. I considered a suitable Pensacola May Day message. The atoll below had no name. The only geographic point of reference was a long smudge thirty miles to the southwest: the backbone Highland Ridge of the main Island of New Guinea.

My port wing tip vanished. The Japanese gunners' diet was obviously perfectly in balance. So was the Avenger, but the only direction it wanted to follow was Down.

Nineteen, eighteen, seventeen, sixteen . . . like the lead-in of a training film, except that the morale boosters never showed this bit. They always cut harmoniously to the liquid-shit voice of the narrator summing up "The combat lessons we have now learned to beat the Jap."

At fifteen thousand feet the God in whom Americans trust provided a miracle: a layer of rain-soaked cloud. When I came out of it the Japanese gunners were gone.

But dead ahead was a mountain where no mountain could be.

The chart on my waterproof kneepad proved it. The nameless atoll behind. The vast unexplored cannibal blank of New Guinea ahead. Only blue water between . . .

The unpleasant impossibility of rock vanished back into the cloud layer. At fourteen thousand feet it reappeared. Now the impossible was close enough to have sheet-ice on it — at the equator! — and a faint plume of something which looked altogether too like the smoke streaming out of the Avenger's blunted wings.

"Mayday! Mayday!" the pilot intoned as taught by Pensacola to an unheeding ether. "If I miss the fucking crater, will attempt a pancake with Avenger on the side of a volcano."

In the absence of any answer or tactical improvement we plunged a third time through the cloud layer towards the cannibals' un-named cooking pot. . . .

Howling through the cloud, the great engine shut off, water vapor streaming with dumped fuel from the wings, I could see nothing in front. Nothing below. Only a gray blackness with occasional nauseating whiffs of sulphur mixed with Av Gas. We must be passing directly above the crater. To eject now would be to jump into the very gates of hell.

But to stay . . . ?

If the monster sent out a single volcanic spark to join the fuel the darkness would be final —

Sunlight!

Only for an instant, then back into the cloud, but enough for me to see that we had cleared the highest crater wall. That was east. The western lip was directly in front. Teeth would be more accurate. A line of jagged lava pyramids, any one of which would rip the belly out of the Avenger. And meanwhile the cauldron was below us . . . a dim red glow through the clouds reflected in the Plexiglas of the cockpit.

The aircraft lurched downwards.

The lava teeth must have us! A slamming fist smashed the fuselage behind me. The remnants of the wings shuddered so violently that all the rivets popped. Nothing responded to the controls. I glanced in the combat mirror. The Turkey's tail was gone.

The nose pitched even more steeply. It was impossible to eject. I could do nothing but ride the whirlwind down to become one of those skeletons with dog tags discovered, if at all, half a century too late for a mother's grief . . .

The canopy shattered. Eye sockets in a human white skull jeered at me. White teeth filed to cannibal points. I thought of my mother and *Smoke Gets in Your Eyes*, and grabbed my little Yo-Yo.

The day went black.

Island

Three

BELOW THE CANNIBAL'S LEERING SKULL WAS A NECKLACE OF WHAT seemed at first to be dried figs. As my vision cleared I saw that they were human ears. Leaving the cockpit to join them wasn't a much better choice than leaping into the volcano. In the *Boys' Own* yarns of Croydon and Choate the word "cannibal" was always in the plural. Pensacola's Survival Manual tried to put on a pleasanter gloss with "In the event of a forced landing in the Pacific Theatre the natives will usually be friendly" — but the natives were still plural.

Fortunately the Manual came with a nine-millimetre Smith & Wesson. The magazine contained sixteen rounds. I had a spare magazine. Saving the last bullet for myself I could take thirty-one cannibals with me. This keen mental arithmetic didn't allow for the shaking in my hand as I tried to draw the pistol. Or the wobbling in my legs when I tried to stand up in the cockpit. But at least the canopy had removed most of itself on impact. I brushed some shattered Plexiglas aside.

The man fell to his knees — I can be certain of the gender: this was the first moment at which I realized that except for the ear necklace, and white paint on his skull-face the cannibal was stark naked — then scrabbled to his bare feet and ran off at flank speed into the cloud, screaming.

I sat down again and tried the radio. Not even static. Every tube was smashed. The cannibal didn't come back. Fear of the unknown is a two-edged weapon in psychological warfare. Although it didn't seem possible, obviously at the moment I was more terrifying to the cannibal than he was to me. I had only to maintain that state of mind to keep the upper hand.

But if I did it here I would die of cold. A case of out of the frying pan into the freezer! I had survived the largest cooking pot on earth to find myself on a glacier. Not a large one — this was the tropics — but ice about a foot thick for as far as I could see. When I stepped down from the cockpit my flight boots skidded out from under me. How the cannibal could run in bare feet down a one-in-three gradient was a sobering mystery.

Only a few yards from the ruined Avenger the mystery steepened. The volcanic gradient changed to one-in-two. Forty-five degrees.

I crawled back on hands and knees to the Turkey and removed its Survival Pack. In one of those bureaucratic blips which are inevitable in a truly Global War, in addition to the universally helpful Spam and Band-Aids I discovered nylon stockings and French francs. I had been sent into the South Pacific with a Landing in Occupied Europe kit.

There was a mini phrase book to ask "Where is the pen of my Aunt?" in French and German. Not a word of Pidgin English. My mother could have used the kit against the Gestapo. I hurled it into the sulphur-stinking void, then sat and wept for both of us.

Not a grown-up action I admit, but I've referred to *Boys' Own* comics. Although I was dressed as a man, with a gun, and flew a man's machine in a man's war, your would-be-hero was in fact only eighteen and a half years old. To paraphrase the Bible I had neither given up the toys of a child nor stopped thinking like one in a tight spot and therein probably was my eventual salvation — and such small repute as I may have gained since in my subsequent career of Off-the-Beaten-Track explorer. I was not my mother's (and various fathers') son for nothing.

I resolved to treat the whole thing as an Adventure.

I wiped my eyes — and the Smith & Wesson — then checked the cockpit for anything useful which Naval Procurement might have left there by accident. I had been sitting on the first thing all along: my parachute. It provided me with both a tent and a life line for lowering myself down the glacier. The radio was shot but I decided to take the Very Pistol and its flares to signal my Fleet rescuers whom the Survival Manual said would be circling overhead before you could say Commence Pilot Recovery Operations!

As if to prove it the sun broke through again. I looked upwards. A single wheeling buzzard-cum-vulture stared back at me with a six-foot wing span and distinctly morbid curiosity. (This was also the start of my minor contribution to ornithology. Even as I shuddered at the sight of the vulture-buzzard's enormous hooked beak I remember making a mental note to record finding such a raptor at so great an altitude. See under "Cathartidae of the Pacific": *Cathartes Bretonii.)*

The clouds closed in again to deny my future namesake its potential dinner. My choice of actions was limited to one: there was nothing except death by frostbite and buzzards to be gained by sitting still or moving sideways; moving uphill across the ice-sheet was impossible as well as suicidal. I wrapped one end of the parachute cord around the crushed starboard wheel strut of the Avenger and began lowering myself down to face the Unknown among the cannibals.

Backsliding and scrabbling down the glacier on the volcano . . . it seemed to take a day before both the cloud and ice began to melt. In fact, my watch — an Aviator's Special — which was still working showed that it had only been two hours from the pre-breakfast moment of engagement by the Japanese gunners until now. The cloud-ice mix was vanishing under the power of the tropical rising sun.

Instead of a frostbitten foreskin, prickly heat in the crotch caused by chafing of the parachute harness was now my medical problem. "Buggers' Itch" in pilot's parlance.

A zip pocket on my left sleeve had a tube of ointment. The slope of the volcano eased to nothing worse than looking down from the top of a roller-coaster. There was even a level patch of smooth lava before the next wispy bank of cloud. I belayed the parachute line around an outcrop with glinting flecks of mica in it, unzipped the sleeve pocket and then the front fly opening of the flight suit.

The sun on my genitals had the warmth of life. I took a pee of relief and luxuriated for a moment in my escape from certain death . . . before beginning to apply the itch ointment to the affected area. This massage combined with the sunshine to produce an entirely predictable, but considering the surroundings still remarkable, physical result. Tumescence on a gratifying scale for an eighteen year old. Urged on by nature, and a memory of a Silver Screen cover of Betty Grable, release was in my grasp when —

The last cloud lifted. The full vista of a South Pacific paradise was laid out before me. That glory at a distance must be delayed however for a description of the sight closer to hand. Not the proud eighteen year old's member I was grasping — although seen from the opposite perspective that is precisely what

Even so many years later I am still almost at a loss to describe.

Clinical exactitude and dispassion is required:

The moment the cloud lifted was that precise second at which I ejaculated. What I then saw was not the distant vista of the island but its cannibal inhabitants ranged in a row a scant ten yards in front of me.

What *they* saw — well I don't think that leaves much to your imagination. A young man with his pants down, applying a medicinal cream to his testes with the left hand, while the right . . .

No!

Like me at the time, you have leaped to an obvious, but erroneous erotogenic conclusion. What the cannibals saw was the climactic fulfillment of a prophecy.

As I didn't know this when it happened, what I saw was my volcanic friend of the skull face with a dozen others looking even more terrible in white paint and red feathers. I couldn't know, either, that what they had put on was a once-in-a-lifetime finery to welcome a God.

What they had put on was very little. In fact they were wearing considerably less than I was. And where I had merely applied some Naval Issue ointment they had stuck what looked like orange chili peppers a foot long! And if that wasn't enough, between the chili peppers and the feathers they had pasted French francs and Johnson's Band-Aids (from my discarded Occupied Europe kit) in the most extraordinary Pablo Picasso designs. And for their pièce de résistance, as they fell in unison to the ground and banged their heads on it while wailing something like, "Boniya! Boniya!" I saw behind them a very creditable imitation of the Avenger made out of palm leaves and grass.

Of course it didn't have a propeller or a tail — since both were missing from the original — and only a vague idea of the canopy as most of that had gone too; but there was a pilot's seat made out of some kind of giant toadstool, and a white star for Uncle Sam painted on the side of the grass fuselage with the same clay they used for their bodies. And on the front of the palm-leaf nose, as a crowning touch, set in like eyes, my two discarded cans of Survival Spam.

How the cannibals had recovered them from the void was less of a wonder than creating the entire spectacle in so few hours — and from a glimpse of the wreck in the clouds which could only have lasted seconds. The savage brain behind the skull face clearly possessed a photographic memory. Below it, a Survival Nylon Stocking around his naked waist now supported his phallic chili pepper.

I could appreciate the cannibals' artistry and hard work. From their humble and prostrate attitude they appeared to appreciate me. That still left the always vexing problem of communication between apparent

God and Man. The useless Franco-German phrase book was stuck in an appropriate spot: the starboard interior panel of the grass cockpit where the "Pilot's Body Waste" receptacle would normally be housed.

Even had I possessed the Pidgin-English edition it would have been useless. I realized intuitively — my subsequent career owes everything to this truly God-given ability to feel the emotions of so-called "primitives": no doubt an intra-uterine gift from Madagascar — the feathered fiendish forms in front of me had never seen white skin, let alone heard a word of English. And my skin *was* white — at least that portion from the waist down, more the centre of their attention than my tanned face.

Being clinically exact again: at the precise moment of contact between our two cultures, the tip of their focus on my godlike anatomy was a turgid crimson, but in comparison with the blackness of their prehistoric skins the penile shaft and rest of me was driven snow.

"Boniya!"

The skull-face fellow was pointing at my penis tip. As a last seed-pearl dropped from it the other cannibals raised their scarlet-feathered heads from the ground long enough to look again and groan before banging their foreheads back on the lava. The skull-face continued to stare. The object of his concentrated study was rapidly shriveling. (Compared to the chili-peppers it had been bush-league from the start!) I pulled it back into the flight suit, zipped up, held out my hand, and smiled.

"Hullo," I said, tapping my chest in the manner of Johnny Weissmuller in Sunday evening Tarzan films at Choate. "Me, Teddy. Who are you?"

The kneeling skull-face reached his hand forward . . .

Our fingers touched . . . to close a gap of fifty millennia.

"Me Teddy," I repeated, giving his hand a firm squeeze. "How do you do?"

He squeezed back.

With a howl so loud and dreadful that I almost fainted from the shock of it, the others leaped to their feet and began brandishing their weapons —

I haven't mentioned the weapons. Bows and arrows, clubs, spears, their brandishers only wore feathers but they were armed to the filed points of their cannibal teeth! As they rushed towards me it was small comfort to note that I was going to die in the Stone Age: there were no metal edges or points on the arrows and spears.

I couldn't use my gun. Skull-face still had my right hand in his iron grip. A jagged, stone-bladed dagger was tucked into his new nylon-stocking waistband.

"*Boniya T'd'i.*"

He spoke my name. And I had the instant foolish thought:
That means they won't eat me!

Inches away, the others halted.

"B'longa O'l'e." The rest of the group retreated behind the grass imitation Avenger. Skull-face patted his own chest and repeated, "B'longa O'l'e."

(The true dialect pronunciation, in syllable form, as I was later privileged to record their language for posterity was *Oh-ah-li-ya-i.*) I stood there, grinning inanely, while another Choate-Sunday movie flashed through my head. Laurel and Hardy doing the same inane thing.

"Hullo Olie," I said.

"H'l'o T'd'i."

Where I have written apostrophes, he put in a sort of aspirate for the absent English letters with their corresponding sounds. The missing links came out as wafts of his breath on my face. Slightly rancid, slightly sweet.

Cannibal breath . . .

As I had this thought the rest of the group returned at a howling rush. They carried something with them. A cross between a First Aid stretcher and wicker throne. They dropped it in front of me.

Without releasing my hand Olie the skull-face pulled me forward. Other hands pushed me down on the stretcher-throne. They lifted it.

Olie coughed.

It was such a human sound. I had been so overwhelmed by their cannibal filed teeth and hideous, mythologic painted masks — to say nothing of the foot-long orange chili-peppers sticking upright from their loins! — that I hadn't observed the physical reality of my new friends. They were small men, barely to my shoulder when standing, and once they began moving off down the mountain more than half of them had hacking coughs. While their arm and leg muscles were highly developed their anti-bacterial defense was weak. (Olie's sunken chest and coughing reminded me of TB patients in Pensacola's sanatorium.) Wearing no clothes did nothing to protect them against the cold at this altitude.

But they were as sure-footed as goats on the volcano. It had been a long morning since my dawn patrol started. At this prehistoric end of it I was grateful for the ride. Aboard my swaying stretcher-throne I leaned back on an elbow and carefully surveyed the paradise island that was now my prison home.

Island
Four

THE CANNIBAL WARRIORS WOUND THEIR WAY DOWN THE SIDE of the volcano without a pause, but making frequent hairpin turns. Each time they did so my line of sight from the stretcher-throne swung through 180 degrees. The result was a terrifying but unparalleled view of the western half of the island.

The volcano formed the eastern half. To the south and north its flanks eased to a more gentle pitch that at their extremities were almost flat before they plunged again, vertically, into the sea. The western half was dominated by a second mountain, not quite so high (there was no snow on it), and geologically much older. Its sides were almost precipitous, once-white limestone, eroded in fantastic sharpened promontories and fissures. There was no wisp of steam from the saw-toothed top. At the base of the precipices the land again provided some leveled area, and then again straight down black-lava cliffs to the Pacific.

Between the twinned peaks was a saddle valley divided almost exactly in half by a silver flash which began as a trickle, broadened to a stream, then to a rushing river shortly before it too plunged into the sea. The distance across the valley from my present elevation — halfway down the volcano — to a similar height on the other peak I judged about three miles. From coast to coast (North and South) a little more than double that. Assuming the island to be circular gave a total area less than forty square miles, two thirds of which was vertically uninhabitable.

The cannibals' diet wasn't solely human flesh. Neatly arranged garden patches covered the more level area in a quilt of varied greens and rich red soil flanking both sides of the silver river. This was clearly not enough to support the island population. As my feathered bearers made another hairpin bend an astonishing bit of agriculture came into view. A terraced garden had been carved into the mountainside which was so steep that its gardeners had to swing themselves back and forth across it on plaited ropes of vines fastened at the top to hand-chiseled bollards of lava rock.

As we passed the closest vine the gardener turned to stare. The naked figure on the vine had breasts. Pert ones, with neat nipples —

"*Boniya!*" bellowed Olie. The young woman swung her face towards the mountain — but when we made the next hairpin bend she was staring open-mouthed at me again.

No Japs have been here.

Delayed shock or stupidity? . . . it was the first time since my crash landing that the thought which should have been uppermost since impact finally came into my mind. The Enemy from Tokyo might not possess the fiendish slit-eyes of the Pensacola training manuals, but there was no doubt that their Yellow-Devil hides would have been just as miraculous to the jet-black cannibals on first sight as the mottled pink blotches of mine. The bare-breasted young woman's reaction verified Olie's and his warrior gang: I was the first pale skin the island residents had ever seen.

Effective communication was our major problem. I at least had the benefit of Robinson Crusoe and the Choate Tarzan movies. I knew about swinging on vines through the jungle and how to keep one's sanity by recording minutiae on a desert island. The cannibals not only lacked those advantages from a higher civilization (while I admit finding interesting alternate uses for its canned Spam and nylon stockings); they didn't even possess half the rudimentary vowels and consonants of European language. It took several months to get the crudest transmission of ideas — *viz*, the similarity, yet crucial difference of chili-pepper and Yo-Yo for penis — between us. But we hadn't even that first day to waste on semantics. I arrived in the cannibals' village to find myself part of a war within a war!

There was no outward sign of a serpent in my unfolding Eden. Like Hawaii and New Zealand the island had no venomous snakes at all. As our small procession moved further down the easing slopes of the volcano the panoramic view became obscured by trees. The typical rain forest mix of towering mahogany, teak and gum, plus a thousand other tropical species of orchids and undergrowth adapted to this locale. What made this forest unique was the narrowness of its jungle: no more than two miles from the point at which my stretcher-throne entered the green canopy until we emerged again into the patchwork quilt of gardens. Looking back, I saw that the forest circled the southern side of the volcano like one of the rings on a lemur's tail. No lava flows broke through it. Though the monster wisped at the top it had not been violent for eons.

Their fearsome cannibal decorations and weapons notwithstanding, the same seemed true of the human inhabitants. Women cultivated peacefully on their sweet-potato patches. Men lounged, chatting to each other, idly observing the pigs rootling freely among them. As pork was — is — the island's chief currency, the scene looked for all the world like Wall Street traders gossiping in a Market lull, while at the same time keeping an eye on the tickertape state of their assets.

This languor shattered with my arrival. As Olie and the others bore me through the gardens towards a village of thatched huts each male we passed dropped to his knees and repeated the "Boniya!" forehead-banging (among the heedless pigs) I had already encountered on the mountain peak. The women remained upright, but turned their heads away. Welcoming a God was clearly for men-only. Their pot-bellied children seemed exempt from religion; running alongside my stretcher throne displaying a mixture of awe and giggles.

I waved to a couple, then gave it up. By now I was exhausted. The full blast of a tropic sun at noon beat down on my bare head. The huts and humans shimmered in a vague haze. I fell off the stretcher . . .

Olie caught me. (Considering that he had been up and down that mountain twice this morning — with a tubercular cough — his stamina was amazing.) The bearers set the portable throne in the shade of a breadfruit tree near a smoldering campfire contained by a circle of lava rock. Dead chunks of whitish wood and twigs were scattered around it. Olie helped me to sit down with my back to the breadfruit's trunk. Disturbed by the commotion an enormous purple-velvet moth purred past my head into some higher branches. Its wing span was at least twelve inches. (*Blatta Bretonii*. You can see one at the Smithsonian.)

The village was situated near the point where the silver stream became a small river. I gestured at the water and my lips. As the stretcher bearers all had their heads down in another *"Boniya!,"* Olie got me some water himself, using half a dried melon gourd for a container. The gourd had a slight crust around the rim but this wasn't a moment to stand on the niceties of galley hygiene in a Flight Officers' Mess.

The water was cool and sweet. My head cleared. I could see the pattern in the breadfruit bark and leaves. Flakes of charcoal in the fire. The porosity of the confining lava rock. The shapes of the scattered white firewood.

The hair on my neck prickled. The shape of the closest bit of fuel was not of a log but a leg bone.

A human femur.

Until that moment I hadn't truly believed it. Now there was no doubt. Behind their welcoming feathers and skull masks my worshipers *were* cannibals.

The legbone was next to a piece of pelvis. What had looked before like twigs were bits of human ribs. I sat under the breadfruit tree and tried not to think what would happen when it became obvious to the cannibals that they had snared a mere mortal instead of a god. It was only a matter of time — not much. Olie was no fool. When whatever miracles they expected from their catch failed to materialize . . .

A shrunken head was hanging from a doorpost of the closest hut.

Nature intervened. My bowels moved.

"Olie," I murmured, "I need to use the head."

A forlorn request. Nautical terminology for a water closet wasn't the issue. Olie still couldn't understand *any* blind word I said! We made my predicament and its solution clear through sign language. I pointed at my arse. Olie pointed at the stream.

I stood up and moved towards it. No one tried to stop me. The stream bank was about fifty yards away. On the opposite bank was an identical pastoral scene: thatched huts, men lounging, women cultivating, pigs rooting, children playing. The only difference was that the Other Side people — while pointing predictably at my pale complexion — didn't go through the "Boniya" head-banging routine. I squatted on the edge of the bank to commence my bodily function.

"*Naga!*" Olie gestured southwards, indicating "Go further downstream."

I was happy to comply. It allowed me to retire around a bend, out of sight, where I could think. It wasn't my privacy they were respecting: God or no god, they didn't want me shitting in their cannibal drinking supply.

I took my time doing what I had to. The physical result was satisfactory but thought achieved nothing. I couldn't do my normal act of self-preservation: simply blend. (Being a Choate chameleon or a Naval one was trivial: here my pallid coloration stuck out more glaringly than the orange penis peppers!) I couldn't hide from my captors; they must know every inch of their island. I couldn't swim to Australia. The

Avenger couldn't fly. Escape seemed impossible.

I decided to take advantage of my relative freedom and reconnoiter downstream. The river at this point was still barely more than a creek but around the next bend it widened abruptly, then entered a gorge. A path had been smoothed by human — cannibal — feet along my eastern edge of rock. I followed it through a profusion of orchids and enormous butterflies. The air filled with mist, and the roar of an approaching cataract. Another hundred yards and I came to the head of it: the falls I had seen on my way down the volcano plunged before me into the sea.

The cliff was vertical. I couldn't observe any steps carved into it. The height was too great to repeat my trick with the parachute harness. No escape that way except the Void. Eighteen is not a pessimistic age. I wasn't ready for the convenience of self-inflicted death. Besides, I still had my Smith & Wesson.

I began strolling back up stream towards the village. As I came through the orchid and butterfly patch Olie met me. His white skull makeup was wrinkled in a frown of concern — obviously considerable, to crack that mass of clay.

"*Boniya naga soa!*" he said, or thereabouts.

"I was looking at the ocean," I replied, with a waves-breaking-on-the-cliff sort of gesture. To my astonishment this threw Olie into a paroxysm of terror.

"*Naga soa! Naga soa!*" He grasped my arm and tugged me back towards the leg bones around the cannibal fire.

"It's only the sea." I made paddling motions. "Do you have a canoe?"

The paddling gesture heightened his fear, if that was possible. His hand shook on my arm. "*Naga basas!*" His voice trembled also. The butterflies took off in a cloud of gorgeous yellows and iridescent blues filling the gorge like a spilled box of Treasure Island jewels.

His anxiety didn't subside until we got back to the narrower stream where I had performed my ablutions. Fifty feet past it, a yard-long arrow whistled by my head and sank up to its feathers in the red earth.

Compared to what was going on in the rest of the Pacific the bellicose activity between the cannibals might seem like a *Boys' Own* game . . . but an arrow past your ear does concentrate the mind.

Island
Five

ON OUR SIDE OF THE STREAM . . . MY FORMER STRETCHER-bearers were pointing at the other side, issuing apparent gibes concerned with inadequate masculinity, interspersed with rather lackadaisical jumping which made their penis peppers flop absurdly up and down. (Except for the forward thinker who had appropriated the Survival Kit nylon stocking around his waist.)

On the far bank — which is to say, a mere thirty paces — about a dozen of the Other Side People were doing the same things (but without the nylons). Now and then someone would shoot an arrow more or less at random. Two spears were wasted, touching down in no-man's land in the middle of the stream. So far there had been no casualties.

"Why are they fighting?" I asked Olie (using bow-and-arrow gestures) from the slim protection of an immature banyan tree.

"*Naga bilonga boniya Tedi.*" Pointing at me. "*Aga yogo bogo.*" Pointing at a dead pig lying on the Other Side People's part of the sylvan battlefield. This was our longest conversation to date. What it meant was that in celebration of the God's arrival on Our Side, Olie's chief sidekick had loosed an arrow into the air with less aim than exuberance. It had fallen to earth, Guess where! Thus adding insult to the Other Side People's grievance at not being vouchsafed a new God of their own.

(There may also have been something to do with a girl in a potato patch and a cuckolded ancient husband but that part — like the causes of all wars — was never completely clear.)

"We must stop it."

I made a restraining gesture at the closest bow-and-arrow. Olie shrugged and let out a blood-curdling yell. The Other Side People warriors ran part way up a low hill, waved their peppers in my direction and yelled something bloodcurdling back.

"If the only way to stop this is for me to go over there, I'll go."

I could afford to say it because no one understood it — but when I moved towards the stream Olie grabbed me back. I was their treasure on earth, worth dying for, which an unfortunate fellow on our side began to at that moment.

Where the cannibals had lethal aim against a deliberate target, hits from an arrow in this random form of warfare — which was more a ritual form of display, like their minor forest god, the Bird of Paradise — seldom struck a vital organ. Death came slowly, from septicemia, or a little more quickly by a follow up if things got hand to hand, using a spear. The chap on Our Side would probably have been all right if he hadn't rolled on his back to make an obscene gesture at the Enemy, thus forcing the arrowhead deeper, into his heart.

Olie stared pensively at the man, as though pondering the Great Question of human existence in a heedless universe. The women on both banks wailed briefly in unison. The Other Side People went back to lounging and cultivation. The War was over. Once more, Peace prevailed.

There was time for observation — Olie's second-in-command sidekick had obtained the Parker propelling pencil from my Pilot's Kneepad and stuffed it through the septum bone-hole in his nose: the HB leads had been extracted and passed with needle precision through apertures in his ears — and time for reflection. I realized that what I had been witnessing in the capering and taunting up hill and down dale was the Battles of Homer. This surrealistic feathered dance, not the massing of Bronze Age Legions, was the original art and form of war.

Meanwhile Olie and his opposite number from the Other Side People came to each of their respective banks to arrange the Peace Settlement. An expeditious process — two pigs from Our Side for the one on theirs. The uncertainty about the potato-patch girl was put off for another day, by which time her ancient husband would have died of natural causes, she would have severed two fingers for remembrance, and the young man who caused the problem was able to marry her: the League-Of and United Nations could have learned something from it.

I was too young myself to learn much and I hadn't been married. My mind could accept modern warfare across the Pacific, or the English Channel: I couldn't grasp the prehistoric idea that people no further apart than a New England village green — or the distance from a grocer's shop in Croydon to the Post Office's scarlet pillar box — could be mortal enemies one minute and friends again the next.

I left the mopping-up operations and went for another walk along the river. The sun had moved west, there was more shade. The jeweled butterflies stayed on their mud banks and the decaying intestines of a large water rat. I came to the waterfall and stood for a moment gazing down at the Pacific to ponder a Great Question of my own . . .

How did the peppers stay on?

Even more existential: how did they stay upright?

And finally the Insurmountable: how did they do it running up and down the slopes of a volcano with no nylon stocking to hold it in place?

Prehistoric man must be made of sterner stuff than Choate's. I couldn't maintain an erection for more than half an hour. Given the present state of Olie's and my linguistics the penis-pepper mystery would have to wait until the language one was solved. The dorsal fin of a huge shark cruised below me, its dark shadow blunted at one end in the lethal form of the Greater Hammerhead. I wondered if this could be the reason for Olie's inexplicable terror of the sea. His ancestors must have come here by canoe. Could they have been capsized, and seized by those great jaws?

The sun was halfway to setting, obscured by towering anvil clouds of a sudden tropical squall. Even as I watched, a tendril touched down, then became the whirling vortex of a waterspout. The storm was moving towards the island. I turned to take shelter — and noticed that where on my/our side of the river the cliff was impassible, on the Other People's Side was a crude set of carved stairs down to the sea.

A possible escape route! And as I saw it, I remembered the inflatable dinghy beneath the Avenger's pilot seat. If it had not been punctured on crash landing . . .

I crossed the river using natural stepping stones. The crude stairs zigzagged across the cliff face to lessen the angle of descent but carrying the dinghy down them would be a difficult task. More daunting still, the stairs stopped forty feet above the surf. The waves broke full against the lava.

Hopes dashed, my spirits fell too. The waterspout was only a quarter of a mile off shore. Part of my mind actually considered waiting, and leaping . . .

The other part got me — using Flight-Deck parlance — the fuck out of there!

And none too soon. The rain overtook me. By the time I reached the dead water rat the river had already risen enough to wash free its rotting body. It was only at this point that I remembered I was on the wrong bank.

I couldn't cross back. The river was still rising. Striations along the rock walls of the gorge showed that the level could go higher than my head. I began running inland, towards the villages. Lightning revealed a cataract and a million drowning butterflies. Nature is profligate in the tropics. What was I to it? Thunder crashed as though all the rocks of the gorge were tumbling from heaven. The rain so solid, it might have been the river. I stumbled. Fell. Recovered. Saw a skull face in front.

"Olie!"

But this skull had green feathers, not red. The Other Side People. The wrong side. My fate seemed re-sealed.

"*Boniya!*"

A second miracle in one day.

With more anthropological experience I could have guessed. The power of myth resides in the clash of opposites. Where Olie and his people had been waiting for their Salvation to descend from Olympus, this green-feathered bunch — the Other Side People — expected Him to ascend from the Styx.

Fortunately for me, in the majestic currency of myth or the petty cash of real life, Divinity doesn't have to account for its inscrutable behavior. The mills of a God must ever be prepared to grind the unexpected.

DAVID GURR

E.P.B. Le Breton
c/o The National
Westminster Bank
Stoke-on-Trent Trustees &
Investments Branch
Hanover St
Newcastle-under-Lyme
Staffs 5T5 1AP

1/8/1987

Dear Mr Gauer:

Your <u>unstamped</u> letter dated July 2nd eventually reached me at the end of last month via your solicitors & the Executors of my late father's will. As you say after fifty years it was very much a Bolt from the Blue. I don't know what you really hope or expect from me. However as you seem to have gone to inordinate amount of trouble and expense for as you put it "biological background information for your children's benefit" and your own very understandable curiosity — I will do my best to throw what light my memory & I can on the story you have unfolded.

1)   My Family Tree
        a) Grandfather — Staff Commander EDWARD PARKER Le BRETON, R.N
b)   Father — Capt. HAROLD BEAUCHAMPS BRISBANE-Le BRETON, RN
        (Died 5/11/'76 aged 97)
        Mother — Ruby Brisbane-Le Breton
        (née Clark — died of Cancer 1934 aged 50)
c)   b) had two sons
        <u>self</u> EDWARD PARKER Brisbane-Le BRETON — Born January 1913
        Harold BEAUCHAMPS   "   "   Born March 1916

My brother & I did not like our unusual Christian names of "Parker" & "Beauchamps" (ordered by our Grandfather at birth — they were too liable to produce derision & so away from home we often used to use other Christian names. He may have called himself "Teddy" amongst others. I myself have been known as "Tony" for the last 50 years.

2)   It is quite true that some lady came to see father sometime about 1935/36 claiming my brother had put her in the family way. I never saw her or knew the "ins & outs" of their story; nor do I know what happened at this meeting with my Father other than he later told me the matter had been settled. However in retrospect in all fairness to my Father I would point out — my brother could not have been aged more than 19 (a minor) and as a very young junior trainee of the Imperial Tobacco Co did not earn enough to keep himself let alone 3 people. My Father was Retired & virtually broke — thanks partly to the medical expenses from my mother's long

167

illness — and then it was of course the time of the economic crisis of the 1930's & jobs were far from easy to get.

3)   I was employed by the Asiatic Petroleum Co first as an Overseas Trainee & subsequently abroad. I left England in January 1937 for Egypt & because of the War etc I did not return to England again until 1945. I was stationed in Aden during 1944 & I met my brother for a few hours in Aden harbour on board a Convoy ship carrying troops from India for the North African / Italian campaigns. It was the first time I had seen him since I left England in January 1937 & the last time I saw him alive. My brother had married somebody called Nesta in 1938. He told me she had left him for somebody else: they had separated but not yet divorced. They had no children. No mention was made by my brother of the lady involved in 2) above.

4)   Well that is about all I can tell you: it may be of some help. You will of course make your own deductions — but taking into account what your mother has told you, what I have written above & what your Solicitors have gleaned from searches into my father's & other Le Breton wills etc — it would seem possible even likely that my dead brother was your natural father — although it cannot of course be conclusively proved. However that said as it would seem you have had a happy family life for the last 50 years * — I cannot for the life of me see what possible benefit it can be to you & yours to bring out from the cupboard into the light this very old & long forgotten skeleton which has done you no harm all these years.

Yours sincerely
EPB Le Breton

*as David Gauer
P.S. Re my grandfather — I don't know about Canada but he did a lot of Survey/ Charting work for the British Admiralty off the East Coast of Australia between 1864-1880. My father was born in Australia.

P.P.S. to Panda and Rabbit:

We've been played for suckers, P&R!
There's one born every minute!
P.P.P.S
Out of wedlock, which is almost prestige.
Almost.

IT'S A BARNUM & BAILEY WORLD...

Saddled with Jim's music hall beginnings, a bastard son of Nelson expects circus Bunkum to drift in with Flotsam & Jetsam to Sing a Song of England, complete with double entendres and off-key. We can even see the comic side of Charlie specializing in Adoptions for twenty-five years before she dropped *her* bloody Letter! — but this latest micro-handwritten missive turning our toy-cupboard world upside down makes us cry Uncle.

A personalized "c/o Trustees & Instruments" referring in barely detectable script to "my dead brother" can't be our Live Father. As for an Edward Parker being a *"Tony"*? And HAROLD BEAUCHAMPS being *Teddy*?

Rabbit : *(Ears totally drooped)*
> "Isn't any of it true? Olie and
> the Cannibals sounds as real as
> Aunt Dorothea's Little Pliny and
> Vesuvius."

Panda : *(Eyes doing a brown-button roll)*
> "Not Olie. He means Mummy never
> said anything about an Uncle
> Harry."

Owner : *(Head split as usual)*
> "Uncle Bullshit! — but on the
> other hand — Charlie never said
> there wasn't one. She just leaves
> bits out. Until I find them. And
> then she weaves the new bit in as
> though it was always there. Until
> she drops the next one."

"What are yew thinking?"

It's time for more True Confession. Yes, we're back on the Couch — half a continent removed from the first one, but we can hardly tell the difference. The "yew-for you" accent is the same Jewish South African: only the names have been changed to protect the Innocent Until Proved Guilty of fathering-before-murdering Willum.

"What are yew thinking?"

Blame it on Amelia Earhart or the Celery Flossing incident. We flew the Cooped Up with Strangelove in Victoria to land ourselves flat on a shopworn scrap of Turkish carpet staring five days a week at a statuette of Freud in the pose of Rodin's *Thinker* beneath assorted Certificates for Studying Fifty Minutes of Madness before Our Time Is Up in the Nation's Capital. Ottawa, city of dogshit after endless snow.

"What are yew thinking?"

Very subtle. Guiding us from Thinker to thinking without skipping a broken heartbeat. Other Sigmundian relics abound, not least a windup gramophone with a 78 disc in place that truly does deliver His Master's Voice, scratched needle and all.

"What are yew thinking?"

This broken record never stops playing — except when Dr. A-for-Apnean Abe takes a deep sniff in the gloom behind us, usually after a series of sleep-apnean snores. We have never actually *seen* the Illegal Substance being snorted, but it would hardly be surprising if such a devotee of the Viennese School of Rudely Intruding followed Siggie's example of seeing if things that go bump in the night went better with Coke to keep himself awake. Even the Couch we lie on was bought (like the Scrap of Rug which covers it) at a Fraud auction in Vienna where it was described in the Sotheby's Catalogue of Sins as a True fragment of the Freudian Cross.

"We have a very angry Yew today."

The endless interrogatives are bad enough, but when Abe makes flat statements after Sniffing it really pisses us off.

"Yew were describing thissss letter from your possible father's brother, complaining about having to pay for a stamp."

The totally infuriating thing about that being: we not only HAD stamped the bloody letter to his bank, we even included a ditto, self-addressed envelope for a reply, which got lost by his lawyers.

"And thissss is why yew feel angry?"

The accent really will drive us crazy! We're already halfway there from having to repeat everything we already spilled to S-for-Strangelove. But those Victorian sibilant Sessions about Crustacean Curiousities were only once a week. Analysis for five Ottawan days out of seven is a very different stinking kettle of Freudian fishing for Lobsters in waters out of our depth.

"Yew displace hatred for abandonment by your possible father, onto thiss possible Uncle for still not recognizing yew, and thisss is why yew have 'abandoned' a third attempt at your blocked novel, which again portrayed an idealized Mother — but this time in a lesbian relationship, with Amelia Earhart — and a delayed-adolescent preoccupation for the mechanics of cannibals' penis gourds?"

For the third time of not asking: WE AREN'T BLOCKED!

The slight pause in our half-lived Boys' Own Island yarn is more accurately described in the Psycho-Analytic Krazy List as Displacement-out-of-Guilt for Knowing-all-Along more of Mr. Snodgrass's recent story than Owner let on even to Panda and Rabbit. During that Dickensian Expedition down to the Blitz shelter of Somerset House, which dug a putative Uncle out of Probate, D.D. had also unearthed:

> Harold Beauchamps Brisbane-LeBreton, Captain South Staffordshire Regiment, killed in action, 8 October, 1944. Last address, 47 Westbourne Gardens, London W2. Verbal Will only. "Words spoken by the deceased to his brother, Edward Parker Brisbane-Le Breton on an occasion towards the end of March, 1944, at Aden: 'I am leaving you everything I have got'. Amount 2354 pounds, 12 shillings and sixpence. The Residuary Legatee and Derrsee named in the said Will now resides out of England."

Residuary & Derrsee is a worthy Legatee of Jarndyce vs. Jarndyce — though a wee bit rough on an ex-wife "somebody called Nesta" — but par for the course of such a close-knit Trustees & Instruments family. By whom, in a tiny crabbed hand: "no mention was made by my brother of the lady involved in 2) above." either.

Et tu, Teddy versus *Fuck You, Charlie!*

Their disbarred issue writes off the 2000 patrimonial pounds (from a man who counts the cost of a stamp?) but during our two days off the Couch we brood over the lost twelve shillings and sixpence because Canada's War-Baby Bastards are in the *NOW* News.

One sharp-toothed sound byte from the CBC Weekend shows a found-and-reunited fifty-year-old MacTavish from Loch Lomond stepping off the plane in Halifax to be greeted by 250 of his Nova Scotian Tribe — plus Barbecue! Encouraged by this Hibernian display of clannish generosity, Only-Nephew D.D. sends an intimate Anglican follow-up c/o the Nat West's Stoke-on-Trent Trustees in Hanover Street at Newcastle-under-Lyme, asking Only-Uncle E.P.B-LeB by proxy:

"If we could perhaps speak man-to-man on the phone?"

In the (Greenwich) Mean Time . . . our Weekend relief from Abe's dishonest dissection of our Boys' Own Half Life disguised as fiction . . . we continue to ponder what naughty part our Unconscious played in connecting Penis Gourds with Pilot-Teddy's throwaway about losing a Little Yo-Yo, and the two halves of *Singer & Keyes* having only three balls between them. Which takes us back to:

Jim-and-Ginger (Grimsby) Session

My testicle wasn't removed. It just drained itself away through a catheter in my scrotum down to a container on the floor. Horrible black stuff came out. Awful for the nurses. A swelling twice the size of an orange. A bacilli-something jumped in somehow from my colon. I'd been at a swimming pool twenty-four hours before, in Grimsby. I was staying at the Travelers Hotel. There was a convention of bankers or top people present as well. I collapsed and had to be carried out by stretcher. I begged the ambulance attendants to use the back door. The doctors, a father-and-son team, refused to believe me. I kept telling them I hadn't had sex. If there had been I would have used a rubber. **Your Mother says the doctor told me I wouldn't be able to have children? Now I *do* need a drink!** About wearing rubbers, it could have been something telling me I didn't want kids. Your sister was the first time in my life I hadn't used a rubber. I thought, it would have been nice to have a kid of my own. The old Aunts were delighted. They used to say in hushed tones, "This is the room where She was conceived." **Charlie says I said we never used birth control? — this is Liquor Control Board Rye — Having your sister was a complete surprise? — I haven't had LCBO for years.** The songs were for Travelers'

Dinners, strictly for the Boys, boosting sales. **I did the Yo-Yo one after I married Gladys.**

    I'M SO SAD AND DISAPPOINTED
    I'M AS SORE AS I CAN BE
    WHEN MY WIFE FINDS OUT WHAT'S HAPPENED
    SHE'LL BE MOST UPSET WITH ME
    IT'S BOUND TO CAUSE SOME TROUBLE
    AND IT'S SURE TO CAUSE SOME STRIFE
    BE--CAUSE I'VE LOST THE ONLY THING
    THAT SEEMED TO CHARM OUR MARRIED LIFE!
A bit more ginger for the Chorus!

    IT MEANS WE'LL HAVE TO PART
    IT'S SURE TO BREAK HER HEART
    WHEN SHE FINDS I'VE GONE AND LOST

       MY LITTLE YO! YO!

With my first marriage, I had to find digs. I made a friend, Glynn Jones — a pharmacist's traveler with a beautiful Rover convertible. He was associated with a woman called Mickey Wildgoose. I was eighteen. She was twelve years older. Desperately unhappy. I was too. I had a room. Nothing else. I married her. For nine or ten years. Her mother was common as shit. Awful woman. Nag and Hag saved her brother Len from dying with pneumonia — this is back in Liverpool. Len had a pony and cart and sold vegetables on the other side of the Mersey! This didn't lift me up in life at all! I must be fair. She did the damndest she could, Mickey. Our wages disappeared. I was taking anything I could in any town I visited. After the Aberdeen Concert party I met Gladys Knight again — the contralto from Moisevitch's Leicester Concert, when Hag refused him the ride up to London because of no insurance. **She had a nice squirrel coat.**

> I COULD DO ALL KINDS OF TRICKS WITH IT
> COULD TWIRL IT ROUND AND ROUND
> COULD SWING IT UP — COULD SWING IT DOWN
> COULD TRAIL IT ON THE GROUND
> IT REALLY WAS A BEAUTY
> AND THE PRIDE AND JOY OF ALL
> BUT NOW I'VE GONE AND LOST IT
> WELL! MY WIFE IS SURE TO BALL

Next Round Chorus!

> I'VE HAD IT THERE'S NO DOUBT
> AND SHE'S BOUND TO THROW ME OUT
> WHEN SHE FINDS I'VE GONE AND LOST
> MY LITTLE YO! YO!

Because I already had a divorce, Martin and Newman fired me. In London, Gladys had been telling untrue stories to the boss.

> I SHOWED IT TO "MATILDA"
> SHE'S THE BARMAID AT THE "CROWN"
> I TAUGHT HER HOW TO PLAY WITH IT
> WHEN I TOOK HER UP TO TOWN
> IT FAIRLY TOOK HER FANCY
> PERHAPS — SHE'S STOLEN IT FROM ME
> BUT — I DARE NOT TELL THE WIFE
> IN CASE IT CAUSES JEALOUSY!

The boss was a woman — stories about my separation from Mickey. I was invited with Brother Reg, he was also working for M&N, to the boss's Knightsbridge flat for a cocktail.

> SHE'LL SHOOT ME THERE'S NO DOUBT
> WHEN TONIGHT SHE WILL FIND OUT
> THAT I'VE BEEN AND GONE AND LOST
> MY LITTLE YO! YO!

DAVID GURR

Reg was told, "Here's your new contract."
I was told, "You're fired!" That's
when I wrote — **Time, Gentlemen!Last
Round!** — Charlie hated it — *"In My Dreams"* —
Charlie Thomas, not your mother.

> I DREAMED OF A LAND--WHERE ALL SORROWS
> WERE BANNED
> WHERE THE RIVERS WERE COW-JUICE AND
> HONEY
> WHERE THE BIRDS FROM THEIR THROATS--
> UTTERED TEN DOLLAR NOTES
> AND THE FIELDS WERE ALL BLOOMING WITH
> MONEY!
> IN MY DREAMS--IN MY DREAMS--IN MY
> BEAUTIFUL BEAUTIFUL DREAMS!

**Sometimes for the songs I borrowed the
words.** All my own tunes — unless I used a
standard like Onward Christian Soldiers.

> THERE WERE GOLDEN HAIRED FLAPPERS--
> WITH CROWNS ON THEIR NAPPERS
> WHO FED ME ON PEACHES AND CREAMS
> WITH A WONDERFUL GIRLIE--I SAT DOWN TO
> SUP!
> IT WAS NECTAR WE SIPPED--FROM A BIG
> GOLDEN CUP
> BUT MY WIFE STARTED SNORING--SO OF
> COURSE I WOKE UP!
> FROM MY BEAUTIFUL BEAUTIFUL DREAM!

I was down and out in London. I paid 7/6d
a week for a room over a fish shop on
Thayer Street in Mayfair. But Wolsey's
didn't know it was a fish shop. They just
thought it was a "splendid address in
Mayfair." I got the Wolsey job on the
strength of it.

> WITH TOOTHACHE LAST LENT--TO THE
> DENTIST I WENT

WELL YOU KNOW WHAT THOSE PAINS IN YOUR
TEETH ARE!
HE SAID — GAS OR COCAINE?
I REPLIED TO STOP PAIN!
HOW HAPPY — I WOULD BE WITH
"ETH-AH"!
IN MY DREAMS —

Wolsey made the best stocking on the market. They were in Ideal House, Great Marlborough Street next to the Palladium and the Greater Metropolitan police station. A friendly sergeant used to call me up for good cases: **"Four queers in a toilet. Iron railings!"**

I CAME HOME ONE NIGHT — RATHER MERRY
AND BRIGHT
I WAS MET AT THE DOOR BY THE
MISS-IS
SHE SAID JIM — YOU ARE BLIND — BUT MY
DEAR I DON'T MIND!
AND SHE GAVE ME HOT TODDY AND KISSES!
IN MY DREAMS —

I was in night clubs for a year and a half. The Albemarle Club. One night I'll never forget. A ten pound note fell onto the keys — I got four pounds a week! — I looked up. It was Gladys! She was living with another pianist but she couldn't sing in key. An ear-respiratory thing.

THEN SHE WHISPERED MY HONEY — I DON'T
WANT YOUR MONEY
I JUST WANT YOUR LOVE AND ESTEEM
I LIKE YOU TO GO — WITH YOUR BOY
FRIENDS AND SOAK
WHEN YOU'VE SPENT ALL YOUR MONEY — I
THINK ITS A JOKE
THEN SHE GAVE ME A CLOUT IN THE EAR —

AND I <u>WOKE</u>
FROM MY BEAUTIFUL BEAUTIFUL DREAM!

Gladys was half a bloody note out — **Forget
the time! Let's have another LCBO!** — she
missed the Albert Hall by miles!

    I'M RATHER A SPORT — AND A TICKET
    I BOUGHT
    FOR A SWEEP THAT THEY HAD IN CALCUTTA
    AND A "GEE-GEE" I DREW — A HOT
    FavourITE TOO!
    CALLED "<u>MELTED</u>" "<u>BY HEAT</u>" OUT OF
    "<u>BUTTER</u>"!

Cissie Murray was the business agent for
Harry Gordon. He opened as an evening
Pierrot in Aberdeen. Of course he bombed.
Cissie Murray hired us, "Singer & Keyes"
for a hundred pounds a week! Next I took a
job solo with the Llandidno Pierrot troupe
in Wales. "The Folderols." Fourteen Darkie
Minstrels, singers, musicians on the Pier.
**They were sponsored by Gracie Fields — I
accompanied her on piano. The high point
of my life!** I met Gladys again in the
show. It gathered speed.

    I DREAM'T IN MY FABLE — THEY BROUGHT
    ME A CABLE
    I FELT THAT I WANTED TO SCREAM!
    I READ IT — AND HAPPINESS MELTED AWAY
    IT CAME FROM MY DARLING WIFE'S MOTHER
    TO SAY —

Gladys only appeared once a week with the
darkie Folderols and went back to London.

    THAT <u>SHE'D</u> WON THE <u>FIRST PRIZE</u> — AND
    WAS COMING <u>TO STAY</u> . . . !

Then she wrote from Llandidno, "I'm not coming back." **My beautiful Steinway went up in smoke!** She walked out — I walked out. I don't know where the furniture actually went.

WHAT A BEAUTIFUL-BEAUTIFUL DREAM!

Thank you Mr. Snodgrass! Canada Dry tonight! I don't mind if I do! Now you see this other Gladys Knight on TV. Gladys and the Pips. We had a flat in Holborne. Underneath lived Ralph Richardson. He had a very nice open seater Bentley. At eight or nine he'd shoot off to Elstree. At first I thought he and Gladys had a thing going but it was Charlie Forward. A bloody marvelous pianist with a wife and six kids. He made good money. We had to meet on social occasions. It was awkward. Everyone told me what an idiot I was. With Gladys. We were happy for two or three years. The Profession was soulless. They meet a producer — Artistes — their life is changed overnight. My family never approved. Why the hell should I give a damn? I was of no consequence at all. I was merely a child produced from some sour scene. They were hypocrites of the first fucking water! I think Richardson had an eye on Gladys for a while. This is the Theatrical Profession — **It's hard to beat Canada Dry** — you don't have to screw anyone — **ask your Mother for some more** — but it doesn't take a second.

> NOW THAT I'M OLD AND FEEBLE
> MY PILOT LIGHT IS OUT
> WHAT USED TO BE MY SEX APPEAL
> IS NOW MY WATER SPOUT!

I set this one to the Dead March on the back of a Trocadero menu. I was on my arse in London. Brother Reg never came to see me. Nag and Hag had broken up. He ended up as a night watchman in a hut with a fire in a barrel, watching road works. He was taken to a pauper's hospital. Double pneumonia. Reg said, "Will you come?" I borrowed money. We went to the hospital. Nag was saying, "Is he dead?" Nell — Reg's wife — was saying to me, "Why are **you** here?"

> I USED TO BE EMBARRASSED
> MAKING IT BEHAVE
> FOR EVERY SINGLE MORNING
> IT WOULD STAND AND WATCH ME SHAVE

The words were fudged from the Readers Digest. I saw Hag alive for the last time with eight or ten students standing around his bed. They covered him up. I looked at the poor bugger and in fourteen hours he was dead. I went with Reg. "What arrangements do we make?" Nell had covered the old bastard with a twopence-a-week Prudential. They wheeled out the body. His nose was straight. They'd bent it! They said, "We'll straighten that lot out." At the funeral a Seventh Day Pastor Craven — I'd lived with them for two and a half years in Cheadlehume, Manchester. A few other Seventh Days showed up — he conducted it nicely — to see the old man lying in the box. I thought, What a bloody waste of a family. I said to Reg, "We'd better square off with this bastard." He wouldn't take a nickel. Nag nearly threw a hernia. *"He's gone!"* They didn't belong to me. I didn't belong to them. **I've had more love shown to me by my dogs.**

THE CHARLATAN VARIATIONS

```
BUT NOW I'M GROWING OLDER
IT SURE GIVES ME THE BLUES
TO HAVE IT HANGING DOWN MY LEG
AND WATCH ME SHINE MY SHOES!
```

Quite a touching little "ODE"! I used to
have a routine, I'd pick a name, there was
always a HOWARD! HOWARD! **HOWARD!!!** Would
you mind very much <u>not</u> fooling around
<u>under</u> the table with **Olive!** That kind of
behavior gets you into "Church" you know!
Thank you Sir! Thank you very much indeed.
This will have to be the last one — Then
the Music Intro — **Don't drown it!** — But
The Birdies was my own. I have the score
here somewhere on a photo negative. "When
The Birdies Get Together." **Words and Music
by James Gauer.**

```
You and I have always been companions
A boy and girl affair, it's plain to see
But now the time is here when birds are
mating,
So won't you take a chance and stay with
me...?
```
Drink Canada Dry! Here comes the Chorus!

```
When the birdies get together
It's the time for love.
Say goodbye to stormy weather,
It's the time for love.
As the sun shines in the sky
It must be clear to you and I
That happy days are coming by and by
Just for we two.
Say goodbye to all your troubles
It's the time for love.
Take a lesson from the birdies
In the branches above.
I will build a love-nest for you
We'd arrange for a stranger or two,
```

DAVID GURR

So when the birdies get together....
LET'S FALL IN LOVE!!

Then came the bloody Gladys Divorce!
Before the Honorable Sir bloody Alfred
Bucknill, Knight — I've got that damn
thing somewhere too: "between Gladys
Evelyn, Spinster, and Hugh Courtney
Gauer," I wasn't James then — for
"Celebration of Adultery," in Admiralty
Court! Another year in London picking up
anything I could from people at the Club.
As a pianist you can always get a pickup
or a meal. At the Christmas Carol Concert
at the Albert Hall a French conductor
would invite the audience to sing. Then
say, "Would you like to hear it properly?"
Then the choir would sing Once in Royal
David's City. Give you bloody goosebumps.
**Jesus — Ask your Mother where she's hidden
another bottle of the Kelowna — this is a
hell of a session!** With Gladys gone I was
broke, out of a job. I got three quid a
week playing the clubs. I met your mother
in the Albemarle, near Harley Street. One
more step and you're in Scotland Yard.
They used to do a beautiful sole. I was on
from ten till two in the morning. By that
time you're playing to nothing but a bunch
of swaying drunks. Charlie was alone in
the bar. I'd seen her before. She liked
Bacardi's rum cocktails. I said, "Let's go
out to Barnet and see the Air Force Boys."
She had a lot of Bacardi's and got sick
as a dog. She said, "You'll never want to
see me again." Next we went to the Wigmore
Hall — a woman cellist. Your mother left!
She was an usher, not in a cinema, but
in Haymarket Theatre. Dressed up with a
bow at the back of her head and little
shorts. I used to meet her at midnight
when the show was over. Weekends we'd go

181

and hear Hutch. At Boundary Road we went
every Sunday morning at 10:30, to a pub in
Hampstead. Hutch dressed like a ragamuffin.
He was black but fabulous at the piano. And
the voice. Everyone went. He sang Trees,
Because, For You Alone. Not good enough ·
for the mob. They wanted something else
besides. Your mother says she'd never been
to — **Look under the counter!** — a music hall
in her bloody life until she met me. We
went to hear that jazz violinist, the one
still playing. What's his name? Grappelli.
Charlie came and stayed as a boarder with
us for a time at Boundary Road. Sometimes
if he got in late I shared the bed with
him — **The bloody counter next to the Dog's
Bed!** — Charlie Thomas. You always had a
room of your own, little Dai-Dai. There was
the ARP Colonel with his bowler hat. It had
a tin helmet inside! We were issued steel
tables for cellars. Under Boundary Road
was the tunnel going into Euston Station.
Big Bertha gun on the rails. They'd roll
it out to fire — it shook the whole bloody
street to smithereens! — then roll it back
inside. There was Joan Cross, the soprano:
One night she pointed at you and said,
"I've come for that boy. I have a feeling.
I want him." She hugged you under the
table all night. The homes on each side
were destroyed. We walked every Saturday
night to Maida Vale — fifteen blocks,
that's where we saw Grappelli for the first
time — and the Red Hot Jazz Orchestra
from Paris. We got home and heard a hell
of a thump. A direct hit on the Maida
Vale Empire! In ten minutes, another one
on the Queen's Hotel. It could have been
us. The incendiaries. Your mother used to
bring the damn things in from the garden!
**Charlie, where the hell is our bloody
Kelowna?**

From the garden

JOSE ITURBI

Tempus fidgets while we have fun . . .

There will be a Time Gentlemen, Please! for all of us, P&R. It's come to pass already for Jim and T.S. Eliot. For Charlie it comes slowly; dropping the soft shadow of death one harsh hemispheric stroke at a time — while her laptopped son betrays her, and complains to Monsieur Laurillard's successors about how much it hurts to do it.

> **Rabbit :** *(Ears still totally drooped)*
> "I think Teddy the Pilot definitely
> met Jim and Olie."
>
> **Panda :** *(Eyes still doing a brown-button roll)*
> "I don't remember Him ever wearing
> a Rabbit suit to School."
>
> **Owner :** *(Head still split as usual)*
> "Us in the Brown Bunny costume was
> Charlie's Black Book reminiscence,
> not Teddy's — but it's easy to get
> them as scrambled on the hard drive
> as they are in our brain."

"What are yew thinking?"

Honest Abe is remorseless on Monday mornings because he doesn't need to snort to stay awake. A double-shot Espresso from the Lebanese café on the corner keeps the snores away for our Fifty Minutes of regurgitation about Three Charlies in the same bed in Boundary Road, and Jim not even using the name until he added it to Hugh Courtney to become "James-with-the-Aunts" in the bloody Black Book.

"Photographs bring back memories. Nostalgia can disturb."

The pictures lie. Jim-at-75, in his Lawrence Welk cum Liberace ("*From Bach to Bacharach!*") Canned Music Outfit for Weddings (silver-and-black herringbone jacket, blue-ruffled-satin shirt) with his Captain Kangaroo Haircut over his eyes . . . it can't be the same man as the Brylcreemed Young Horowitz-at-30 in white-tie-and-tails in love with Jose Iturbi and Noël Coward —

Can it?

N-for-Nostalgia . . . reminds us of Nan.

"Thisss 'hockey-playing' aunt who loved you."

Now that we are sinking about it (on a Tuesday afternoon), when she said goodbye to us at Liverpool, Nan did look a bit like Amelia Earhart. Gentle snores behind the Couch encourage us to reflect.

Harley Street, 1944. Charlie's sister "former hockey-player, gym-teacher Nan" is by then a physiotherapist ("perhaps something closer, though I can't imagine her and sex") for an Orthopedic Surgeon pioneer, and has a flat above the Great Man's consulting rooms. Only Nephew's visit to Only Aunt in London, manages to coincide with the volcanic blast from the first of Hitler's V2 rockets during Sherbourne's Mid-Term Hols.

"V for Volcano — perhaps this bomb blast memory is where 'I for Island' got blocked?"

Abe's abrupt queries coming out of snores with no warning (on a Wednesday) are highly disconcerting. In real life, Doc, the V2 blast didn't *block* fuck all! A coffeepot flew in magically through a fortuitously open window and a fabulous model of Sir Malcolm Campbell's racing car, Blue Peter, landed undamaged in the street. We celebrated with Marmite-Fried-Rice and Brandy Snaps, and coffee from the blasted pot. Also a delayed birthday copy of Priestley's *The Good Companions.*

" 'Good companions.' You were so close to your aunt, and yet it was thirty years — with you on 'this side' of the Atlantic, and she on 'the other' — until you met again?"

You have to look at *both* sides. (Which couches us through Thursday & Friday.) She got married, late, to another Uncle serving the Empire: Engineering, the Assam Bengal Railway Battalion; and bridges in Nigeria; a pleasant fly-fisher, with a cardigan made of his favourite-dog-hair. She only visited us when she became a widow of 72 —

"I'm sorry, our time is up."

Ours isn't! Another Weekend gives us too much time to sink. Despite an enduring antipathy to Jim — "I still loathe the man for calling me Nanny-Goosegog!" — she sold her house on the Welsh border and moved to British Columbia, where, at Only Nephew's suggestion, she buys "The Cottage," a triangular property between Cadboro Bay and Telegraph Cove, in Victoria. Here she creates a West-Coast-English garden, and then paints it.

As Only Aunt was also Official Keeper of the Dearest David Letter (prior to the Disclosure Lunch), the Addressee decided to discuss its Darling Willum content with her in the skewed light of Charlie's first Black Book Chat. Nan has her own Early Days collection in a Gray Book — the same colour as the cover of the All Saints Nursery College postcards. Our title for this one would be:

DAVID GURR

No-No Nanette!
*White Cottage, green trim to match the Lawn; Michaelmas Daisies
and Dahlias, real and water-coloured; Trug of Wilkinson garden tools,
trowel, fork etc; 2 weathered Cape Cod cedar chairs; 1 Charlie Letter.*

About you not knowing about Jim...? My dear
boy, I was *appalled*! When I first came out
to visit and Charlotte told me she hadn't
told you, I simply couldn't believe it!
She said it was because of what the Social
Agency people she worked with as Head of
Adoptions would think if Jim told them of
her past. I said, "A child out of wedlock
in this day and age? Absolute rubbish!"
After she wrote the letter I kept begging
her to tell you but she still wouldn't.
She left it with me because she didn't want
Jim to know she'd written it. I've no idea
what on earth finally persuaded her. All I
can say Dear Boy, is that I'm jolly glad
she did! — Ah! This is Daddy. **[Seated Man,
dark three-piece suit; hair centre-parted;
detachable round-point collar, right hand
(with cigarette) stroking a brindle male
Bulldog, its front legs draped over his
left knee]** I don't remember the name of
the bulldog, but isn't it funny how people
do look like their pets? The way the sad
eyes and mouths turn down. Because we were
both so young when they died I remember
very little about Mummy — I don't think
Charlotte remembers either of them — but my
father, Henry Egerton Harvey — his stage
name was Henry Howard; Charlotte took it
as well when she had you — was nice and
pleasant. He only became irascible at the
end as his Graves Disease took over. This
is him as Abraham Lincoln in Medicine Hat.
**[H.H. standing in Tailcoat, floppy bow tie,
holding Abe's Top Hat; snow, & Stage-Door
iron Fire-Escape behind]**

And there was gas or something equally frightful as well, from when he was a Major in the War. I spent many summers with him until he died, about 1921. Because they were both Theatricals I was born "on tour" and put in a skip as a cradle. This is Mummy as Mary Queen of Scots. She really is beautiful. **[Young Woman in Coronet, oval face framed by lace, heavy Elizabethan brocade costume, huge sleeves (fur-trimmed) and Throne Chair; Jacobean stage-paneling backdrop]**

You didn't know they were both actors?
Daddy made several tours of Canada — I
suppose my being born on a tour of
Yorkshire is why I'm so fond of 'The
Good Companions' where Miss Trant finally
gets married and Oakroyd the odd-job
man for the concert troupe emigrates to
Canada. I gave it to you as a birthday
present once, I don't suppose you still
have it. But getting back to Daddy, he
was also the Company's business manager.
His partner, Esmond, was the father of
Lawrence Olivier's first wife, Jill,
before Vivienne Leigh — but you probably
know more than I do about Olivier from
Charlotte. **[Gloomy Victorian facade in
Chelsea]** Between tours we lived in London
in a succession of rooms in Elm Park
Gardens. That awful Chelsea red brick
and we played on asphalt. Numbers 43,
81, and Number 36 at the top, where we
saw the Zeppelins. Our Grandfather Harvey
was a GP in Hampstead with a French R.C.
wife — but this is Kythe, of course.
**[Upper-Middle (but impoverished) Young
Woman, 1912; some resemblance to Coronet
figure's eyes]** None of Mummy's beauty. Poor
Kythe had absolutely no chin. Your Great
Aunt from the MacKenzie side — although we
never met then. She was being secretary
to Owen Nares, the blue-eyed boy in No
No Nanette. What else is there to say
about The Aunts? **[Two Young Women, 1890;
Upper-Middle-Nursing Costumes (costly);
ruffled white gauze caps, white gauze
bows, dark taffeta dresses, white linen
aprons]** Elspie is lovely, even Dorothea
looks quite pretty. When you see them
here you can see why they might have been
in love — I know Charlie can't believe
it, she's very blind sometimes. **[Group on
Porquerolles]** By now Dorothea is vast,

189

always in her cape; and Elspie still tiny
in her buttoned boots. Me looking fat and
Charlotte, looking cross. Porquerolles was
marvelous, but going back through Paris,
those bleak suburbs. Drab. It was always
drab going back to All Saints. I loathed
it. Charlotte didn't seem to mind. What a
life she led! This is her on Balaclava.
[Fox-Hunting Young Charlie on Large Horse]
A terrific jumper! I only learned about
her "Condition" when her friend Pauline
got in touch and said, "Charlie's working
at Woolworth's in the Edgeware Road." I
went around, not having seen her for a
few years and saw no one looking like
Charlotte anywhere. There was a fashion
then you shouldn't have a high colour, and
if you did green powder would lessen it.
Behind the counter was this green object.
I thought, Ye gods! It *is Charlotte!* And
then "The Meeting With The Aunts."..! **[Aunts
Driving in Trojan]** Those enormous wagon
wheels, with wooden spokes. Their club was
the Cowdray Club, for professional women.
They were "country members." They invited
me and Charlotte for a Royal Command Meal.
Elspie said, "You're putting on a bit of
weight aren't you?" Charlotte denied it,
trying to hide everything in her Jaeger
coat — but a letter came in the afternoon
post from Dorothea saying, "It was all
too obvious that, etcetera." I wrote back
denying — but the next step was the Aunts
arriving in London at Charlotte's last
known address, where the landlady said,
"Oh yes, Ma'am. She's just arahnd at the
'orspital — 'avin' the by-bee!!" **[Trio in
London, 1940; Full Summer]** The three of us
off to the Wedding. Charlie in her Ascot
Hat, and Jim with his boutonnière. I went
with Charlotte as moral support to the Old
Admiral's lawyers, but I never met Teddy.

As for Jim, I admit I thought he was God-awful! It wasn't just his deciding to call me "Nanny Goosegog" — I've never had the remotest idea why! — I simply couldn't stand that Brylcreem Lounge Lizard sort of man.

Off to the Wedding

"WHEN THE BIRDIES GET TOGETHER"

You and I have always been companions

A boy and girl affair, it's plain to see

But now the time is here when birds are matin

So won't you take a chance and say with me ..

(CHORUS)

When the birdies get together

It's the time for love.

Say goodbye to stormy weather,

It's the time for love.

As the sun shines in the sky

It must be clear to you and I

That happy days are coming by and by

Just for we two.

Say goodbye to all your troubles

It's the time for love.

Take a lesson from the birdies

In the branches above.

I will build a love-nest for you

We'd arrange for a stranger or two,

So when the birdies get together .....

LET'S FALL IN LOVE♪♪

Our Kingdom, for a Lizard, P&R!

We should have been an actor . . . it's truly in our genes. A flying DD visit to the Provincial Archives mausoleum in Victoria confirms everything Nan says about Willum's Maternal Grandfather. From *Who's Who in the Theatre*:

Henry Harvey-Howard's Canadian Theatre Tours took him (1914) to Montreal, and Quebec (February 16th) where he played *The Dear Fool*; and (1920-21) to Regina, Saskatchewan. "December 30th to January 1st: *The Law Divine*. Original London Company." And also in 1921, closer to home: Vancouver, British Columbia. "January 14th. *Eliza Goes to Stay*, with Henry Howard."

And then another genetic bull's-eye. "Eliza In Victoria, on Sunday, Jan 15th, at the Royal Theatre."

From *The Daily Colonist*, January 20th, 1921:

"Henry Howard was an excellent type of elderly uncle, who though seldom on the stage was decidedly a personality."

He played his way out through Calgary, Alberta; Regina again, and Montreal (March 14th to 19th, the day before Charlie's 9th birthday), then sailed for England. He died shortly after his return.

And if she'd told us, Panda and Rabbit? . . . Your Grandmother was Queen of Scots! Your Grandfather played on the very same stage! . . . where Willum's Impersonator steals a scholarship thirty-one years later for Best Actor (as a Welsh Poacher, in "Birds of a Feather," with an unctuous Bishop) in a Provincial Drama Festival —

We might have stayed in the grease-painted Life of a Ham that Music Hall Jim never wanted us to be . . . instead of a monogrammed ghost of What Might Have Been.

P&R: *(In rare harmony)*
```
"We love ghost stories! What puzzle
letter comes next?"
```
Owner: *(In dislocation by association)*
```
"F for fog and fuck it."
```

"What are yew thinking?"

Another Monday bloody Monday, dragging us through to Friday, with Dishonest Abe pretending for each 50 Minutes-worth of angst for hire, that he doesn't know thissss What-If sssshit is ALL we think about. Half-Howard? Half Brisbane-Le Breton? Half MacKenzie of Gairloch? Half God knows what! Five halves don't make us whole. Obsession is the only real name we can answer to.

"And where do the 'Ancient Kings of Scotland' fit into thisss search for an identity yew can call your own?"

Och aye! Between yon sniffs and snores, once in a blue Ottawa moon, Abe comes through with a zinger that's a wee bit uncanny: as though Monsieur Laurillard's South African successor really *does* know how we are sinking into despair at ever being able to do Proper Writing.

"Another start at the novel thisss weekend, perhaps?"

After three F-for-False Starts, we haven't had the foggiest Bleak Housed idea where to go next in a Fraud's Progress through fiction — until our ghostly *I-for-Id Lit*, lights again on the original source of borrowed Inspiration for a Con Artist's Memoirs. *A Hundred Years in the Highlands*, subtitled, An Autodidact's Family Bible.

For David
from his great aunt !
Kythe MacKenzie
December 1947

This was written by yr
great, great, great uncle in 1921!

Osgood Hanbury MacKenzie
of Inverewe
with Illustrations, and a Preface

My uncle, Dr. John MacKenzie, having left behind him ten manuscript volumes of Highland Memories, covering the period 1803 to 1860, and I, who inherited these manuscripts, having reached the age of seventy-nine, it has occurred to me that I might make a book which would give pleasure to those who reverence ancient customs and love the West Coast Highlands.

I make no pretence to the art of the writing man

"So working backwards — once again like your childhood fictional friend, Mr. Lobster — first there was acting in the 'proper' side of your family, now writing. And your Great Aunt made you aware of thisss?"

Kythe was an ancient Highland custom. When Jim called her Old Trout it made her so furious she'd have an extra shot of gin in her sweet vermouth to give herself a heart attack. It was just angina, she lived to be eighty-plus like the rest of them, but it looked alarming because her false teeth would fall out. Charlie pretended that she didn't know I was illegitimate but Kythe wasn't stupid — she'd been Lord Haldane's private secretary, and various other things in India. She gave me a copy of the Gairloch MacKenzie genealogy showing my place on the tree. And a signet ring with the family crest of a stag's head. And the motto backwards. *Non sine periculo.*

" '*Not Without Risk*', backwards — but I'm afraid our time is up."

Allowing another Lost Lobster Weekend for the following MacKenzie family mess of Pottage & Haggis:

Kenneth is Fighting Jack's younger brother *
yr gg gfather's (on the Roman side !)

Kenneth MacKenzie, born 1765. First
considering the Holy Church as a career
(a youthful letter from Rome while on
Tour, admires the Jesuit Order) given the
exigencies of the time he turned from
religion to serve as a midshipman on board
the *Egmont*, 74 guns, at the relief of
Gibraltar by Lord Howe in 1783. Promised
a commission in the 73rd Regiment (now
the 71st), then in India, on occurrence
of a vacancy, he landed in Madras in
1785. Whilst so waiting, he was offered a

commission in the Madras Artillery, which
he joined in 1787 till the vacancy occurred
in the following year. He served with
that regiment, of which Sir David Baird
was lieutenant-colonel, throughout the
campaigns against Tippoo Sultan, ending in
the first siege of Seringapatam; afterwards
acting as brigade-major to Sir David
Baird at the reduction of Pondi-cherry,
held by the French, in 1793.In the same
year he got a passage with other officers
in the *Scorpion* sloop-of-war sent home
with dispatches; but in a dark night of
October, when off the Azores, they found
themselves surrounded by a large French
fleet without possibility of escape, when
they pitched their despatches overboard
and hauled down their flag. The French
fleet being bound for America they were
landed in Virginia on parole. After an
embargo by the American Government, for
some time, they were allowed to depart
in May 1794, when he and his fellow-
passengers in the *Scorpion* — Captain
Braithwaite, 73rd, Captains Oakes and
Manning of the Navy, and an officer of
the *Winterton*, East Indiaman, wrecked a
year before on Madagascar — crossed the
Atlantic alone in a small vessel belonging
to the British minister, and after some
hairbreadth escapes, landed in Cork in July
of that year. After some years service with
the Rosshire Militia till its reduction
at the Peace of Amiens, Captain MacKenzie
settled down on his brother's property
in Gairloch, where he built the house of
Kerrisdale. Though still Roman Catholic he
was appointed a Deputy-Lieutenant of the
County in 1809. Died in 1861, aged 96, and
was buried in Gairloch.

DAVID GURR

One day you __must__ write a rattling
good "yarn" about all this! K
* they both lived to almost 100!!

Jesuit Fervour & the Madras Artillery went to sea! Wrecked for a year on Madagascar, courtesy of Absent-for-the-Weekend Abe, now at least we know where our intrauterine Island fixation came from.

And thanks be to thee, Old Trout for our next installment of potted inspiration. May your Highland bones rattle on in the toy cupboard with the rest of the skeleton family Signet Ring, arse-backwards.

Danger for Nothing.

Following in our gg gfather's brother's example, we're cutting ourselves adrift from the past is Prologue to the man. Fuck the Old World's building blocks. Bring on the brave new one's Gold Bricks.

DAVID GURR

Aunt Dorothea reading you Pilgrim's Progress

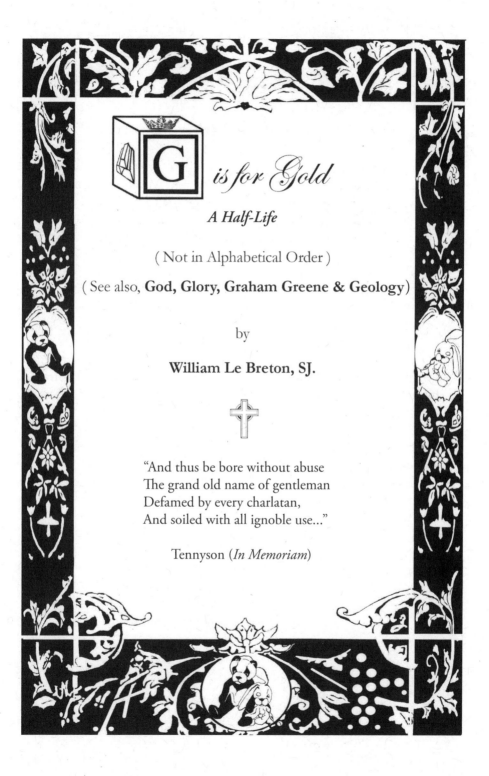

G is for Gold

A Half-Life

(Not in Alphabetical Order)

(See also, **God, Glory, Graham Greene & Geology**)

by

William Le Breton, SJ.

✝

"And thus be bore without abuse
The grand old name of gentleman
Defamed by every charlatan,
And soiled with all ignoble use..."

Tennyson (*In Memoriam*)

Gold
Preface

It is true I am a god — His Holiness called me "Mio Ciarlitano!" when I received my Red Hat — and who can disagree with the blessed conceit of a former-playwright Little Father who made himself God's Polish Vicar on Earth to those millions of the faithful illiterati who still believe in a wave from the Balcony?

The Power of Rome! Humility may stand highest in the Christian graces of Ralph Waldo Emerson but Sherlock Holmes is a truer judge. "Mediocrity knows nothing higher than itself, but talent instantly recognizes genius."

I offer that direct extraction from Sir Arthur Conan-Doyle's *Valley of Fear*, at secondhand, because it was the last thought but one to enter the mind of a lost soul; a young pilot's, fighting to regain control of his plunging Avenger fighter aircraft before both struck a New Guinea volcano. . . .

I was given the Grace to grant him Baptism into the Catholic and Apostolic Church, and Absolution of his sins, in absentia of the corporal remains.

I dedicate the world of the flesh in this book to my old friend of the Faith, in letters, Graham Greene.

And after the temporal, the spiritual.

I said, a last thought but one . . .

Of Him,
Paternoster,
that alone hath
the Power and the Glory.
Amen.

Gold
One

THE YEAR WAS 1963. THE TIME, LATE SPRING—NOVEMBER— or early summer; in the Antipodes all seasons run together. I had abandoned Missile Crises and Presidential Assassinations to bring the Grace of God south for the Society, to a still undeveloped world.

My unseen destination had not existed in Western cartography or consciousness until twenty years before. It had apparently been sighted in a final dreadful moment by an American naval pilot, and faithfully reported in the line of duty before he crashed into its unknown mountain and so met his salvation and our Lord.

By some accident — probably topographic — the lethal peak had no strategic value to any of the belligerents waging war in that part of the Pacific. The mysterious island and its possible inhabitants slept on — but it had been given an outside name by those final flaming moments: the pilot's name. Le Breton Island. And that was what now drew me to it, standing in the bows of a trading lugger under sail, staring forward through an antique telescope with a cracked eyeglass. Call it the Christian's Hand of Divine Providence or Carl Jung's co-incidental Synchronicity: whichever of those vast agencies directs our human fates, I was here because the name of the fallen pilot and the island was my own.

But had you asked me at that moment why I was on the heeling teak deck of the lugger there would have been no existential confusion in my answer. I was a Jesuit. Even more than my vows of poverty, chastity, and obedience to a reigning Pope, the mission of the Order of Ignatius Loyola was to promote Christian dialogue with the pagans of this world.

"Land ho!"

So had Ulysses heard it. And Saint Paul —

Through the cracked glass I could now see an object. Tiny, yet triangular. A shape unmistakable to a mountain climber in British Columbia or a priest in Tokyo. I had been both. The shape was a volcano.

"Range about fourteen miles, Father," said the lugger's captain, a weathered half-breed Baptist from Truk. "Horizon distance to the binnacle is seven. That means she's a big 'un."

The overloaded lugger — a mix of salt and pungent copra in her hold — was making a bare five knots. Arrival at my destination would still be another three hours . . .

Which gives us time for My Early Life: superfluous to me, but obligatory I am told, in a work of this sort.

In brief, as a youth I was everything that a Jesuit is not.

"Filthy rich, unchaste in the extreme, and bloody disobedient."

Those words of my instructing chaplain should be carved on my tomb. He blamed it on my parents — a sin of pride on his part, if not blasphemy. "Mum and Dad they fuck us up" as a recent British poet wrote — but mine were only responsible for having the money. Like my classmate Graham Greene, what I did with it was my own weakness — triads in bed, bi-sexual at first — not for those who let it all hang out on today's televised Talk shows.

I have confessed it all to Almighty God, if there is one — and if lightning doesn't strike the screen after that there probably isn't. Like Larkin, various schools of psychology have blamed Mum and Dad equally.

"Your bastard's anger and rejection of the world are fury at your mother's apparent prostitution" was one of the more memorable Freudian exaggerations in my analysis. "Your adoptive father was her pimp" was not a bad runner up.

Today I accept that my parents were human. And their parents before them. The chain is endless and times were tough. Outside our Holy Family, platitudes really are the best placebos.

"It doesn't look good, Father."

Our range from the island had narrowed to five miles. The captain was pointing at black-lava cliffs rising sheer from the sea. They were dwarfed by the volcano. A cone as perfect as Mount Fuji's, called "Mother's Breast" by the Japanese. To the west of it soared a second peak, somewhat lower, of limestone, truncated and irregular.

"Like the tits on that cheating whorehouse cunt in Port Moresby," one passing seaman — a Tahitian, named "Tango"; he had once been to Paris — said to another swabbing down. "That one with her left nipple cut off by the barber."

"Watch your fucking tongue!" bellowed the Captain. "Don't you scum know we've got a goddamn priest on board? Sorry, Father."

Ignatius left us the Prayer for Generosity. *To give and not to count the cost* — or as the nursery rhyme has it, *Sticks and stones may break my bones but names shall never hurt me.*

The brothel invective my parents hurled at each other with such abandon means nothing any longer. My true identity has been forged by war and the Church. *When I go to my stake I shall know who I am.* That credo of the Society is the legacy of every Jesuit. What heathen stakes lay at the top of those black cliffs only God could tell.

On this southern side of the island where the prevailing wind drove the swells against it, the black cliffs were unbroken, yet often in the South Pacific a reef forms off-shore on the northern coast, in its protected lee. The captain put the lugger about and sailed east . . . but a complete circumnavigation revealed only a closed circle of those forbidding lava walls. Their battlements were the reason civilization had stayed out. Yet I was determined to my core that the Society, and not the business-suited clones of Joseph Smith, should be first to bring His word ashore.

Pride, not lust, is the most ineradicable sin.

"This waterfall's where we started," said the Baptist lugger Captain. "The cannibals might have a trail beside it we can't see. The weather's fair. If you're game for the whale-boat, Father, I don't mind trying a run inshore."

I was game and he was brave. Though the word "cannibals" was doubtless an exaggeration, only two years earlier young Rockefeller had vanished among the head hunters in the untracked marshes on the main island of New Guinea. But that native population had been previously provoked by Australian prospectors whip-cracking for gold. This unexplored dot in the Pacific could have seen no living white man before me. The lugger crew manning the davits were unimpressed, already calling the island "Two Tits" —

"Swing her out!"

The whale-boat eased off its pads, rocking to the swell.

"In you get, Father."

I climbed aboard. The Captain followed. "But not the guns," I said.

There were two Lee Enfield rifles in the bow.

"But if you get ashore and something happens, Father —"

"It would prove God's will. I shall not be responsible for bringing them to Him unbaptised, my son."

On a page the words of a priest seem pompous as well as cliché. In a swaying wooden boat facing the unknown in the middle of nowhere, they still retained a hint of that Higher Power which transformed this world before the Book of Mormon. The bowman — Tango, who had visited the "Barber's Nipple" in Port Moresby — by crossing himself now and saying, "Bless me, Father," was surprisingly revealed as a practicing Catholic.

The Baptist Captain said gruffly, "Put the guns inboard, lads," wiped a tear as the Enfields were handed back to the lugger, then barked, "Lower away!" and finally, "Let go!"

The boat fell with a crash on to the top of a swell. The oars bit deep. In a single swirl of foam the lugger was behind us. The wave carried us forward to the waiting cliffs which loomed higher by the second. For a last few moments I could see the southern half of the island as a whole. The twin peaks with their curious dissymmetry. The higher tip of the volcano to the east was wreathed in cloud. Halfway down the flank below it was a circle of green jungle, then a patchwork of vegetation which might indicate primitive cultivation. The ground between the peaks took the form of a saddle plateau, too high off the sea to observe whether it held any human habitation. The plateau was bisected by a river. Through the cracked telescope the cataract at the river's end was splendid but also forbidding. I could see no path on either side of it.

"There is a beach, though." A tiny patch of black sand protected by a hook of fallen rock which formed a breakwater. "To the left, Captain."

"Ease up, Port. Give way Starboard!" The point of the bow swung west. "All together now. Steady as she goes!"

The bottom of the whale-boat's hull was flattened. We rode the swells as though on a huge surfboard — that shrank to infinitesimal dimension against those immense cliffs.

"Cease rowing!"

The Captain timed it perfectly. A final wave carried us past the breakwater, then, as the wave receded, deposited us with a feather touch upon the black sand shore.

"Tango, hold her fast! The rest of you lot, keep a weather eye for fucking cannibals! Sorry, Father."

I ignored his profanity and followed the advice. It proved unnecessary. No part of anything human revealed itself on the cliff or the cove. The only footprints were those of the crewman holding the bow line. At close range I was able to study the rock previously obscured by spray from the cataract.

"How does she look for climbing?" asked the Captain.

"The first twenty feet are sheer. Only cracks in it. Above that there could be a shelf. Hardly big enough to stand on."

"Let me have the glass, Father."

Expecting nothing, I passed it to him.

"You must have been saying your prayers, Father."

I stared at him. "You think you see some way up it?"

"I don't bloody think. Any boy seaman could do that lot in two lashes of a cat's tail." He turned to the crew in the boat. "You, Midships, bring that coil of manila. First Stroke, unship the footboards, we won't need 'em heading back. Tango, run the ladder up."

The sailors didn't seem to share his optimism.

"Jump to, you flaming scum, or Jesus won't have your guts for garters before I do!"

They jumped to. In a matter of minutes a highly professional rope ladder had been formed out of the manila and footboards. Tango secured the upper end to the rock shelf. The Captain tried the ladder first.

"Steady as a battleship's bell. You could pitch a bloody army camp up here, Father. Come aloft."

I've heard some gross falsehoods in the Confessional but that "battleship" stability beats them all! The rickety ladder was bad enough. The campsite at its top barely allowed the Captain to stand by himself.

He supported me with one arm and pointed upwards with the other. "If you're determined to go up there, God's on your side."

By His agency, natural stairs had formed in the lava rock.

"I'll check 'em out." With that unexpected dexterity often found in burly men the Captain bounded into the mist and vanished from sight. I heard his footsteps, then only the roar of the cataract . . .

"Plain sailing." His disembodied voice echoed down from the mist. A short time later he reappeared unscathed. "There's a river bank, straight and level, Father. I found a broken arrow shaft. Are you sure you don't want us to go back for the Enfields?"

"Quite certain, my son. I must go alone."

"Bring up the Padré's kitbag!"

There was a break in his voice as he bellowed. I felt a curious mixture of fear and calm. I ascended the natural steps. Behind me the "kitbag" — my Society portmanteau — was passed up hand over hand. At the top the Captain gave it to me. We could only see each other dimly in the swirling mist.

Despite the equatorial heat, I knew by some Loyolan instinct, that for the next unfolding of my Mission, I must dress the part. I took the robe — white, not black; this was the tropics — and vestment. I held the breviary in my right hand, with the embossed gold cross on the cover to face forward as I advanced.

"Thank you, Captain," I said. "And your men. Without all your splendid help I could never be here."

At which this bluff seaman, a heretic Baptist, fell to his knees and kissed first the vestment, then my hand.

"Say one for both of us now and I'll have 'em say another just for you back on board, Father."

I did not give him a lengthy Litany for Our Lady, nor allow him the full Act of Contrition he so richly deserved for his profanity. I gave him something simple and ecumenical, something for both of us on land and sea.

"O my God! I am heartily sorry for having offended You, because You are all-good, and because I love You and want to love You for all Eternity."

Gold

Two

IN NOMINE PATRIS, ET FILII, ET SPIRITUS SANCTI . . . I WILL GO IN UNTO *the altar of God. To God, the joy of my youth* . . . With my back to a precipice and facing the uncertainty of that heathen wilderness I fell to my knees to recite both the prayers and responses of what might be my last Mass, to the greatest sinner I could encounter:

Myself.

And after the Kyrie, before the Gloria, studying the vanity and wickedness of my own heart in the shadow of a volcano . . . I was reminded of Dante, that most infernal of all heretics, who, whilst seeking vainly to emulate Ulysses cast himself down to the eighth balcony of the eighth circle of Hell in opposition to God. I thought of Dante at that moment only to postpone my own step into this Pacific heart of darkness.

In fact it was bright and beautiful. Sun as golden as the cross on my breviary shone upon iridescent birds and flowers beside the silver river. Picking up my portmanteau I set forth along the bank.

The going was easy in the way of the Lord. The crooked was made straight. The steep sides of the gorge gradually drew back to reveal the inland saddle plateau. Its patchwork quilt was human cultivation. The river narrowed to a stream. On either side of it an irregular pattern of tiny gardens stretched up the slopes of the twinned mountains until gravity defeated agriculture.

There are souls here to be saved!

As an antidote to pride I recited the rosary aloud. First, The Five Joyful Mysteries; from the Angel Gabriel's Announcement . . . to the Boy Jesus in the Temple. The mingled smells of wood smoke and roasting meat provided final confirmation of human activity. A less worthy thought intruded.

Is the roasting meat human . . . ?

The Sorrowful Mysteries — Jesus Agonizes in the Garden, is Scourged, Crowned with Thorns, Carries His Cross, is Crucified — proved how little it would matter if I were to die, but did not solve the question of the nature of the meat.

Sweat ran down beneath my robe. One corner of my vestment caught upon the prickle of a type of wild rose. I heard voices — and then a terrible scream. Cut short by a gurgle. It seemed to go on for two decades of the rosary while I forced myself to contemplate the great mystery of my redemption as a sinner . . .

The gurgle ended. Holding aloft the breviary's golden cross I rounded a last corner.

Thatched huts. A slaughtered pig, not a person. Chattering and laughing, mortal men, women and children, going about their domestic tasks, naked as Adam and Eve — albeit with a strange collection of objects as facial and genital adornment — on both banks of the stream.

They saw me.

Their chattering stopped. In the sudden silence I heard the roasting pork sizzle and then pop. The men reached for adjacent bows and arrows.

I began the Glorious Mysteries . . . *His Resurrection — to obtain increase of a live faith.*

The warrior savages fitted the arrows to their bows. I recited His Ascension, *for grace now and glory hereafter —*

The arrows flew high into the air. I prayed for the Descent of the Holy Spirit upon the Apostles.

The women — too often the cruelest torturers of male martyrs — began a warbled screech. For their pagan salvation I recalled the Assumption of the Blessed Virgin.

The men ran forward, howling. I waited for the arrows to strike with Our Lady's Crowning, *to obtain Her grace of perseverance in the faith. That another may come after to convert these poor heathens —*

The men fell prostrate. The poisoned arrows landed harmlessly among some saphron orchids. In what can only be called a miracle of Divine comprehension the savages had understood the nature of prayer and now responded with their own.

"T'rkee Boneeya! Em i cum Tee Dee frum P'nskola! Boneeya Tee Dee!"

Their chanted syntax meant nothing to me yet, but its sentiment was clear. The Seed of God had landed on a garden of most fruitful soil. As His humble cultivator of the Cross I was welcome to grow the True Faith among these simple and already-trusting friends.

Taking me by each hand they led me into their village — or villages, for the habitations were bisected equally by the stream. A tiny island in its centre divided the two sets of thatched huts. At the edge of the bank my escorts knelt, indicating that I should do the same.

The sight in front of me was so unexpected that my knees bent of their own volition. The natives on both banks bowed towards the island and began to chant again towards an object whose function had to be devotional.

"*Tee Dee Boneeya!*"

The savages' primitive altar was nothing less than the reassembled wreckage — complete with white star on its fuselage, and a black-feathered and red-wattled turkey hand-painted crudely on its crushed nose — of an American fighter aircraft.

Wine can be the blood of Christ or the source of a debauch. Alcohol among the savages of "Two Tits" Island served the same duality of purpose that it does for Vatican Popes: a measure of our human frailty in the face of temptation. My new flock were abstemious except on special occasions.

My unannounced arrival from the sea appeared to be as special as occasions got on Le Breton — to give my new parish its proper Western cartographic name. The parishioners, of course, had their own name for it which, like everything else in this volcanic place that Western time had forgotten, remained a frustrating mystery. (The greatest of which was that wreckage reassembled as an altar.) To pass on the Word of God, I had to learn their language.

The Tribe of Loyola may have lacked the milk of human kindness at certain inquisitorial points of history: ignorance of logic has never been a fault of the Jesuit mind. I had come prepared with all that anthropology could provide about New Guinea in 1963.

This was remarkably little. Flickering film images of Australian prospectors making first contact in the Highlands (circa 1938) before shooting the inhabitants (more-or-less in self defence). Some papers by the Anti Slavery Society (Bulletins 3 & 4, London, 1935). And my most valuable temporal resource, *Growing Up in New Guinea*, by Margaret Meade (from her year in the Admiralty Islands, in 1930), which provided insights in its Appendices to everything from the Guardian Spirits of specific householders, to the *tchani* blessing of a boy leaving the happiness of his homosexual adolescent relationships for an approved Tribal marriage.

No detail was too small for Meade — but because they dealt with specifics of life in the Admiralties they were only of general use here. The body painting of the warriors and the separation between the sexes might seem approximately the same, but the inhabitants of Le Breton ("Two Tits") Island were as different in their behaviors and reactions to events as the French and the Finns. And in their language.

You may think from television commercials that Pidgin English is a universal standard. In fact, there are as many varieties of it as those birds themselves in Trafalgar Square. It took me three months to realize that a form of Pidgin was embedded in the two local tongues —

They shared nothing in common linguistically except the "T'r'kee" and "Tee Dee" which they chanted at me and the altar of the American naval aircraft.

It was also our Rosetta Stone . . .

But when the savages first led me towards it, the flesh of a Jesuit being as weak as any other man's, I thought again that I was to be sacrificed on the fuselage and prepared to fortify my spirit with prayer.

Having called upon Thy holy Name, we pray Thee, O Lord, our God, to sanctify the victim of this offering and, as a result —

"T'r'kee!"

The ancient savage holding my right hand in his left used the spare one to pat the crushed nose of the aircraft. It did not seem a killing gesture, but that was still far from clear. He patted again, and repeated with the patience which comes from dwelling in a land without clocks,

"T'r'kee."

He released my hand and made wing-flapping gestures, then patted the nose for a third time — at which my terror was replaced by logic. Or as my first Chaplain would say, "The penny's dropped!" The savage hand was stroking the painted feathers and wattles of America's Thanksgiving Bird.

"Turkey!" I exclaimed.

A file-toothed grin of pleasure cracked the severity of his white clay face. He beat his breast, saying, "Frum Tee Dee P'nskola em Olie."

At the "Olie" he tapped his breast bone with an arthritic finger.

Using an amalgam of Margaret Meade and Anti Slavery I pointed at him and said slowly, "Yo nem bilong yu Olie."

Other than God's grace, no mortal pleasure is greater than recognition of the Self. From my repetition of his name a bond was woven between us . . .

Olie led me through the rest of the kneeling natives — still calling out their "Boneeya Tee Dee's" like penitent Benedictines — right up to the ruined cockpit which was protected from further disintegration by a small roof of thatch. Olie reached inside, lifted a dried pandanus leaf and reverently brought out what must be some priceless relic.

I expected the unfortunate young pilot's head.

"HOW TO SURVIVE IN OCCUPIED EUROPE!"

Oh ye of little faith!

The pages of the guide were stained and rumpled from constant damp and drying out. *Issued by Base Printer, US Naval Air Station, Pensacola.* The 1944 Edition gave me my third word.

"P'nskola," I said to Olie.

He smiled in gratification, but that was not the miracle. He retrieved two more twenty-year-old objects. First, an Armed Forces paperback of Sherlock Holmes stories stamped, Return to Fleet Library. On the cover of the second document my name stared me in the face.

Flight Log of:
Lt. (J.G.) W. (Teddy) Le Breton, USN

Its first page formed the start of a rudimentary journal:
  "This last direct extraction from Sir Arthur Conan Doyle's
  Valley of Fear . . . "
But even my name was not the miracle.
The face in the cracked sepia photograph marked Pilot ID was my face.
I could not prevent a superstitious shudder. In pagan myths like *The Tales of Hoffman*, to confront our Doppelgänger is to meet our living death.

Gold
Three

AS THE LATE DISCOVERY OF PAPAL INFALLIBILITY PROVES: NO doppelgänger belief is so bizarre that it will not find its time and place in one or another of humanity's misguided religions. Worship on "Two Tits" Island . . . brings us immediately to a second proof of my opening proposition. That brothel name of Tango's — the Tahitian seaman on the lugger, who had once visited the Follies in Paris — uncannily resembled the native inhabitants' own name for what the outer world knows as Le Breton Island.

Pok-Tet-Im-Bilong-Sky-Ma. The pagan logic behind this pidgin-mouthful was as impeccable as any Loyolan's. (Students of Trans-Pacific migrations will get its similarity to Japanese Shinto immediately: "Teats-on-the-mother-pig-goddess" is an approximate translation.) Pork was the currency of both god and mammon on the Island; principal Feast days imparted a two-in-one meaning to our phrase, Bringing Home the Bacon.

They organized such a feast for my arrival — but I want to leap six months beyond it: to a time when Olie and I could communicate on the level of abstraction demanded of any formal study of the pigmy place of human beings in a Divine universe.

Olie was the island's Chief of Chiefs — which is to say he was a few moons older than the Head Man of the Other Side People who lived across the stream. In our Gregorian measure Olie's age was deceptive. He looked seventy; but from the earliest celestial event that he could recall — the lesser Mentor's Comet of 1915; South Sea islanders are phenomenal astronomers — was no more than his middle fifties. Which had made him only in his thirties when my namesake predecessor crash-landed the Avenger.

"Ted Dee Frum im T'rkee bilong Misis Merka."

The islanders' cosmology being matriarchal, this endlessly repeated phrase of Olie's eventually revealed that the pilot and his aircraft were the personal property of Eleanor Roosevelt.

(That formidable First Lady was also credited with inventing nylon stockings: a piece of Island arcana which will be made clearer when we come to the delicate matter of Genital Decor.)

The pilot had crashed on the volcano — Im-Bilong-Big-Tet, the masculine higher of the twin peaks; the lower limestone one to the west, being feminine, had no Proper Name — above the ice line, itself a wonder in the tropics. Olie's village, the Our Side People, living on the volcano's (now Mount Le Breton) side of the stream had tribal preeminence. This had led to a prehistoric condition of spasmodic but endless warfare between the villagers.

"Im Pearl nogo bilong Tee Dee Frum," Olie would patiently explain until I comprehended:

Pearl (Harbor) stood for war. The arrival of the pilot, Teddy-From (anything to do with America) had stopped the cross-stream fighting.

"But how, Olie? Why im nogo Pearl Tee Dee?"

Fortunately the savage was far quicker to grasp my Jesuitical fractured syntax than I was with his. To cut a six-month story short enough to proceed to the vital but terrible matter of the gold:

The Our Side People believed that a god would one day descend from the clouds and provide a limitless supply of Peace and Pig. Once annually, on their (Southern Hemisphere) shortest day of the year, their Chief (Olie) would ascend alone to the ice line to deliver prayers for the god's arrival.

The Other Side People's tradition was Neptunian: their god of peace would arrive from the sea. On the same shortest day the Other Side Chief would go alone to the Cataract to pray for the god's ascension from the foam.

(Students of Judaism may be interested to note that for reasons lost in the mists of time both sides had a mortal terror of the ocean and never went down to the shore: eating any creature from salt water was believed to cause instant death.)

The arrival of the Peace god in both appointed spots on the right day answered Both Sides' prayers. To paraphrase the psalm: *There shall be no more Pearl.* Warfare-without-end on Two Tits Island stopped. Now they waited for the heavenly largesse of limitless pork.

Nudity and modesty made strange bedfellows on Two Tits Island. I raise the matter of savage nakedness not from Western prurience, but because in that unfathomable way of He whom I still call Lord in the privacy of my sinful soul, all that subsequently occurred followed from a routine expedition to collect fresh *kot'kas*: the objects our anthropology calls Penis Gourds.

In my time with them, I never attempted to clothe the inhabitants. God had seen fit to keep the concept of bodily shame from those in this Eden; it was not my place to correct His handiwork. The first curious fact of their nakedness was that it was not total: both sexes actually wore an equivalent of a "fig leaf," but askew so to speak. Most of what we think of Occidentally concealing, they revealed.

The men wore the *kot'ka*, which housed the shaft of the penis but left the scrotum not only unhidden — and excessively vulnerable to any passing Devil Thorn bush, Whiplash Vine, etc. — but had the effect of drawing attention to it. (More so as the gloss-purple genital areas of both sexes were virtually hairless.)

The married women wore the *yokal*, a grass mini-skirt, but again placed ninety degrees out of phase — borrowing from electrical mathematics is appropriate: the placing of the garment was done with a Vernier scale precision — so that most of the covering occurred on the side of the hip, leaving most of the vagina and buttock-cleft exposed. Virgins wore the *thali*, a "micro-mini" whose mathematical placement and cleft revelation were even more critical.

To the outside eye, the support of these pubic coverings on both the men and the women broke all the laws we know of physics. Which returns us to the matter of Olie wearing Eleanor Roosevelt's nylon stockings.

I observed this phenomenon at the first big feast given in my honor. No other male had so much as a cobweb to hold up his *kot'ka*. As the average length of the yellow gourd was fourteen inches, and the weight, even when dried, three-quarters of a pound — 860 grams in Metric measure — I could not help but wonder how the *kot'ka* suspension trick was done. I concede that we lace-cuffed servants of Rome may be more conscious of matters of dress than our drab Baptist brothers (the denial of Sisters in the priesthood is a matter I leave to Polish Papal infallibility: that Little Father in White would be delighted at the Two Tits Island rhythm method; no sex for three years after childbirth) but any denomination would have noticed Olie-and-Eleanor's stocking!

He had three others. My predecessor, the pilot, Teddy-Frum had been issued two pairs of nylons in his Occupied Europe Survival kit. Olie kept them with his other relics from the prehistoric past and Pentagon Procurement, in his *w'sa* (sacred place), the remains of a honeybees' nest, halfway up a giant Casuarina tree. (His late father's

Smoke-dried body and spirit — *Aduarit* — resided at the top of it.) I asked one day why he had decided to break *kot'ka* tradition of his Smoked ancestor in so radical a fashion?

Olie thought for fifteen minutes (a brief moment to him; I have already said that this was a land without clocks) then began with the ritual greeting, "Tee Dee Father-Frum im bilong pyop up-top" — roughly, "Father from Heaven, I honor your feces" — "Kot'ka im hunt too much bilong go flip-flop."

I could believe it. "And not only while hunting" I replied with a man-to-man laugh. "But why don't the other men follow your example with their gourds?"

"No bilong Missis Merka n'lons."

"They could use slim vines," I suggested.

Olie thought about this for half an hour, then tapped his chest above the heart to indicate his soul. "Olie im go adu'rit lak ka'n kok." This meant that only after he was dead, and his bodily remains became a Smoked Man of Great Influence, could his spirit be asked for permission to adopt this new ritual.

"And if the Smoked Man spirit says no, Olie?"

"Im bilong kot'ka g'ruba!"

The consequence would be appalling. Any matter to do with redesign, or even collection of penis gourds, without the Other Side People's full agreement with Olie in the Spirit World . . . would reignite a cross-stream war in this one!

Value for money — the Holy Grail in Western spiritual life now that shopping malls have replaced cathedrals — was another concept unknown to my simple pagan souls on Two Tits Island. The myth-fulfilling god, Teddy Frum, had introduced paper money (French francs from his Survival kit) to them twenty years earlier but they had used it for ceremonial decoration. Because of their terror for the sea they did not even have *keena* and *toya* (Cowrie and Conch shells), the traditional trading currency of New Guinea. For the major transactions in their village lives, marriage and death, the only medium of exchange was Pig.

This digression into economic theory was prompted by a wedding. Olie's youngest daughter was to be married to the elder son of the Other Side People's chief. Such an occasion required not only the slaughter of half the island's pork but the obtaining of a new *kot'ka* for the groom to wear. Collecting it was the duty of the bride's father. Thus, almost immediately (twenty minutes) after raising the prospect to me of a cross-stream war being started by the collection of fresh Penis Gourds, Olie proposed we should go alone together on just such a mission!

Preparations for the wedding were already under way as we left. Two lines of slaughtered or still-squealing cash on the hoof formed a grotesque avenue of evisceration leading towards the stream. (In a bizarre aside I noted Olie's First Wife — my pagans were polygamous — placidly suckling twin piglets at her breasts as their own parents were felled on each side of her by the ritual slaughterer's axe.)

Queen of virgins, pray for us.
Lamb of God, who takest away the sins of the world;
have mercy on us.

Sacrifice is central even to the Rosary. I raised my crucifix in a blessing as I always did entering or leaving a village. Little by little, faith achieves its healing work. But Salvation is still to come: Olie and I crossed the stream . . . and this was my first intimation that our Kot'ka collecting meant treading on the Other Side.

We exchanged greetings with its Chief — Olie's future in-law — and requested his permission to proceed. In Island time, the exchange took only a blink of the eye. By my Society watch, it lasted for an hour.

"O'a'lee im go bilong Kot'ka Bon'ya Frum Papa." the Other Side People's chief finally intoned, in a fair imitation of Gregorian chant.

My understanding of the Other Side language was still rudimentary. The last clause, *Bon'ya Frum Papa* (God Man from the Pope) was me. The first, *Olie bilong Kot'ka*, gave him the right to get the gourd. I grasped that we had the Chief's approval: not its full implication.

We set off through the Other Side gardens, which looked just like Our Side's. At first the ground was level, then it began to rise to a point at which agriculture seemed impossible but in practice was not. This also was identical to Our Side topography and cultivation. Then things changed. Where the volcano's flanks were circled symmetrically by their girdle of rain forest, this lower mountain's trees grew intermittently in its gorges. No two seemed the same. I recognized a few familiar trunks, then could only keep track of the number of different species. The same was true of the Other Side flowers, birds, and moths. The profusion, and difference in so small a linear distance, was beyond even Darwin's imagining.

By now we were climbing almost vertically. Olie went ahead. I followed in my robe, envying him his nakedness. The sun beat down with tropic fierceness. We came at last to a small plateau. Olie paused at the edge of a tiny clearing. I heard a whistling warble. Then a coo. Olie pointed. A pair of the most splendid birds — feathers of an iridescence that made peacocks pale — performed a ritual dance.

"*Lahml'y kree'o'pan*," Olie whispered.

Later I came to know the islanders believed the eggs of this gorgeous creature to be their world's greatest aphrodisiac. Now, alas, the Kreeo Pan has been reduced to the edge of extinction and a plebian nom de plume, the Le Breton Bird of Paradise . . .

We ascended another minor precipice. The limestone was eroded to an outer consistency like the crumbling bark of an ancient tree. And extreme age, I realized, was the key to this mountain's geology. Where the volcano was comparatively recent in its origins, the crumbling rock under my hand had been laid down by the sea before the volcano burst from the ocean floor.

"*Kot'ka!*"

Olie pointed at the top of the next ridge. I saw a clump of vegetation with thick, water-gathering foliage, like Japanese Jade plants. The yellow phallic gourds were their fruit. Olie took a flint knife tucked into his nylon-stocking waistband and severed the new gourd he needed for the wedding ceremony. I reached to grasp a rock outcropping and haul myself up beside him.

Olie cut a second gourd. "*Kot'ka im bilong Papa Frum.*" He held it out to me.

The vision of myself wearing only a rosary and a penis gourd to perform my first Island Christian marriage caught me off balance! My hand missed the rock I was reaching for. I felt myself falling backwards. I grabbed again. My left hand lodged in a crevice. The pain was excruciating, but the action saved me.

"Olie. Your knife."

He passed it down. With my right hand I pried the left one loose. A chunk of moldy limestone fell away into the shadow below. In the blaze of sun, the ground before my eyes shone gold.

Gold . . .

Gold
Four

I T WAS GOLD. THIS YELLOW GLEAM BENEATH MY HAND — THIS metallic stuff of love and avarice — was the engine which drove the ancient and modern world. From Midas onwards . . . kings and popes, like mortal men and women, couldn't get enough of it.

Olie was indifferent to it.

"Ya'la." He gave a shrug towards the bulk of this Other Side peak below us, saving his attention for the true object of our expedition, the wedding penis gourds. "Im bilong n'ga."

"The whole mountain!" I exclaimed. "You cannot be serious!"

He merely kicked an adjacent ridge of crumbling limestone with the horny callous of his heel.

Again the yellow gleam!

I took his flint knife and stabbed the rock twenty feet away. *Gold.* Fifty yards. *Gold.* One hundred yards, across a gorge of Rosewood trees and Crimson-Throated hummingbirds —

More gold.

A thirteen-thousand-foot mountain of gold was beyond even Midas's madness. God's hand had led me to it, yet further revelation of my accidental discovery — reporting it to the Society, as Loyolan regulation said I must — could only bring disaster to the island from the outside world.

This logical conclusion was a test of faith which would have taxed Ignatius. I could only follow my Saint's example: drop to my knees and pray for Divine Guidance to escape His latest trap for doubting souls . . .

Our Father who art in Jail . . . !

Jim's legal trials catch up to our fiction's. Pause for prayer on an imaginary isle is derailed by a sentence passed down from the Vancouver Island Glen Lake Bench. "If it was only the lobster, I could remit you to the care of your loving wife. However, the added drugstore Gold Goblets give me no option: In consideration of your advanced age and lack of any previous convictions, you are hereby ordered to perform six months of Community Service that makes best use of your talent. To wit: Piano playing on Sundays and Thursdays for the enjoyment of the residents at the Silver Threads Recreation Centre."

"Of course he only went once for the Ga-Ga's," Charlie reports, with something like pride in her voice at the end of the Probation period. "The cunning old bugger got his doctor to excuse him for a bottle of Scotch and arthritis in his fingers. Plus a good word from the Langford priest who buys his Irish Sweepstake tickets."

The local beak got it right about the Prisoner lacking convictions. While Catholic family assistance works a miracle for Remittance Man Jim, Graham Greene's self-adopted Apostolic Church has almost been the end of us since Charlie dumped Darling Willum back on the nuns for six weeks to set herself straight.

> **Rabbit :** *(lost, again)*
> "Does He mean Mother Superior and the swallows?"
> **Panda :** *(morose, again)*
> "More likely His little Roasted Ass or Jim and the Hollow Buttocks thing."

"What are yew thinking?"
Stay out of this, Abe, it's none of your monkey business.
"What are yew thinking?"
Alright, already! We're sinking into the goddamn Convent in Duncan episode — which wasn't the swallows. It was their nests. They built them under the Convent eaves — the place was called St Francis of Assisi Academy, I went there because the son of the Gentleman Drunk who owned the farm that Jim wanted to be partners with, was Catholic

and already attended — and one day I noticed a couple of gardeners knocking the mud nests down with rakes. I said 'Why are you doing that?' They said, 'Mother's orders are none of your goddamn business, Limey. You ought to be in Morning Chapel.' Which I couldn't be, because Heretics weren't allowed in for the serious black-magic Hail Marys, we had to sit outside, even if it was raining — so I went to the Mother Superior's office and told her that I didn't think St Francis would say knocking down the nests was a Christian act.

"And thissss association of your toy Panda's 'roasted ass' with Jim's 'hollow buttocks' fixation?"

Abe the smarty-pants. Jim made a point of dropping his pants at parties or walking around the house with his lower-half nude, but I never knew he only had one ball. Monorchid, like Hitler, going on endlessly about my 'hollow buttocks' in the bath with my sister, or swimming in the creek. Of course, I see the Oral sex connections and projections now, but the Roasted Ass has nothing to do with my bum. When we left the farm at Duncan and moved down to Langford — thirty miles south — maybe a year later, I was hitchhiking. The local priest stopped to give me a lift and after he asked my name, 'Ah yes, the heretic from St Francis. One day for your sins, you'll be a proper little roasted English ass.' I laugh about it every time I see Monty Python do their Spanish Inquisition.

"And now you see your latest attempt at 'proper writing' blocked by the character of a Father Confessor."

What we see is the Pythons' audience of morons wildly applauding brilliant shit they can't begin to understand. Blockhead Abe just can't get it through his frontal lobes — WE AREN'T BLOCKED!

But don't look where the last laugh has got us. To Dante's end of the earth, and our front-row seat on the rim of the Inferno; trying not to watch a mother dying in slow motion while she considers euthanasia with chocolate pudding — in plastic Tupperware pots — and a borrowed copy of Final Exit . . .

Thank God it's Friday! — which means we have another weekend to ourselves, free from the Inquisitorial insinuations of pseudo Father Confessors. The Convent Expulsion was what prompted Old Trout to give us our bastardized (hand-annotated) MacKenzie Tree to foster the Roman half of our Family Pride.

You are descended from a Master of Restoration Comedy.
This is still Fighting Jack yr gggfather

General John MacKenzie married **Lilias**, daughter of Alexander Chisholm XXII. of Chisholm, by whom he had one son, **Alexander**, an officer in the 90th Light Infantry, who died in Melbourne in 1852, where he held the appointment of Colonial Secretary and Treasurer.

By his marriage in 1839 to **Wade Ellen**, daughter of George **Huyler**, Consul-General of the United States in the Bahamas, Alexander had issue: **George William Russell** MacKenzie, an Episcopalian clergyman.

yr g.grand father
*the Congreves were Army. My friend Lady Congreve
was the only woman ever to be Daughter, Wife, and
Mother of a V.C. (Victoria Cross)! They also go back to
the Writer so you are related as well!

Rev George William Russell MacKenzie* married *Annie Constance Congreve**, 2nd daughter of Congreve of Burton, Cheshire, in 1876 and had 3 daughters:

Dorothy Lilias, yr grand mother
Kythe (me yr Grt Aunt) and Marjorie MacKenzie.

*Daddy became a Royal Naval chaplain on
the last wooden battleship, in Ceylon — before he shot
himself on a platform of Paddington
Station.

The Modern Era

You will have to fill the rest in yourself
Yr Grt Aunt K

Fill in the rest! What else have we been trying for the last three years of shrinking and four literary abortions? Reading between the lines again, our Grt grnd father Chaplain probably shot himself on the Paddington platform because he was queer like the Cardinal's secretary, in the Liver Dock Club bath house, that we cut out of G-for-Gold —
   "What are yew thinking?"
No rest for the blessed. We carry Monsieur Laurillard's Couch

nailed to our back like Pilgrim's Burden. The strange thing is, we don't seem to mind Abe's funny accent any more.

"Do you think all priest 'fathers' are homosexuals?"

Abe's pointed questions remind us of Michael Redgrave's gramophone needle. From what Nan didn't say about Lawrence Olivier, it's obvious Charlie was fucking him as well.

"You remember playing with thisss gramophone?"

I don't *know* Willum played with it. I can only remember the music. Schubert — dum, dum, diddle-iddle-dum — and The Last Time I saw Paris, which Jessie Franks, the buyer from there, used to sing in French to me, along with Noël Coward. But I'm sure that was as David. I *do* know they never used birth control, at least after we came to Canada. Like all fixated adolescents I looked through their drawers for Sex. The Glen Lake bathroom was tiny. It didn't even have a medicine cabinet. A diaphragm would have stuck out like a sore thumb.

"Or a gramophone needle. So a novel which starts with a Jesuit 'Father' gets blocked by Convent memories of a 'Superior' mother."

Another Laurillard window nailed shut by Abe's Father-Figure broken record. The next time I have a goddam Chat with Charlie, I'm bloody well going to tell her outright, every time she contradicts the fucking Letter!

And next time we bloody do it! Like a proper bastard.

In lieu of their Black Book photos, inserting Boldly:

["Typical Ghost-Remarks" — Under our breath.]

```
The Admiral father was good-looking
but bad-tempered. ["In 1935 he was only
a retired Commander."] Teddy liked
rugger and cricket — the Wills Tobacco
people's annual Firm Tournament at their
country house. He had brownish-fairish
hair, gray-blue eyes. Good looking, not
remarkable, but he had a nice colour in
his cheeks. Not too bright but I adored
him. ["Unprotected? — after the 'Stock-
broker Thing!'"] I'd missed two periods
but I didn't realise the true significance.
Pauline suggested the Button-on-a-Thread
test to see what it would be. Circular,
counter-clockwise meant A Boy. Back-and-
```

forth like a pendulum was A Girl. Pauline
said, "You should go to a doctor." Teddy
was aghast. "I can't marry. Daddy wouldn't
let me." So in about my seventh month I
went on my own to beard the Old Man at
the house down in Watford. He was very
firm — On the Quarterdeckish: "No way my
son will ever!" — but uncomfortable as
well. What happened next...? **["What did the
bloody Button say?"]** A Boy! You weighed
six-and-a-half pounds. One of the Royals'
doctors doing volunteering delivered you.
I was kept in hospital for three weeks.
["Only two in the Letter."] Nan and
Pauline and all my friends visited — but
not Teddy. I have to think. Time is funny,
it runs into each other. **["The syntax
makes it harder — telling a Jimmy from a
Teddy."]** On Circumcision? Somewhere I'd
got the idea that it should be done. I
know Jim wasn't — but Teddy was. So you
were. **["Thanks for nothing!"]** While we
were still in hospital, I also spoke to
a Something Association for Mother-&-
Child who were useless but they knew two
ladies in Sussex who needed a housekeeper.
Meanwhile, postpartum, I went for two
or three weeks with you back to Nan's
best friend Kita — and John — Corbett.
The Corbetts were kindness itself. I
left you there **["Enjoying the comfort
of strangers"]** and went down to visit
the two Sussex ladies in a dear little
house with a most dreadful ghastly oil
stove with only two burners. I took the
job — with you along — but trying to cook
was impossible. We were totally isolated.
When I told the ladies I was leaving they
seemed resigned. Their meals had been
pretty awful. I took you back to London
and my earlier bed-sit, in Oxford and
Cambridge Terraces. Everyone was young.

Redgrave and all those. ["**Those what?**"]
Great camaraderie. I don't really know
what we lived on. ["**The wages of Love,
perhaps?**"] When Nan and I each reached
twenty-one I think there was a settlement
as a war orphan, a thousand pounds, a great
deal then. I went back to modeling but
the hours were too long. Auntie Rita was
doing your looking-after — and sometimes
Granny Monk, and there was also an Auntie
Kate — but I really wanted to be with you.
You were a darling baby. ["**Really-truly,
Mummy? — our Auntie Katie's someone new.**"]
I decided to be an Odeon Usherette, part
time, evenings. It worked very well. I was
with you all day. We went to Kensington
Park every afternoon, just the two of us. I
used to call you ["**Darling Willum, we know
that broken record by heart. And in the
Letter there weren't just the two of us in
the Park. A bunch of Nannies bending over
being goo-goo'ed at by God knows who!**"]
One day Teddy dropped in and "visited." He
was sort of fascinated by you. We never
slept together again though. He came in
to play with you the odd time. There was
a little café behind St Mary's Hospital
on Prade Street, run by two sisters. All
the youthful gang ate and met there — it
was the original meeting place with Teddy.
["**You met Jim there in the Letter — and
you didn't name the street.**"] All the food
was home cooked. And we used to eat at
Berterelli's, on Charlotte Street, a huge
plate of spaghetti for one shilling. Up
the street was a notorious club for all
the lesbians and homosexuals. ["***That's
where you met Jim!***"] James doted on you.
It was you he wanted — he adored you. You
were about two-and-a-half. At weekends we
used to go to the country for picnics.
["**And thinking of his wet-bread-moustache**

kisses still makes us feel sick!"] Jim was disentangling from the singer Gladys Knight, his second wife — she was a queen to him. He was her lackey. I had a lot of boyfriends. I attracted them like the proverbial **["Bumble Bee, another broken record"]** but they were casual. Kita's (Nan's best friend's) husband, John, was a bit of a roué. Half-uncley. He took me out to dinner. Then, "May I come up?" And then we opened the door — and there was Nan sitting in the armchair!! She never mentioned it again **["Casuals? You'd just been Uncle-ing the husband of your sister's best friend!"]** Teddy came around again one afternoon — and this time Jim was sitting in the armchair. **["Still casually...?"]** Teddy said, "I won't stay." He came once more, alone, and said, "I came to ask you to marry me." But by that time I was really involved with Jim — as James — he seemed to offer so much security. I was afraid to gamble on Teddy. I didn't dare to trust it. Looking back, you should go with your heart and not your head. **["Thomas Jefferson wrote it first, for *his* Love slave, Sally Hemmings."]** Jim continued to live in his flat in Sussex Gardens. You and I — as Mrs. Henry Howard, a War Widow — in Oxford and Cambridge Terrace. He decided we should go to share a common apartment as Mr. and Mrs. Gauer. From the beginning, Jim insisted that no way would he again get married! That was Boundary Road, in Hampstead. He was insanely jealous from the start about my behavior with all my friends. I gave him no cause to be. I never tried to contact Teddy. **["Good Girl!"]** I did have a small fling with the pilot, Timmy Vaughan, your godfather. He was killed in the Battle of Britain. **["Just another fucking casualty."]** One night Jim got into one of his towering rages, throwing things — I didn't know anything about psychology — he stalked out in his stocking feet and sat on the steps in the rain. Why did I stay...? [**"The Pleasure Principle, Mummy."**] I was really afraid of Jim. He would threaten to tell you that you weren't his son. [**"This is the Madness. All four of us knew from the start that I wasn't!"**] Teddy looked like that host on the Nature series — sort of a Robert Redford face without the blond hair. Charming. And then the fact that Jim made me get rid of — burn — the pictures of Teddy. And I had pictures of other friends that had to go.

There was one of a most beautiful Edward — Edward Bach, he was on the Stage. He used to walk through the park with us and all the ladies would whisper, "That lovely silver hair!" Most of the time he was "resting" between engagements. Another Teddy. [**"Another one! Just how many casual Timmys and Teddys are we talking about?"**]

In 1939 'or '40 when you were evacuated the First Time to Reigate I took a job with a pony and cart delivering bread in Golders Green. I loved to be with the horse, but the basket was huge and had to be carried up all the back lanes — because one had to go around to the Servants' Door. Jim was always so proper and old-fashioned about appearances. His brother, Reg, really thought that I was Mrs. Henry Howard, a widow. **["Playground 'Even-Steven'! Little Dai-Dai thought Brother Reg really was an Uncle."]** For your Second Evacuation — for our marriage — I was really torn, but it seemed the best thing. I think. Sending you down again to Nurse Crowe. In the bombing Jim just decided: "We should get married!" All his friends begged me not to. "Look at the history. Like the War, it won't last a year!" **["History is bunk. Henry Ford was right."]** After the start of the Real War we used to try and visit you

in Reigate on weekends. The thirty-mile
trip by train took eight hours! Then Jim
was called up — recruits had to wait for
their number. He said, "What shall I ask
for?" His "frightfully-frightfully" artsy
friend Bob Coxedge, who made the beautiful
leather belts said, "You've always liked
the Navy, James." So he asked for the
navy. They put him in the Marines. [" 'The
ball was in Hitler's court'. A line
straight out of Beyond the Fringe."] Your
Adoption Proceedings were at Marylebone,
in Closed Court, in the Blitz. We all sat
in front of a judge — just the Your Honour
kind, not a My Lord — you and Jim and me. I
think he asked you to go up to him so that
he could ask James some questions. "Are
you going to love this boy and take good
care of him?" Jim said "Yes." "Are there
any names you want to give this boy...?"
["Which Blitzed boy are we kindly talking
about, Your Honour?"] I don't really know
how we changed over from Willum. Perhaps
just, "You're going to have a new name."
Not Dai-Dai, you weren't David then. Mainly
we called you Snod, for Mr. Snodgrass. I've
no idea why. You know how strange Jim was
with names. He certainly never read the
book. Perhaps at Christmas, Pickwick Papers
on the radio, after the King...?

GOD SAVE US!

... From the reality of coagulated chocolate pudding in the fridge in
Euthanasia Cottage at Cadboro Bay — which Charlie and Jim move
into after the sudden death of Nanny Goosegog. Genuine heart attack.
Plain cremation. No funeral hymns please.

What a Friend we have in JESUS,
All our sins and griefs to bear —

"The death of your Aunt, still hurts you deeply."

Christ save us! Abe's back in the thick of things we'd rather forget.
Such as, it's another Monday-bloody-Monday.

Rabbit : *(the blue-eyed slow learner at Sunday school)*
    "He always liked chocolate pudding."
Panda : *(a quick brown study)*
    "But not with euthanasia."

"And you fear your mother's death — but I'm sorry our time is up and the next two weeks will be August vacation, which of course brings more separation anxiety."

A fortnight off for bad behavior on our own doesn't bother us. What scares the hell out of P&R's Owner is the Nembutal. Charlie always kept a supply at Glen Lake for putting down the 'beloved animals' in the basement. The number of times she told Nan she wanted the old bugger dead I used to think any day we'd hear that Jim had 'gone to sleep' there. And we've forgotten to ask Mother one more nagging question of Theosophy left over from the Chat before this one: the part about 'a sleazy bundle of rubbish with wandering hands'.

"Uncle Rex, the Vicar at Stowe-on-the-Wold, Aunt Grace's husband. No, that was the Bishop of Newbury."

Memory in our laptop is a fixed quantity. With Charlie now, recall is random. Keywords help nudge her stricken central processor. Sticking with Sexy Uncley Rexy. You 'shuddered to think what he got up to with a crazy curate and a cat'.

"Did I?"

O what peace we often forfeit,
O what needless pain we bear . . .

It reminded you of Kiff poking the stick up Babette's bum.

"That was at All Saints, with the housemaids."

This one was after 'some monkey business in the Vicarage'.

"It made an awful fuss about nothing in the end. He insisted on an Ecclesiastical Trial. Helen — she married Archie the farmer, and wouldn't do the dishes but could follow the Latin and Greek — said it was like something straight out of the Middle Ages. The Curate was put on trial, his name was something typically double-barreled C-of-E, like Gorse-Prickling."

Charlie fires her Luddite's look of distrust at our Laptop,

"I've told you before, if you'd write things down properly, with a pencil, you wouldn't make all these mistakes your poor editors have to pick up. It wasn't the curate on trial. That was the mad part. They tried the cat."

THE CHARLATAN VARIATIONS

Have we trials and temptations?
Is there trouble anywhere . . . ?
You bet, P&R! It makes the *THEN* Church Times.

A Hung Verdict in Animal Heresy
. . . For reasons of ill-health, Mr. Thornethwaite-Barqhuar, who brought the Feline Apostasy charge (last date, 1736; unique in Modern England) has elected temporarily to retire on the grounds of ill-health, "from my perhaps sometimes too-active, though I trust never less than truly zealous (in the Hebraic sectarian root-meaning of that word) part in defeating the Devil and all his works in Church or Vicarage affairs."

Rabbit : *(looking troubled)*
        "With 'Feline Apostasy', does it
        mean Jim-Puss, at Barton-Olivers?
        I don't understand this mad
        Prickling-Cat part."
Panda : *(looking pained)*
        "That's because He only saw Krazy
        Kat at Boarding School without us.
        The Feline thing doesn't matter.
        We weren't even here yet."
Owner : *(tired of looking for Abe On Vacation)*
        "Precisely, P&R — and don't even
        ask why the Aunts' black cat has
        the same bloody name as Our-New-
        Father-in-the-Gown-Trade!"

The final Jim & Ginger ghost-session with the pets' bête noire is even more rambling than the early Dai-Dai meanderings of Lingerie & Music Hall appreciation and invective which have come to pass as Normal Charlie-Jim.

He tires quickly in his fragile last months, and the death of Nan the year before, as always with the loss of a lifetime enemy, has made him miss her more than he could ever have admitted while she was still there to kick and bite when he called her "Goosegog."

Most of the fires of his Lear's rage are burnt out — but re-ignition can occur without warning from spontaneous combustion (set off by a handful of incendiary documents he has unearthed) between Rounds . . . and one last song before the closing bell.

Our Father in the Gown Trade

"SALARY OR COMMISSION" — Just a Small One — I wrote it to the "Vicar of Bray." We had Champagne at the Trocadero for lunch. At the Registry Office, Nan and Jessie Franks — the Paris Wolsey buyer, she loved speaking French to you — were the only witnesses. The Troc Band Conductor had been tipped off as we walked in — "Here comes the Bride" — just the four of us. Nan was a hard cookie. This Teddy you're asking about — I swear I knew absolutely nothing about the man. I

never asked her a thing. Charlie. I never
saw a picture. I never knew you had a
name — William Whatever — you were always
Snod, for Mr. Snodgrass. When you were
adopted, that year that was the Christmas
present! Once I had fallen for you, it
was like falling in love with a person.
Not that small! Charlie says once I saw
Teddy sitting in an armchair in our flat.
She says on purpose I wanted to forget all
those things. Didn't **want** to remember you
weren't my son. If anyone had said so — if
they had? — **I would have chewed their
bloody balls off!** Once — with Gladys, just
before I met your Mother — I was living
in a room on Hervey Close — Same sound as
her maiden name, different spelling. Next
door there was a man who sold surgical
appliances. Or at least he took the money,
but there was never anything in the shop.
I said, You'll go to prison. He said, "I
have been!" I made up a song, *"You're in
the Hoosegow now."* **He used to say, "Shhh.
Stop it, Jim. That's too close to the
bone."**

> WHEN I WAS A LAD AND FIRST LEFT SCHOOL,
> THE SMART BOYS SAID, I WAS SURELY A
> FOOL--
> TO WORK FOR A WEEKLY PAY,
> FOR "YOU'LL EARN MUCH MORE--
> SO THEY SAID TO ME,
> IF YOU QUIT THAT GAME AND WORK LIKE WE--
> (ON COMMISSION)

What an abortion! No ice! Coming through
Streatham on a Sunday afternoon, after
going down to Reigate to collect you from
Anne Crowe we were nearly strafed. They
hit the bloody lines on every side of
us. We had to stop in a tunnel. You had
your First Haircut, at Austin Reed's,
Piccadilly. First Dinner-in-a-Train, going

up to the Aunts. Arrived at Gloucester
station for the change to Ross-on-Wye. I
had to get a taxi. Fourteen miles worth!
Arrived in snow in time for dinner. A warm
reception from the Aunts, and Nan was
there. Froze to death upstairs! Coaxed the
old girls into coal for the fireplaces.
"There *is* rationing, James, you know."
    WHEN I WAS A MAN I HARKED TO THE BOYS
    WITH THEIR TALES OF THE ROAD,
    AND ALL ITS JOYS
    AND I GAVE UP MY NICE LITTLE WEEKLY PAY
    AND WENT ON COMMISSION —
    (ALAS THE DAY!)
I wrote it for the Hudson's Bay. I found
it with my old Employment History.
"James H.C. Gauer, 2975 Glen Lake Road,
R.R.6, Victoria B.C. Telephone GR — for
Granite — 8-2468. Born Brighton, England,
June 20th, 1905. Graduating from
Stamborough Park College age 19½ (Senior
Matric). Commenced my selling career in
my father's business — " That Matric was
laying it on with a trowel! **While you're
filling me up again as Junior Sales Rep, my
own territory, the Midlands in Hosiery,
Furs and Gabardine, take a look —**

With Messrs. Rossi & Company Ltd., 129 Mildmay
Road, London, E. 1 (7 yrs) - Ladies' Gowns (day &
evening) and evening Wraps & Capes.
- - - - - - - - - - - - - - - - -
Resigned to accept appointment with Messrs. Martin
& Newman Ltd., 65 Conduit Street, London, W. 1 -
Silk Lingerie, pajamas. (7 yrs)
- - - - - - - - - - - - - - - - -

**Resigned to accept position Sales Manager
with Messrs. Hygrade Lingerie Ltd.** — a new
company — **Thanks, Dai** — I was traveling
Monday to Friday every week for Hygrade,"

your Mother sold ties in Austin Reed's. We
were in London Saturday and Sunday. The
Finsbury Park Empire. Jack Payne was on. I
remember it so well. The last house of the
show. I flaked out in the toilet. Your Mother
and Brother Reg went back to the flat. The
night watchman found me. I went home in a
taxi. **This was the Battle of Britain!**
> SO I SOLD MY JALOPY AND BOUGHT ME A
> CAR —
> LARGE AND SHINING — BRIGHT AS A STAR,
> IN WHICH TO SWEEP UP TO EACH CUSTOMERS
> DOOR,
> AND SELL THEM APPLIANCES BY THE SCORE!
> I BOUGHT ME A HOUSE TO ENTERTAIN IN
> RICH LADIES AND GENTS
> (BUT THEY'VE NEVER BEEN)

**Hygrade couldn't get enough material
for lingerie** — by '42 the factory was
three-quarters in work for the armed
forces — that stuff that creaked as you
walked. **Taffeta was the problem.**
> A BENDIX, PIANO AND ORGAN I'VE GOT
> AN IRONER, A RADIO, I BOUGHT THE WHOLE
> LOT
> AND HOPED FRIENDS WOULD ASK,
> AS THEY SAT AT THEIR EASE
> AND WHERE CAN I BUY ONE OF EACH OF
> THESE?
> (WISHFUL THINKING)

**Ask your Mother — "Poor Dad poor Dad is
just a poor weak dog"** — if that really
**is the end of the bloody sherry she can
fiddle us another at the liquor store.** Then
the Marines. "Served 4 years (Rank W.O.1)
Pay Corps and Drafting Office (England
2 years, Ceylon 2 years)." We went out
on the old — **Fetch us the last of the
rye, it's by the postcard** — RMV Athlone
Castle. Warrant Officer was stretching it

again. Lance Corporal, I played piano in the Troopship Band with Jackie Thomas and Wally West, had a hell of a good time. **"We're here because we're here!"**

We hadn't been told where we were going. When we left Capetown the convoy split in half. One part went to Burma. I was bloody lucky. We got Ceylon and malaria. In hospital half the time. A few were heroes — crashed Yank pilots, one of ours — prayers by the Duty Chaplain. **The poor sodding Yank drew a bloody Rabbi! — Employment Record, "Remarks as to ability, special qualifications including Shorthand" I didn't have it, this'll tell you.**

. . . .

HQ,,RM
East Indies
Marine Ply/x.109102 J.H.Gauer
13. 3. 45
24. 10. 45
Drafting
Clerk
Has been sick for a large part of the time he has been here. He has, however, remained cheerful throughout and has always worked with a will. Willing and quick to learn.

. . . .

Signed Hoskins. That was the Piccolo Player, Ted. We were there to guard Mountbatten — it was his headquarters — and the High Mucky-Mucks. We used to watch them picking tea in the fields.

The women were good looking but black as your hat. They smelled terrible. In church they used scent — perfume — which made it worse. It made me feel sick. **Your Mother says she doesn't imagine they ever went to church with Royal Marines? The General himself said I put up a damn good show!**

David Gurr

On the successful conclusion of the war with Japan, many members of the staff of Headquarters, Royal Marines, East Indies, will be leaving for duties else-where, or to return to civil life.

While the staff is together I would like to give you this memento of our service in Ceylon.

I think we have worked, and played, as a happy team. We have maintained the efficiency of the Royal Marines serving in the East Indies and I hope that we have made them all feel that they have been members of one Royal Marine Family.

They have completed every task that has been given to them, with success.

In that you have played your part I am grateful. I wish you luck wherever the future may lead you.

> Yours very sincerely,
> W.G..L Melbourne-Marmaduke
> *Major-General, Royal Marines*
> *East Indies.*

The Happy Family's over. Back to bloody Civvie Street — with only a Certificate of Character from Dear Old Marmalade — in spite of what your Mother says about the stinking women he gave me a "Very Good." Signed by a "Major Fitzwilliam." In '46 the smart salesman was the one who could sell nothing! — They wanted two-hundred pounds? You sold them twenty. You were good! **As little as possible to keep them happy**.

>   THE END OF THE MONTH IS 3 DAYS FROM NOW--
>   FROM MY WIFE I AM IN FOR A H--- OF A ROW,
>   THERE'S A PAYMENT TO FIND ON THE CAR,
>   AND THE HOUSE
>   THE BENDIX, THE PIANO, I FEEL SUCH A LOUSE,
>   THE ORGAN, THE IRONER, THE RADIO TOO —
>   SO WHAT, I SHOULD WORRY,
>   (I HAVEN'T A SOU)

I got it typed by a woman at Langford — the Employment History. "Return to Messrs. Hy-grade Lingerie Ltd. upon demobilization in former capacity, resigning shortly after one year's resumption of business to emigrate to Canada with wife, son and daughter (and dog)." Getting you kids out of England to Canada was the best thing we ever did. At Sherbourne, when we came to get you, the Headmaster said, **"That boy would get more good out of a bowl of stewed bones with you at home than anything we could give him."**

    MY COMMISSION IS HAYWIRE
    I'VE NOT SOLD A THING
    FOR MY BREAD AND MY BUTTER,
    I'LL JUST HAVE TO SING

I'd only like to go back to England if I won Loto. I buy twenty dollars worth of tickets a week. Sold bloody Irish Sweeps all my life — but never hit! Well that's it. I've lived too damn long. **"The Lord said unto Moses, All the Jews shall have long noses. All excepting Aaron, And he shall have a square'un."** I'd like to see the steps where I stood in a sailor suit with my mother. **And my Prize Money. After all we went through, the cheap buggers in the Admiralty wouldn't part with a bloody nickel!**

THE DIRECTOR OF NAVY ACCOUNTS
(Branch 3B)

Sir,
Regarding your application for Naval Prize Money, your attention is drawn to the Regulations laid down in the Royal Proclamation of the 4th March 1949 viz:-

    "Participation shall be allowed to
    each individual officer and man who
    performed service at sea for a period
    of not less than 180 days between
    the 3rd September 1939 and the 2nd
    September 1945."

According to Admiralty records you did not
complete 180 days at sea within the above
war period and I regret, therefore
No more ginger? Signed by a bloody
Obedient Servant! Defence and War Medals
instead of my Prize Money! *You can bet
your bottom dollar, bloody Mountbatten got
it!*

He charmed the bloody snakes out of the
trees in that Admiral of the Fleet white
suit! Twice a week, rain or snow. We were
absolutely determined to get you in the
Sea Cadets. I don't know why in God's
name you ever left it. The Navy Pension.
Never mind the stripes! All that security.
Chucking it all up to build. People
don't have the money for those damn great
houses. Well, it's seven o'clock. I'm off
to bed. **Whether you like it or not, in
Sales, you go where the bloody market is.**
   AND I'LL SIGH AS I SIT IN MY WEE PRISON
   CELL
   FOR MY LITTLE JALOPY--I LOVED OH SO WELL,
   AND I'LL YEARN FOR THE TIME
   I COULD HAPPILY SAY —
   TOMORROW IS TUESDAY!
   (PAY DAY)

I suppose now it's Goodbye Mr. Belham. I
mean who is this latest William Breton
book? And here's the bloody Athlone
Castle. I can't keep track of all the
names. . . .

May-Day pot calling the kettle black!

Rabbit : *(as puzzled as Jim)*
```
"I got lost in the General
Marmalade letters about the
Pirates' Prize money. Does May
Day mean the Mother's chocolate
Tupperware pot?"
```
Panda : *(pretending not to be)*
```
"You don't say goodbye with
euthanasia."
```
Owner : *(still dodging)*
```
"With Nembutal for fuck's sake!
She had the powder in a sandwich
baggie."
```

"What are yew thinking?"

Abe's back on our case. Bright eyed from Vacation, with the same cracked record. "What are yew thinking?"

Forget Charlie's Chocolate Pudding preparations, in Jim's Ginger Sessions it's the bloody NAMES that matter. Another TED, *par example*. Popping up as a Piccolo Player from the Marines, like the apocryphal Black Captain of Jim's Mersey Whaler who popped out of a teak hatch as our Jesuit's Baptist Skipper from Truk.

"And a 'Boy's Own' story about Gold perhaps gets blocked by your stepfather's letter about being denied 'prize money'?"

Stuff & Nonsense but Abe just won't get it. With Jim's "Goodbye Mr. Belham" — which could have been a Music Hall closing line for Singer & Keyes — the problem isn't knowing our names, we've worn them all: it's having only one personality to wear with them since Darling Willum's Hampstead balcony scene. Which doesn't bother Charlie. When third parties are present, Mother refers to her Dearest David as "This one," as though there are multiple versions of us hanging around like the Bishop's household at Olivers, to be pressed into service for special occasions.

"Yew feel thisss hostility from the abandonment of the Vacation."

As usual, Guillaume's petit anger is diagnosed displaced.

Off target, Abe. The object of our current displacement is another crab-handed letter from Uncle Not.

Photo (b)

DAVID GURR

E.P.B. Le Breton
c/o The National
Westminster Bank
Stoke-on-Trent Trustees &
Investments Branch
Hanover St
Newcastle-under-Lyme
Staffs 5T5 1AP
October 27th 1987

Dear Mr [crossed out] Gauer
I must apologise for not having replied to your last letter but I have been feeling
a bit poorly of late. Nothing too serious — just a complaint sometimes associated
with old age: I am 75. The answers to your questions are as follows:

<u>Photos</u> a) Brother. Enclosed is one my brother sent to my father from India in
1943 — the last I imagine taken of him. He would have been 27. As regards
physique — He had blue-gray eyes, just under 6' tall and very powerfully & stockily
built. A first class County rugby player and swimmer.
b) Father. Here are two covering the 1st & 2nd World Wars. During the latter he
was NOIC at two or three submarine bases on the coast of Wales. (You may keep
all the photos if you wish)

<u>Brother's Death</u> I was told he was shot by a German sniper while on a motorcycle
carrying despatches from one area of hostilities to another. He is buried at Rimini
in Italy in a War Graveyard.

<u>School</u>   My brother & I were both at the Imperial Services College near
Windsor — a school for the sons of impecunious Army & Naval officers. ISC does
not exist any longer. As a matter of interest it was formerly the United Services
College at Westward Ho — the venue of Kipling's book 'Stalky & Co'.

<u>Brisbane</u>   The name was first given to my father presumably because he was
born near there when my grandfather was doing Surveying / Charting work in East
Coast Australia.

<u>Australian Connection</u>   Yes I was aware of the Tree. The Australian branch
was founded by my Grandfather's brother, Heriot Percy — a pioneer (Gold Rush
days) who landed in Australia aged 20 in 1852. Apparently later he did well cattle
farming. Heriot (& my Grandfather) were the sons of Lt Edward Parker Le Breton
RN. (Born 1791). The latter's brother Frederick was Master's Mate on board the
S/S Northumberland which escorted Napoleon to St Helena in 1815.

Well I have given you a brief résumé of the Le Breton family history. As you will see
the naval tradition goes back a long time. In fact my brother & I were almost the
first to break it — I partly because I was short-sighted but mainly I think because

247

after her experiences in the 1st World War my mother would have none of it for either of us.

Yours very sincerely

EPB Le Breton

P.S.:

I have done the best I can to satisfy your very understandable curiosity. Now it is my turn to be curious. What if anything are you going to do now that you have all this information. For example, do your children know of your story? If so how do they react?

P.P.S.:

Of course there is no need for you to tell me anything at all: but I do confess to being curious as to the end product of all the time and trouble you have taken to investigate your possible background.

EPB LeB

Photo (a)

Post Post Script

If Ifs and Ands, were pots and pans . . .

There'd be no trade-in What-might-have-beens! to exchange for Aunt Elspie's Kill-me-quicks. If Only-Uncle E.P.B-Le B can refuse to divulge his whereabouts — or even a phone number; for a man-to-man call, at our expense — we can refuse to talk further to a [**crossed out**] Stoke-on-Trent Trustee & Investment Branch at Newcastle-under-Lyme.

    But if—

Rabbit : *(helpfully)*

    `"We'd known about the Navy?"`

Owner : *(furiously)*

    `"That I was related to four`
    `generations of naval officers going`
    `all the way back to St Helena. And`
    `that the Canadian Navy's main West`
    `Coast anchorage which I must have`
    `dropped anchor in a hundred times,`
    `was named for my Great Grandfather`
    `who surveyed it, I might — I mean,`
    `I just wish, like the MacKenzie-`
    `Harvey Acting side, Charlie had`
    `told me . . . "`

Panda : *(practically)*

    `"We'd still be stuck between two`
    `half lives."`

The proof of which always manages to arrive by post on a Friday afternoon, leaving us stranded with no Abe to go off the Couch-rails at for another lost weekend of Catch 22 all by ourselves.

MINISTRY OF DEFENCE
Bourne Avenue Hayes Middlesex UB3 1RF

Your reference	
Our reference	
88/49408/CS(R)2b/8	
Date	
25 November 1988	

Dear Mr. Gauer

Harold Brisbane-LE BRETON
South Staffordshire Regiment

Thank you for your recent letter in which you ask for information in respect of the above named.

I have to advise you that the personal records of ex-servicemen are held in confidence. It is therefore the policy of this Department to disclose details from these records only to the ex-serviceman himself or, if deceased, with the written consent of his legal next of kin, i.e. wife, children, parents etc.

It is also necessary for you to provide us with documentary evidence of the relevant birth, death and marriage certificates.

I regret I must therefore refuse your request. However should you be able to furnish the necessary consent, your enquiry would of course be given favourable consideration. I have to say that we could not undertake the task of tracing former servicemen or their relatives for this purpose.

Yours sincerely
KG NEAR (MISS)
for Departmental Record Officer

P.S. to P&R: No Bastards need apply . . . !

Egged on by our obsession . . . *taking full disadvantage of Abe abandoning our ship for another Lost Weekend:* we stare at Le Breton photos of (b) Father & (a) Brother. For Christmas Last we gave Charlie a new Framed-Teddy with an inscription: "To replace the burned one."

"Which after a little sob," Guillaume pettily betrays to Monsieur Laurillard's current incarnation when Abe deigns to reappear for a fifty minute hour on Monday morning, "she immediately hid from Jim. And don't bloody ask what I've been sinking!"

Two THEN-Pictures . . . Dearest David & Teddy, taken when they were twenty years apart in age (7 & 27): we set them side by side above a tabloid "Obit for Anastasia: Was She The Last Romanov?" We also study old film. Pathé News. The Eyes and Ears of the World . . . !

Rabbit : *(with nursery excitement)*
        "Are they like ours?"
Owner : *(with clinical dispassion)*
        "There's a science of Matching
        Ears. Except for a few hairs in
        extreme old age, our lobes defy
        the years."
Panda : *(with unexpected heat)*
        "Not when they've been shaved."

"We still have a very angry Yew — but I'm afraid our time is up."

We're happier letting the pictures lend us their Ears. The DD & Teddy Left ones stick out identically. The Rights are trickier because while Dearest David-at-Seven stares straight at the lens, Teddy turns slightly away — the Standard Officer's Portrait Pose: Three Pips on the Shoulder and a Rugged Briar between clenched teeth, which avoids the embarrassment of Smiling in Uniform. DD can't use that excuse: wearing only a white shirt, unbuttoned at the throat, below unsmiling Cupid's —

The line of the upper lips . . .

Another dead ringer, P&R. The hair is less certain. Both part on the left, but where Teddy brushes back, Dearest David's wing drops forward.

"A Noble Forehead!" Chinless Old Trout used to whinny to her

Great Nephew between toothless attacks of Gin & Angina. "Like your forebears, the Earls of Ross and the Barons of Kintail." Thirty MacKenzie generations; no whisper of Le Bretons.

"Yew whisper in these exchanges with your imaginary animals."

Another brilliant observation from Nosey Parker Abe, on another drab Ottawa Tuesday afternoon

"Have yew decided whether yew want to continue for next year?"

We can't believe it's been twelve months of getting absolutely nowhere since we switched to Abe from Strangelove. But through the magic of fifty minute hours we don't have to make the Decision today because our time is up and we can return to our clinical study of the photographs. Inter-ocular distance is the second definitive measurement of genealogical science, and there's a Charlie-colour match, 'eyes Blue-grayish'.

The eyes have it. But only DNA could prove it . . . and DNA says Anastasia was no Grand Duchess. Just a Jewish-Polish factory worker who fooled half the world for a lifetime of mental illness called Wishful Thinking.

Our Grandfather Admiral is a different kettle of fish.

The uniformed Figure (b) standing with polished feet braced elegantly at right angles against the ship's roll, on a planked deck in 1919, knows exactly what he is: an Englishman ordained by God to wear three gold stripes on his sleeve and keep his hands in his pockets while he does it. Any rank below him who did the same would be thrown in the brig of *Pugnacious* at His Majesty's displeasure.

Taking Grandfather (b) from his lounging group we blow him up enough to see the Left Ear and white kerchief flopping from his breast pocket . . . but the eyes remain in shadow beneath the "scrambled eggs" on the peak of his Commander's cap.

The mouth's distortion negates the gleaming shoes' assurance; an inner reflection of things to come, or already at hand. A wife dying of cancer, retirement on half pay, educating sons to replay Stalkey & Co.

Both our Grandmothers died of Cancer . . .

Ignorance isn't blissful, P&R — but in a fool's lotus paradise like Charlie's Victoria, or Abe's Freudian Ottawa Chamber of Horrors, there are Tupperware morgue secrets it's better not to know.

David Gurr

Commonwealth War Graves Commission
2 Marlow Road Maidenhead Berkshire SL6 7DX

	Your reference
	Our reference
	ENQ2 HSO112
	Date
	1 December 1988

Dear Mr. Gauer

Thank you for your letter of the 8th November 1988.
I am able to give you the following information
from our records concerning Captain Harold
Beauchamps Brisbane-Le Breton.

Captain Harold Beauchamps Brisbane-Le Breton,
149955, The South Staffordshire Regiment attached
1st Battalion 2nd Punjab Regiment, died on the
8th October 1944, age 28 and is buried in Plot 6,
Row D, Grave 9 in Forli War Cemetery, Italy. He
was the son of Captain Harold Brisbane-Le Breton,
R.N. and Ruby Le Breton; and the husband of Nesta
Winsome Brisbane-Le Breton.

Forli is a town at the junction of the main roads
from Ravenna to Florence and from Faenza to Rimini.
The war cemetery* is about 3½ kilometres south west
of Forli and a little to the west of the road to
Predappio (Pierantoni)....

I hope I have been of some assistance.
Yours sincerely

Marjory Smyte (Miss)
for Director-General

* The cemetery was formerly a cherry orchard,
and many of the original trees remain along the
boundaries.

Addendum: Extracts
THE CAMPAIGN IN NORTHERN ITALY
FROM ROME TO THE ALPS

THE associations of the land of Italy and its people with England and the English are ancient, profound and various. The fortunes or the tastes of many of our northern race have led them in one way or another to that southern country and accustomed them to her classic inheritances. In the first half of the twentieth century this course of life was interrupted, and for the first time it became the lot of the Briton to appear in Italy as a fighting man . . .

The Allied Armies had won a great success, but at high cost, and they were unable to follow it up as they would have wished. The Eighth Army had advanced about 48 kilometres in less than a month, and hoped now to be able soon to reach the Po; but apart from their battle casualties, they now lost the 4th Indian Division and the 3rd Greek Mountain Brigade, ordered to Greece, and they had not the reserve of manpower to keep up their strength. Moreover, they had now come to a region of innumerable water channels which proved serious obstacles in the very rainy autumn weather, and the German determination not to yield a metre of ground without fighting for it was almost fanatical. So it was that during October the Eighth Army gained only a few kilometres of rain-sodden ground. . . .

. . . The total Allied casualties in killed, wounded and missing were 312,000; of these 42,000 of the killed belonged to the forces of the Commonwealth.

On many of their headstones some inscription from one of our own poets has been engraved. Those who recall the elegy written in Italy in 1821 by one of the English residents for another, of peculiar valour of disposition, who died young, may have in mind, as suitable to the whole company of the fallen, these lines:

> *They borrow not*
> *Glory from those who made the world their prey;*
> *And they are gathered to the kings of thought*
> *Who waged contention with their time's decay,*
> *And of the past are all that cannot pass away.*
> *Shelley "Adonais" (Stanza XLVIII)*

Stories, stories everywhere . . . !

We can no longer tell the difference between them. Kipling's Stalkey, or Miss Smyte's Shelley's, with its Chekov's Cherry Orchard, or our four alphabetically Aborted Teddys' (plus epistolary Trustee Uncle Tony's); or Jim & Charlie's, or Panda & Rabbit's, or Willum & — the Half-Tales all seem to hang with the same albatross dead-weight around our neck, more real than our own Ghost Life.

"What are yew thinking?"

Our Father which art in Forli, forgive us our trespasses.

"A feeling of guilt for being alive when confronted by a parent's death may not seem rational but it is normal. And now I'm afraid —"

Our week is up. Thank yew, Abe! Another three days to think off base.

My Father's House hath many mansions . . .

But why Teddy Elgar's elegiac variations of love and loss should be written at a Cotswolds cottage with the same name as Charlie's Teddy's last rest; Forli, Plot 6-Row D-Grave 9, is an enigma beyond solution.

"I go to prepare a place for you . . . Hear now the Gospel for the Ember days. 'And He said unto them, I beheld Satan as lightning fall from heaven' . . . "

In what monstrous God's name do these random fragments come from to rain terror into our hard drive? Ex-Choirboy Owner can't remember even hearing of bloody Ember Days — though a flicker of Anglican Then-service, "we fast and pray on the Wednesday, Friday, and Saturday after Whit Sunday and St Lucy's day" comes echoing back from Sherbourne's Abbey. Like a headmaster's bowl of stewed bones for Snod. Or is that another Dorothea, and Oliver Twist? But Churchill's V-for-Victory was real: Beethoven's Morse-Coded Fifth before D-Day, on the BBC.

"It has just been announced that a Landing . . . "

The Monster is silent again. The Last Ember Day, on Hold for another endless moment. Leaving us to contemplate the remote possibility of a Daddy who was a Hero instead of a lingerie salesman.

BACK WITH HYGRADE

Just back from Ceylon after four years with the Royal Marines, Mr. J. H. C. G—— has taken up again his position with Hygrade Lingerie, Ltd., Leicester, as sales manager. He tells us they hope to open a new London West End showroom again soon to replace the one that was blitzed. Miss Jessie Frank will be in charge of it.

RP 1091
HS 1001
10th January 1989

Dear Mr Gauer,

Further to my letter

WITH THE COMPLIMENTS OF

to you dated 9th January 1989 (reference RP1091),
I realized that I omitted to enclose
the general view of Forli War Cemetery, Italy as I
said I would.
I therefore enclose it with this compliments slip and
with apologies for my oversight.
If you wish a Close-up of your Father's Grave, it can
be taken by a member of the Commission Staff on
their next visit. Please provide a postal order in the
sum of £1 per picture.

COMMONWEALTH WAR GRAVES COMMISSION

2 MARLOW ROAD

MAIDENHEAD BERKSHIRE

SL6 7DX

Yours sincerely
Marjory Smyte
(Miss)
ENQUIRIES

P.S.: I do hope it will help you.
People do find visiting the actual site brings a sort of
contentment.

Our true struggle for a foothold in European history . . . is always against names. After her General View of the cherry trees, and the white stones in the grass, we return (Miss) Marjory Smyte a note of thanks with a money order to Enquiries for a Grave Close-up. It arrives in God's good time, via monstrous snail mail. At first sight of the inscription . . . *Here Lies . . . and a single red poppy* . . . all the clichés flee away to where they belong in the trash heap of our mind. Raw emotion grabs us by the throat. SEEING . . .

Le Breton, and Captain —

It's the carved granite HAROLD that sticks in our craw.

How could Charlie not know that her Teddy was a Harry?

The plot sickens.

Our doubts crawl back from the trash heap. We can't repeat family history by burning the photo of Grave 9, Row D, at Forli, but we lock it away, like Monsieur Laurillard nailing our window shut, and listen to Elgar's newly-unearthed-and-patched-up "Uncompleted" Third Symphony.

Out of sight, not out of mind. A counterfeit key to contentment.

"Perhaps another way of thinking of thisss contempt yew feel for Jim is possibly displacement for anti-semitism yew feel towards me?"

Oy vey, Abe! Or perhaps it's just another way of saying D.D. can't be bothered to dig up a fifth hard-driven fucking revelation from a laptop. Genug! Enough already!

Which leads to Mutiny on the Bomb Shelf.

Pair : *(in Highland rebellion)*
```
"We don't care about Harry. If it
isn't Teddy's Treasure Island we
won't play any more."
```

So play it again, Mr. Belham. We're here because we're here sitting shiva. Forget Charlie's chocolate pudding in Euthanasia Cottage. Write k-for-kosher and be damned already!

Formerly a cherry orchard ...

Plot 6, Row D, Grave 9.

$M is for Money

A Half-Life

(Not in Alphabetical Order)

(See also, **Marlon, Madness, Midas,** *already!*)

by

Schlomo "Lucky" Gur,

Dream Management Inc.

*"Poets are people who despise money —
except what you need for today."*

Jim Barrie

Preface
About Money

So it's true I'm a god — "Meistersinger Marktschreir!" Lennie-baby used to nail me from his podium — but who's blaming the yiddisher poppa of Radical Putz for Young People going a little over the wall after those first West Side Story reviews of Candide?

The Best of All Possible Worlds down the tubes for Bernstein, over my extra 5 per cent! You want a better Agent? Let Humility go stand in the Christian graces of Ralph Waldo Emerson with Shylock!

Sherlock sells better.

Quote, Mediocrity knows nothing higher than itself, but talent instantly recognizes genius. End quote.

End argument.

Or go ask the A&E Channel!

Money
One

I WAS BORN FOR BUSINESS . . . AND EXCEPT FOR THIS OPENING TIME-
-out, I don't use the past tense. A Mega Match-Maker for *The
Misfits* (Monroe and Gable) lives in the present. "Sweetheart," I tell
Marilyn, "with all the Great Deals, either it's happening Now!— or we
close Ten Mill higher next week!"

My first memory of hard cash is the $5 bills from the johns crash-
landing on my baby-buggy blanket when I'm parked at the bottom
of the fire-escape stairs. The johns are heading up for lunch-hour
quickies with my mother. And that's all I'm dropping about the early
nooners — except between us, Mom'n'Me strike it lucky enough times
to move to the top of the staircase, and then buy the building.

Location! is the key to everything from New York tenements to
New Guinea gold mines. NASA has the photos to prove it; you can see
Vulkan's operation on Le Breton Island from the planet Mars.

So how, you ask, does a moniker like Lucky Schlomo's also show
up on Vulkan's letterhead?

Roll credits for the Seventh Day Adventists and a client of my
mother's. But here I have to tell you, Mom was English, not Jewish,
which strictly speaking, as the Chosen People hands itself over for
protection on the mother's side — *it's a wise man who knows his own
father already!?* — means I'm out of it also in the Yiddisher Momma
department.

What makes the mix weirder, Mom calls herself "Mrs. Le Breton,
a War widow from London. This is my son, Billy," when she takes us
shopping: how she got to working 42nd Street we don't ask. The old
john taking charge of the rest of my young life was called Moussy —
plus five syllables of Polish you can look up in Schwann — who smokes
huge Cubans and tickles a Steinway for a living. A good one!

A weird thing about Moussy — even to a five-year-old Anglo-
American — a Jew he obviously is with us, showing off the Friday Night

chicken-soup scene; but *Oy vey!* Outside, he plays he isn't Jewish.

"My folks hid me with some Seventh Days, in a Pogrom," he explains one evening in our kitchen over matzo after balling Mom. "No Pork, and Sabbath on Saturdays, are the Days' major rules, Pipik, so it's dead easy you can pass."

"But I'm not Jewish, Moussy," I tell him.

"Not to worry, Pipik, by the time it matters, you will be."

Moussy plays Rachmaninoff from memory, which is impressive even to adults. Whole concertos, yet! And setting another thing straight for the record: I hit the Loud pedal with the Yiddish for sound business reasons. Ari Onassis plays his Greek Peasant. With me, it's the contrast between Catskill and fucking the world's Top Coloratura. (Who just happens to live next door.) People who can afford Contentment get a kick in reliving escape from the Borscht Belt.

I start out dreaming I can make it as a piano player like Moussy. By the time he's through balling Mom a few more freebies, she trades "my son Billy" for "Pipik" on our shopping expeditions, and I know from one end of a keyboard to the other. Moussy gets me going on his traveling one. It's short three octaves and can't make a noise while they do.

"You have to be dedicated, Pipik," Moussy says on his next way in to visit Mom. "So show me dedicated. Finish the Chopin before I come out."

I finish Chopin with enough dedication to raise an eyebrow on Rubenstein. I meet them all, and not just piano merchants. Even Cassals, although he's too old to do anything more than just admire Mom's well-turned ankle in front of his cello.

It's hard to describe what my mother had. Not from embarrassment — I've never been ashamed of what she did for our living: keeping Carnegie artists at the top of their form isn't in the same league as 42nd Street hooking. In the years since the fire escape I try to figure it out, staring at the faces in the Louvre or the Metropolitan. The Great Courtesans look like any woman in Isaac Bashevis Singer's Cafeteria . . . but after one of their blow jobs Napoleon or whoever hops out of bed and beats the shit out of Russia. Or if he's religious, he makes Pope.

Getting down to it — after it — I have to buy Mom's last "Oy vey!" on the subject: "Sex is always more in the mind than in the box."

Getting back to *What's In A Name?* Shakespeare lobs the question; I need to catch it. Roses may smell sweet but a Jew doesn't in the $5 Gentile world of my youth.

"Moussy," I tell him, some time around age nine, "thanks awfully, but if you don't mind my saying so, I don't think I really want to be a Kike. Not even the Seventh Day kind."

Mom is mortified — prejudice is bad for business — but Moussy just laughs it off.

"The Lord of Moses only makes his play when the time is right. But Pipik, forget with the performing," Moussy advises after another drop-in to Mom, at the end of the War. "The Moscow Competition is murder and you don't have it — but I've told your Mother: this boy was born to be an Agent. Now he needs a hot name. There's too many Steins in the Music Trade already. And don't go goy, everybody's doing it."

"But where would I find such a name, Moussy?"

"Not under the bulrushes, dumbchuk. Use the newspapers."

Which isn't as crazy as it sounds. *The New York Times* is the Chosen Daily of Record and in Israel, there's a war on.

TANK BATTLE AT NAZARETH

GUR SLAYS NINE

A photo of "gallant young Israeli Captain Schlomo Gur" grinning out of a conning tower doesn't look so far from my adolescent face. When Mom sees it, she has a smile with tears in her eyes, but I don't think we can read anything into that.

As a consolation prize for giving up my piano and deciding to be Jewish, for my sixteenth birthday, Moussy writes in "Seventh Day Adventist" under Religion, in my new American passport, and takes me with him to judge the murderous Moscow Competition where —

Stalin dies!

Or is maybe murdered himself by his doctors. Either way, all public musical events are banned. Moussy gets asked by Melodiya to cut a record for their label. I've never been in a recording studio. The experience is a revelation. The anechoic silence. The calm. Compared with the Synagogue coughs and candy crackles of a concert hall, the studio is an empty Orthodox cathedral. For real. While Moussy cuts his Tchaikovsky in a single take, and the crowd waits out in the cold for his autograph . . . with borrowed wisdom — Schlomo after all, means Solomon — I get the Concept for Dream Management:

Hide the Artist. Scrap live performance. The less you give people what they want, the more they'll pay for it.

Moussy gets paid not with rubles, but gilt and silver icons, which he gives me one of with his blessing. "A piece of old Mother Russia so you can start your own nest-egg, Pipik. Money turns into wheelbarrows. Banks fail. A Leonardo is always a Leonardo for a rainy day. And Pipik, take it from an expert, pogroms never happen when the goys are at the beach."

Back on the Free side of the world (after I put the icon with my Seventh Day passport, and a collapsible umbrella, at my mother's, ready for a 42nd Street pogrom getaway), my Concept dream becomes reality when I meet — and then sell it to — one of Moussy's protégés. A Toronto kid not much older than myself but a light-year more neurotic:

Glenn Gould. Schlomo Gur's first client.

By my mid-twenties people have wanted so much and received so little of Gould since his Goldberg Variations, I can afford privacy outside the recording studio as well as in. We're talking early Sixties — and then come The Beatles, who, after Ed Sullivan, and fucking the screaming broads of all ages from New York to Los Angeles, just have to get away. They come to me. And after the Beatles comes the need not only for privacy, but Security. Kennedys get assassinated in America. Kidnappings break out all over Europe. The targets become as desperate for solutions as Vivienne Leigh in A Streetcar Named Desire.

At which point, I get Brando and people start calling me, "That lucky Gur fucker. He just falls into it."

"Lucky" Gur. I keep the nickname — in Hollywood, Irving Lazar has his "Swifty" — but ask any sky diver: falling with only luck for a chute is asking to get killed. I know what has to be done. After Marlon's Last Tango, I begin to scout the right location.

It takes me a whole decade of looking and right timing to quotes, *just-fall-into* the slice of luck and sand the people now living on it call "The Miracle of Contentment."

Money
Two

RULE ONE WITH MIRACLES . . . FIRST, SOMETHING BAD HAS TO happen! Like Dickie Burton and my other Dream Management clients with a Swiss Resident permit, while I'm socking my own percentage, from the growing "Lucky Family," into Switzerland and dying of boredom waiting for the bad things to click . . . there's also, even in those days, a cloud no bigger than a needle casting its shadow over the tax-free Alpine paradise. Hypodermic syringes sprout in the manicured civic parks and chocolate-box town squares of Berne on Saturday mornings.

America gets its warning bell with the Watts riots. I'm staying backstage as usual, at the Ritz Carlton, Pasadena, signing Andre Previn to play the Hollywood Bowl — substituting for Oscar Levant, a sad in-house example of the hypo problem — and I come out for breakfast on the hotel terrace to smell smoke instead of Orange Blossom. Personally, it doesn't bother me, the Riots. I'm still young, not living in L.A., and the flames at night are barely visible on the horizon.

Instead, I watch the Pasadena Permanent Money — the guests who keep the year-round suites and golf-course memberships — being scared shitless by the hotel's Latino gardeners after dark. I think about what Permanent Money wants beyond dodging Death duties to keep it happy in Paradise.

It wants Climate (Los Angeles or better). It wants Location (as close as a skipped heart-beat to the Good Life Support of the USA); it wants Facilities (Golf and Financial) —

But:

Permanent Money does *not* want to pay more than minimum wage for Paradise, and it needs a Buffer Zone to do it. The Guest Workers maintaining Paradise have to ship out at night. And even if those big Buts are covered, there's a final Joker 22 in the pack: to pass Paradise Laws you have to be able to make your own Rule Ones.

Paradise has to be a Sovereign State.

The Dream Solution would be Florida with a draw bridge and its own seat in the UN. With that option foreclosed by the Louisiana Purchase I look at the Delta Airline route map in the Ritz Carlton lobby.

The Baja Peninsula is almost a natural — below California, no shortage of gardeners — but buying it from Mexico is out of the question, and America's border with that Sombrero State is notoriously porous. Heading north, Whidbey Island has proximity (to Seattle) and separation (a single bridge to the Mainland, through an Indian Reservation) but not far enough off shore — and a North-West Rain Forest climate is hardly Los Angelene.

I shift back East. The Caribbean has a million islands, all of them in someone else's hands. Former Colonies like the Bahamas that could have been perfect a generation earlier — the Brits were desperate for cash flow after the War — now are knocked flat by their population explosions. The cautious Dutch never let anything go, and most of their holdings, like Curacao, are uncomfortably equatorial. The Jonestown Massacre wipes Kool-Aid South America off the map.

Cuba has Castro. And U.S. Embargo.

My search is resembling the endless spiral of a hurricane — another real estate hazard to consider when you're thinking Permanent — and that's exactly what leads me to it.

Hurricane Edward.

The fifth tropical storm of the '86 Season. And right under the eye, just north of Grenada . . .

Hudson Cay.

An island — but almost a peninsula; only twelve miles (the magic legal limit for Sovereignty) of perfect coral reefs separate it from Jamaica. Formerly British, now independent, and broke beyond fiscal repair through one-too-many IMF loans, the Hudson population — a mere thousand — is less than a drop-in-a-drop of any Caribbean bucket. And the natives speak English.

"No better than Cambridge, I'm afraid," the Prime Minister tells me in his charming Carib-Oxbridge accent, when we meet for our first working lunch in the United Nations' private dining room. "Reading for a first in Greek Philosophy, at the college of Maynard Keynes, and listening to Glenn Gould. I have all your clients' records."

Which helps explain the economic chaos of his Cay's exchequer.

All I've seen of the island itself is a sexless shot in a National Geographic. " . . . *These two old sponge fishermen smile in placid contentment as they repair their woven baskets for their next catch*" with three ritual palm trees in the background.

The island has an airstrip big enough for Piper Cubs but Hurricane Eddie has put it out of business. The only way across is a chugging Jamaican lobster boat with its bilges awash with salt water and fuel. It lands me at a dock where the same two old spongers are still at it with the baskets. A pile of their last "next catch" dries hopelessly in the sun. The only sponges in the world's supermarkets these days come courtesy "the placid contentment" of Du Pont.

The island has nothing else to offer except white sand, scarlet flowers, and a gentle green hill dominating its soft centre. The hill even produces fresh water year round, from three springs. With a change of name, Hudson Cay is a buyer's wet dream.

But:

Since Genesis on Day 7, there's always a But. Offer human beings a shot at Paradise — they'll Putz it up. If it isn't lust, the snake called Greed slithers into the frame.

Like Oliver Twist the Prime Seller wants more. We've agreed on British passports all round; ten million American dollars for the PM himself (plus one million each for his tri-partite shyster Cabinet); and $2000 in passage money to the UK for each of the thousand other Hudson Islanders.

"Fourteen million US is the maximum leverage I can swing, Prime Minister — and even that means mortgaging my Swiss chalet beyond the point of any hope of return."

"My dear chap, I'm so sorry, but America's debt ceiling has just gone through three trillion. The dollar is falling like a stone. For my people's protection, our transaction must now be in pounds sterling."

More Maynard Keynes than Aristotle rubbed off at Cambridge while this bastard listened to Gould.

"Prime Minister, double my offer isn't possible with this Market."

"My dear Lucky, you deal with artists, not stockbrokers. Instead of the Market consider Marcus Aurelius and his Meditations: 'Do not think that what is hard for thee to master is impossible for man; but if a thing is possible and proper to man, deem it attainable by thee'. Forgive me if Aurelius is Roman, not Greek."

I no longer give a shit where the Prime Ministerial crook in front of me acquires his philosophy . . . but on the long flight home to Berne my mind turns over what he said.

Contentment *is now* possible; it only needs the proper cash to be obtainable. Flying over the Azores I realise I can raise another two million by selling my Moussy Icon collection, which also includes rare books, but it would take the right buyer. Looking down on the Italian Alps, my mind drifts from the word Roman . . . to the ancient city itself, now visible on the horizon . . . then to the Vatican . . . its Bank . . . its Library —

I make an instant turn around at Berne.

The following morning I present myself for a meeting with the Library's Chief Purchaser of Antiquities. He's held up by a computer glitch.

"La IBM è grande, Impresario, but is preventing the transfer smoothly of a large number of Jesuit documents physically . . . "

He means from a place of humid decay beside the Tiber, into the air-conditioned eternity of the Church's new Archives within the walls of Vatican City. The contrast of Ancient and Modern scrolls before my eyes on La IBM's è grande screen.

St Ignatius's Last Epistle to the Cardinal of Venice, The First Society Expedition Among the Iroquois, Conversion of the Head Hunters on Le Breton Island —

What's in a name? . . . The power to arrest your eye in an instant when that name started life as your own.

William Le Breton , S.J.

My Lucky moniker was handed to me from a *Times* pic: the hand of the G*d of Moses has led me just like Moussy said it would, when H*s time was right — to this kosher heart of Gentile religion.

When the Chief Purchaser returns to study my Collection list, I ask him for the Head Hunters' document in exchange. We each keep our paperwork overnight. All he gets out of it is another handful of Gutenberg relics nobody will ever read.

I get Our Father's keys to the kingdom.

Money
Three

I FLY ALONE TO MY GOAL IN THE SOUTH PACIFIC. FOR ACQUISITION Rights to two paradises, on opposite sides of the globe, a rock-solid position is prudence, not greed. Taking even one on-line geologist to see what I suspect from the Jesuit's report will be like letting a platoon of Peeping Toms into a women's ritual *mikveh*.

I need a visa. In the two decades since the priest's arrival, Le Breton Island has been taken into the Papua New Guinea Protectorate, co-administered by Australia and abbreviated by everyone to PNG.

"We don't want a bunch of condos plonked down on the beach overnight," a Tourism and Development drone warns me in Port Moresby, the capital. "We keep reminding the missionaries, let Indonesia rape their Irian Jaya, our PNG Abos have to be eased from the Stone Age into Time-Share."

On Le Breton Island there's no risk of plonked condos. There's no beach. Nor an airstrip. I have to land from a chopper. Its Crocodile Dundee pilot is reluctant.

"Too right I don't like it, Lucky," he twangs over the intercom. "With Two Tits she's tricky enough dodging the fucking volcano in a chopper, but if the Mormons haven't even got there yet, we could find ourselves looking at the wrong end of a cook pot in the billabong!"

To me it looks almost as familiar as my mortgaged mezuzah front door frame in Berne. I've read my birth-name's report so often. Nothing seems changed. The twinned mountains, the ring of forest on the dead volcano, the limestone gorges on the lower peak. The hanging-gardens in their green patchwork quilts. Twin villages also, separated only by a stream no wider than a blade on the helicopter's rotor.

"Kee-rist!" my Dundee pilot points down. "A fucking Turkey, or I'm an Abo!"

The reassembled wreckage of the World War Two Avenger still holds centre stage on the water meadow in the middle of the stream.

"Looks as good a spot as any, Lucky. At least it gives us room to see the poisoned arrows coming!"

"The priest's report says they've stopped fighting."

The dark-skinned figures below us run in circles as we hover. The males are buck-naked except for ritual penis gourds. I see a Christian cross beside the wrecked Avenger. Prehistoric shields and spears form a mini Stone Henge circle around it.

"This place is over the Jesus rainbow. Those cannibal fuckers with the dick-covers haven't even seen a bloody chopper. Say a Jewish Hail Mary for us, Lucky. We're going in."

The grass flattens on the water meadow. The undercarriage touches. The pilot keeps the rotor turning. I step out. Only one native doesn't scatter. An old, old man, with a white-skull face squatting next to the Avenger.

I hold out my hand and say in guide-book Pidgin:

"Moning, Olie. Yu stap gut. Yu sav'e?"

His hearing seems impaired by the noise of the rotors. He holds a wrinkled hand to the pierced lobe of his left ear. A corroded, "Property US Navy," Biro pen sticks through it.

I repeat more loudly, "Moning. Mi Lucky. Yu Olie?"

A smile cracks the white clay mask. A tear runs from one eye. With arthritic slowness he stands up — then falls back on his knees. "Boneeya" he makes the sign of the cross. "Boneeya Luki cum bak Tedi Frum!"

My Crocodile pilot shakes his head in disbelief. "What the fuck kind of pidgin shit is this boneeya crap?"

"It means you can shut the rotor off. They think I'm the returned spirit of the Avenger pilot. We're home and dry, already."

Naked savages close in all around the chopper, forming a concentric circle with their Stonehenge spears and shields protecting the Avenger. The Jesuit's wooden Christian Cross, its white paint faded, stands bizarrely at the centre. The Christ-figure carved on it from black ebony is in the image of the local population.

"First time I've ever seen J.C. with a pecker," says the pilot. "Where do we go from here, Lucky?"

"You guard the chopper. I have to look for a Bird of Paradise." I turn to the old Chief. "Mi cam Amerika gosee yu Olie Tedi Kree O'pan."

Olie smiles his slow smile. The Dundee pilot drawls, "Last place on the planet Coke hasn't got to go Best at. The old bugger's got all his cannibal teeth left."

I say, "Migo yugo tude, Olie? Okay?"

Today is okay. Olie nods. Then he begins to mumble.

"H'leem'reemuv'rg'd . . . "

He repeats it until even a Seventh Day Jew can decipher Hail Mary. After however many additional Mother-of-Gods he needs for a Rosary on Two Tits Island Olie concludes, "Amen Luki migo Kree'o'pan" and climbs stiffly to his feet.

Twenty years earlier the Acquisition round trip took my Loyolan predecessor two hours. In the priest's Journal, Olie did all the leg work. Now he still has his teeth but two decades of advancing arthritis slow our progress to a crawl. The trees and insects haven't changed. Every minute detail of a purple moth's giant wing matches the priest's description. I can't keep back my excitement. If the Jesuit got it right about moths and beetles —

"Kree'o'pan." Olie points before I hear the whistling coo of the dancing Birds of Paradise. His eyes and ears are still as sharp as his teeth. I remember every word of the Journal:

We came at last to a small plateau. Olie paused at the edge of a clearing . . .

We're there again.

Another minor precipice . . .

I scale it.

The limestone was eroded to an outer consistency like the crumbling bark of an ancient tree. . . .

The rock breaks away beneath my hand.

In a blaze of sun —

I take out a vial of sulphuric acid and apply two drops to the fractured rock. The limestone fizzes green. What's left stays yellow.

A mountain of Gold!

All I need now is an X.

Money
Four

I'VE SIGNED BRANDO AND RINGO, LENNIE AND MARILYN . . . EVERY Lucky Family Name on all the dotted lines since Gould and the gross percentage won't add up to the hourly interest I can earn from this New Guinea Fort Knox. It takes all those years of playing it cool for me to stop sweating long enough to sell Olie on an Interim Development Contract disguised as a "Letter imfor Tedi Frum," followed by a first chopper ride out of the Stone Age.

Olie in his Penis Gourd and Skull Face comes through his prehistoric encounter of a Higher Economic Order with greater gravitas than its bankers. The Tilley linen suits from Tourism and Development are used to having their pictures taken standing next to a nude cannibal: for the pin-stripe-trousered female representing the air-conditioned National Westminster banking empire in Port Moresby the experience is an obviously disturbing first.

"Tell Mr. Olie," she says to the Tourism translator, as small beads of perspiration pop through the powder on her upper lip, "that he is signing what in effect we may call a Deed of Mortgage granting all Development Rights in perpetuity to Mr. Lucky, on his island. But that he is still in effect their Owner — in the same way as the Duke of Devonshire owns London — every ninety-nine years it all comes back to him again."

God knows how this is getting through in Pidgin, — *I* know inside, I'm a nervous wreck! — but Olie seems calm. He listens closely, nodding once or twice . . . until he shakes his head.

"Cum Minster missis nogo im yokal imgo thali?"

"Do we have a problem with the Term?" The Nat West woman is having a problem with the penis gourd: she can't keep her eyes off it. I'm trying not to go into a tailspin while I wait for that last X.

"It isn't the mortgage," says Tourism. "Olie wonders why you aren't wearing either the married woman's grass skirt, or that of a virgin, to signal the state of your vagina."

The banked perspiration turns to sweat patches under the pinstriped Nat-West arms. "Tell him because I'm in a serially monogamous relationship with — Christ, this is fucking absurd!"

It's vital for Contentment that everyone floating it stays on board. "Explain to Olie," I say to the Tourism translator, "that Missis Minster puts on her thali when she leaves the office."

He finds this compromise entirely reasonable. We proceed to a reading of the entire document, aloud, in pidgin. I'm lost after the Date, but Olie follows the "imgo whereto's" and "em bilong therefore's" with no trouble.

"Thank God," says the NatWest woman. "Now just get him to bottom-line after you, Lucky."

Somehow I manage to sign as though it's nothing bigger than a routine Hollywood poolside closing for another *Gone With the Wind*. But Olie's shaking his skull face again. The tip of the penis gourd wobbles beside the banker's hand. Then he speaks for five minutes, ending with a solemn, "Dukminster adu'rit Lond'n lak ka'n Luki kok."

"The first part was a just quickie history of his ancestors," Tourism translates. "The end could be a bit more of a problem. Olie says he's going to be a Smoked Man long before the ninety-nine years so he won't be around to get the Developed island back from Lucky. He wants to know what London magic the Duke uses to keep control of Westminster in this kind of situation?"

"We've already covered that." The NatWest woman flips her hand to point to the document. "The Heirs and Assigns Clause, or if he wants it tighter we can amend to use Legatee in Derrsee."

Instead of the clause, her hand touches the gourd tip. The translator translates. The banker's nipples shudder slightly. Olie frowns. I can feel Contentment slipping into the cannibal cook pot, with me following. I pray to Moussy, who got me started, to send some Seventh Day words to save the deal's bacon.

"Explain to Olie," I hear a voice which sounds like mine telling the translator, "the Mortgage Term is like the Turkey. An act of faith. In the same way that the Father Le Breton from Rome returned after twenty years, and now me after another twenty, every ninety-nine years the Time-Shared Turkey Island of his sons' sons will come back to them just like the spirit of Teddy Frum."

"Timeshared Turkey?" it's Tourism's turn to get rattled.

With all the deal-making magic of Yiddish Cabala and Moussy behind me, I say, "An Avenger aircraft from the US Navy. Details! Schtemails! Olie understands from Teddy. *Oy vey! Sign, already!*" The Moussy magic works.

(After one last-minute Freudian slip . . . as the Nat West woman, reaching for her pen, grabs Olie's gourd instead.)

X marks the G-Spot. Now I have to make sure I haven't bought a Timeshared pig-in-a-poke to support Contentment. A high-powered geologist from UCLA is on a $1000 per diem holding fee in Port Moresby but before we can get going — Olie wants to go shopping!

The clash of cultures is maybe worth a mini-minor book option. I only mention car buying to show how swiftly technology leaps the gap: Olie is nobody's Stone Age fool. He knows what we've signed. He doesn't know how much —

I don't know how much! That's why the per diem geologist. We're walking together as a trio in Waigani, on Melanesian Way, past the Australian High Commission. The Government District of Papua New Guinea isn't called "The Canberra of the Tropics" for nothing: Los Angelenes or Londoners go out of their wired minds — but to Olie every rusted Toyota 4 Wheel Drive that zips by (with two of the four out of commission) is like Ben Hur's Original Chariot to a Telaviv archaeologist.

When we get back to the Town commercial district I buy Olie a new one, loaded, with a compass and CD player.

"You've got a happy camper there!" says the Aussie salesman. "But if you're heading for hill country, take plenty of insurance. The manufacturer only gives 90 Days in the Highland District of PNG — and the warranty voids if he goes over the edge."

Olie strokes the Toyota and says, "Em tenkyu Luki," so often that it even gets through to a car sales mind.

"'The Lost Beatles' producer! You're *that* Lucky? Man, what an autograph on the contract!" He produces an HMV jewel box from his desk and pops the Fab 4's CD into the Toyota's player. "A real collector's item!"

Rule One from Day One of Dream Management is hiding from fame. Avoiding too-close encounters of this Toyota kind is my driving force behind Contentment. But it takes the expression on Olie's white-clay face as he studies the Listening Dog on the HMV box cover, to bring home just how great the Dream has been to abandon live performance.

"It's more magnificent than Fuji!" . . . My UCLA geologist is blown away by the volcano. I've only spoken to him in generalities — a possible Cruise line Dock, maybe a Hot Springs Lodge — I haven't even shown photographs. From a thousand-dollar per diem I want an honest first impression.

"The American fighter pilot who crashed here in the forties recorded in his flight log seeing a wisp of steam," I tell my hired gun now, as we approach the peak with Olie, in the chopper, "but a priest making contact twenty years later has no mention of steam in his journal. I need to know it's really cold. We don't want to get started on a Hilton Sauna and find we have another Krakatoa."

"There's certainly been no major activity in the historic era, Lucky. My initial judgment — this is shooting from the hip, to confirm we'll have to walk the ground — your idea for a Springs Resort is out. There hasn't been anything hot here for at least ten thousand years. Which is as close to inert as vulcanology gets."

Olie hasn't been so close to it since his ascent as a young man to rescue the Pilot-God and bring back the Avenger. As we circle the peak he stares down from the chopper at the dead bowels of the crater and begins to chant a prayer. I recognize an occasional "aduarit" for Smoked Man, and frequent "Tedi Frum's." A fifteen-thousand-foot monument to your ancestors is enough to make even a born-again Seventh Day reflect on their hereafter, and sit shiva.

"How about the blob on the Other Side for my Hot Springs?" I ask the geologist, in a super-cooled Royal Flush bluff. "It seems to be limestone."

"Which backs my shot from the hip," says per diem UCLA. "What we're looking at with the Other Side peak is the remains of a caldera — an enormous explosion, probably far bigger than Krakatoa — that blew the lid off leaving behind only part of a core. The sea covered it for a couple of million years, which explains the limestone coating. Then the Asian Plate moved north, lifting the old core back into sunlight and the normal forces of erosion."

"And the volcano?"

"Secondary activity. Like a pimple on a boil."

"Anything else?"

"Not from up here." The expert shrugs his per diem shoulders. "When we walk the Other Side, there's always a Loto possibility of some residual concentrations. The odds are a billion-to-one against it, but with cores like this if you find a vein sticking out, sometimes an old lava tunnel of top-grade precious-metal runs right the way through."

"Kree'o'pan, Luki!"

Out of a hundred indistinguishable gorges, Olie's ancient eyes have picked the Priest's plateau of the dancing Birds of Paradise.

I remember two drops of sulphuric acid. And a hiss, before a golden Lotto gleam . . .

$10 *LOTTO 6/49 *BIG ONES!!

Mayday, it's happening NOW, P&R . . . !

Now the day is over,
Night is drawing nigh,
Shadows of the evening
Steal across the sky.

Hymns of childhood crowd us in even as Jim celebrates his last birthday run of luck in his diary. Alas, like Yorick (played by our maternal "Henry Howard" stage-grandfather) poor Mr. Keyes never did hit the Big One. We mustn't read too much into the Loto asterisks — but it's odd that at the end Jim — who as "the-James-sounded-better" Hugh Courtney Gauer took the L*rd's name so often in vain — follows the habit of Observant Jews in replacing the central, awestruck character of G*d.

> **Rabbit :** *(bubbling Occidental optimism)*
> "Aunt Elspie always said, Miracles
> do happen."
> **Panda :** *(stuffed with Oriental pessimism)*
> "Dorothea called Jim a Traveling
> Disaster!"
> **Owner :** *(filled with uncertainty)*
> "An eternal optimist in such a
> pessimist, but . . . "

"What are yew thinking now?".

Death is too much with us. Like yew, bloody Abe! So fuck off!

" 'Lucky' lottery tickets block a story with a 'Lucky' Jewish protagonist. Anger at death can displace fear of it. Perhaps like your loathed stepfather's 'Jewish' use of asterisks?"

Yew can't play the Fear & Loathing anti-Semite card with us. First to go was Nan, lapsed Anglican, last year, but for twelve months of fifty minute sessions we've refused to talk about it. Or our Fifth Unlucky Abortion of a novel.

"And now?"

DAVID GURR

Now the darkness gathers,
Stars begin to peep,
Birds, and beasts and flowers
Soon will be asleep.

Like Abe, who can stuff displacement up his asterisks in his leather recliner — but at eighty nine, Jim may be changing at least one of his spots.

JAMES GAUER
The Wedding Reception
Music Specialist

FROM BACH * * *

* * * TO BACHARACH

Your Favourite Groups and
Big Band Sound Played on
Stereo Tape Equipment.

—— ·· ——

On the back of which we find this hand-lettered ode to G*dliness.

I'LL KEEP IT CLEAN "Mr KITCH" !
I'LL KEEP IT CLEAN
MY SONG NOR I
MUST NEVER BE OBSCENE !
BUT ITS JUST A MILLION PITTIES
CAUSE I KNOW SOME FILTHY DITTIES .
BUT I'LL KEEP IT CLEAN "Mr KITCH" !
I'LL KEEP IT CLEAN ! ..
HOWEVER HARD FOR ME -- TO YOU IT SEEMS !
NOTHING NAUGHTY WILL I UTTER
I'LL GET MY MIND OUT OF THE GUTTER
I'LL KEEP IT CLEAN "Mr KITCH" -- I'LL KEEP IT CLEAN !

"I'm afraid our time is up. And as thisss is the start of August vacation, yew have the number to call in case of an emergency?"

281

Comfort those who suffer,
Watching late in pain;
Those who plan some evil
From their sin restrain.

Yessss, Abe, we have your number. Little enough to show for our fifth year of Couching.

Pair: *(breathless with anticipation)*
> "It's Holidays! What shall we write next?'

Journal

AUGUST 13 . . . . Saturday.
In Paris . . . humidity reducing energy to write this short scrawl. Much has happened since last entry (Bastille Day).

A call from Gotch/Mother that there was a marked change came in at 1700. By 1800 I was actually on an aircraft; the quickest move I have ever done. Not quick enough. I had the feeling that he had died as the plane was descending over Harrison Lake, bright gold in the setting sun, with smoke/mist in all the valleys. On the ground in Vancouver, when I phoned Victoria's General Hosp, Info said — in response to my query: Is he still alive? "Yes. In critical condition." The ward nurse said, "No he isn't. I'm sorry. He died an hour ago."

Owner : *(almost — but never quite — speechless)*
> "My God. He's really gone . . . "

In Abe's absence sur les vaconces, said more as a long-ago whisper to Monsieur Laurillard . . . while we stare down at the open mouth on the hospital cot, from whence all breath has fled.

She said Jim — you are blind,
But my Dear I don't mind!
Then she whispered My Honey,
I don't want your money —
I just want your love and esteem

How much of either we are left to judge for ourselves by this last guilt-inducing page in his diary, recorded one month before his death.

Jim's Diary

1994

*June *LOVELY SUNNY DAY AGAIN TODAY****

Quality is not an act.
It is a habit.

I GOT MY TILLEY Aristotle.
* HAT FROM "CHARLIE"
" OUR BIG DAY "
* Monday 20 * * * ON OUR OWN * * NO ONE HERE " *
* Morning * * MY BIRTHDAY TODAY (89) * * * *
* DAI CAN ? — COME — HE WILL BE IN THE USA
* * " OUR ANNIVERSARY " * *
* Noon *   — ("DAI" AWAY IN THE USA
MAY COME — OTHERWISE ITS JUST CHARLIE AND I *
* Evening x WE HAD A PRAWN SUPPER FROM
COCKNEY KINGS*
* Tuesday 21   Summer Begins
* Morning
* SHOULD HAVE A RIDE AROUND THIS MORNING TO START *
* THE DAY — IN MY CART THIS MORNING ROLLING *
   * AROUND — *
* Noon
* IT WAS THE POOREST BIRTHDAY "WE" EVER HAD (22") *
* Evening TRY AND EXCHANGE MY TILLEY FOR SMALLER SIZE *
* Wednesday 22   ANOTHER BEAUTIFUL SUNNY DAY *
* Morning
   * LOTTERY DAY: —

Where is Abe when we need him? We had no sooner suffered indigestion from this Prawn Supper of scrambled guilt, courtesy of Cockney Kings, than we were sandbagged by a further velum scrap of faded MacKenzie deluge de grandeur:

Our right to The Throne of Scotland, à la Old Trout.

David Gurr

For David from his Great Aunt
with all my Love — K ("Trout"!)

Abstract Genealogy

OF THE

Kerrisdale-Gairloch Branch OF THE MacKenzie Family,

As taken from Family Papers, as also from the History of the Family
by Alexander MacKenzie, published in Inverness, 1894.

Kenneth, *18 generations (if I haven't lost count) to your grt grnd father*
or **Coinneach,**
> **1st Baron of Kintail**
>
>> *Killed by Robert the Bruce*
>> *in the church of Dumfries, 1306.*

John Maccoineach, *(or 17 gens. Grandson of Olave the Red King of Norway?)*
> **2nd Baron of Kintail**, through the Thane of Argyle.
>> *Gave shelter to Robert the Bruce in Ellandonnan Castle,*
>> *and led 500 of his vassals at the Battle of Bannockburn.*

Murdoch MacKenzie *(Murchadh is 14 gens)*
> **5th Baron of Kintail**
>> *Was at the Battle of Otterburn, or Chevy Chase, 1388.*

This bit missing but Murchadh
>> *Married Fingula, or Florence, daughter of*
>> *Malcolm Macleod III, of Harris and Dunvegan. By this marriage,*
>> *the blood royal* of the Bruces was first introduced*
>> *into the family of Kintail. Buried at Beauly Priory.*

* so You too are Blood Royal !!

For those closer to home base than the Gairloch MacKenzie Family graves of Dumfries Abbey and Beauly Priory — and in the continued carefree holiday absence of Dr. Anal-ist Abe — Owner and Charlie have to make simpler Obituary arrangements in Victoria's *Times-Colonist*, and Cadboro Bay's Cottage Garden.

> ### For Nan: Friday, January 8th, 1993, Aged 86 years.
> *Who went for a walk and sat down on a rock* . . . at the corner of Aspen Place, which her Only Nephew subdivided, built, and named; after resigning from the Royal Canadian Navy in a fit of pique because Lester B. P***son, Prime Minister, took away our Blue Uniform — *but we kept the sword Nan gave us when we were granted Her Majesty's Commission, and wept real tears, and got drunk on Air Canada: too late to be there, either, when she died* . . .

> ### And James: Thursday, July 21st, 1994, Aged 89 years.
> *A month and a day past his and Charlie's 54th Wedding Anniversary* . . . ***a date and number which his widow can never remember*** *— which amnesia his son by adoption without permission leaves for Monsieur Laurillard's successors to sort out.*

> ### And Charlotte: Born, March 20th, 1912 —
> Not yet!

That merciless last Sting is still only stroking Charlie to death where the bees hum, in (date left blank) her late sister's easeful garden. While the chocolate pudding waits in the refrigerator, sunshine and her "rummaging at random" throw additional light (and/or confusion) into odd-corner memories of the Black Book, next to her copy of Final Exit. . . .

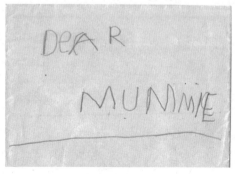

You sent me this when I was in hospital
having Bun **["You've never shown it to me
since!"** *viz* **6 year old's crudely lettered,
DEAR MUMMY AND BABY SISTER LOVE DAVID]**
so you weren't Willum then. I've always
been hopeless with dates. So much was
going on. When was Jim's divorce from
Gladys Knight granted? **["1939, Mummy, you
know that."]** But then it took a year to
get the final decree. And the names! I've
always hated my middle one. Nan tried
explaining how Daddy gave me two spellings
for it. The birth certificate is Charlotte
Iseult Harvey. Then on the Aunts' Legal
Guardian papers, he put it Isolde. In
these two letters I have from him **["You've
never shown them, either!"]** he calls me
"Bill"— and asks if Nan is fat. There's
only one letter from my mother — but I
don't think the Bill is why I called you
William. I just liked it. When was the
Autumn war broke out? **["The same bloody
time you beat out Gladys."]** Jim's call-up
papers were served in Nottingham, for some
reason. So I went up there that first time
with him — he signed the papers but didn't
get called — I didn't take you. **["Why
the hell not?"]** We all thought there was
going to be bombing any minute, and your
old friend Ann Crowe had a place in the
country, the White House, down at Reigate.
["My *old* friend?"] You already knew each
other from the time I left you with her
for six weeks when you were six months and
I was looking for a job. It seemed natural
to evacuate you there the first time.
**["And naturally the second — to get rid
of the little bastard for the Wedding."]**
A week after Jim's Gladys Divorce was
final, at the Marylebone Registry — I've
never been able to remember Anniversaries
either **["And you say it every year! June**

20th, 1940."] we had the Reception at the Trocadero and decided to bring you back to London. Just in time for the real Blitz! That night Joan Cross held you under the stairs, the houses went on both sides of us. I went out and dumped a pail of sand on an incendiary in the garden. I could hear them whistling down all around. I had the absolute certainty I was going to be killed. I don't know exactly when your adoption and name change from Willum happened **["Don't ask me! Entry #66984 of Vol 134 says October 2nd, 1940."]** or where Jim got the bee in his bonnet about David. **["We do. *viz moldy sepia of Haywagon 1918 Wales: Farmer Jones, Young Jim with pitchfork, and 'My best pal Dai.'* "]** Afterwards, as Raids were going on night and day we sent you back down to Reigate for the third time. You used to tell me about the dog fights with the Spitfires. When the bombers came over Nurse Crowe would make you all lie down on the lawn under her cape to be safe, like baby chicks, before you tried to run away with that little girl in the photo, I don't remember her name. **["It was Lucy!"]** They found the pair of you by the gate at five o'clock in the morning. You had your suitcases packed, very businesslike.

Just look at you both. Like stockbrokers
going up to the City. 'Two Little
Runaways.' We went down to Reigate by
train and had a conference. The two sets
of parents plus Nurse Crowe. [**"With what
conclusion?"**] You didn't seem sad or
frightened, but we needed somewhere to
live if Jim was going to be called up, so I
went ahead from Nottingham to scout out the
Aunts at Barton-Olivers Whitchurch — they'd
never met either you or James. I don't
remember. [**"*viz* Us-on-the-Toboggan. It's
Winter, 1940-41."**] January could be right,
there was lots of snow on the roses. Jim
collected you from Reigate by himself — the
Two-Of-You on the Blitzed-Train-in-the-
Tunnel horror story. The time I couldn't
speak was much earlier. [**"This new revealed
horror leaves me speechless!"**] We had
just moved in with Jim, the first flat on
Boundary Road. He said we couldn't afford
it unless I went back to work. He insisted
I send you to a nursery school run by Nuns.
I wanted to look after you myself. [***viz
Charlie sitting on steps in Flowered Frock,
showing Gorgeous Legs.***] We had a terrible
row. Calling me the usual things — "You're
a whore, a slut, a cunt!" I simply couldn't
speak. The words just wouldn't come out.
[**"For Christ's sake! — how bloody long?"**]
It seemed forever. Perhaps a week. Finally,
Nan got me to go to St Thomas's Hospital.
There was a doctor, but not in a white
coat. He could have been a psychologist
I suppose. He gave me some medicine in a
green bottle. It tasted awful. He said if
I took it for a few days I would be able
to speak again. And I could. [**"Obviously
a shrink."**] Looking back, it must have
been very frightening for you but you
were happy with the Nuns. This is one of
your earliest ones, when you were still

Willum. It's Us-and-Nan in Kensington Park. [*viz **Summer 1937; grinning Nan-at-31 holds squinting Toddler-Willum-with-curls; wooden deck chairs and starched white table clothes in background.***] And the organ-grinder's monkey you used to feed bananas. Poor Nan was between Jilters — fiancées who dropped her. These few are Jim with his mother and maiden sister. [*viz **Sooty Liverpool Row House (Haunt of the dreaded Nag!) sepia little old lady, taller Auntie Nina (spinster); both frowning with (unfortunate in a woman) Jim-faces and (even more-so) moustaches.***] Jim had told me the Diamond-Ring-slapping Story about his mother umpteen times but I'd only met the old woman once. You didn't until the last week before we sailed. Whether they really could have been Jewish, before the Seventh Day Story, I've no idea. Of course, half the people in the Gown trade and Music Hall were, and the couple who ran our local pub. I don't think I ever met any before — this next is the first of You-with-Jim. [*viz **Summer Interlude, 1939, James as badminton Athlete-about-Town.***]

Of course he hadn't been to a school
within a hundred miles of a blazer -- I
think he had the pinstripes made after
I told him about my friend at Rugby. He
didn't really play with the racquet.
[*Summer's End. Scotty Dog on park chair;*
Rocking Horse on wheels; last glimpses
of Happy Willum's London.] You-and-Me at
Boundary Road. None of Teddy because Jim
made me burn them. And Ginny, our Scotty
who was stolen. They broke into Jim's
car, parked in the West End outside his
tailor. You were heart-broken. [**"The first**
horror-story where I wasn't happy!"] Until
you mentioned it, I've never thought that
the Not-Speaking episode might have had
something to do with when my mother died.
The ones before Us are Me with my best
friend from school, Morna. [*viz* **Charlie-**
at-16, striped bathing costume.] Morna's
father was Provost of Edinburgh. She
still asked "How is Willum?" in Christmas
Cards, until she died a few years ago. And
dearest Lefroy, who loved you. [**Lefroy**
really did." *Pensive, ethereal young*
woman, seated on grass, holds Panda and
Rabbit on her lap, David stands on guard
beside them in front of the Summer House.]

The Summer House had a thatched roof and it was on a turntable so it could follow the sun. Beside the pool with the kingcups and waterlillies. [*viz* **Frowning Dorothea.**] Doodlie again, at the window where you threw out the fatty bacon. There was a terrible row, it was scarce as hen's teeth on the rations! [**Frowning David.**] In your Monmouth Grammar cap for your First Day at School. Then Us doing the Snow-Man, and you with the black cat. [**Frowning Puss clawing Rabbit.**] And another of the Little Runaway girl at Reigate. How did she get here? And the two older girls, Tatyana and Irena, who had their bedroom next to yours. ["**Where sex first reared its tiny head.**"] They were some kind of Russian nobility in exile, staying with the Aunts. Here we all are, on the lawn, playing tennis and croquet. [" **'1941: Charlie's Boys of Summer'.**"] Anthony, Nanky, and Harry Styles were down on a Commando Officers' course in the area. The picture on the right Nan called "Jim on Monday Morning." Going off in his bowler and starched cuffs with his sample case of lingerie. The one with me standing in the middle is Jim's best friend from the Trade. He had a wife with a Gown Shop somewhere. Anthony and Nanky Poo are doing the ballet clowning with me. [*viz* **Civilian Jim watches.**] Nankivell was his actual last name. Cornish. Jim added the "Poo," I suppose from the Mikado. Anthony you know, from our early days at All Saints. He wasn't Bun's Godfather — what am I thinking about! Of course he was. Now that you mention it, Jim does look odd man out. ["**Did I really have to mention it?**"] After you had whooping cough but before you sicked over them so they all had to be washed. [**David with (unshaved) Stuffed Menagerie.**] That's Anthony again doing

the Heil Hitler. Nanky never made passes.
A really nice, gentle sort of fellow. The
two of you do look happy together. Harry
Styles was up through the ranks. Very
rough. A good solid soldier. [*viz Male in
Underpants*.] The sunbathing one isn't
Harry. That was Scottie. Red hair and a
beard. He was an editor for the *Daily
Worker*. We met Scottie in a London pub and
I suppose said get in touch. He was going
through the counties to sell memberships of
the newspaper — I can't imagine he found
many communists around Whitchurch — anyway,
he just showed up at Barton Olivers and it
was a sunny day so he took his clothes off.
On the lawn! Aunt Dorothea saw and called
out in horror! I couldn't believe it. Jim
wasn't there. I guess I told him to put his
clothes on. He got the next bus. Anthony
and the others did the Dieppe Raid. This
is the absolute earliest of You as Willum
at six months. [*viz Locket oval of Baby Boy
in Curls*.] I think it's rather sweet. And
Anthony again, safe back from Dieppe with
his Captain's Pips — and Jim in his Marine
Private's Battledress, so he must have been
called up by then — and Uncle Christopher
who came over again for a visit carrying
his Knight of Windsor Cocked Hat with
the Egret Feathers! [*viz Gentleman Jim in
Jodhpurs-and-Pipe*.]

Jodhpurs to build the Aunts' henhouse!
With his mustard waistcoat and pipe behind
the chicken wire. He always tried so hard
to impress them that he was a gentleman.
Old what's-his-name, the Gardener, said
about the henhouse, "Her won't never
hold up, buildin' on top o' that there
cesspit." [*viz Happy David ("At no longer
being an only child?") with-Mummy-and-
New-Baby-Sister.*] Look at me after having
Bun — actually, Jim called her Rab first,
for Rabbit, with her baby teeth — in
those bellbottom slacks! [*versus Swim-
suited Nan with Naked David.*] Bathing in
the River Wye, that's when Jim first began
his endless going on about your "hollow
buttocks." The henhouse on the cesspit
didn't fall down, here are the chickens.
The reason the Aunts sold Barton-Olivers
Whitchurch and moved to Burton Bradstock,
in Dorset, after Bun was born was to be
near Margery and Rhoda, their sisters, who
were already at Swyre.

We were totally isolated on top of the cliff. The other villa and bungalow were completely empty for the Duration. There were some soldiers at a gun emplacement underneath. I don't exactly remember — **["You remember, Mum. 1942, the year after vizing the Boys of Last Summer."]** — but the sensible thing seemed to be to send you both back to Nurse Crowe at Reigate during the Dorset move. Bun created such a fuss — not eating, and constant crying — Anne said, "I can't keep her. You'd better come and collect her." We all met on Paddington Station. I hadn't expected to meet you there too — but Ann said "I thought it would be nice for Willum to see you" — she only knew you as William. I felt simply awful leaving you on the platform, as the train was pulling out, but you didn't seem to mind. You just took Nurse Crowe's hand and walked away. **["Doing our Command Performance as The Happy Anglican."** *Next viz shot: David in Battledress, flanked by matching Tommys in Tin Helmets.*] So many uniforms — but everybody was in uniform in those days. I sewed you your own khaki battledress to be like the Dorset soldiers manning the gun emplacement on the cliff — here, playing with the Searchlight group, next to my darling Dickie, in his American Sergeant's "pinks." [*viz American Sergeant, Formal Portrait; brown-ink inscription (barely vizible against sepia): "Here's to you. Mr. P."*]

I'd forgotten it was signed. That was
Jim again, giving everything nicknames,
like you being "Mr. Snodgrass." With
Dickie — Richard, Dick became "Mr. Penis" —
"Mr.P." The same as calling it a Japonica;
when Jim saw one in the Aunts' garden the
shape of the flower reminded him — but he
didn't know about us then. We weren't
having an affair. Yet. The first time the
gun on the cliff was fired, the entire thing
collapsed! [**"Play it again, Mr. Keyes:
THANK YOU, MR. PENIS!"]** Dorothea couldn't
usually stand Americans — she always
switched off the wireless if Bing Crosby
came on — but the Aunts were completely
charmed by Dickie. He brought more food
from the Camp than they'd seen since the
War started! One didn't feel guilty.
Everybody who was separated for two or
three years had affairs. People turned
a blind eye. There were enough spare men
around for even the plain girls. Two "dark
ladies" moved into the village for the
soldiers. They didn't last long! I suspect
the Army moved them out. I don't think

they were Gypsies. Darker than that. I never actually saw them. [*viz* **Tanned Dickie in white Lastex Jantzen swimsuit, with Pipe, on grass in front of pup tent. viz Smiling David standing behind, watching Mr.P touch Sister's hair.**] What I mean by no guilt — it's so hard to explain now but things were just different then. Bombs were falling. Everyone you knew was getting killed — or might be. Time was different too, it's why I can't remember exactly when we got married or went to war. [*viz again*, **Wedding Day Trio (Nan, Jim, Charlie) against railings in treed London square.**] Things had been going on for so long it was a relief to finally get it over with. Like the rehearsals for D-Day. The Army just showed up at the door of Barton-Olivers, all by itself on the cliff, and asked how many of us there were? The household was the Aunts, Us — you me, Bun, Sammy [*viz* **Pekingese and Goat.**]

Sammy the Peke — I've forgotten the name of the goat — and Doreen, Bun's Nanny, who was the niece of Mrs. Westover at the Dove Pub — which later was owned by the brother of Jim's doctor in Langford. It's amazing how small the world is! The Major said, "You can stay but you can't say a word of

what you see. Or use the phone. If anyone
does, you'll all be moved out." And there
we were. Stuck. [*Pekingese and Sister*.]
You crawled along the cliff ledges while
the American Rangers were climbing them!
The grapnel hooks came up with rockets.
And all the Ducks — amphibious landing
craft, I've forgotten the exact initials.
And then The Day...! [*Pekingese and Blur*.]
The gliders went over for hour after hour
from the fields behind us. We could hear
the guns on the other side of the Channel.
Suddenly those thousands and thousands of
soldiers were all gone. All the rest of
D-Day, nothing but that empty sea.

And that evening there was the terrific
storm and the Carrier Pigeon arrived on the
ledge of your Nursery window with the band
on its leg. The Army came and collected
it. I often wonder what the message said.
["**Next cheap shot:** *Royal-Marines-at-Sea.*
This viz message (to Jim) is quite legible.
'*Yours rhythmically, Wally*'."] I never
noticed that inscription before, either.
"Yours Rhythmically, Wally!" — they were
together in the Marines' Dance Band with
Jim's best friend, Jackie — Thomas, but not

the Charlie one of Singer and Keyes — who
was a hairdresser, and their pet monkey in
Ceylon. It stole things and took them up
to the top of a palm tree but they didn't
know it was the thief. That caused quite
a fuss apparently. [*viz* **Marines-in-Ceylon:
Succession of vized Elephants, Pagodas,
Snake Charmers; vized Jim with shirt
off and Pipe and —**] Those ridiculous
long shorts above the black girl cutting
straw — I'd never heard that Women
Smelling Awful in Church story. I still
can't believe they ever did go to church
with Mountbatten — Kythe knew his wife,
Edwina, and swore she was a lesbian. I
often wondered about Kythe herself. Most
of the time in Ceylon Jim had malaria,
or that horrible skin rot. Leaving the
Aunts was nothing to do with me and Dicky.
[*viz* **back to David and Sammy in Dorset.**]
Moving to Sherbourne was for you to go to
school there — as a Weekly Boarder, the
fees were less and you got to come home on
Saturdays. The horrid part was the Aunts
making us give back Sammy. You adored him.
They said it was because he still belonged
to Marjorie and Rhoda, who gave him to us,
and he couldn't live in a town — it's so
difficult to sort these things. But yes,
there were two Sherbourne houses we stayed
in. I got them through an Agency; one had
to, accommodation was hen's teeth. We left
the first place — where you learned to ride
a bicycle — because the wife got annoyed
when the husband liked you better than
their own son. [**"Liked who? This is where
we came in!"**] The second house, where you
had this tent in the back garden, was
owned by the Mad Professor. Not sex but
weird — like Alex Guinness who I've never
been able to stand, in that film about the
old lady and the robbers. Our Landlord

Professor seemed to live just in one room
and had a habit of knocking on the door
at all hours. [**"The Guinness film was *The
Lady Killers*, with Peter Sellers. *VIZ*,
Mr. Penis in his Jantzen Lastex in front of a
garden tent."**] When I knew Jim was coming
back I took Bun up to London to find us
a flat. You stayed down at Sherbourne as
a Full Boarder. The flat was the one in
Finsbury, near Alexandra Palace, on Ferme
Parke Road, where the landlady's mother
died, and was laid out on the kitchen
table. We were there, just me and Jim and
Bun until you wrote the letter from the
infirmary saying it was impossible, and
the Sherbourne Matron asked us to take
you home. So we changed you to University
College in Hampstead where you got the
trots. [**Last *viz*, *Reunited Family Gauer at
Alexandra Palace: Civilian James-with-
pipe, Tight-skirted-Charlie, Always-
Happy-David, Pig-tailed-Bun, and Honey Bee
(Golden Cocker Spaniel).*]** I suppose it was
too much to ask. The Ferme Park place was
tiny and Jim had been in the Marines four
years, two overseas in Ceylon. Families
all over the country broke apart when the
fathers came back. No wonder I have that
'where am I?' look. I don't know why I
stayed with Charlie except for you kids. I
should have taken you and run.

"I should have taken you and run."

Amen and/or Oy Vey to all that . . . !

There are no Stars of David in the MacKenzie Family Plot at Beauly Priory. Whether one of Charlie's Other Teddy-Might-Have-Beens was a kosher Mr. Lucky remains an open question . . . buried in the rest of the avalanche of names played around with so much by all the players — concerned, and otherwise: Real or Imagined — that we haven't a ghost of a chance to sort them out.

> **Rabbit :** *(out of his depth in the Home warren)*
> "Could Charlie's Teddy be
> American, like her Dickie?"
> **Panda :** *(disgruntled on the Incendiary shelf)*
> "I'm still lost by her as Charlie,
> staying with Charlie."
> **Owner :** *(over P&R's heads: for M. Laurillard's)*
> "That name game at least is easy
> to explain. Like the Curious
> Lobster."

"What 'lobster' name game do yew mean thisss time?"

O frabjous day! Callooh! Callay! — we're chortling with joylessness because Curious Abe has deigned to come back from vacation to where we left off. More annoying is his curious new habit of tuning in to our playlet conversations without so much as a What are yew thinking?

To make an impenetrable marital arrangement imperfectly clear: we've just remembered that the Author's Dedication page in our copy of The Curious Lobster's Island reads, *"This Book is for CHARLOTTE"* so no wonder we loved it. Jim called Charlie, Charlie, *instead* of Charlotte, because of his Music Hall partner, Charlie Thomas. Freudianly speaking, 'John Thomas' is lower class Brit for prick, and they used to sleep in the same bed — as Singer and Keyes, if Thomas got pissed — in our flat in Hampstead. Charlie-Mother called *Jim* Charlie as a term of derision — being 'a proper Charlie' is like a North American dumb asshole. In the Glen Lake kitchen it wasn't a problem. Jim would say, 'Where's my goddamn rye and ginger, Charlie?' And she'd say to Nan, 'Don't pay any attention to Charlie. Just let the silly old bugger drop dead.' Where outsiders got confused was when she switched herself to Gotchie.

"'Gotchies' worn by 'Mr. Penis' under his American Sergeant's 'pinks'?"

And before Mr. Snod can say Why didn't *we* think of that . . .?

"I'm afraid our time is up. Also, I shall be away at a conference next week — but perhaps your mother has more to tell you?"

On a lovely late June evening . . . when Dora the Home-Care has left to look after her own, Petty Guillaume skirts the E-for-Euthanasia chocolate pudding waiting in the fridge and finds the courage to confront his stricken Mother full-frontally about a lot of other previously unmentionable Black Book *viz* loose ends like:

["Why You REALLY Left E-for-England?"]

For lots of reasons — but nothing mysterious like bigamy, or stealing shillings from the gas meter. This was my first Post-War suit. **[Some Last *viz* Pics of 1947: *Charlie-in-tailored-suit, white-sandals & shooting-stick by Ford Anglia*]**

Material was still almost impossible to come by. We got it from Jim's West End tailor. He was good at that sort of thing — like getting a new car when nobody else could. The Anglia is the last English picture. Mostly we left for the endless Rationing — you even used to queue for horsemeat. And whale meat. A terrible winter. We had to get water from a pipe in the street, and the landlady's mother, old Mrs. Fairlambe, laid out as stiff as a plank on the kitchen table. This was the last straw! [*viz* **Barren shot of Sussex Down**] Not being able to build in Sussex. The Aunts had given us a piece of land, we had the bungalow designed — you loved looking at the plans — and then Labour froze it in a Green Belt. But the main reason we left, as Jim always said: "It was for you children." [*viz **Empress of Canada: Mother-&-Half-Siblings, standing at the rail*]* Jim must be taking the snap. Six days at sea. Such an enormous country. Seven more to cross it, counting Christmas on the train.

["What about my NAMES — and Teddy's?"]

Well yes — you knew he was your father. You were told, "This is Daddy." and whenever Teddy came around to the flat or we went out in his car — there was never any more sex between us — you called him Daddy. You always called Jim James. You called all the others by their names. Until in front of the Judge. I don't remember exactly — it's so long ago! — but I think the old Judge asked you to come up to him and sit on his knee. And I think the Judge wore a robe. I know it was just the three of us in his chamber. And he probably said something like, "James — Mr. Gauer, is now your father. And you're going to have a new name: 'David Hugh Courtney' to be like Jim."

["What about THE STOCKBROKER THING?"]

Well you know there were some others before Teddy. My first real lover was John Bishop, a Pilot Officer — not the R.A.F.,

a real pilot, of an American airliner,
landing at Croydon. When he was passing
through London we used to meet. But I know
exactly when that was all over. The Silver
Jubilee Night. The old King, George the
Fifth. After the Jubilee I only saw Teddy.
I don't remember the date but it was long
before you.

["How long EXACTLY?"]

I was never good at Maths. Until I went
to school we had different governesses.
Miss Wright wore button boots and those
net collars high up her neck. Her dress
always trailed on the stairs. As we walked
down behind her we used to put our foot
out to catch it, and then say "Sorry,
Miss Wright." When she left All Saints
she asked the Aunts not to tell any of us
kids she was going in case we threw stones
at the taxi. You know that film you went
to see the other night? — where the New
Zealand girls kill one of their mothers
and record everything in a journal for the
police to find —"*Beautiful Creatures*" — How
did they actually do it to the mother...?
A brick in a stocking. Of course it
doesn't upset me. I'm only interested
because I kept a diary.

["What bloody DIARY?"]

Didn't I tell you...? Of the men I went out
with — Not only lovers, there also the
Uncle kind who just wanted dinner. I had a
sort of code. Very simple. "LMV" — For "Lost
My Virginity." And the name — for instance,
John Bishop. The American airliner Captain
at Croydon. Before the Silver Jubilee and
Teddy. It didn't necessarily say if I
actually had sex with the others. Kythe and

her Edwina Mountbatten lesbian stories in
India could be a real 'Always a bridesmaid'
bitch!

["Did Kythe know I WASN'T JIM'S?"]

I was always sure she didn't. She hadn't
met you until she came to stay at Burton
Bradstock. I suppose she might have
weaseled it out of Nan or the Aunts. You
know what a gossip she was, endlessly
stirring up trouble. You had your own kilt
in the Family Tartan, made specially in
Edinburgh, you looked really good in it
when you were little. I don't remember
Kythe giving you the MacKenzie signet ring
with the Stag's Head on your twenty-first
birthday to get over being illegitimate. I
just wish you could finally be happy....

["What about your VIRGINITY DIARY?"]
I kept it in our flat. Not locked up or
anything, and one day I couldn't find it.
I thought I must have lost it. Nan and
I went around to see the Old Admiral's
lawyers. I think there were three of them.

```
They all seemed really old — terrifying!
just like Rumpole of the Bailey. "The
party of the first part, signs here." Dear
Nan was there for moral support. And then
one of them simply held it up! The Diary!
Teddy had stolen it!
```

After the purchase of some more Gravol by the prosecutor (to be taken only as directed "for relief of nausea" by the defendant), and in the Sunday absence of home-caring third parties like Dora — or eavesdropping anal-ysts like What are yew sinking Abe via an unexpected Conference call to say whatever crap the Post-Freudians are examining under their Projection microscopes will take another bloody week! — the Rumpole interrogation continues down P&R's Chocolate Cottage Bailey:

Milords Panda and Rabbit, Owner now shows the Accused a road atlas and her Birth Certificate: CHARLOTTE ISEULT HARVEY. *Born at "Dickoya," Quickley Lane, Chorley Wood.*

```
These damned names! The house one,
"Dickoya," is a bit like Dickie, I
suppose . . . And Chorley Wood being
only four miles west of Watford, in
Hertfordshire, where Teddy's old father
the Admiral lived. A sort of circle,
that's rather strange. But not if you
believe in reincarnation. Did I already
ask for Gravol before you leave for
Ottawa? I only need it now and then.
```

Milords, prior to our departure on a two-week summer vacation, we now present in evidence the final photographs in the Black Book: Both are tiny, cracked, and faded. The first is labeled, "Nan (8) and 'Bill' (3) with Father in gloomy garden." The second, "Father and Mother on beach at Porquerolles, 1914."

```
I remember so little about them. Enjoy
your holiday, you deserve it. My knee is
just such a crashing bore — not being
able to drive again — but otherwise I'm
```

fine. Dora looks after everything. She's a
treasure. Don't hurry back on my account.
Two weeks is no time at all.

If Your Lordships please, this picture shows Lilias (Willum's grandmother), jumping from a rock. Her foot splashes. Henry (Willum's grandfather), grasps his young wife's hand. Milords may also be interested to observe that the primitive box-camera still manages to freeze even the drops of water as the Accused wipes away tears.

Is this the only one of them together...?

In summation, Milords: by the calculation of Prosecution's Expert Witness in analytical geometry, the Silver Jubilee of our late Sovereign, King George the Fifth, occurred on or about the exact day of said Witness's conception.

But it wasn't just the *Day*. Or Jubilee
Night. The parties went on for the whole
week — and whether stealing the Diary was
Teddy's idea...? No, Teddy was too thick.
I can't believe he thought of it himself. I
think the Father or the Brother put him up
to it. But of course the horrid lawyers used
it as proof of my promiscuity and him not
for your Paternity. Poor Nan was speechless.
Personally, does it *really* matter?
[pregnant pause]
I suppose to you it does.

Milords, the Prosecution rests on the volcanic lip of a millennium.

UNEXPECTED EXHIBIT B
Dateline Vancouver, Wednesday, March 12, 1997

PAPUA WITCH DOCTOR TO PUT HEX ON VSE

Traditional and modern cultures will confront each other in Vancouver this week over something valued by both: gold.

In a display that could turn heads even in the seen-it-all-before Vancouver financial sector, an aboriginal tribal chief from Papua New Guinea and a female witch doctor say they plan to arrive in full tribal dress and war paint to cast a hex on the Vancouver Stock Exchange and to present a protest petition bearing their people's thumbprints.

The South Pacific group is angry because it says one of the VSE's listed companies, Vulcan Resources Ltd., left them high and dry in a gold project located in their homeland, an island country northeast of Australia that borders on Indonesia.

As part of their protest, the landowners will leave gold nuggets, strewn over banana leaves, at the entrance to the VSE. The nuggets, laid down for symbolic reasons, are from the Mount LeBreton property.

DAVID GURR

And now The Verdict, P&R . . . !

Rabbit : *(feeling hung out to dry by the Unexpected)*
    "Banana leaves! You mean all
    along, Olie's been really real?"
Panda : *(feeling like the Morning After mother brought home
    Baby Half-Sister)*
    "We thought you were making it
    all up about the Le Breton Island
    treasure."
Owner : *(feeling a break in Die-Die's split-Life sentence)*
    "I thought so too. But if a Real
    Olie's coming to sue Vancouver in
    a penis gourd, I want to be there
    to meet him. Skip the verdict.
    Let's have the sentence."

DEATH.

Of Abraham — Abe to those who knew him best — son of an Isaac in South Africa, and killed there when the rental car he was driving ran itself into a cliff, leaving us bereft of a man we realise too late, truly has been a father figure for the past five years of fifty-minute hours. Leaving us with an ongoing dread of long distance telephone calls and no life-saving answers to help us when we are sinking under the weight of inexpressible feeling.

Oy vey.

Amen.

And one more Final Exit.

Of Charlotte . . . only one week after Abe . . . August 10th, 1997, a Sunday evening, while watching television. Mother of David (once of Willum) who kissed her goodbye three times before he left for his traitor's summer holiday. And who, after his return (a full week later, not cutting it short to view her frozen body), against her express wishes, read the Anglican service for Burial of the Dead, the unrepentantly out-of-fashion Aunts' Version, to her grand-and-great-grand children, as her ashes went into the dirt of the flower bed already containing Jim's and Nan's, and Badger the Dog's and Sascha the Cat's, at the end of the Cadboro Bay Cottage garden.

Concluding with the planting of a Chaste Tree as a bastard's token of remembrance; and these words left behind in her own strong right hand before the strokes got at it:

> I said to the man who stood at the gate of the year " Give me a light that I may tread safely into the unknown ." And he replied "Go out into the darkness and put your hand into the hand of God. That he shall be to you better than a light and safer than the known way ." Churchill used this in dark times in one of his speeches.
> It is many times with me .

And this faded clipping, stuck on with Scotch tape:

BOOK THREE
"I returned and saw under the sun, that the race is not to the swift, nor the battle to the strong, neither yet bread to the wise, not yet riches to men of understanding, nor yet favour to men of skill; but time and change happeneth to them all . . . "

— ECCLESIATES

Time for you and time for me,
And time yet for a hundred indecisions,
And for a hundred visions and revisions,
Before the taking of a toast and tea. . . .

...DID SHE REALLY DO IT WITH CHOCOLATE PUDDING?

In a post-mortem search as vain as all the preceding ones D.D. goes first to Dora the Home-Care to dig out the dirt of the Final Exit question:

"No. It was the sugar bowl. That was the first thing I saw when I came in the next morning. The sugar bowl on the table beside the chair. To hide the bitter taste. Because of course she didn't take sugar any more with her tea. She used to talk about it a lot. On a Sunday, I wouldn't be here. But how it would be difficult to find the right time because David — you — could drop in any moment from your studio next door."

A teaspoon of sugar dissolved in a sea of guilt.

As always, Charlie leaves no hard evidence on her plate, just more half truths. The quote wasn't used by Churchill. It was George the Sixth, in a radio broadcast to the Empire for Christmas, 1939 — which must have been spent at Nurse Crowe's White House, but D.D. can't remember. The poet was Minnie Louise Hoskins, born 1875 in Bartlett's, date of death still not recorded in the Centennial Edition. The title of the [1908] proem was *God Knows*.

With a regal conclusion which Charlie omitted:

So *I went forth, and finding the Hand of God, trod gladly into the night. And He led me towards the hills and the breaking of the day in the lone East.*

D.D. follows her spirit there, along the Old Pipeline Trail behind Glen Lake, where mother and son used to ride together in his adolescence, before Panda and Rabbit got lost.

Time for you and time for me . . .

Three years together before Jim — and three years after. The great sixty-year wheel of Cathay has gone its full circle, P&R, but your Owner still can't believe in reincarnation. This is our last Evacuation: this time she won't be coming back.

P&R . . . ?

The pet voices of our past have faded out again.

Taking with them the Strangelove shadow chorus called Paternity: their names Teddy, Larry, Nanky Poo or any other G&S walk-on from that midsummer night's dream dropped in my lap above Greenland's icy mountains. The balcony window-nails are withdrawn. The Blitz is over.

No more Family History Revisited Abortions masqueraded as stillborn half-fictions for Abe. I know who I am. And what I am: Builder, Father, Sailor, Tango Dancer and ghost-free Writer. Free to record A-for-Adventure's gilt volcanoes in a bleak or joyful progress all my own.

Con Brio

An Entertainment

Con Brio
One

GRAINGER DIDN'T HAVE THE TALENT — NOT WITH THE BIG T, he was honest about that. He was honest about most things: Marriages, Women, Houses, Lack of Conviction, Level of Dance, which was what made him a good spy.

In Ballroom he was Bronze. There had only been two marriages. The first was for sex. Baby naval officers of his Midshipman's "snottie" generation weren't allowed to sleep ashore in an unmarried state. Nor granted divorce after it; at least not a decree nisi combined with any hope of promotion. Sliding from the navy into spying with a mid-Atlantic accent solved both problems of his youth but created new ones just in time for a Third Millennial mid-life crisis.

His second marriage postponed it for a while. He couldn't honestly have said at the time, This is for Love, with a Big L, but it was comfortable and might have lasted if the other vagaries of spy-life hadn't made his second wife say, on the third Sunday afternoon in April, four years ago, over a perfectly ordinary brunch in a café disguised as a bookshop in Santa Barbara, California, "I'm sick and tired of seeing you stare me in the face with those blue eyes looking at Architectural Digest and tell me there isn't somebody else when it's obvious you're screwing yourself blind on all these so-called building trips — or what other possible excuse is there?" And as he wasn't screwing anyone — or only in moments of espionage extremis, like the Balkans, when exploding bombs and dumdum bullets really didn't seem to make anything else matter — and couldn't honestly lie to her, "If that's what you want?" which understandably drove her further up the wall to his second divorce. But he still didn't think it was fair that she took the dogs.

He loved the Afghans. Notwithstanding the inconvenience they caused by jumping six-foot fences to outrace passing trains. They couldn't have won in France, but this was a Canadian backwater line with a single-car, morning run that went north at 8:05 after the dogs' breakfast, and south after their supper at 6:17.

He had come home from a particularly dull, and thus celibate, Washington D.C. spying trip to find his chewed-up dance shoes in the dogs' plastic bowls. Otherwise, the house was empty. The shoes were German, hand-sewn, with suede soles and Latin heels; cost, two-hundred U.S. dollars. Meaning $300 in domestic currency for the Separation Agreement, given the Canadian rate of exchange.

He couldn't afford to make a fuss about the shoes for the same reason that he couldn't accept a Silver Certificate from the American Ballroom Society although his West Coast Swing was more than adequate. Don't draw attention was the first of the spy game rules. My friend will pay, in as many languages as possible, was the first professional advice he got for playing Men-will-be-boys in the Navy. Nautical demands on male intelligence never swung much higher.

After the opening, "Father's first name?" "James." "Do you know what this is?" he was asked by a green-striped psychiatrist when enrolling for his Midshipman snottie stint. "A sword." Grainger replied to the obvious. "And this?" "A tennis racquet." "Fine. No overwrought imagination. You're in."

Not quite. The Captain of the Board asked, "Ever played rugger?"

"Only a rather bad Scrum Half. And second-string in the Mile." With a Sir tacked on, that was all it took. The same with spying. You could tell the ones who wouldn't make it by their excessive imaginations or lies. One couple used that combination plus a pseudonym to slide sideways and end up in the CIA's library of Espionage Fiction, much of it commissioned in-house.

"Anyone can get found out when it's sleeping-with or stealing-from," his Spy Nanny had advised during the probationary period. "Much better to have the One Big Lie. Your father's first name, for example."

"What?"

"Well you must know it isn't James."

Grainger didn't.

"But of course you have known he isn't your natural male parent?"

Grainger hadn't, and was floored. Spy-Nanny was delighted.

"Plausible Bastardy Deniability. The best Big Lie is invariably so petty to a mind outside your own that the odds of stumbling across it with the Detector running are astronomical. We need a Minimum of Convictions and Never take a Second Thought. And of course it's a major plus for the Trade that you don't have kids, but for passport purposes you'll need an honest job. Architects and builders can travel anywhere they make cement. Trot along between Not-too-Dull and Life-of-the-Party, you won't slide off the rails."

He slid into building because there was no other way except treason that he could afford a home worth living in. He didn't have to be Lloyd-Wright. And being minus children hadn't bothered him in his delayed naval adolescence. When his first wife found she couldn't, tests showed he was potent. Her infertility was a one-sided domestic tragedy. When his second wife said, She Wouldn't, at an age when a man wants to pass something on, it was only out of female vanity, and hit home. Taking the Afghans made it a double hit.

"Two wives but no mess in divorcing, honesty's always our best policy." Spy Nanny had summed up briskly between aphorisms, wearing tartan-wool plus-fours for a round of Far North golf played in Ottawa's tropic-summer humidity. "And Bronze Level on the dance floor's not too flashy — but we have to watch the music, it can be Achilles' Heel. Remember Orson Welles getting tripped up by that damned zither in the Third Man. With Mr. Blanding's Dream House under your belt, you're par for the course except the name."

"Grainger?" said Grainger.

"The Stuart. You can't be ignored at a cocktail party when you're a film star."

"That was spelled Stewart, no i in Granger, and he's dead."

"Not on the late show. I saw Caesar and Cleopatra three nights ago, and people don't know the spelling when they only hear it in the Club Jacuzzi. 'Adam and Eve and Pinch-me-not!' We can't be too careful when we go down to bathe. What were you at school?"

"Grainger," said Grainger, beginning for the first time to query his mid-Atlantic shift of professions.

Spy Nanny was a film buff when he wasn't Mother Goose. "You must have had a nicker, like Mr. Chips, it's part of the Old School drill for Class War. And you did go to an Old School. That's why you're in. Think of Sam Goldwyn's immortal 'Include me out.' Or imagine yourself at a cocktail party in the Browning Version."

Grainger made an honest effort to show less conviction than Michael Redgrave. "Grainge," he said.

Spy Nanny broke the Never Think Twice Rule by invoking a third one: "Don't be hidebound." He looked around his Ottawa Headquarters office (disguised as the Clubhouse Manager's) and pointed at an object on the wall between pictures of Lord Mountbatten teeing-off at St. Andrews (with Charlie Chaplin) and Checkpoint Charlie in East Berlin. "That's more like it."

"A midshipman's dirk?" Shades of the psychiatrist returned.

"Dirk Grainger's a born natural. Think of me as your Snottie's Nurse." Which was the first hard evidence Grainger received that the Spy Nanny knew his job. In fifteen years of spying against enemies and allies on both sides of the North Atlantic Treaty nobody ever asked Good Old Dirk if he was Scaramouche or the Prisoner of Zenda.

But now there was no more Checkpoint Charlie and he was still stuck with the nicker but not the Class War pension to go with it. In a barren season for good spies the few Big T's of deception left for greener Corporate Espionage fields of the Early Nineties on their own. The Spy Nanny's successors, taking their cues from Tabloid TV, retained the noisy least competent. Grainger and the other quietly solid performers were Outplaced through System Re-Engineering.

Stripped of euphemisms: he was fired.

Pissed-off at being passed over, Grainger wrote it all down under a pseudonym and called it a novel, but as telling the honest truth about spying required no imagination, it went from printer to remainder with a single accurate review from the publisher's first reader: "Grammar better than usual. Should try ghost-writing. Too dull to sell on his own." The 20 listed under Sales to Libraries on his one royalty statement were just to disguise the CIA's copy.

It was no consolation that he emerged from the Ottawa Clubhouse phase of life as a builder with his One Big Lie intact. Through all the inevitable Where Have You Hidden the Papers while crossing the borders of inhospitable spots of bother like Xinjiang and Iraq as a free-lance architect for the United Nations and passport purposes he was never once asked, *Who is your real father?* If he had been, he could have told the machine in all honesty, *My mother didn't know.*

His lack of Legitimacy never used to bother him.

Chatting casually to people like Saddam's Butler while a cruise missile wandered by, tended to focus the mind on more important matters — Where have *you* fuckers hidden the Bomb from the U.N.? It seemed to be a combination of his mother's death with the Golden Handshake that brought out the Bastard issue.

And really only on dark midnights of birthdays cusped at a vanishing decade. Or Party Life moments of boredom even more acute than copying statistics of Soviet Tractor Capacity versus Vodka Consumption by Missile Crews while the Deputy Minister responsible was peeing the latter down the Kremlin drains.

This was one of those birthdays. It was also a Mission Test.

Farewell to 49 on the Absolut Scale and a warm hug from Taitinger against the hollow freezer-chill of his turning Big Five-O. The man paying for tonight's champagne was a British Peer of the Realm, not a commissar, and the venue had switched to the Grand Ballroom of the Plaza Hotel in New York, but this Mission journey, to New Guinea, began two months ago, in Dallas.

Through the unattributable word-of-mouth that passed for normal conversation in the spy trade, Grainger received an invitation to visit the richest man in the Wall Street world of 10 per cent derivatives, Gustav Rufus.

Ruffian would have been more accurate, from the original Greek-Bulgarian. A former Colonel in the Athens Junta, with a squat body still resembling a hirsute (except for his shaved turret-head) version of one of the Junta's American Army surplus Patton tanks in an up-to-the-minute Gentleman's Quarterly three-button Armani suit, Rufus couldn't afford to forget his roots. Despite a personal wealth beyond counting, he always carried enough gold on him to allow an emergency exit, and let no fair-fight Queensbury Rules stand in the way of profiting from the other side's weakness. Failed brakes on Rolls Royces. Decimated stands of ancient redwood trees. Whatever weapon came to hand for a hostile takeover. Greenmail or black. The method was immaterial, sometimes it even included a velvet glove.

"Like now," Rufus said, staring from his bronze-triple-glazed window above Dallas, while Grainger's tongue tried to filter the grounds of a second demitasse of honey-sweetened Greek coffee, thick as mud. "Why you think, Mr. Grainger, I pay for a CPR tub worth only scrap — as much as for renting QE 2?"

Some tub! A photo showed the *Southern Cross* to be a nautical buff's gem: renamed into a cruise cliché, the liner was the last of Canadian Pacific's White Empresses from the era of solid teak and polished brass. Grainger put down the demitasse and offered, "Generosity, I suppose."

In the Derivative trade, things were no more what they seemed than in spying. The walls of Rufus's oval office appeared to be rock-solid: constructed of shiplap-channeled redwood planks, clear edge-grain, standing floor-to-ceiling, twelve inches wide by sixteen feet long, worth a lumber baron's ransom. But the light steel drywall studs supporting them hadn't been cross-braced to take the added weight of so much wood. Each time the matching planked door closed the walls shook as though they were part of a false-fronted mansion from one of Spy Nanny's back lot sets for *Gone With the Wind*. If a tornado swept in on its way up from the Gulf, the strewn remains of this sanctum would look like any Southern trailer-park's. Similarly, Rufus's "Mister" before "Grainger" was only apparent politeness to subordinates involved in hostile decimations.

"'Generosity I suppose.' Very good, Mr. Grainger. We get on well." His Old School cool earned him a Rufus laugh, gold escape-hatch wisdom teeth exposed. "I ask you another simple question. What is secret of How to get rich in stock markets?"

An honest spy wouldn't try to outsmart it. He offered the obvious from First Year Economics, "Buy low, sell high, I guess."

"You let me have punch lines, Mr. Grainger. Good mostly. Not always." Rufus's turret-head swiveled. His dental fortune vanished, to be replaced by a gleaming Zeus medallion previously hidden in the grizzled hair on his Armani-armoured chest. "You know answer is Sell short. Don't, not joke me, what is word —?"

"Humor me."

"Okay. Now answer first question. No more of 'I guess.'"

Grainger had to dredge back through the coffee grounds to recall the first question. Paying too much for a CPR tub: Renting the *Cross*. He said. "You paid top dollars for future scrap metal because you think the Market in commercial paper's going to crash."

"Not think. I know — but Crashing is always Time." Rufus slammed a fur-knuckled right fist backed by a solid gold Rolex into a left palm guarding against future losses with three over-sized rings. The spot for one on his tanned wedding finger was marked instead by a white circle: the end of that marriage must have been more recent than Grainger's. "Only Lord God's Lady Luck can know Time. I bet. You understand?" Heaven provided no clue to understanding: the Dallas skyline was unusually pristine against a clear Texas sky. "Lord God happens to be my neighbor, in Contentment," Rufus continued. "Godfrey Bowman, M.P. From your work backstage at Westminster, have you met?"

Grainger shook his head. "I know the name." Like the rest of the wired world he knew a Tabloid Legend's virtual reality: from Member of Parliament, to Embezzlement *cum* Sexual Excitement (in *Regina versus Bowman*), to three years of Confinement (politically suspended), to Remorse and Re-Instatement by a Knighthood, and finally to Off-shore Investment beyond the dreams of avarice — by writing about it from a tax-free mansion on Contentment Cay often and badly enough to earn a Coronet.

"Bowman speaks baby talk 'nickers' codenames to dodge libel and tax," Rufus said. "Not always successful. I am 'Ruffles' in his computer. 'Lady Luck' — Freda' — is his Swiss shrink, and also his new wife. He calls her orgasms 'Lady Godiva's Big O.' I get such inside information from his new Research Assistant, 'Miss Montana'. She tells me Lord God needs a new 'Holy Ghost' to help write the latest schlock plot. Ghost writing is what you do."

Grainger was swamped, but he realized that they were almost down to the Industrial Espionage ground floor: why Rufus really wished to hire an antique spy as well as a cruise liner.

"Always at ends of cycles, Mr. Grainger, comes a Bubble. I think the name of this one's is like Freda's lucky orgasms. Con Brio."

"The gold mine in New Guinea?"

"Maybe mining gold. Maybe salt."

He said, "Salt meaning, 'Somebody's fiddling the Assays' — ounces per ton in the core samples?"

"I know Assays meaning, but finally you ask right questions. If before the Dow Jones hits ten thousand, just do for me, Gold or salt, find which? and you will never have to 'suppose' my generosity." Rufus's turret-head brought Grainger in its sights and locked on target while his three-ring hand fondled a glittering string of 20-Karat worry-beads. "Assuming you get hired by Bowman, as what you would call 'cover', for this mission, there is still a downside for both of us. Although the company denies it, gold or salt, this Le Breton mine is on a floating dead volcano coming back to life."

Frontal attack on the mountain proved out of the question. Vulkan Extraction Inc. had Le Breton Island padlocked with a private army for Security: Pitcairn Proprietary. Using Gulf Surplus supplies of ex-Special Air Service Paras and napalm, Pitcairn fought small counter-insurgency wars for free enterprise in the South Pacific.

"Pitcairn's primary target on Two Tits," an Aussie informant from the company's PR division told Grainger, "is Tree Huggers screaming the usual Green bloody murder about displaced butterflies and Abos. Pitcairn's Secondary target is Tab Shits."

Tabloid Investigative Journalists. Investors were allowed guided glimpses. The liner hired by Rufus was booked to take a Blue Chip boatload of ex-movers-and-shakers from their tax-sheltered condos on Contentment Cay in the Caribbean to celebrate the Dow Breaking Ten Thousand while they eyeballed what was bluntly pitched in the prospectus as "A South Pacific Mountain of Gold."

Grainger couldn't book passage as a Major League Investor: answers to the inevitable questions about Where he hid his money? would require too much imagination at the Captain's Table. Bullshit was Bowman's stock-in-trade. As a pulp Top Ten Author with a peerage "getting colour for my new novel which happens to have the same bloody name as your mine!" at the same bloody time His Lordship was buying Brio stock faster than Vulkan could print the certificates, Bowman was a shoe-in to dodge any Pitcairn SAS goons checking the passenger list.

A tougher step was getting hired by God. Grainger hadn't counted on wearing dance shoes for the job interview. Which brought him back to the Plaza Ballroom in New York, and the woman he was relying on to provide him with his second layer of Mission Cover.

Pamela St. Deney (rhymes-with Mandalay) was the cool British private eye pitching the hottest gossip in America via *Vanity Fair.* Her BBC Morning Show accent and deportment came from Cheltenham, a cucumber-sandwich town once known only for its Edwardian tea dances and College for Young Ladies. The school was still there but the town had acquired a growth industry for the 21st Century. Cheltenham osmosed itself into the electronic nerve centre of British Intelligence. Pam had been seduced and/or recruited in the Service of Last Resort as Spy Nanny's swan-song at her Tea Dance graduation. She and Grainger had laughed and worked together in his Checkpoint Charlie days.

"As one tit-for-Tattlering Old Spy to another," she told him, "I can help you now with Bowman, to be his current Holy Ghost — blame the Tab Shits for the job description, it goes with being part of what they call God's Entourage — but you'll have your work cut out. I only met His Lordship for the first time in the flesh, at a story conference this afternoon, and his subjects and predicates are even more fucked up on paper than at the dinner table. The odd thing is, watch him in front of a camera, or on the hustings and he seems to make perfect sense. It must come from having snake-oil DNA in the family tree."

"And the good news?" Grainger asked.

"People never work for Lord God twice. Even if they can stand his bloody knickers names, His Generosity doesn't believe in sharing the wealth. And we'll have a few laughs again along the way. To cover your Bowman's Ghost cover you feed me what's happening on the So Cross under the Captain's Table. I've always adored Julie Christie in the blow-job scene from Shampoo — blame that on Spy Nanny — and don't worry about libel. I'll give you a laptop ThinkPad you can scramble."

Lord Godfrey Bowman's live presence put Grainger in a real-time double bind: he not only had to listen with the sycophantic politeness of a good butler to more bullshit than Saddam's, he had to do it in the full glare of Head Table publicity accorded an Author at the top of the *New York Times*. The acuteness of his Big Apple boredom from Bowman's mind-numbing monologues on the art behind best-selling World Class fiction to the masses (for a *Vanity Fair* Special Issue Profile) was just beginning to exceed the Kremlin's Tractor Capacity ennui when the Ballroom P.A. announced an excuse for a pee break:

"And now, the finale in Argentine Tango!"

The crystal chandeliers went out. In contrast, and despite floating waterlilly centrepiece candles on the Plaza tables, the room seemed black. Bowman became just a voice babbling in the dark.

"I don't see it myself — dancing — but that's the point about talent with a Big T. Generosity. World Class writers pick it up out of what's the word for German shit? Rhymes like zoot suit. Pam-Pam, before Van Fair you worked at Time for Rupe?"

"Zeitgeist, and it wasn't really working at, Godfrey darling, so much as passing through while Rupert was merging with Vanity Fair. But I do agree that your *Death Dance at the Palace* before the actual Princess Di awfulness happened in Paris was absolutely brilliant. And miles ahead of the competition, wouldn't you say, Dirk?"

He could barely discern "Pam-Pam's" up-market Lancôme eye-liner winking behind the floating lilies but as she had got him this far in his Holy Ghost job interview, Grainger agreed without regard for a passing critic from the *New York Literary Review*.

"Brilliant," he repeated to Bowman's starched dress shirt, suddenly luminescent as two ultraviolet spotlights flashed on. "*Death* deserved every week it stayed at the top of the Times List."

"Month," Bowman's disembodied voice said, in a tone which made

Grainger fear he might have overplayed things with His Lordship in the Vanity department. "*Palace* stayed thirteen **months**, which was and still is the record for creative World Class fiction. Although I shouldn't give it away for a song, I'm going to let you in on Sid the Yid — my first agent's — unprejudiced secret of Big S success."

A drum roll and puff of dry-ice smoke obscured the first part of Sid's secret. The computer-controlled spots swiveled from stuffed shirts to a pinpoint focus at the far end of the dance floor. A trap opened in the Plaza's simulated Louis Quinze parquet beside the knothole.

" . . . Do it again," Bowman was saying as two frozen Latin Lovers arose from the dry-ice and the drum roll subsided. "Sid told me that whenever he wasn't drying out. You can't beat a drunk's remorse for sound advice. 'Give them what they want until it's coming out of their ears and both orifices' — if dancing's what's still selling — and Ballroom is mega at the moment, isn't that right, Pam-Pam?"

"*Mega* mega, Godfrey darling. And the new title's fabulous. 'Chasing Con Brio'. Throw Salsa in the plot and I'd even add stellar."

"Would you?" Bowman's voice had the same vaguely threatening note, which Grainger now realized was just His Lordship's unprejudiced way of taking a moment to steal somebody else's better Big Idea before slapping his own nickname on it. "Doing it again with Salsa, I don't see how we're going to work in a Cuban Fred and Ginger eating each other's nachos at the bottom of a New Guinea gold mine for Chasing Brio but that's what genius is all about — "

"*Repeating their triumph in Buenos Aires,*" the PA hyped, "*our Grand Winners are. . . !*"

"Product Endorsement!" . . . capitalized by Bowman, invisibly chasing genius.

"*Antonio and Maria in their ¡el Tango Volcánico!*"

The title came up in scarlet on a Hitachi big-screen. The computerized star-spots changed from chilled ultraviolet to blood-throbbing infrared. Wreathed now in crimson smoke, the ascending pair of Latin figures remained frozen as the unseen elevator brought them level with the parquet floor. The haunting notes of a bandonéon merged with, and then replaced the disintegrating wisps of artificial smoke. Grainger recognized *Otoño porteño*, one of Astor Piazzolla's collaborations with Anibal Troilo. He wouldn't have classified its languid lilt as volcanic, but all tango lyrics had the same underlying Argentinean molten core of betrayal, criminality, and raunch. Which neatly described the career of the best-selling arsehole he needed to glue himself to for the next five weeks.

"We've already sold the movie rights to 'Brio'," Bowman said to Pam, "and sex isn't a problem for Hollywood with a PG rating. Black satin sheets and Che Guevara — that's how we work the Fred eating Ginger angle into Salsa! And quoting Goldilocks: 'Who's been spilling the milk in my bed among the fucking nachos?' — which is where the Spell Check needs checking and this one does his Good Old Dirk act to play the Holy Ghost."

Grainger realised that 'this one' meant him, and probably a job offer. His second layer of Mission Cover was in place and heating up. The female Follower half of the frozen tango duo began to melt. Her mesh-stockinged right leg stretched back from her slit skirt to what seemed an impossible length for a woman of medium height. The stiletto point of her black patent heel hovered like the tip of a scythe. Bowman was expecting some kind of intelligent response to his "Salsa in satin sheets with Che Guevara" gibberish.

Grainger borrowed from Spy Nanny's Hollywood training aids. "The only gold mining choreography I can think of that rang bells at the box office was Chaplin with the Dancing Buns. I guess if you want, I could talk around and see what else I can dig."

"That digging is what I want — but there's no question on a Bowman Project who's doing the talking. Anybody in the Industry or at Westminster will tell you: play fair with the Member for Lady Godiva and you couldn't ask for a better partner in a dark corner of your cell. There are no Free cock-horse Rides either. I paid my price to society for the Commons Stock-split fuckup in Community Service. I'm prepared to buy you as a ghost on Pam-Pam's say-so and show you on the books to satisfy the Cayman accountants for tax purposes, but the inside scoop of Cruise Life has to be the real thing. Widow Bonking. Of course it would be child's play for me to pull strings to get you on board but the bottom line is, we all work our passage. Grammar don't buy the Guccis when you're going for broke as First Elected Provost of Edinburgh without a bloody word of Bonnie Scotland to beat Sean Connery."

"What Godfrey *means*, Dirk darling —" Pam unfractured the last part of Bowman's parliamentary syntax — "combining his electoral experience as a former M.P. with his 'Brio' Advance he can buy being Provost but you have to land the Gigolo job as a Dance Host aboard the So Cross on your own."

The scarlet title on the Hitachi screen unexpectedly dissolved into the steam of a darkly brooding volcano. The Lead half of the tango team did a forward lunge with his left knee in the woman's satin crotch. She tantalized his foot with a *parada* sandwich of her leather instep, then whirled temptation away with a boleo revealing a flash of inner thigh as he led her in three whip-lash strides completing the *salida* to the Cross.

Or double-cross?

For the instant that the tanguera poised on her left toe, Grainger wondered at the co-incidence of Pam's shorthand for an ocean liner's name — So Cross — bumping up against the Christian undertow of a gangsters' dance, with him as its Host . . . *Just a gigolo in Guccis* . . . the Hitachi volcano belched flame, and the soundtrack melded inevitably into *la Cumparsita*, the most famous of all tango tunes. To the strains of The Little Carnival Procession, the couple rotated their hips counterclockwise into an intimate *cunita* of penultimate betrayal.

Now he only had to sell his soul as a Dance Instructing gigolo, to complete his Mission Cover as Spy Nanny would wish: minimum three layers deep.

The volcano erupted on the Plaza Ballroom Hitachi. The soundtrack accelerated from languid salon tango to the military march-beat of a milonga, played-off for the Nineties against a digitized background blend of *Don't Cry for Me, Argentina*. The lyrics wailed as always about small-time macho thieves being stabbed in the heart before carving vital organs out of their opponents and *chiquitas*. The woman Follower did a *gancho* with her scythed patent heel which threatened to spike her Lead partner's virility.

Bowman picked up non sequiturs where he'd left off: "Widow Bonking and Sean Connery. If there's a Big E that got me where I am today it's Empathy. I use Churchill's standup desk, the genuine Sweat and Tears article, from Chartwell — you're going to see Godfrey Bowman genital grammar warts and all before this trip's over. Just ask Miss Montana or my little Pam-Pam."

The Leader on the dance floor saved his masculinity in the nick of time by pinioning his partner's lethal heel with a lightning-fast leg wrap. Grainger did a rough calculation of the nautical distance to Papua New Guinea divided by the Maximum Speed of the good ship *Southern Cross* multiplied by the Bowman empathy just spouted and poured himself another long flute of the Plaza's best champagne.

"I can't speak for Miss Montana's research, but I *think* what Godfrey's saying about 'genital grammar', Dirk —" Pam re-arched her Lancôme eyeliner across the flickering waterlillies — "is while you cruise for the Dow breaking Ten K on the So Cross, with the Contentment Top Five Hundred, we don't want any American useage 'maybe's' instead of British 'perhaps's' to rock the boat for his Vanity Profile ."

"I *know* what I'm bloody saying." Bowman snapped. "Heathrow or JFK, the airport lip-readers aren't totally fucking stupid. As I found to my cost with that cunt and the French hooking episode — of which there was no single grain of truth, Dirk, as God is my judge, and Mags backed me every step of the way, bless her, no matter what those Party arseholes on the Ethics Committee said and did. Show me one of the Westminster bastards who isn't shagging everything from a slippery sheep to their grandmother and I'll say you've done the impossible and found an honest politician! But that's water under Tower Bridge. I told my wife, Buying the bitch off is the obvious thing to do. With a three-book deal for seventy-mill, US, and a peerage, what's ten thousand Euro quid for a whore in the scheme of things?"

About half his ghost fee, Grainger thought — wondering at the same time how any woman could put up with even one empathetic sheep-dip from Bowman for any hourly rate. Seventy-five million for unreadable books was equally unimaginable.

"Think of it like Monopoly money with no Mr. Tax Man looking over anyone's shoulder — or between the legs, that's the beauty of Contentment. The Cay scenery isn't Tahiti but Congressional Medical Consultation without Taxation makes up for a hell of a lot of coconuts if you're worried about prostate. I wouldn't be asking an Old Sherbournian to break his balls for me if there wasn't a bonus. And this is strictly, absolutely between us. '*Entre Nous*', as they say in Simenon's frog pot boilers, like that Diva movie thing. The nigger singer was gorgeous, but where was the plot? And the characters? Three cardboard thugs in an underground parkade is not Godfrey Bowman's idea of deep psychological motivation! We need to know what Big Dick *makes* Ginger spread her creamy thighs on those slippery black satin sheets for Fred and Che Guevara. And if I catch you reading my bad reviews you're off the case quicker than Bobbit could say Ouch!"

The *Diva* film wasn't a Simenon and there were no good Bowman reviews. Grainger had waded through them all, plus the Securité report from Paris about the "creamy thighs" and the actual cost of hushing up the grain of truth: "the French hooker episode" was trans-sexual.

"I guess what Godfrey *means*, Dirk," Pam gave him her Cheltenham upper-middle gaze implying the opposite before it was spoken, "about Mags and Mrs. Bobbitt: we don't want any real names like Bill and Hill — "

"There's no question what I *mean*, you can't hide voices like Mags under nickers, she'th an Icon and the fucking crithics are all thits." The tango pair locked thighs. In moments of molten emotion, Grainger noted, Bowman had an Alfred Hitchcock lisp. "After theeing the real Inthide of Palace life after Death if I found myself stepping in Corgi thit up to my ankles every time I got out of bed — but we're getting off track with the Royals. I told Pam-Pam when she mentioned your name at our Vanity supper last night, and the Old School popped out with the Lemon Tart: a Fellow Therbournian who ran the mile with a nicker like Good Old Dirk is my ghost for Chathing Brio."

With his Ghost job doubly confirmed, Grainger took advantage of a lull in the empathy — the arrival of another Monopoly-money bottle of the Plaza's Taitinger — to check the lisp-volume-level of the voice-activated Sony micro-recorder in his dinner-jacket pocket, followed by a mental note to check His Lordship in the Old School records.

The tanguera's skirt ripped to show scarlet satin panties at the end of a Rear Corrida. While the audience and Hitachi volcano exploded in synch Bowman dropped a World Class bomb.

"You can teach that move to Mags. She's going to be with us for the cruise."

The Sony's red light winked off. Grainger accepted a flute refill from the Plaza's black waiter. Switch-hitting "perhaps's" into "maybe's" for North American lip-readers at airports was one thing: playing a Dance Host Valentino for former female Prime Ministers, recently widowed, was a boatload more of *Blood and Sand* than Good Old Dirk had bargained for when he became Gustav Rufus's tame rat.

"Just make sure you don't flunk the bloody Bonk Test," said Bowman. "HIV Negative Hosts and crew sail from Miami. The rest of us come aboard at Contentment, to dodge the Customs Hassle."

"And I really ought to dash — " Pam glanced at her Cartier Pasha, from Mark Areias, water-resistant to 30 meters. "*Perhaps*, Godfrey darling, and I'm really *not* being picky, we should get down to Dirk's bonus nitty-gritty?"

"Call a spade a bloody shovel." Bowman leaned across the black waiter. "Entre nous again, Old Dirk, and this one is going to be hard for you to swallow, but you heard it here first. *When we get our arses Over The Rainbow your bonus is a goddamn mountain of Twenty-Two Karat gold!* You can put that in italics and smoke it. Also, as our friends with the funny hats on Fridays would say — and some of my very best friends really are Jewish, and I'd be delighted for my daughter to marry one with the name Rothschild, if I had a daughter — 'I can get it for you wholesale' from my next-door neighbor. In this case, ten per cent margin. Deferred. As derivatives. Take it from the horse's mouth or whichever end of Wall Street you think you can believe: that kind of leverage when the shares are going for sixty-eight cents on their way to sky's the limit and Bobbit's your flipping Market uncle. Just ask little Pam-Pam."

"I don't think there's any more I can add to that except, Kiss-Kiss you both and Many Happies, Dirk. Max love to Miss Montana when you meet." Bending to kiss-kiss she added, "One more fucking Little Pam-Pam and I'll give him Mrs. Bobbitt!"

Pamela St Deney flicked a final Lancôme wink of lashes across the waterlillies and departed as *¡el Tango Volcánico!* ended with the Hitachi erupting shooting stars and Maria doing a ripped-skirt leap to straddle Antonio's out-thrust thigh in a scarlet-pantied *sentada*.

"Encore! Encore!"

The dance pair took bows and bouquets of red roses from the Plaza fans. In place of the volcano, the Hitachi screen showed a montage of sepia images from tango's Golden Age. Singer-composers and band leaders like Gardel, Canaro, Di Sarli, and swirling crowds of thousands in the Dance Halls of Buenos Aires in the 1940's. The sound track sang in Spanish, Discépolo's scratched-lacquer lyrics selling the soul and raffling the heart at 78 rpm . . .

"Ladies hold tight to your partners!" Antonio clutched the microphone in a phallic grip leaving nothing to the ladies' imaginations: *"As a special and unique experience, Maria will choose and dance la Cumparsita once more with a lucky Gentleman of you so wonderful audience!"*

"Dago hoke. Good old Winnie! Ask what they were doing about Adolf in bloody Buenos Aires at the time of his Big V as in Victory churning it out at the bloody Sweat Desk for the Few." Bowman accompanied this Taitinger incoherence with a crude Churchillian two fingers.

Maria had worked half the Plaza Ballroom crowd, allowing her volcanic *sentada* to rest for a moment on wannabe *Malevo* lotharios dressed in Tino Cosima white scarves and trilbies from George Raft gangster movies — before dismissing them with a flick of her spiked heel that sent them back to their life-sentence roles as Big Apple accountants.

"You."

She stopped in front of the head table. Bowman leered at her scarlet satin.

"No. Him."

Her hand reached for Grainger. Top female dancers had an uncanny ability to sense skill in a male, and be ruthless when it was otherwise. He had to respond. Either way risked Drawing Attention. If he refused her invitation, he would be exhibiting unpardonable bad manners — in the Malevo days it would have earned a knife between his ribs — but if he accepted he would have to walk a tightrope, never deviating one step higher than Bronze. In foxtrots and cha-cha's of American Ballroom there was no problem, he just had to follow the judges' rulebook. But Argentinean tango flew without rules. It had the music.

"Pull the bloody finger out. Pussy's dripping. Call it your Bonking dry run. Let's see you get it up."

Bowman blurted crudeness as naturally as breathing. Grainger rose to his feet. The simple act got him too much applause for a spy.

"You know steps?" Maria smiled at him, nodding in the direction of the Hitachi screen. The volcano was back. Music started, just an underlying beat, faintly.

"No volcañicos," Grainger said. "A few basics."

"Good Basic can be greatest."

That was what he was afraid of. The dance from the slums of la Boca had more complexity than all of Arthur Murray. She was still waiting. He saw a flicker of second thought and took her in the Embrace, right arm behind her spine. Left hand holding her opposite one away from the body, forming the Frame. He flexed his left fingers to relax them. Her eyebrows lifted slightly. *La Cumparsita* started.

He knew every note of the Carnival Procession. The conventional basic opening to *salida* was *el retroceso*, Lead's right foot backwards. Instead, he opened sideways, in double-time to his left, three steps to her two, forcing her to syncopate to make the Cross, then quick-quick-slow to *resolucion* beyond it.

She was weightless, her eyes half-shut in satisfaction as he swung her right to Close the Box — but this was the next test.

Skill would break out. Average would go around the box again.

He went around and sensed her disappointment. He eased out of the second dull basic with a simple rock-step left turn that brought her in front of him. Then some safe back *ochos*, a figure-of-eight pattern retreating as he advanced in a stolid side-to-side, barely moving his feet. Again he felt her disappointment.

They had reached a corner, beneath the Hitachi. He had to turn. Average would be simple Left again. He was about to do it when she stole the lead. Another knifing offence in a dark alley of Buenos Aires. She took a Front Step to his right, forcing him to pivot and *sacada* between her legs in rapid succession.

She smiled.

It was too flashy. He locked her for a moment in a *calecita*, pressing her breasts tight against his chest in a milonguero holding-pattern invisible to on-lookers, then deliberately started another basic.

She stole again. Holding his right foot between both of hers.

"*El sandwich*." she murmured. "Eat me."

He broke with a modest hook behind her calf. She gancho'd so high in return that he felt her heel flick his cock. By defence reflex, he did a reverse leg wrap, she front boleo'd, he lunged —

Applause.

They were out of Bronze territory, heading through Silver; if he did the Curving Rear Corrida her body was begging for they'd be halfway to Gold stars. An impossible situation for a second-rate Dance Host. He couldn't stop the start of the curve, or the check-and-balanceo, but where he should displace Right . . . he stuck out the wrong foot.

She still got around it. She was marvelous. He would have died to dance with her all night. But not on a Mission. He stopped for a moment, while he appeared to be trying to remember, and gave her an amateur's apologetic smile.

She returned it gracefully, like a pro. *La Cumparsita* ended. Their Little Carnival was over. He kissed her hand. The audience applauded, but only for a job well Bronzed. In the middle of the clapping she kissed his ear, and breathed in Spanish,

"Malevo. Betray me again one day in Buenos Aires. And next time, don't cheat."

At the head table Grainger's high-wire act went safely unnoticed. Between the World Class waterlillies, Lord Bowman of Misappropriated Churchilliana had flaked out.

Con Brio
Two

MIAMI WAS A FIRST COUSIN OF THE TANGO. BOTH SHARED A Latin sense of imminent explosion from mundane sub-tropical artifacts. Spike heels on a dance floor: whatever came to hand in that moment after orgasm's *petit mort*. An everyday pistol from a pawn shop got Versace. This morning's headline Florida killing was a hand grenade inside a lover's breakfast grapefruit. Grainger read about it in the *Herald* as he waited for his gigolo audition.

"Next."

The word echoed in the vastness of the Boarding Shed, disturbing pigeons beside the ventilator grille of a fan that didn't work. Grainger recalled Jacques Brel's song about soldiers waiting for their moment in the Army brothel. The figure in front of him moved through a rippled-glass doorway from a Bogart movie, leaving behind the smell of booze.

"Next! That's you."

The male voice had a hint of Continental, to hide the Bronx. A plastic badge ID'd its wearer as Ricardo Avar ("Dr. Salsa") Dance Director. The Old Spy net had confirmed that the party of the first part of Ricky Avar had managed his initial Arthur Murray franchise as Ronald Evans in Tribeca.

"Last Name?"

"Grainger," said Grainger, with the shade of Spy Nanny hanging over him again from another film buff's maxim. *"Never trust a man with a Vincent Price moustache."*

The hairline above Avar's upper lip was pencil thin. And dyed.

"Grainger ees good for the weemin name. What ees First, then Dance Experience, Straight or Gay, includes Bi, with recent Negative blood test, and can you be Bonded?"

"Yes, and I'm Straight." Grainger produced a bona fide Negative lab report — Bowman hadn't been bullshitting about HIV. "I've got Society Bronze for Instructing anything in Ballroom. Lambada, I picked up on my own. And some Salsa, in Cuba. The first name for a bonding query is Stuart, otherwise it's Dirk."

"Forget Cuba and salsa. Am I 'earing a Brit accent?"

"Mid-Atlantic. Half-and-half."

"Straight Negative, wiz Dirk, ze weedows will go gaga for Lambada on ze gin. Better being Gay Positive if you want sleep. Show me your Bronze. Naturally I 'ave Gold."

Avar's accent slipped when the Dance Director got down to business. And if "Dr. Salsa's" dye-job was anything to go by, the Gold was tarnished. Grainger produced a genuine Bronze Certificate, obtained during his second marriage, before the Afghans ate his shoes.

"Okay. Bonding happens by computer. If eet checks, you can sail. Our contract covers cleaning. You provide your own cloze. Here's the list. Four changes minimum for tropics. Be back to board by six. And no fun stuff in the garment bags. Customs use dogs. Next!"

Outside the boarding shed Grainger stood in the shade of a Florida Palm and studied the Wardrobe List for a maritime Dance Host:

Black Tux

White "

Blue Blazer

Lounge Suit (super lite)

Costume Ball

NB: Re Decorum. Nothing suggestive.

(For Trannies: No flaming. Keep it in the closet!)

He'd guessed the first four and didn't need the final warning. The Costume Ball was a problem. Plenty of Fancy Dress shops in the Greater Miami Yellow Pages offered "Special & Exotic for the Love Boat" — one even had "Fig Leaves for Cruise in the Nude" — but by the time he crossed off anything that might be Flaming in Avar's rule book (transvestite Popes and Cardinals), or Draw Attention in his own (too tall to be Napoleon), he was left with Zorro and Scaramouche. Zorro in black would be too hot. He took his namesake's likeness. The store clerk had never heard of either.

"Like a pirate," Grainger said.

"How about Admiral Nelson?" The clerk dug out a catalogue glossy of Laurence Olivier promoing Vivienne Leigh in *Lady Hamilton*. "Here's an eye patch. And Long John Silver's crutches."

Grainger compromised with the Nelson patch and a poster of Douglas Fairbanks Jr as *Sinbad the Sailor* without the pantaloons.

"You want Sinbad in riding breeches?" said the clerk.

"Plus a blouse shirt and a bandanna." And thigh-high, vinyl boots from the Three Musketeers with D'Artagnon's rubber sword.

Spy Nanny would have loved it. Grainger needed a stiff drink.

He returned to the dock fifteen minutes early, expecting a handful of crew members. Instead, he found four thousand sweating passengers in the frantic state between over-exhaustion and Lost Luggage. Two Love Boats on turnaround were scheduled to sail at the same time. Customs and Immigration had geared for one.

The 5-Star Treatment promised in the brochures only started at the head of the gangways. Pandemonium reigned inside the Boarding Shed. Grainger barely managed to get himself and his Host wardrobe through the crowd to meet Avar's deadline for departure. Inside the rippled glass door the Dance Director was watching the Exploding Grapefruit as The World at Six headliner for local news.

"You're late." Avar flicked a remote. Entertainment Tonite. Without warning, Grainger saw his cover blown up instead of the grapefruit. The screen revealed him tangoing at the Plaza as a voice-over said,

"Last night's Latin shindig for celebs like Lord God —"

Avar hit mute to kill the sound byte. But if the picture showed a Dance Host applicant quaffing Taitinger with Bowman . . . ?

Tab Shit TV stuck with a zoom of Maria's scarlet panties. Grainger was only a pointed shoe between her legs. The point where he deliberately forgot the step. A sudden cutaway shot caught the embarrassed-amateur smile on his face just as Avar looked up.

"Some nerve," said Rickie, between accents. "You play the Plaza and can't triple sacada? Zeeze iz ze difference between Hosts and Directors. Your Bonding checks. Get on board right away."

"How?" Grainger pointed past the rippled door at the abattoir scene in the Boarding Shed. The sweating throng had grown even denser and more stunned by jet lag. A group of Mature women wearing We Love our Love Boat tee shirts were in tears.

"Forget them." Avar produced a *Dirk: Your Bonded Dance Host* piece of plastic and jerked his head towards a second door, with no glass, in the wall beside the TV set. As Grainger opened it, Entertainment Tonite panned from Maria's underwear to offer voyeurs another fifteen-second glimpse of fame with a Big F. Bowman flaked out, face down, at the Plaza's head table.

The second door let in fresh air. It carried the timeless smells of harbors — salt and tar, plus fish in subtly changing shades of decay — overtaken by the toxins of marine technology: Diesel and bunker oil. Four degrees north of Cancer, Grainger's nose also caught tropic hints of rotting fruit and flowers. Heaped in mounds against the back wall of the Boarding Shed he saw Frangipani necklaces and orchid corsages; wilted reminders of Paradise on cruises past. His future was parked dead ahead.

PRINCESS LINES
No Boarding without DEA Clearance!
SHOW PASSES

The twinned bulk of two Love Boats blocked out Miami's skyline. The Space Age vessels could have been Las Vegas hotels waiting to be fired into orbit as crew quarters for Star Wars: nothing marked them with sailors' ageless life at sea except the rat guards on their massive polypropylene hawsers.

"Hold it. Let's see your ID."

He produced his Bonded Host plastic. A mongrel working for the Drug Enforcement Agency sniffed at his Scaramouche garment bag. Both operatives were satisfied. The human waved him through. The canine waved its tail.

"Not that way. Pier Eighteen for Southern Cross." The DEA guard pointed to starboard of the Love Boats. "Better hurry, the tugs are on overtime."

Grainger slung the Scaramouche bag over his shoulder and set off along a concrete jetty with grass growing out of it. Halogen lamps starkly defined the blades and cracks. In the few minutes since leaving Avar's office night had descended on Miami. With the Love Boats behind him, he could see the neon pulse of Entertainment Ashore. Already it seemed remote. The sea was calling.

Southern Cross
Crew Only

The sign was hand stenciled and the last Empress looked like a ship, not Las Vegas. Rows of round portholes instead of plate glass windows. Three funnels doing the work they were designed for: transmission of sea power from steam through smoke.

A puff of white proved the steam was real. A millisecond later the siren's upper blast hit his ears, then the bass resonated in his gut. Two toots on a tug's whistle answered the pipe organ. A buzzer buzzed. A red light flashed on a crane about to raise the gangway.

"You with the bag! Get the lead out!"

The crane-operator gave him a Bowman two-finger salute for

causing the delay, but slacked off for a moment. The end of the gangway entered the ship's side two rows of portholes below the upper deck. An officer with seadog written on his face took one look at the Bonded Host plastic, said "Last one's always a bloody dancer!" and waved him by, just fashionably late enough not to draw attention.

Cover intact, he was afloat.

Con Brio
Three

THE FITTINGS ON THE *SS SOUTHERN CROSS* BROUGHT BACK THE Gilded Age for one last run before Designed-by-Silicon took over life at sea. The gold-leaf rim around the plate supporting Grainger's breakfast sausage was the real thing. Unlike Ricardo Avar's Ballroom Certificate: an overnight enquiry via Pam's ThinkPad returned a verdict of "Not Completed" from the Dance Society's Central Registry on Ronald Evans, who only got his Silver thanks to some dodgy footwork on the part of the former Arthur Murray Bronx franchisee.

Nothing was phony on the *Southern Cross*. Even the letters before her name meant what they said: *SS* for Steam Ship. There were three boiler rooms, one for each funnel. The watertight compartments were just that. The portholes were brass. The three propellers, bronze. The Promenade and all other decks on her upper works were solid teak. The Famous Passengers' signatures on the last Empress's cabin door portraits of "Larry" Olivier and "Viv" Leigh were certified by Sotheby's. From Captain down to the newest watch keeper, the *Southern Cross* officers all had their Master's or Mate's Certificates for blue water sailing and the certificates were vouched for by the British Board of Trade.

There was only one nautical storm warning in such competence: the Blue Ensign streaming from the stern signaled to the maritime world that the Master of this vessel had once served in Great Britain's Royal Navy. Captain Philip Dawson-Harris even took a one-year course at Greenwich Naval College before it was turned into a tourist museum. The problem confronting Grainger as he finished his breakfast banger was that they took the course together.

Dawson-Harris knew him as 'Grainge'. Dr. Salsa Avar, as 'Dirk'.

There was no way around it. A Dance Host didn't get an Outside Cabin on A Deck but he ate his meals with the grownups; in the Main Dining Room. When the Ladies joined the voyage he would rotate in accordance with the Seating Placement notice posted daily in the Purser's Office. For this breakfast the great room was cavernously empty, only two of forty tables being served. Himself, in solitary at the

Chief Purser's Number 22 — only ten feet away from Number 1.

The Captain's.

He had dodged the Entertainment Tonight risk of Blown Cover by blind luck. To be an honest spy this morning, he would have to meet the crisis in the time-honored manner laid down by the Navy's Rules of the Road for moments like Mess Dinner bun fights in the Painted Hall at Greenwich.

When in danger or in doubt,
Wag your dick and go about!

In those far-off, pre-Spy Nanny days of life as *The Winslow Boy*, Dawson-Harris was Young Dorkers when Good Old Dirk was still plain Grainge. He laid down his linen napkin as Midshipmen were instructed in Mess Dinner Etiquette by the Chief Steward — "not folded neatly, Gentlemen, this isn't a whore's drawers in a Fiji bang-bang shop! Just drop your wiper like a bleeding pocket handkerchief beside the plate. Thus." — stood up, and walked three paces towards Harris's starched white back. Four gold stripes gleamed from the epaulettes on each squared shoulder. The stripes had no curl. That tiny difference represented the gulf between Merchant Marine and Royal Navy. In Harris's case the professional gulf was wider: where Grainge had been Regular Force at the Bun fights, Dorkers was only in the Reserve.

Naval snobbery from the past might not add to his Twin Identity problem today but Etiquette was still a force to be reckoned with: a Dance Host couldn't be the first to say Good Morning to a Captain. Instead, he took the junior officer's approach, standing tactfully to one side of his superior's right shoulder, waiting for the moment to catch his eye.

"I wondered how you'd pull that off." Harris gave him a nod, and small smile, then gestured at an empty chair. "I saw 'Grainger' on the manifest last night and looked up your likeness on the Security computer file. Except for the new nickname, you haven't changed much. Curious how the world goes round. Join me for a coffee if you're not already awash."

Even if he was, a Dance Host wouldn't refuse the invitation. Grainger sat down in the chair, and while the Steward filled his Wedgwood cup from a sterling silver pot, considered the circularity of fate that had made Harris come to resemble Robert Donat — the Winslow lead — and more seriously, how to play being honest?

"Victim of the Golden Handshake, I suppose." Harris said. Captains of cruise liners overloaded with widows become past masters at tact. "I'm glad it doesn't seem to have shaken your self-respect. Don't let it on my account. We're all gigolos for the Company once we come down from the Bridge."

Their conversation steered into the usual doldrums of male mid-life; names remembered, some achieving, others dead.

"Any kids?" Harris asked. Grainger shook his head. "Four in my case, a mixed blessing. Two daughters are all set, both snapped up by Merchant Banks. These days it's the boys who have the problems. Bright lads, but no sense that doors will open —"

"Excuse me, Sir." The Chief Steward lowered his voice and spoke into Harris's ear. "First Officer says his compliments, and we're approaching the Hudson Limit."

"Very Good." Captain Dawson-Harris dropped his napkin like Young Dorkers' bleeding pocket handkerchief, and rose from his seat in a single action. Grainger followed suit, then stepped back a pace. "If you've nothing better to do," Harris said, "join me for the run in to the Cay. It isn't driving destroyers but momentum versus inertia of twenty-thousand tons can provide their own thrill."

Grainger hesitated. As Grainge he would like to watch it. Dirk the Dance Host shouldn't.

"If you're worried about your Director's Instructions, don't. First, Señor Avar isn't aboard — Doctor Salsa has a pattern of joining late to dodge US Immigration — and as far as your future partners are concerned, being seen on the bridge will give you a considerable boost in the estimation of the handful who may prove eligible. Looking at the Golden gift horse head-on, isn't a bad motto."

As they walked from the Dining Room to the business part of the ship along companionways paneled with clear-grain mahogany and rosewood inlay framing Larry & Viv, Grainger asked, "Did you mean that these widows' runs lead to genuine romance?"

"Subject to tax advice. They aren't all widowed. In this money league, the weaker sex can abandon ship and spouse at home ports of their own choosing."

Hudson Cay was only a faint thickening of the horizon when Grainger followed Dawson-Harris into the Captain's kingdom of an ocean liner's bridge. This one was complete even down to the obligatory three red-painted buckets of sand for fire-fighting as demanded by Board of Trade Regulations before automated CO_2 systems became the fashion:

smothering engine rooms with Carbon Dioxide — hopefully after their crews had left to join the rats.

Communication between the brain at the top of the ship and its beating heart ten decks down was still by Engine Telegraph: rotary brass handles and ringing bells made familiar to a landlocked movie generation through the latest reincarnation of *Titanic*, but every fitting on this bridge was made in Belfast, to Harland and Woolf's instructions, not Hollywood's. Yet somehow the very genuiness of the articles made Grainger's situation more unreal. He felt as though he was part of an Agatha Christie rerun on A&E: at any moment the waxed points of Hercule Poirot's absurd moustache might appear towing Miss Lemon and a teacup of *tisane*.

He blamed the adrenaline rush of being back at sea for his overactive imagination. Nostalgia was the most debilitating of Nanny's spy-movie vices. It would have to be reined in.

"Hudson Limit, Sir. Range to the Cay, three miles."

The thickening of the horizon became a green smudge on radar, crescent-shaped, with a notch in its middle. Everywhere else in the maritime world, twelve nautical miles had been adopted as the modern standard for national boundaries: in this left-over corner of the Caribbean a mixture of history and chicanery had kept limits down to three. Contentment, like Puerto Rico, was part of the American Way of Life only when it suited both parties to be united.

"Take off her way."

The telegraph bells clanged in response to Harris's order. If Grainger gave the same command in a destroyer, physical objects like parallel rulers would roll off the chart table as the warship stopped. Aboard the *Southern Cross*, nothing happened, except that the radar smudge got a mile closer.

"All engines, half-astern."

The order was repeated by the watch keeper, and telegraphs. The smudge became a dotted line of palms punctuated by typical condo-resort development. A floating coconut bobbed eighty feet below the elbow Grainger was leaning on the wind baffle of the bridge wing.

My port of last resort . . . ?

He didn't like the way his mind was drifting this morning. His concentration should be for the job at hand. That was the problem: he didn't like the job. It was fine to be towed along in the captain's wake, but for the rest of the voyage there was no disguising the looks from real working mariners for a piece of flotsam tagged Dance Host.

"Stop all engines."

More clanging bells.

"All engines stopped, Sir."

The liner hadn't seemed to go astern, but the coconut was bobbing in the opposite direction.

"Let go!"

The shuddering rumble of anchor chain through hawse pipes transmitted itself to his feet. The *Southern Cross* came to rest precisely where she should be: anchored five cables off-shore, centred in the radar notch. By eye, it was a marina behind a breakwater. A deluxe launch headed towards them.

"Time for all of us to put on our dancing shoes." Harris gave a friendly nod of dismissal that put each of them back in their place. "The Dow's rising again. More than I can say for the barometer."

Catering to the embarking passengers' main concern, a digitized stock-ticker had been fastened to the bulkhead above the old-fashioned red fire buckets. The tape's dotted line showed . . . 9448 . . . for Wall Street's Opening. As Harris left the bridge an up-tick made it an even 9450 over the three buckets. Nanny used to compare spying to running by The Board of Trade Rules:

"Seventeenth Century sand for ships entering the Twenty-First seems stupid on the surface of things, but every time you trip across one of the sods in the dark of a Mission Middle Watch it acts as a reminder. Good cover must be three layers deep. Four's better. Five perfect. Just keep them straight. No trips."

Translated to this Mission, his top cover was Bronze Instruction of widowed weemin in the fine art of dancing to keep out the dark that lay ahead. The fine line of Ricardo Avar's, née Ronnie Evans', upper lip was visible through binoculars. The Dance Director stood next to a spectacular female shape in the waist of the approaching launch.

The second-layer cover was ghost-editing the "maybe's" out of Bowman's potboiler, Chasing Brio. Covering *that* was his Third Layer contract with Pam to report faithfully enough on all the backstage "perhaps's" aboard the Vanity Cruise of a Lifetime to titillate magazine lip readers who couldn't afford the tips.

Layer Four was Gustav Rufus, and the Mission focal point: confirmation of the bursting of a Bubble in time for the richest man in the Derivative world to leverage another incalculable fortune from everyone else's Crash.

Layer Five — was coping with the Unexpected. On this Mission that could be Mags: dancing on a burning deck with a widowed Prime Minister hadn't been covered in Spy Nanny's Winslow Boy syllabus. With the layers straightened out in his head, Grainger went below to dream up his first ThinkPad slashed gossip to Pam.

```
//From the horse's Golden arse: the Chief
Steward. Dr. Salsa is tarnished silver.
(The Chief just had a new bridge installed
by "Bill & Hill's" Dentist). Nobody
believes the party or the Dow will ever
end at the Captain's Table. The Marconi
Room has framed photo of Signor M with
Mary Pickford and direct sat-link to feed
latest Two Tits Assay reading from New
Guinea. I sank half your Fair advance in
Brio last night and it floated from 72
cents to 5 bucks with the coconuts this
morning!

          Cha-ch-
```

A syncopated knock on the cabin door interrupted the last cha. Grainger said, "Just a minute!," keyed **//pam @ van_fair.com**, into the ThinkPad — before he could click Send, the door opened.

"Hi. I'm Randy." Male, bucktoothed, with a ponytail on the wrong side of forty. Also dyed, blond, not recently enough to be convincing. "Last name's Smith, but we make it Randall Smythe for the program. I play piano. The Purser's Assistant screwed up last night. We're sharing."

Grainger had shared accommodation from Mongolian yurt tents to Inuit igloos but his fellow occupants on those occasions couldn't interpret if a spy spoke in his sleep. Smith-slash-Smythe looked past him at the ThinkPad.

"Seems like you're a writer when you aren't dancing. What have we got — the Great Cruise Novel for Vanity Fair?"

"An E-mail about my subscription." He zapped Pam's text into a screensaver of luminous fish chasing winged toasters and wondered where to find the line between suspicion and honest paranoia about the Assistant Purser. It wasn't Unexpected that Vulkan or Pitcairn Proprietary could have a Counter-Intelligence vet to check the livestock before this ark beached on their Golden Mountain.

"Don't mind me." Smythe-Smith dumped a Yamaha with dangling patch cords, labeled KARAOKE IN and OUT. "I'll just leave the keyboard.

It's for my yodel practice while you're giving your rumba lessons to the Blue Rinse crowd. I have to grab my other bags. Back in five."

Grainger allowed ten seconds for the ponytail to round a corner of the C-Deck passage . . . then stepped into it, locked the cabin door, pocketed the key, and set off to exhibit some artistic Song and Dance temperament at the Purser's Office.

The Assistant was dressing down a junior steward about "Sex in a linen cupboard on Company hours!" The Chief Purser tossed breach-of-discipline aside and picked up Cabin Allocations.

"I can guess what you're here for, Mr. Grainger. Sorry about the cabin sharing foul-up, but I didn't realise until breakfast that you and the Captain were old Naval hands. We're traveling light anyway for this Dow run, normal complement of passengers adds another hundred. I can't come up with Winnie's favourite — Lord Bowman's just taken the Churchill, as well as the Olivier — but I can give you an Outside Deanna Durbin to yourself on B-Deck. It faces north once we head east, which keeps you in the shade until we cross the Line. At least you'll be spared bloody Randy Karaoke."

The Chief Purser looked sharply at the junior steward. "And you stay out of bloody linen cupboards any time. Now shift Mr. Grainger into Deanna Durbin, and look sharp about it. He's got to make the Bonking Rules."

The Bonking Rules, otherwise known as Dance Deportment On & Off the Floor, was scheduled by Avar for the Antares Lounge at 10:00. A list of topics was posted on a notice board resting on an artist's easel beside the Orion's Belt Bar. The major constellations formed the ceiling — deckhead, in navalese — of the Lounge. Grainger found his twelve fellow Hosts under the Seven Sisters of Pleiades. A silver-templed gent in a Lounge Suit (super lite), stepped forward.

"Jonathon Trimble, Union Rep. Welcome to the Bonkers' Dozen, you make us Lucky Thirteen for this trip. Only one ground rule: we ignore Doctor Salsa." Who arrived at that moment. The handle of the Big Dipper pointed at the Dance Director's Vincent Price moustache.

"Zeeze eez ze List of ze Do's and Dont's for JHosts." Ex Ronnie Evans had added a Spanish soft 'j" to his accent. He jerked his head at the easel. "Zoze of you who 'ave JHosted already may sink you know all ziz by 'eart — well, forget it!" Avar's Latin touch cut to a Bronx cheer. "This time you'll be hosting Real Money so don't any of you think you can make the usual play for it. Keep your cocks at half mast at all Workshops. That includes the Lambada. Say you love Lox on a Bagel, even if you've never goddamn heard of it already! And no Jack in the Box unless the Lady puts it in writing. Yes means Yes. Witnessed by her lawyer. As Director, I get first crack at the Privates. Eez ziz clear?"

The Bonkers Dozen ignored ziz with a collective shrug. Avar ran down another JHost list of Required Steps and Degrees of Difficulty. "A final note for ze bizness side. First dance on board will not be until tomorrow but zere will be a party ashore tonight which means three Workshop volunteers. You, you, and you."

Grainger found himself part of a phrase he hadn't heard since he passed the Snotties' sword-and-tennis-racquet test.

"Sun's over the yardarm, Gentlemen."

He hadn't heard that one since he swapped his commission. The Orion's Belt barman placed a bowl of plastic-parasol swizzle sticks in front of him and said, "You look like you could use a long and strong after Doctor Salsa's first crack at the Privates."

True, but Good Old Dirk shouldn't let his face show it. He accepted the drink and sat back to pick up the Dance Hosting background dirt that counted.

One third of the gigolo crew had sailed together on previous voyages. Another third had sailed with Señor Avar separately. The rest had done neither and had a table assigned in the Lounge with a place holder labelled "For Virgins Who've Never Bedded a Cruise Widow." Dirk drifted towards them in time to join the Bonkers' Union Anthem, with Randy Karaoke's ponytail at the piano.

Although the job is hateful
The ladies are so grateful,
And someone's got to do it
When the Old Man bellows screw it —!

"This must be the workshop on Political Correctness." said a female American voice. "I'm Lord Bowman's Research Assistant, Holly Briar."

Code name, Miss Montana. The Bonkers Dozen stared opened-mouthed beneath the Seven Sisters. Grainger turned his head to be honestly charming and found himself swept off his feet.

Miss Montana was long and blonde, plus a perfect profile. An American Beauty Queen from *State Fair*, with a genuine-rhinestone-tiara smile and an accent trailing Big Sky spaces in the shadow of the Rockies. She wasn't charmed by him. Her hand, with long fingers and perfect nails, was extended to Avar. "His Lordship would like a Romeo to give a tango lesson to his wife before tonight's party," she informed the Dance Director. "He sent me to pick one out who can blend." She finally turned her green eyes in Grainger's direction, and said as though Juliet couldn't care less, "This one will do."

The Bonkers Dozen resumed as she left:

Fuck 'em all. Fuck 'em all,
The wizened who can't even crawl . . .
We'll get no promotion for showing emotion,
If they're halt and they're lame, fuck 'em all!

Grainger said he had unfinished business with Deanna Durbin.

Cabin B-109 had an autographed publicity still of the Star of *Lady on a Train*, only one bed (maple-burled, queen-size), and his effects had been transferred. The screensaver fish were still chasing toasters on the ThinkPad. He clicked to a rhinestone web site for Miss Montanas. Holly Briar's tiara was genuine, and came with a Harvard scholarship in Modern History & Music.

He pursued her through the Swimsuit Competition (one-piece), and Talent (2nd Oboe from the Billings High Band) to her birthplace, Great Falls, on Christmas Day, which according to the Year Book Sweetheart explained her first name. Her first love was horses. He clicked off, brought back Pam's gossip and added //: Just met Miss Montana. Lost for words.

He gazed for a moment at three unhappy palm trees through a porthole, signed off in Spy Nanny-approved code, via double-encryption for the triple password, put the Sony mini-recorder in his Super Lite host pocket, prepared to go ashore and blend with Holly Briar.

Con Brio
Four

CONTENTMENT WAS A MAIDEN AUNT AT A HOME WALTZ: barely rotating banked passions of silent partners with numbered accounts, a light-year and ninety nautical miles safely quarantined from the tango of Miami's melting-pot. When Grainger stepped from the launch in the late afternoon, nothing moved on Hudson Cay except the sprinklers. Even the flags on the putting greens were immobile: drooped in the thermal tropic moment between Viagra prescriptions and offshore winds.

A battery-driven golf cart waited on the jetty. The cart had no driver, but its exhaust-free engine was running. He was reminded of the sole TV series that got Nanny-approved for spy audiences: *The Prisoner,* with Patrick McGooghan waiting to be trapped again in The Village by the lethal balloon of Number One.

"Over here!" His rescuer was Holly Briar, emerging with Lauren Bacall's stride from a palm-thatched hut behind the golf cart. The hut had a small sign, Snacks and Security. Close enough to read the fine print for Contentment Environmental Rules on Emission Control, the palm leaves on the roof became ceramic tiles. Mini-Surveillance lenses peeked out between them.

"Residents don't have to go through this," she told him, "but as a Visiting Alien you'll have to step inside to have your hand read. The monitor is next to the Live Bait. Make sure all five fingers touch the pad or it'll squawk."

Holly Briar also had Lauren Bacall's voice. Grainger felt the red-cells remaining in his blood stream rising. He placed his hand next to the Live Bait. A green light flashed.

"Open sesame," she said. "You made a good impression, but I guess you Host guys have to go through a lot of security shit getting bonded."

If Miss Montana with all her State Fair female antennae for judging men, bought his cover, Vulkan's Para has-beens should be a pushover in New Guinea. She matched him stride for stride back to the golf cart.

"I hear you met Godfrey at some dance show in New York while I came down ahead. How about Freda?"

Grainger said, "Not yet," and tried the impossible balancing act of honestly noticing, but not crudely staring at, the way Holly Briar's Lycra-cotton Lands End shorts pushed against her perfect crotch as she pressed a Nu Buck sandalled foot on the golf cart's accelerator.

"One hired hand to another, I guess it's only fair to warn you again about all the names being 'knickered' by Lord God." She gestured at million-dollar cottages of former chief Democrats or Despots eking out their Indian Summers with absentee tycoons who only showed up for the pages of Architectural Digest. " 'Ruffles' lives over there, but he's mostly in Dallas, managing the Rufus Boomer Fund. That fuchsia monstrosity is 'Wee Willie's' — Vulkan's CEO, Williams; he's physically huge, but don't expect any big tips. And he won't be at tonight's party, he flew back to Le Breton last week. That newest one's Chateau Mags, beside 'Animal Crackers'. Sorry, I mean the priest, not the house." She dispensed a State Fair smile for a skeletal nonagenarian clad all in black, shakily supported by Anglican bishop's gaiters. "A combination of Canterbury and Rasputin with Parkinson's, he used to be Chaplain at Chequers. Harmless except about sex between household pets."

The mad priest used Latin to address a longhaired Himalayan cat halfway up an Avocado tree. The cat gazed back impassively — then jumped over his head into the middle of the road. Holly Briar slammed the brakes. The priest warded off the Himalayan's devil-blue eyes with a shaky sign of the cross, saw Grainger staring and responded with a querulous, "*Maleficium diabolicum per . . .*"

The Himalayan took the last word as gospel and sauntered, purring, with its chocolate-tipped tail in bottle-brush attitude into the Chateau garden. "At least you won't have to worry about Mags for a client," said Holly Briar. "She's missed the boat, on a book tour. But how are you on Nordic mythology?" The loony priest's Latin malediction faded as the golf cart hummed on past more rising monuments to duty-free money chasing *Brio's* bad taste.

Grainger said, "I'm only here to teach the tango. How long have you been a Research hired hand?"

"Exactly two days and I've yet to meet my employer face to face. Godfrey's still somewhere between the Big Apple and Contentment. He doesn't do anything by the book. I was hired via one conference call with his agent."

"Sid the Yid."

"The 'nickers' thing gets cruder the more up-close and personal you get to Bowman," she said, as the golf cart arrived outside a pair of gates with another ceramic-thatch roof and mini-cameras over the arch. "Freda does this Jungian 'Frey-and-Freya in Valhalla' act between them on the speaker phone when they can't have afternoon sex. God-frey, Frey-God, don't sweat it."

That was easy. Spy Nanny's Intelligence generation trusted nothing Germanic. Another Miss Montana smile at a mini-cam opened the gates. As they drove through she said, "I don't see Freda doing tango on a heaving deck but the Argentine version's something I've always wanted to learn. If you have time between rich widows and New Guinea, how about teaching me?"

She stopped the cart under a pink stucco portico guarded by nude cherubs of the same material. Double front doors behind them were hand-carved imitations from palazzos in Venice, modified for rot resistance and electronic anti-intrusion. The nudes had already begun to shed their stucco skins from too much Caribbean salt and sun. East of the cherubs a computer-designed addition the size of the main building was slowly morphing into Marie Antoinette's playhouse from Versailles. An imported Jamaican framing crew taking an extended lunch break sat on the plans.

"That's the new Blenheim Wing, from Brio's advance. If you need to wash your hands, there are five bathrooms, but the closest john is off the hall, by the Chartwell Study." Holly Briar pointed a perfect fingernail due west. "If we see the red light on over the study it means Godfrey's doing his Churchill Dictation act, which means he'll want me like yesterday, for Corroborative Detail. As you've been bonded, I guess I can leave you to find Freda without stealing the Probable Van Gogh and the Genuine Goya — his first go at a Naked Maja."

She bestowed her tiara-smile and left him to wash his hands under $500 Kohler gold taps that dripped for want of a twenty-cent washer.

He emerged and found Freda. He couldn't have missed her. The newest Lady Bowman wore a Day-Glo-Purple muumuu and weighed at least three hundred pounds.

"Purple is the colour of my aura and you are Mr. Grainger. Shall we dance?"

Freda's invitation didn't fit anywhere on Avar's Bonking List of Deportment Do's and Don't's. Even a Buenos Aires pro would boggle at sacadas with a Full Size novice and her aura.

"How much Argentine Style have you already done, Doctor —?"

"No titles between us. Paraphrasing what Carl Jung himself so beautifully said: 'A week of Freud is enough for all the penis-envy before thirty. Then we have a lifetime to find our Archetypal Whole.' Mine is still virgin to the goddess Tango. For dancing, like love-making, I am Freya, you shall be my Magic Dirk."

He did a mental search for a magic Rear Opening with the least risk of being trampled to death — then spotted a CD of Di Sarli on a Bang and Olufsen player. *A la Gran Muñeca*. Big Doll. He hit the play button and waited for the beat.

An elephant could quadrado to Di Sarli's 1940's baton. Grainger assumed the most Open Embrace possible. To get his right arm even partly across her purple back meant being engulfed by the Moo Moo chasm between her breasts. The thumping of her heart was picked up by the red light of his pocket Sony.

"We'll begin with a walk. You step backwards. Take the longest paces you can. Toe first, imagining a hole in the floor of a dark attic you wouldn't want to fall through."

"You have a so-Jungian gift for description, my Dirk." And she had the balletic lightness that often accompanied bodies of great weight. Their procession was heading for a corner, under the Maja, which would normally call for a rock-step turn. He took a leaf from the *Southern Cross* approaching anchorage and led her into a slow curve. "New learning experiences in our sexuality should be always this pure pleasure," Freda confided to Sony. "But already I have given away too much with my 'So' for our first tango, have I not?"

Goya's Pubic Maja passed safely behind his shoulder. Lady Luck's Zurich accent wasn't her major problem. Interpol said her Archetypal Whole existed as a clinic in Küsnacht specializing in De-Tox for Tax Evaders under the guise of Jungian Dreamers. Bowman got to Swiss care-giving from the Tranny-hooker nightmare in Paris that cost him his last wife.

"Do you not ask yourself, my Dirk, as a magician with no father — 'Who were these paternal containers who gave us our genes?' "

There was more to Freda than psycho-babble. Grainger's Big Lie (about 'James', as his father's name) wasn't an open secret; the facts of his illegitimacy could only be accessed by a Freedom of Information request.

He steered her past the Probable Van Gogh of a canal barge being towed by a wall-eyed horse, and said, "The difference between this dance and Ballroom is that we can be out of step in Argentine tango."

"Changing the subject, this is so Freudian. I told the poor man who discovered Brio last week, 'Fear of death with four wives is nothing to be ashamed of astrologically. But as a Scorpio, dear Mr. De Cosmos, you should be prepared for the tax bite, and alimony increases will also be natural from the world's richest gold mine'."

The warning light over the Chartwell Study door was red.

Bowman must be back. Time to tread even more carefully. Grainger did a Cross-footed syncopation which brought him out on his vast partner's left side, where the Lead didn't have to think about tango and could concentrate on Brio. The claim was spiked months ago. The bigamist who visited the Cay last week was the Mine's principal geologist — in a head-hunting state of anxiety or De Cosmos wouldn't have been consulting Contentment's only shrink. Who lived two pink-stucco'd archways down the yellow-brick-road road from the bigamist's boss: Vulkan Mining's Wee Willie, who hightailed back to the headhunters immediately after the Scorpio visit. Freda sailed on with her Archetype's life story. "In my case, Oedipus and Elektra were disposed of at the age of six weeks when Baby Freya was found —"

"For Christ's sake, woman! I can't hear myself bloody think!"

The door to Bowman's Sweat & Tears sanctum crashed open. Grainger found himself in line-of-dance with the Battle of Britain Desk. Freda came to anchor under the Maja.

"I've had a brain wave," said *Chasing Brio's* creator. "We add the Southern Cross as prologue, cashing in on Cameron's Titanic."

Inside the study door, Holly Briar caught Grainger's eye and gave a blink covering a wink. She said to her employer, "The note you left for me about Brio said, 'Like Conrad'."

Bowman took her Research assistance straight. " 'Nostromo for the Nineties.' Talking to L.A. we'll have to make that the Millennium. The weird thing — and this is how I know it is Art with a Big A: Genius anticipates. I already had the first draft before the stock was even being traded! In the exact part of the globe. Plus or minus, no one's going to quibble over a thousand miles of trackless pollution for the Discovery Channel. I had the Brio story and then De Cosmos strikes the Mother Lode —"

"*Rest!*" Freda's aura swept forward in a purple bow-wave that gathered Bowman's nickered genius into her muumuu for a Valhalla afternoon.

Alone in Contentment with Holly Briar and the possible Van Gogh, Grainger hoped that the Big L moving his anatomy was only the lust for life and beauty that any man his age would feel stuck on a desert island where even the golf flags drooped. Lust he could handle: Love was that Miami grenade in the grapefruit. Pull the pin and blow the Mission.

"How about a first lesson here? We can make it a cash transaction. What's your going rate?" She stood between Bang and Olufsen's technology and the voluptuousness of Goya's Maja. Her tone matched the Boarding Officer's for a gigolo arriving late.

"Tango rhythm has to match personality," he said, trying to convince himself that her putdown tone was only playing Bacall in *To Have and Have Not*, daring Bogie to whistle. "Di Sarli was fine for Freda, but his Big Doll doesn't suit you."

"And my going-rate dig was a cheap shot. Sorry. Let's see what else we've got." She gave him a Bacall friends-again smile and waved her hand at the B&O. The player's glass doors slid open. With electronic magic and Danish design its carousel rotated to match the twirl of her finger, like the action on a Bogart movie dial phone. She checked a CD label. " 'The Tango Lesson' sounds perfect."

"Sally Potter used some great tunes," he said, "but we'll skip the free form. Astor Piazzolla's too difficult for beginners."

Her dial finger stopped at track 19. " *'I am you. You are me'* . . . *and Yo-Yo Ma's cello*,' " she read from the box. "My oboe did five minutes with Piazzolla in a summer school Master's Class at Julliard. Try me on something too difficult for a beginner."

Grainger felt more Retirement rust in his gears. He should have followed her Billings Yearbook Tiara Talent from the High School Band to catch the Julliard. He had been tripped up once at the Plaza when a tango pro stole the march. For this amateur round, there was no point in explaining syncopation to a Master Class partner. He played it as Bogart: a pattern of movement as old as 4/4 time, with no questions asked about sexual harassment. At the end of a digital three minutes and five seconds her cheeks were flushed, her eyes still closed.

"Hit repeat," she said in Bacall's voice — but it was her own voice, and Circe's, calling all sailors. Grainger looked for a safe way out. "No more Piazzolla until you learn how to really walk the walk."

Her green eyes opened and stared straight at him. "The Churchill Sweat and Tears desk is only a copy. Tell me honestly, are you really just a Host?"

He shook his head. "Honestly, I'm an ex-navy carpenter who learned how to join split infinitives."

"So that's why God hired you — for referee when Frey and Freya Scrabble. I have to change for the party. If you need a ride back to the ship, use the go-cart."

She escorted him to the double front doors. The Prisoner's cart was ready-and-waiting, with its emission-free engine running, between the corroded cherubs. Holly Briar gave her open-sesame smile to the surveillance camera, which relayed it to the ceramic-thatched gates. They parted with a hum to send Grainger on his way, dreaming too imaginatively of a last grab at eternal youth reflected by a Caribbean sunset in a Martini-glass slipper . . .

He almost ran over the priest.

The lunatic stood in the middle of the road, just staring at his face. There was no sign of the cat. He beeped the horn. The cleric didn't move. To get around him Grainger was forced to drive the cart up on the grass as the sprinklers came on. The dreadlocked Jamaican crew framing the Blenheim Wing used it as another excuse to down tools for a good laugh at the Owner's expense.

When Grainger glanced back in the mirror, Animal Crackers was still watching him: oblivious to laughter or the fact that his bishops' gaiters were soaking wet.

Con Brio

Five

HURRICANE HARRY KILLED THE PARTY. GRAINGER RETURNED in the launch to see storm cones hoisted at the *Southern Cross's* masthead. He glanced by habit at the sky. High white cirrus directly above him, blended into copper cumulous banked low to the southeast. The dangerous quadrant for a tropical storm in the northern hemisphere. Dawson-Harris's amplified voice echoed across the water.

"This is the Captain speaking. In view of the weather we shall be departing Hudson Cay ahead of schedule. Prepare to embark passengers forthwith. Come to immediate notice for steam. That is all."

It was enough to convert an ocean liner into an overturned anthill. Anchor cables had to be shortened in, boiler pressures raised, bed sheets turned down, dinner places laid at forty tables for the Top Five Hundred. Dance Hosts and fancy footwork didn't rate.

"You lot just keep out of the bloody way," the Second Officer was advising Avar when Grainger jumped from the launch to the ship's ladder. "If you want to do something useful, help the band crowd secure the armchairs in the Forward Lounge."

"Eez not in my terms of contract." The Dance Director already looked green around the gills. "How close exactly is this hurricane?"

The Second shifted his concern to clenching the cable. Grainger checked the wave action. The surface of the sea had changed from an aqua-marine mirror of a travel poster to a faintly rolling sheet of copper, first indication of the giant swells to come. Hurricane Harry's eye might not strike the island, but Hudson Cay was completely unprotected from the southeast. Dawson-Harris couldn't afford to take chances. Avar found a target for the rage he couldn't vent at the Mate.

"Dirk, you heard that bastard. Help the Band fix the godamn Lounge chairs."

The copper wavelets now lapped the second rung of the accommodation ladder. The launch cast off for its first load of Cay passengers. Dawson-Harris arrived to check things himself.

"Our own boats won't do it in time," he told the Mate. "Call up the marina to organize a Dunkirk, and don't quibble about the cost."

Rufus was paying. A mood of celebration filled the Antares Lounge. A chalked happy-face on the blackboard behind the Orion's Belt bar beamed the message of the day, Bad Weather Means No Dancing!

"Get the armchairs secured, drinks are on the house," said the bartender. The chairs already had chains coiled in canvas pouches slung between the roller-ball casters that normally supported them. It was only a matter of tipping the legs back, pulling the four rollers from their cylindrical sleeve housings, and snap-fastening a brass clip to eyebolts which screwed into threaded receptors fitted into the deck. Grainger joined a duo from the Bonkers Dozen, heads bent, anchoring the Bosendorfer grand piano. Randy Karaoke helped by dubbing *Whistle While You Work.*

"Snow White's not my cup of tea, Tail-Gunner," said a male voice to Grainger's left. "You hired the pony-tailed bugger, Blue Leader," replied the one on his right.

Their heads emerged above the Grand. The first speaker had his photo resting on the easel which supported Avar's Deportment Do's and Don't's.

The Quicksilver Quartet
Music for your enjoyment,
Led by Sir Donald Quicksilver (Baronet)

"Tail-Gunner. Strike that Red Baron moniker, toot sweet!"

Blue Leader was Sir Donald himself. The Tail Gunner was the drummer. Laconic when he wasn't beating rims to death, he had the yellow fingers of a chain smoker with calluses. He took a black felt pen from a Gieves & Hawkes blazer slung over the piano stool, and struck out the bracketed Baronet. The blazer lining had a D.Q. monogram inside; a silver-wired Royal Air Force badge on the outer breast pocket. Its owner sported a silver Battle of Britain moustache to match.

"That seems to be the lot." The bandleader counted heads with his baton, ticking off chairs first, then Quartet members. The baton ticked Grainger as one too many. "Angels Five at Three o' clock, Tail-Gunner. This bird isn't one of ours. A dancer doing a day's work, must be the Old Man's navy pal from the bridge."

Grainger introduced himself and considered this latest moustache. Spy Nanny used to say the Cannes Festival jury was out on that Imperial style of stiff upper lip. "Half the time it may be a genuine Dambusters RAF hero. The other half has something to hide behind the Empire."

"No use for shipboard gossip, myself," said Quicksilver. "Have a gin and squash."

"No squash on tap, Sir Don," said the Orion's barman. "Hurricane Harry's locked up the soft stuff. I can make it straight Pink Gins."

A whistle shrilled on the ship's PA. "Passengers arriving. All staff stand by the gangway!"

The Bonkers Union rep raised a glass to the chalked happy face. "Toast for the Day is Dirty Weather. Good Bonking and No Dancing!"

The scene of women and livestock at the gangway brow looked like Nelson's departure for the Napoleonic Wars in Olivier's *Lady Hamilton* glossy at the Miami Costume Shop. The So Cross *was* an ark: half the Top Five Hundred had brought their pets. Unlike Vivienne Leigh, Freda was too wide for the ship's ladder. A davit normally reserved for a Zodiac inflatable got pressed into service as a crane. A jury-rigged pallet from a load of flour for the galley served as an elevator. Flanked and secured by sailors and Bowman's pseudo Churchill Desk, her billowing purple muumuu rose in a cloud of white dust accompanied by the Himalayan cat (basketed) and a black, Pot-Bellied Pig in a cargo net.

Avar added his two-bits of Dance Direction to this Marx Brothers production. "Don't just stand zere. Be nice to Lady Bowman!" The ship's staff cleared away Freda and the Desk. A second passenger on the flour pallet, previously hidden by her moo moo, was no Nelson.

"Watch your step, Vicar, and move along sir, if you please."

The gaunt, black-clad figure of the mad priest confronted Grainger again, staring into his face. And again, the man just stood there. His skeleton body trembled slightly from his disease but his eyes had the unwavering intensity of a zealot from the Inquisition.

"For Christ's sake," the Officer of the Deck shouted at the davit crew, "what's your bloody holdup with the Dog Collar?"

Two sailors gently manhandled its wearer off the pallet. The Pot-Bellied pig, with only one steward on its rope, fell out of its cargo net and squealed. The cracked priest repeated his exorcism treatment from the Himalayan cat episode: *"Instigante sathana —"*

The sailors cut the exorcist short by depositing his gaiters on the far side of a watertight door, and slamming it shut.

"So long Satan," said the welcome voice of Holly Briar, as she jumped nimbly from the ladder behind Grainger's shoulder.

Freda dusted more flour off her muumuu. It drifted onto Bowman who looked at a Dow ticker above his Churchill desk beside the gangway . . . FINAL AT CHICAGO: PORK DOWN 10 . . . and kicked the terrified Pot-Belly. The dinner gong rang as trading closed in San Francisco. Holly Briar took Grainger's arm, "Brush up your Scrabble. I'm told life with God gets real crazy after supper. They use Nostradamus anagrams to pick tomorrow's NASDAQ flyers."

Except for the priest's reappearance to quaver Latin Grace, it was moderately sane at the Captain's Table. Dawson-Harris excused himself to watch the weather, leaving the Chief Purser to referee the topic for dessert: Hurricane Harry's effect on the Costume Ball. After demolishing the Baked Alaska, passengers chronologically challenged by the Quicksilver version of an Empire waltz demanded the Macarena.

Grainger stood that one out with Holly Briar, former History Scholar, present World Class pulp researcher. Her Julliard quickness for tango rhythm was fabulous. He still wasn't happy about her last name.

"From being born at Christmas in Great Falls, with a mother called Rose," she said when he asked her casually, as Quicksilver vamped the Quartet into *The Way You Look Tonight*. Ex-Miss Montana wrinkled her perfect nose, which touched something too close to Grainger's foolish heart for a working spy. "I guess you still don't get it. Mom was a stripper. 'Rose Briar' was her stage name. She used it on my birth certificate instead of my father's."

"You're illegitimate?"

"Uh uh. They just never got around to marrying. It's what kept them together."

Her green eyes were artlessly wide as she laughed. Kern's lyrics mentioned *thoughtless charm*. Grainger's spy mind recalled Harvard Yard and registered *exceptionally bright*.

Life after supper got crazy but not real. A Technical Investment discussion about Nostradamus's predictions for Dow Jones Chart Patterns involving "breakouts from an Upside Triangle's Moving Average following a Classic Bull's Head-and-Shoulders" was killed by Freda's Jung and Scrabble. Grainger felt sorry for his Sony recorder.

"Religion is myth's worm in archetype's five-letters —"

"Big Apple. That's the difference between World Class and seven-letters Hacking —"

" 'Antigone's Revenge' —"

"Tell that to the fucking Thunday Thupp critics!"

As Grainger fox-trotted Holly Briar to Kern's *Let's Begin,* in the last dance of their first night, Bowman's lisp broke away from Scrabble to direct a closing shot of scrambled syntax at Quicksilver's RAF moustache. "If that queer behind the flue-brush on the bandstand ith a real Thir Donald I'm a monkey's uncle."

The Quartet encored into *What Do The Simple Folk Do?* from a blend of *Camelot.* Grainger double slashed it to bytes of Vanity absurdity for Pam, before he fell asleep alone with her ThinkPad in Deanna Durbin's bed, and the Pole Star due north outside his solo cabin porthole . . . to dream of Miss Montana stripping . . . for one brief shining moment of pure madness that was known as the lull before the storm.

Con Brio

Six

HARRY LASHED THE ASYLUM WITH HIS TAIL. GRAINGER WATCHED it from the bridge, after being thrown from Deanna Durbin's bed when one of the ship's stabilizers failed. In an age of satellite tracking, outwitting a hurricane was still no better than a fifty-fifty proposition.

Tropical storms in the Northern Hemisphere usually curved northeast and spent themselves dumping their last rain on Iceland. Harry was a rogue and ran amok in a straight line across the Turks and Caicos, through Honduras, smashing any hovels or mansions in between, and all the ships at sea.

Dawson-Harris nearly guessed right. For two hours after midnight all the signs were that the storm would take the usual racetrack curve. The Captain altered course a few points south, for travel insurance, and got hammered abeam Snug Corner on Acklins Island when Harry changed its mind.

"A woman's prerogative," Harris said, as a fifty-foot wall of the Atlantic smashed down on the liner's bow. "In the old days, when they had female names, I would have listened to intuition instead of the US Weather Service and dodged the sod completely — but as long as the rivets don't pop, one has to admit the male beast is rather splendid."

The *Southern Cross* shuddered under the shock. Her forecastle vanished beneath solid ocean to the level of the bridge windows. Thirty seconds later every rivet rattled when the propellers came clear astern and their great bronze screws bit into nothing more solid than foam-filled air.

"No dancing the light fantastic in this lot, Captain." Quicksilver joined the show. "I suppose it means we'll be running late for our Command Performance among the cannibals?"

"Not unless she loses a screw. Touch wood!" Harris tapped the mahogany box housing an old-fashioned nautical chronometer. Sailor's Superstition got tossed overboard: a mountainous Seventh Wave stopped the liner in her tracks. Somewhere a passenger's pet barked with a terrified yap.

"Bow-wow and whoops a daisy!" The musical Baronet clutched an engine telegraph for support. "You sure we're not going to run late?"

Dawson-Harris ignored the question. Grainger wondered why it mattered to a man with a Terry Thomas moustache and nothing more important to do than twiddle a baton.

The monster Seventh was the last of the giants. It carried away some life rafts, and all the canvas covers on the forecastle, then Harry couldn't be bothered with them any longer. The swells eased. At 03:45 Grainger went back to bed on B-Deck and slept in with the ghost of Deanna Durbin until 10:00.

He woke to a grinding of gears that sounded like the *Titanic* hitting the lowest base note on the Bösendorfer in the Antares Lounge. He hauled himself out of his queen-sized isolation and peered through the salt covering the porthole glass. The crust was too thick for visibility. He eased off the brass butterfly wing-nuts and opened the scuttle.

The world beyond the glass was black.

He rubbed his eyes, poked his head outside and looked again. The blackness seemed to be a coating of soot that covered everything which had been snow-white the day before. Paintwork, bleached teak decks, even the halyards of the main mast. The top of it was higher than the funnels, and there was no smoke coming out of them. The boilers were functioning with their usual Scottish-built efficiency.

A puff of breeze wafted his cheek. The blackness moved. Grit rubbed like sandpaper under his hand. He brought it in for examination. The soot was pumice: volcanic ash. He closed the scuttle, showered, then went for breakfast and a logical explanation of why volcanic activity dogged him from the Plaza Ballroom to the Caribbean.

"Blame Montserrat," said the duty Steward, with a face and accent from Punjab. "Mount Whatever doing its thingee again to get the lazy buggers on the island another tax Loto from Whitehall."

"That's a bit rough on the old Montseratis, Tail-Gunner." Grainger was also being dogged by Quicksilver: the bandleader joined him for bacon and eggs with the Quartet's chain-smoking drummer. "Share-and-share the Alka-Seltzer on the Morning After is what the Empire's supposed to be about, even if we're all that's left of it."

The baronet's Old School bromides sounded genuine. Grainger still wondered about the title. He had time on his hands to check it: Avar's morning Cha Cha class had been postponed to the afternoon because of the storm. The rest of the ship's business was the usual recovery from its effects, with the additional overload of cleaning up the volcano's fallout. Every fire hose on board was put in service for the wash down. With nothing more honest to do, Grainger volunteered. On the strength of that and his past acquaintance with the Old Man when Dawson-Harris was Young Dorkers, he was invited to the Piddling Dog for lunch.

The Crew's Pub was off limits to passengers, "Sky-Bosuns top of the list, particularly with St Vitus, and we're not too happy about bleeding dancers either, present company excepted." The senior deckhand from Grainger's hosing party offered a pint of Newcastle Brown. "Up your Flying Fish, or Doctor Salsa's, depending on the compass bearings!"

No "Sky-Bosuns" meant a blessedly priest-free zone. Grainger bought a return pint. The beer-talk compass needle swung from Dance Direction to "What the drop in speed's going to do for the bloody Cruise Pot?" Betting on the voyage time to their final destination explained Quicksilver's concern about delayed arrival. The senior deckhand said, "You've been on the bridge, Dirk. Give us the scoop from the Old Man."

"The Captain says we only lost a couple of hours for the storm last night."

"That was before we lost the bifuckated turbine this morning, Mate. They don't like pumice down their bleeding bunghole."

Which explained the Bösendorfer grind that woke him up. Bifurcated turbine blades rotating at 20,000 rpm didn't like anything except superheated steam to touch them.

Pumice threw a final spanner in the Cha Cha Class. Instead of tackling the Atlantic, Dawson-Harris turned his ship into the Mona Passage between Dominica and Puerto Rico, heading the *Southern Cross* straight for repairs in Caracas. Grainger's Tea Dance partners swiveled their blue-rinsed heads from Sweetheart Chase Turns, to chasing emeralds.

"You can't be an honest spy and not not-be a chameleon."

The double negative drifted into his mind as he sat before supper in the Antares Lounge listening to the Quicksilver Quartet vamp Kern's *They Didn't Believe Me*. Spy Nanny started double-life as a mathematician. "After Bogart and Mother Goose, you can't beat Boolean Algebra's double-negations for getting to the bottom of John Buchan's Thirty-Nine Steps."

Buchan still hit the late-show circuit with Robert Donat. Boolean

Algebra was an *Alice in Wonderland* exercise in Truth Tables, tailor-made for computer programmed spying. Nothing was just And/Or. Add an extra Not to anything negative and it became what had just been denied.

"Bifurcation in Venezuela just a two-day fix?" said the inevitably Scottish Chief Engineer, when they met earlier for a ploughman's lunch in the Piddling Dog, "Dirrrk, ye nae canna believe a bluidy word in South America. She'll aye be here the week." The Chief looked like Sean Connery, and shared the same Gorbals roughhouse streak. He was another *Southern Cross* ex-Navy who knew Grainger as a sailor, not a spy. "Help yourself to a second double whatever. The bar chit's paid upfront. Rum bluidy trip. Owners and passengers mad as fucking hatters all round, with more money than alligators in the Amazon. Och, any one of them could have done it with the blades to win the cruise Pot."

"Sabotage?" said Grainger.

"More like suicide. There were blonde hairs wrapped around the starboard generator spindle! None of my boys; Engine Room greasers growing longer than a crew cut all wear nets."

Grainger ordered freebie refills at the bar and said, "What about the turbine blades?"

"Nay black pumice in the bung hole. Pure white sand, from bluidy fire buckets on the Bridge. A couple of grains at thirty thousand rpm turns a bifurcated Y-Fin to a dog's breakfast." Grainger thought of the Afghans and his shoes. The Chief looked across the cucumber in his jug of Pyms. "Number Three unit's still only running at half power in the astern section — and talking of blonde hairs, I saw you tangoing a fabulous looking piece on the After Promenade. Is it true ye've turned into some kind of diddle-fingered poke 'em and forget 'em writer like yon Lord Arsehole who thinks he's fucking Provost of Edinburgh?"

Drifting back from the crudely Piddling Dog to the genteel Antares Lounge . . . the Quartet swung into *Day Dreaming*. From the way its leader looked at Miss Montana *So close to me . . . . I love you tenderly* . . . Grainger felt both intensely jealous on a personal level and satisfied that Sir Donald wasn't gay on the professional. He also observed that Randy Karaoke's faded ponytail looked more moth-eaten than usual. If it had been in the vicinity of a generator spindle the lip-syncher was lucky not to have been scalped.

"Do you know God wears a wig?"

Holly Briar had a disconcerting ability to join his mental wavelength (from ponytails to wigs) unannounced. "Ask the band to play it," he said for cover.

"That one shows your age, honey. Nothing personal. One of Mom's stage-door lines. I like mature men. Take Sir Donald — and don't say, Please!" She squeezed Grainger's hand and sipped her parasolled Margarita. "I mean, here we are working our buns off Chasing Brio for an asshole who didn't even go to Sherbourne, and right there is a genuine gold-star hero."

"Under a phony Battle of Britain moustache?" Grainger tagged the Sony to bookmark her Researched confirmation of his own Old School hunch about Bowman's overstated education, and kept holding her hand.

"Quicksilver earned his Captain Kangaroo tea-strainer," she said. "I double-checked it with the RAF. He flew in Korea. Three Red Chinese Migs, a Distinguished Flying Cross, and a Fifth Baronet playing the foxtrot is backed by Debrett. The British Empire ended with the return of Hong Kong, where he was the Governor's Aide de Camp. The guy needed a job and adores Keats' pest of love. He can quote the whole of 'Endymion'."

So could Spy Nanny after a silly pipe and too much brandy. *Time, that aged nurse, Rock'd me to patience.* Not wanting to be beaten by a Mig moustache, Grainger tried to come up with something honest from Naval College Eng Lit. "All I can remember about Keats is being stuck between Deep Blue soundings and green tea."

"That was in a letter, not his poems. I don't like cynics."

She removed his hand. He switched layers, from a spy's bleakness to Kern's romantic, *Make believe sees me through* . . .

"I've had it with Scrabble after the Dow," he said, "and it's a long run to Saint Helena. How about us doing a Piazzolla night in Venezuela?"

"My tango's still too basic." Holly Briar kissed his ear, and murmured as she left the bar, "Ask the band to play it."

Con Brio

Seven

S ABOTAGE IN THE ASTERN TURBINE WAS BEHIND HIM: GRAINGER'S next Waterloo lay dead ahead. The Iron Duke of Wellington's legendary dance at Brussels on the night before the Battle provided the theme for the Saint Helena Costume Ball. The Main Dining Room was turned into "The Island Prison," credits to the ship's library: a mildewed Napoleonic guide published before the jet age made "the Final Resting Place of the original Bogeyman" accessible to all who didn't know the remains were shipped to Paris.

Music was a problem but the Fifth Baronet Quicksilver gave it his best RAF shot with a specially tail-gunned British Mazurka version of *The Last Waltz With You*. After minor modifications, Grainger's Miami Scaramouche in D'Artagnon's boots and Nelson's Patch became a wounded Huzzar. The dance began in the Last Dogwatch of the evening before landfall.

During the First Dog:

"Lessons in ze Mazurka will be directed by myself, Dear Ladeez, as Napoleon," Avar announced in pin-sleeved uniform and full widow-bonking accent. "Zees will be done in four or eight couples, for vich, eef you forgive, I shall attempt weez only one arm."

The battle for the Mazurka followed historical and musical precedent. "The waltz wiped out the minuet," Holly Briar advised, in Mz Research mode. Most participants admitted defeat before their makeup got smudged. Grainger turned Nelson's blind eye-patch in Avar's direction and had one group of four Contentment couples moving with the required boldness on the third beat in triple time, until a blue-rinsed wave of applause warned him to bow out before he crossed the Thin Red Line of Drawing Attention.

Earlier that afternoon, Bowman hadn't been so lucky.

A steaming tango session with Holly Briar had left Grainger wanting more social intercourse than her offered exchange of Papuan pidgin. He and the Sony were lounging beside the *Southern Cross's* pool of Art

Deco-tiled nymphs lusted for by fig-leaved marble males from Olympus.

"This shall be our floating Valhalla." A dreamily post-"resting" Freda, barely contained by Day Glo Orange polka dots, looked over her Goddess Freya 44 cups as her "Frey-God" went off Valhalla's Deep End in a micro-bikini'd belly flop. The micro inside the bikini provided one answer to Bowman's out-sized ego.

"We do not need to dive for explanations into the *mini-crise* of so Freudian mid-life, my Magic Dirk. I told Louis — 'De Cosmos', we have been calling him for the novel purposes, but really he is neither. One of those English hyphen names, he is in fact the brother of your 'Animal Crackers' over there — I said to him about his four wives: Even in Bali, women of high accomplishment who are *Brio* readers . . . "

Grainger's mind blanked. The tremulous figure of the priest, already in skeletal black costume for the Ball, materialised behind a lusty Deco Poseidon, to stare at him again like an apparition from De Sade. Bowman stayed submerged. A small raft of unwoven hair floated to the surface beside a Deco satyr. The priest advanced, still staring. The scrap of wig got sucked into a filter disguised as the satyr's mouth. The priest clutched the satyr's horns for support and leaned forward. Grainger braced —

A pool alarm klaxon blared.

Bowman's wig had jammed the satyr's pump. The priest's trembling hand slipped from its goat's horns. Two alert pool attendants saved him from drowning. Bowman hauled his micro-empathy out of the water, flopped it in front of a tanning mirror and grabbed a Tilley hat from a demure Deco Aphrodite to cover his micro-embarrassment.

Grainger watched the fragile, yet strangely menacing, black shadow being led away by the attendants. He said to Freda, "Is that true, about the priest and Brio's geologist being related?"

"They both have King Lear's mania and look like Laurence Olivier, but take off thirty years, so do you." Lady Luck shrugged, releasing her monumental left 44 from its Day Glo confinement.

Ball-Wise, a huge success was had by all in costume except the Two Napoleons, Avar and Bowman (with a stand-in wig) who had to split top prize. Scaramouche's patched-up tango with Holly Briar as Evita got a safe Next-Best. The Most Original-but-Why? went to the Chief Purser as a tortoise.

"I'm Old Stone," the Chief had to explain five hundred times, "the original inhabitant of Saint Helena. Legend says I talked to Boney." To Grainger he added, "Our Mags has postponed again. Too many fans on her Falklands Book tour. Her Iron Ladyship won't be boarding now until Capetown."

Another reprieve. A tortoiseshell dancing with Dr Salsa's pinned sleeve was good for a horse laugh. Dawson-Harris played the obligatory reverse-role of an ordinary seaman and got a "Hip-Hip!" for serving drinks to the vessel's most junior sailor — female — cross-dressed as the Captain.

Scaramouche was allowed a last Huzzar's goodnight kiss by Evita to celebrate their prize before he had to change back to a Dull Dirk and another solitary night in Deanna Durbin's bed.

His ghost-visit to Jamestown next morning was Nostalgia with an extra-large N. When he had first contemplated Life and Death on Saint Helena it was the real thing. The Falklands War. Mags' and Spy Nanny's Last Big Moment. For reasons he couldn't define, he'd forgotten that the war's staging base was yet another volcano.

The cliff walls of this one plummeted three miles deep, straight down to the magma waiting in its Atlantic Trench for the next molten round of action. Against that geologic height and time the battlements and moats of Imperial man were ephemeral as rice-paper origami. The handful of inhabitants clung to their newly-granted British Citizenship certificates in cottages painted too brightly blue and pink to make good Local Colour pictures against the pale morning mist and red-oxide lava dust that rose or fell according to the whims of trade winds and plate tectonics.

What the island's famous prisoner described with Marie Antoinette understatement as "not an attractive place" became a Delivery Room for the premature birth of The Next Bowman Novel. Good Old Dirk and Miss Montana tagged along in their professional midwife capacities of Ghostly Research. The Sony recorded the plaintive Bowman squalls of vanity-prequelling Brio II. Otherwise known as The Wig That Failed.

"I'm not just sweating because the Weave cost a goddamn fortune. *The guarantee was waterproof!*" Bowman's World Class bellow echoed off the fortress walls and gun embrasures that once guarded slave traders as well as Napoleon. "For Artsy-fartsy's like that Extinguished Fucking Cross and trumpet over there —" Quicksilver and his drummer, in the centre of the drawbridge, snapping mementoes of Empire with a Baby Brownie from the 1950's — "there has to be some fucking Inner Meaning, quote-unquote, to Poisoning the Bogeyman, so we'll bloody give it to them in the Prequel. Brio Two will put the arsenic in Boney's condoms in time for the Millennium."

The three of them (four, with Stone the tortoise — the real one: still alive and browsing in slow motion on a Marigold) stood next to a clump of maroon hollyhocks in the garden of St Helena's prime attraction: Longwood House, the Bogeyman's Prison Cottage. Holly Briar used state-of the art digital to capture the original inhabitant's drab shell for her Local Colour. "Old Stone does look kind of like the Purser," she giggle-whispered to Grainger. "What do you think of God's new rug?"

A Napoleonic cowlick salvaged from the Ball now protected the Bowman little gray cells. Grainger was more interested in the Cottage background: a pair of fellow tourists from the So Cross lounging over the garden wall, staring intently at Bogey's hand-built goldfish pool. One was Randy Karaoke, still missing part of his ponytail. The other, an Engine Room rating from the ship's Turbine Compartment where fire-bucket sand went down the bung hole.

There weren't any fish to look at: the Imperial pool was drained for maintenance. In the distance, beneath a steeple, the black shadow of Animal Crackers bent like Death's skeleton-scythe over cholera gravestones of the British Empire in St James's churchyard.

Bowman abruptly alchemised his thought-processing from arsenic in French Safes back to the gold of Brio One. "That slice of death warmed over reminds me. The Chase to the mine is okay but we'll throw in a priest having sex with the cannibals before the Pot."

The tortoise munched another Marigold. Grainger positioned himself as an honest tourist in the foreground — with Randy and the stoker in his background. "Snap one of me and Old Stone for the Family album." he asked Holly.

Bowman's big picture shifted to Randy Karaoke. "When we get to the Mine I see De Cosmos as John Wayne in Hollywood, not some queer like that godamn piano player. And forget this living fossil shit — " a swift kick at the tortoise — "Give me snakes. They always go well at the end of a mine shaft, there must be millions in New Guinea."

"None on Le Breton," said Mz Research.

"This is Movies. The shares went through sixty at the closing bell in New York last night when the latest Assay was announced. Billionaire

Bowman has a nice ring to it. Find something that kills with one strike and looks good."

Old Stone took the warning seriously and withdrew into its shell. "Bogey must have had more empathy with tortoises," Holly Briar said to Grainger. "Do you really have a family for the album?"

"Not since they ate my shoes," he replied with an honestly rueful smile.

Back on the So Cross . . . between blue-rinsed Latin Privates for Cumbia and Merengue he used the ThinkPad for converting dross to schlock. In the blink of an eye in the sky the Absolut trivia Pam was paying for joined the other on-line pursuits of vanity to feed the world's supermarket racks. Grainger was left with nothing but an empty screen and an overwhelming urge to fall in love with one last human being before the emptiness spread to him.

Con Brio
Eight

To the strains of *TANGO TANGO . . .* from the movie, *SUR* by Piazzolla and Solanas . . . Grainger did back-and-forward ochos all across the South Atlantic with Holly Briar and still she came no closer to falling in love than a Follower's Leg Wrap in a cross-footed Lead's Left Turn. With dance widows and divorcees looking for lust in every Private bar from Quickstep to Foxtrot he felt the Albatross curse of Bonded Host around his neck.

Time crawled. So did the ship: with her bifurcated turbine blades partially restored — via replacements flown in from Vladivostok — the *Southern Cross* steamed from St Helena to South Africa at only two-thirds normal cruising speed. This meant another day late for her final destination. On the seventh of the crossing, resting for a beat in the middle of a Sugar Push at the end of a Saturday Afternoon Watch class with a particularly demanding Swing widow from Savannah, he saw a familiar cutoff shape outside the Antares Lounge porthole:

Table Mountain, with Capetown at its foot.

The Tavern of the Seas had been hospitable to visiting mariners and their figureheads since Christ was a carpenter: well before Spy Nanny acquired Young Dirk on permanent loan from the navy. Today it was going overboard for an old-age-pensioned Iron Maiden.

"Mags is that rarest archetype, the Dual Anima," Freda confided to baffled Asians riding an afternoon cable car to the Table's top. "I granted her a session immediately after her book signing this morning. The rest naturally is privileged between patient and physician."

Grainger had yet to orbit the pensioned Icon. He stepped from the cable car to view two oceans: the sight of the Indian and South Atlantic swells was breathtaking between sudden sweeps of iced fog across Vasco da Gama's Tablecloth. The fog lifted now to reveal Randy's ponytail unexpectedly on the table.

"Let me guess," said Holly Briar. "You want more Local Colour for the Family Album."

"Fuck it." Bowman told her. "Brio went through seventy at breakfast when the Assay hit two ounces from a nugget that old fart De Cosmos found while he was panning with his pisspot in the river. That's unheard of in the history of mining! I said to Mags at breakfast, 'Placer your bets now. The only chink in your investment portfolio is —' " he broke off, strangely sensitive to looks from possible Oriental book buyers. "For Christ sake, we're not bestselling correctness. That last bloody Chink was a *joke*."

At sea level, offered the charms of the Mount Nelson Hotel, an Old Cape gem on Orange Street, by the Botanical Gardens, Frey-and-Freya predictably lit out instead for Valhalla on American Express at the New Hilton's Nellie Mandela Suite.

The Entourage was excused. Holly Briar said to Grainger at the Nelson, "Meet you in the Rhodes Bar. I have to visit the Damen." He watched her long-blonde perfect back stride past a cardboard windmill in the lobby promoting a Dutch Bulb convention, next to a cardboard Mags doing the same for her book beside a roulette wheel outside the Herren.

Placer your bets.

As he walked into Cecil Rhodes' bar, surrounded by fading Empire photos of Blue Clay diamond mines and pre-Apartheid, all-white South African All Black rugger teams, hung between the Royal Trophy heads of Safaris Past, Grainger realised that panning for placer gold nuggets in alluvial river beds wasn't geologically compatible with cutting the igneous tops off volcanic islands.

Rufus's suspicions of a salted claim could be true. He ordered an on-tap Lion beer from a spigot beneath the mane of a dead one bagged by Edward the Seventh, and wondered further if a wannabe Nostromo for the Nineties knew more about Chasing Brio than just its joke title? Vulkan Mining's trophy-head (Wee Willie Williams, the C.E.O.) was Bowman's next-door neighbor. They shared Contentment's offshore bankers, and Insider Trading was the joke that put God in jail.

"Her Ladyship wants her Privates! Meaning now."

Grainger looked up from his Lion. A Vincent Price moustache stood under the yellowed tusks of a warthog molting its bristles, courtesy the thyroid shooting-eye of George the Fifth. "You've got your booking wires crossed," he told Avar. "Freda's resting with her husband."

"We're not talking wacko Bowmans. The Iron Lady ain't no rusty widow!"

Grainger said, "I thought you were handling the Privates."

"This sounds like a delicate moment." Holly Briar returned from the Damen's. Her Beauty Queen smile even included the beasts, like Avar. She gestured at another male animal behind her. "I found this stray Quixote tilting at a windmill outside the Herren." Baronet Quicksilver — minus the routine protection of his Tail-Gunner, but with a harmonica tucked into his RAF-badged breast pocket — was a seamless part of Cecil Rhodes' memorabilia: "Sir Donald knows all the hot spots left over from the Empire," she said. "He's going to take us to Lu Lu's Shebeen."

"Not tonight, Sweetheart," the former Ronnie Evans snapped back. "You can hustle your tiara to whichever's hiring G Strings, but your boyfriend signed a major fucking contract to do the Hootchi Kootchi back on board."

Grainger decided it was past time for an honest show of backstage gigolo rebellion. "I don't Kootch," he told Avar, "and the contract gives me shore leave, so piss off."

With Dr. Salsa and Mags disposed of for the evening, Quicksilver stroked his Mig-fighter's moustache under the warthog's and said, "One gent to another on safari: Not sure about the 'taking Us', old sport. Lu Lu's isn't kitted out for ladies."

"Nor is the Golden Nugget in Billings," replied Holly Briar. "And as the daughter of a stripper, Sir Donald, I'm right at home with G-strings."

"Donnie, to beautiful gels. What d'ye think, Dirk?"

He hadn't heard anyone say gels for broads since a closet-gay Colonel of Gurkhas showing off his Black Belt in judo at Spy Nanny's Passing-On Party. Lu Lu's had been around even longer. Nautical myth claimed it as Capetown's original Tavern of the Seas. Its municipal address was District Six. In Cold War hot spots Grainger had always found safety in odd numbers. "If Holly can handle Billings on her own, three of us should be okay for a shebeen," he told Quicksilver.

"Good show. Just keep an eye in case the Zulu Boys grab their Chop-Chops. And not to worry —" Sir Donnie Quixote tapped his blazer pocket — "I've brought along the old mouthbox for protection."

A taxi carried them down through the strata of Capetown's three centuries . . . from Dutch Colonial red-tiled villas and cobbles, to rusted hutches and clay lanes that smelled of sewage. Mz Research pointed her

Digital Local Colour at a flyer tacked to a power pole under a tattered picture of Archbishop Tutu getting his Nobel Peace Prize.

DUKE ELLINTON AND WIMEN'S MUDWRESTLIN

"That looks promising. Donnie, I thought you said, No Ladies."

Traditional Shebeens were uniquely South African beer gardens, blending all races with Lion beer and pennywhistle jazz. In post-apartheid Lu Lu's, there was no pennywhistle Ellington and the sexes didn't blend. They arrived to hear Paul Simon's over amplified *Graceland* backgrounded by squeals and roars.

"Three Lions, please."

Grainger upgraded his opinion of Quicksilver. A barely audible request from an Empire relic with a RAF badge got them service fit for the Raj: instant drinks plus a ringside table complete with bonus globs of flying mud.

"Don't you just love it?" Holly shouted in his ear.

He wanted to love *her*. Under the mud, the contestants showed no vestige of racism, or clothes, except for Calvin Klein micro-thongs being used to break the rules which brought screams of pleasure or outrage from their supporters. During a Graceland lull — while the ring was being prepared for the Main Event of the evening, a triple tag-team of six assorted amazons called collectively, Momma Mombassa — Grainger saw a bleached ponytail in the wrong part of South Africa once too often for coincidence. Then unlaundered money changing hands from Randy's to a couple of District Six thugs. Good Old Dirk ordered another round of Lions and asked Quicksilver, "With all these competing attractions ashore, how do you hang on to your band?"

"Usually enough floating talent to keep them happy on board, old boy. Gay or straight."

"And your piano player?"

The Don gave him an appraising look that included Holly Briar. "Gel like that in tow, didn't have you pegged as a left-hander under the blanket. I tell my Tail Gunner: 'Don't mind a feller being queer in the cockpit as long as he keeps his mind on the job.' Randy's problem isn't sex. Bugger can't read music. Has to transcribe everything into F. Hellish key for the rest of us. But any port in a storm. My regular keyboard chappie got blown up by a grapefruit just before we left Miami."

Lu Lu's crowd started shouting for Momma Mombassa. The rhythm came straight from Nanny's favourite scene in *King Solomon's Mines*: the one where Grainger's namesake faced the howls and spears of jealous rivals.

"Donnie," said Mz Research, "I think I'm looking at two Chop-chops."

Machetes, in the grubby hands of Randy's paid-up thugs.

"Time for a grace-note exit, dear gel. Young Keats always has the words for it. 'Pleasure is oft a visitant; but pain clings cruelly' —"

"Fuck poets, man! This here's a kaffir slice-up."

A beer-bellied Boer at the next table grabbed a pair of unopened Lion cans to make a set of aluminum brass knuckles for each fist. Grainger took Holly's arm. The negative bonus of a ringside seat was its distance from the door. The thugs' machetes struck sparks. Don Quixote didn't blink. Quicksilver merely reached for the weapon in his RAF breast pocket.

The Boer said, "Man, are you crazy? A bloody mouth organ can't stop —!"

New South Africa's National Anthem froze the chop-chops in mid air. The six Momma Mombassas released their opponents' Klein g-strings and came with the audience to attention.

In the cab, leaving the charms of District Six behind them, Miss Montana kissed the Fifth Baronet more warmly than Grainger would have wished a man a decade older than himself, with two more Romantic shipboard weeks of Keats' *Pest of Love* ahead of them, and said, "Donnie, now that's what I call racial harmony."

Trapped between a randy devil who wanted to kill him tonight, and the deep blue-green Indian Ocean mixing with the tidal sludge of Capetown Harbor which promised slow death from toxic waste to anyone who fell into it during the graveyard Middle Watch, Grainger listened to the Lounge strains of *Long ago and far away* and confronted his worst fear.

Tango with Mags in the morning.

The chance that she would recognize him from his Nanny Days in Whitehall's spy-nursery was slight, but the lady's Iron Memory was the stuff of legends that made stronger men than Dance Hosts quake in their Church's brothel-creeping suede boots from Bond to Downing Street.

He moved to drown her image in The Piddling Dog. The crew's pub band segued into *Staying Alive*. The Scottish Chief Engineer playing Sean Connery waved him over.

"I hate to be a Glaswegian stereotype of a cheap shyte, Dirrrk, but yon bluidy Rufus has cut off the freebie Pimm's and I've aye run out of credit."

Grainger let himself be sandbagged with honest grace and made his way up four decks to his queen-sized, Deanna Durbin maple hammock.

He found a note on its Irish linen pillow.

Capetown beats the Golden Nugget but I figure I need your Scaramouche Privates to nail my tango. Tonight would be nice. You know the lucky number.

The note was signed not Mz Research, or Miss Montana.

Just plain,

Holly.

He brushed his teeth and showered, then walked along the muted carpets of deserted companionways, past passenger portraits from history — Roosevelt and Churchill after A Day of Infamy at Pearl Harbor — on mahogany cabin doors hiding waterproof-compartments of current loneliness too deep to be cured by any Workshop quicksteps, or whirled away in Nanny's favourite tear-jerker, *The Great Waltz.*

It was a loneliness he had not allowed himself to acknowledge until this moment as he saw the Olivier-Leigh Suite's picture with its Valentine's card signatures vowing *Larry + Viv,* and heard the heart-tugging notes of an oboe playing the soul of Piazzolla: *Tanti Anni Prima's* aching beauty behind a cabin door.

My rendezvous with destiny.

He realised, as he turned the final corner and saw the number of the Golden Nugget cabin — Charlie Chaplain's lucky 7, between watertight frames of Eleanor Roosevelt and the Happy Hooker — that he had played with names and codes so long that his mind only *thought* in other people's sound bytes and Spy Nanny's movie-title scores. His problem was . . . as he knocked, and saw the handle turn . . . that he only *thought* about the tugging of his heart. Until here and now, he didn't honestly feel a thing.

"Hi," she said . . . standing there with the oboe in her hands, while fifty years of nursery-to-cocktail-party Old Dirk chat subsided into a pounding silence pouring from his newfound heart . . . "I'm glad you got my message. Godfrey wants to leave in twenty minutes. The volcano's heating up. We're flying to Le Breton."

It didn't register.

He heard what she said, and saw Bowman standing behind her, but he had fifty years of inertia overcome by momentum behind himself. Instead of turning on his heel and tossing her a dancehall dime, he stayed motionless. Holly Briar's ebony-and-silver wand went into its velvet-and-leather instrument case. The lid snapped shut on the oboe. Bowman continued to sound byte.

"Big Tit isn't going to blow — it's just an excuse to puff the Assays — but sitting on this tub, *Brio's* dripping away faster than last night's Taitinger through Sid's catheter. Just make sure you grab an extra seat in First for my Churchill Desk with Qantas."

Grainger was drowning in words. Back in the passage, staring at Laurence Olivier's face certified by Sotheby's not to look anything like his own . . . he cast Piazzolla's magic-oboe feeling adrift and clung to the spy-trained wreck of his soul.

Adam and Eve and Punch-Me-Not . . .

No Holly tonight. No Mags in the morning. Keep one step ahead of the Unexpected and let sleeping volcanoes lie.

Con Brio
Nine

AT THE BACK OF FIRST CLASS ON THE QANTAS AIRBUS, THINGS looked brighter in the night. Bowman ground his molars. Freda snored over her DDD cups, there was only the Desk to act as a chaperone — strapped into a removed-seat space of its own, against the Coach peasants' dividing bulkhead. Holly Briar murmured, "I'm really sorry about the screw-up with my tango note. Can we still try that Private when we get to Port Moresby? I've got a surprise for you."

Grainger spent the next five hours of cabin semi-darkness looking at the perfect profile of her nose and chin, and slightly parted lips, resting on his shoulder . . . and willed time to last forever. God woke with a grunt at sunrise, demanding champagne for his empathy.

"So that's Borneo. Doesn't look like much from up here. After *Brio* rings the gong as Next Nostromo, we're going head-to-head with those pussy critics who whipped Mailer in New York. Which reminds me about Security." Bowman finger-snapped a flight attendant to keep Brio's prospects flowing. "On Le Breton it's your typical SAS bugger from Eton called Wallers: our code, Knickers. If he's anything like his hairy-ape father — a butcher I sat next to in the Lords for my Maiden — he'll be as much use to literature as a brass monkey's freeze-dried balls."

The globe rolled by. Borneo was nothing to look at from forty-thousand feet because the whole of the Spice Islands Archipelago was obscured by smoke from forest fires. Qantas provided a filler of the Spice Girls instead. In lieu of more breakfast champagne, the cabin attendant presented His Lordship with a fax from the flight deck. "Knickers says the Natives are restless on Two Tits, which means we have to stop over in Port Moresby until Wee Willie sorts out his Vulkan Joint Venture with the cannibals. Of course nobody admits it still goes on — head-hunting — and delay never hurt anyone in a Rising Market."

The Mission signals were as scrambled as Bowman's Chasing Brio metaphors. In the game of Pop the Bubble, delay by Vulkan's CEO might or might not be deliberate: either way heightened chance discovery of Grainger's role in Gustav Rufus's bottom-line investment. And Bowman challenging Mailer's critics to a pussywhipping would hype attention like iron filings to a compass magnet. A spy hiding only in the shadow of a rich man's whim lay somewhere between *The Naked and the Dead* in Papua New Guinea.

A lacklustre group of dancers doing a nude Macarena for a PNG tourist trade already dampened by a string of "im bigpela dan usual" earthquakes rocking Port Moresby's year-round Rainy Season, met them at its airport. So did franchised shoulder-badges for Pitcairn Proprietary, handling Arrivals Security. Air Niugini lost the Entourage's luggage, except for the Churchill Desk which, with a Qantas seat of its own, was treated like a passenger.

Bowman looked vainly for a closed limo to transport it. Grainger kept his ears open for any pidgin hint of local Opposition. Another quake rumbled. The terminal's tin roof crackled.

"Ples nogut," a rep for Air Niu Gini decided.

"Place lousy," Holly said. "How about we find a small re-enforced concrete hotel?"

The spasms in the earth's crust disturbed some green-and-scarlet parakeets into circling a crashed Cessna left to rot on the end of the runway. A ginger-furred pig snuffling beside it took Grainger's mind back to the Animal Crackers farewell aboard the floating madhouse they had deserted at Capetown.

In the middle of a flaming-tranny match with Dr Salsa (about breaches of Grainger's Bonking contract), more vicious than anything at Lu Lu's, the lunatic priest conjured a life-sized model of the Black Pot-Belly carved from six hundred dollars worth of lard by the ship's Head Chef "to simulate the Accused in a Porcine Act of Bestiality as alleged by the Archbishop of Lausanne in AD 1241," according to the Crackers' charge sheet passed from the tremulous cleric's hand to Captain Dawson-Harris.

Total madness — but for a serious split-second Grainger actually considered Freda's suggestion of a shared likeness between his own face and the lunatic's. When he confessed that moment of insanity now to Holly, as they waited for Port Moresby's transportation, she pointed to the drenched naked Macarena dancers and replied with a heat he didn't expect, "Six hundred bucks in lard? That's more than all these people make in a year. We didn't treat our own Aboriginals much better with Custer, but he got his Last Stand, and we should have learned to do more than turn the New Guinea Highlands into Cruise Line welfare bums."

"I've found what they call a cab," Bowman shouted. "He'll take us to the Nelli's Hotel for fifty American."

"Nelli's ples gut. Concrete." Air Niu Gini's rep glanced up at the terminal's still-trembling tin roof, then announced over the PA, "Mosbi Balus ples em close single wan pela bilong repair." When Grainger queried "Imgo just one single day?" for repairing a Jumbo-sized crack in the runway deep enough to swallow a 747, Air Niu Gini shrugged it off as, "Getim redi for im Big Wan."

It was too hot to tango before the Big One came. Frey-and-Freya grabbed the Nelli's only working air-conditioned suite for their Papuan Valhalla. The Samsung unit cooling Grainger's south-facing room had a bird's nest in place of its compressor. Holly's had nothing more than a rust platform outside her window, and a sun-bathing green lizard.

"My shower doesn't work either," she said. "Can I use yours?" He was day-dreaming about her promised Surprise . . . behind the mildewed plastic curtain until a howled, "Jesus Christ I'm scalded! There's no goddamn cold. Only boiling brown like tea."

He went to the lobby to complain.

"Im belong Solar liklik haus." Nelli's desk-clerk stroked a slim white bone piercing his lustrous black left cheek. "Best efficient gutpela in PNG."

Liklik haus meant pidgin toilet: good-fellow argument on solar heating efficiency in the tropics would lead nowhere. "Yumi kissim keys," he suggested to the clerk. "Go wokabaut find cold wara."

"Wannem dring wara?" The clerk went walkabout from behind the desk, stroked his cheek bone again and pointed at a soft-drink dispenser with a faded pink-and-blue poster of a once-crimson maple leaf for DRING Natural BOTOL Spring-Water from CANADA.

"No botol." Grainger made showering motions with both hands above his head. "Waswas. *Cold* waswas!"

The clerk kissimed the keys by removing a ring of them from a hook. Eventually they unlocked a room with two beds where the shower trickle, though still Tetley brown, was bearably tepid. The room faced north. The Venetian blinds didn't. The slats were jammed open. A misprinted tourist brochure of local entertainment next to a Gideon bible showed Moresby Movi of the Week: *As Good as It Gets.*

He helped Holly shift rooms. By the time they were finished, and she had taken her shower, and found him on one of the beds panting like the green lizard, with a forearm shading his eyes, willing the equatorial southern sun to drop, she said, "We're going to have to share resources. I have water, you have shade. Take a shower here and then we'll go back to your place for my surprise."

Cushioned by Qantas luxury, he had dreamed of sex. In Nelli's squalor she took out her oboe and handed him a cassette. "Drop this in your Walkman." *This* was Piazzolla's soul again, his *Quintetto*, put through an electronic wringer. "I got Randy Karaoke to cut the alto sax in Tanti Anni Prima so I could play along instead with Astor himself on bandonéon. You'll probably say it stinks."

He was speechless. The tune came from the end of Piazzolla's composing life: its melodic line drifted from her lips to a sliver of reed, then upward through the gates of an Argentinean Tango heaven.

On Niugini's side of paradise, in a tropic amalgam of humidity and hotel mismanagement, undeterred by a fourth quake, she said, "I have another surprise." Her pubic hair, trimmed far below the bikini line. "I call what's left my tiger stripe. How about we do the same for your Bonking Privates? If anyone asks in the Men's, tell them it's a cure for prickly heat."

She picked up her Lady Schick and with a smile a spy could honestly die for, led him back into the shower of tepid tea.

They lay together . . . watching the sun descend, waiting for the tropic dark, and Grainger knew that this Big-L feeling was love, without limit; not a Spy Nanny-censored frame of lust in a Movi-of-the-Week. From this moment forward, every time he held this woman in his arms, against his heart, remembering her playing Piazzolla's Prima . . .

It would get better.

Con Brio
Ten

FOREVER TANGO . . . GRAINGER FOUND THE SOUND-TRACK IN A Lotohaus kiosk at the end of Ela Beach. A dual cassette, pirate but unaffected by the climate. He bought it as an omen, assured by the kiosk seller that the local "fukfuk god im smilin' lak Brio" and returned to Nelli's hotel for breakfast Kellogg's with Holly's Tiger Stripe — to find Bowman paranoid about Vulkan's Security Knickers.

"That sod Wallers and his SAS paras won't let us within sniffing distance of Le Breton but two can play that game. No more real names. Until we get The End under our belt, we're going Low Profile for *Brio*. I know we're being followed."

Post-Kellogg's, the Entourage did Port Moresby Local Colour: counting the traffic lights that worked.

"Three," said Mz Research.

The downtown loop returned them to the beach kiosk where Good Old Dirk let himself be conned again into a "boomboom box im taptap dek" to keep the fukfuk god happy.

A moulding display of paperbacked *Death in the Palace* made its low profile author ecstatic. "That's the beauty of World Class Distribution Rights. Let me sign those."

Bowman was megalomaniac, but not paranoid. They were being followed, both when they left the hotel and passing the local golf course. Grainger couldn't determine at which Spy Level. The surface seemed a single bumboat souvenir seller trying to peddle Lady Luck a penis gourd "im bilong yu man" to replace her Frey-God's 2 below par, micro bikini.

Freda took it back to Nelli's with a sudden migraine. Barely below the surface, all the gourd-sellers and knife sharpeners had Brio axes to grind. The Lotohaus operator offered Australian Lottery tickets for mine shares at only a fifty percent markup in lieu of stuffed koala bears as prizes for a handheld Gameman version of Brio Roulette.

"Limiting access to the mine can't be to stop us from seeing the hole," Bowman said. "Rupert's satellite does that every ninety minutes. It has to be the Assays again. They must be even richer than Louis lets on to —"

"Not Louis." Holly jogged Chasing Brio's tightened security, "You said No real names anymore. We're using De Cosmos."

Lord God shrugged off his Entourage's cautions with more bifurcated Bowmanisms. "Call him anything between a rock and a geologist. Either way, we've got his number. I've seen his picture, the old sod's a natural for Central Casting. Bearded half-gook, on his fourth Nose-bone wife — and still dropping in for a Quickie with the other three! Scattered from Bali to Borneo. I'll bet you Brio's opening box-office, the cunning bugger stuffs five ounces up his prospecting arse for every ton of shit Vulkan tips in the valley."

"So with the satellites overhead, why hide it?" Grainger asked, as the Lotohaus wheel of Fortune spun.

"Market forces. Tying good news to Ten Thou on the Dow! Everyone from a grass shack to Buck House is waiting for their ship to come in."

The electronic wheel stopped. A naval siren sounded.

"Old Dirk win im bigpela koala!"

HMS *Dauntless* had picked his prize moment to arrive.

The surface reason for the visit of a Royal Navy guided-missile frigate was merely to show the flag in the South Pacific. Her diplomatic purpose was to offset French nuclear tests under Mororea. The sight of *Dauntless's* raked lines and shipshape fittings did more than take Grainger back to his former naval life at sea: the sound of her bosun's-call whistles shrilling across the water made time stand still.

Forever Tango . . .

Another Papuan Siesta. The green lizard was taking one. Watched instead by the voyeur-buttoned eyes of the Made-in-Taiwan koala, Grainger played Holly's *Anni Prima* tape on the boomboom box and made fukfuk love again with her magic Tiger Stripe. They showered afterwards with Tetley in the liklikhaus, then joined Bowman in His Lordship's tea-time treasure hunt along the beach for *Brio* Opposition. (Freya and her penis gourd remained "tropically indisposed.")

The Lotohaus operator had tripled the price of *Death in the Palace*, cashing in on "Lord Bum im sign bigpela imself." The author bought all the autographed copies and then distributed them to a new generation of lip readers on their way to the airport. By nightfall there wouldn't be a Pitcairn ex-para within earshot who didn't know where *Brio's* low profile was hiding.

Beyond the Lotohaus, a gingerbread bandstand, left behind from Empire, stood in a park where real head-hunters had feasted the day before yesterday. Today, white helmeted Royal Marines from *Dauntless* played the Hope-and-Glory of Grainger's life before Spy Nanny. Lord Bum kept time to the drumbeats, one beat out.

"Give me old Elgar for something you can take to the Falklands to bash a few wogs," Bowman said, too loudly, as the last oompah faded into another minor quake.

Grainger considered the presumably innocent faces of ex-cannibal sons and daughters humming Mother-of-the-Free while wearing TORONTO IS WORLD CLASS: LOVE THOSE BLUE JAYS! caps and sweatshirts at a Papua New Guinea Sunset Ceremony rehearsal. Canada's commerce in bottled water was understandable: Toronto's Blue Jays connection remained a local mystery.

Back at Nelli's, the Dow had smashed through 9550 between tremors. Some junior officers from *Dauntless* celebrating it in the Hotel bar fell hard for Miss Montana. Babes of the digital-navigation age were a generation too young to be a recognition threat to Old Dirk. Upstairs in his south-facing room, he turfed out the green lizard and asked Holly to marry him.

"Like now?"

"When we finish chasing Brio."

"And you're away at sea as a Dance Host."

She brushed off his proposal with her Tiger Stripe. He played Piazzolla's *Balada Para Un Loco*. They had more nutty sex and laughs in the face of death. Darkness fell with its everyday tropic rapidity. The sun did set for the Marines but the two of them danced on.

Loco, loco, loco . . .

The lyrics of the madness in a milonguero's life, and Bowman's, and Freda's, and the manipulators mining Brio for the all-or-nothing it was worth.

Loco, loco, loco . . .

"It's crazy," she whispered in his ear, as they curved backwards in a super-close embrace to balanceo nude. "But okay."

Her acceptance of his offer didn't break their rhythm. Piazzolla had them. Tango would hold them to the end.

The pirate tape ran out a minute short. Wolf-whistles followed it through the green lizard's open window. Grainger remembered too late that Nelli's Venetian blinds didn't work.

Below him, he saw the baby RN generation, drunkenly navigating the scrub grass of the hotel lawn for a zigzag course back to their ship. By the time they finished relaying their adventures ashore to their shipmates aboard *Dauntless*, the "messdeck telegraph" of hot gossip would make him as "Low Profile" for his Grapevine Turns among the cannibals as his employer was for freebie ghosted *Death in the Palace*.

Con Brio

Eleven

STILL THE BAND PLAYED ON IN PORT MORESBY. THREE NATIONAL anthems accompanied the raising of the ensign for Colours at 08:00 on the quarterdeck of HMS *Dauntless* while an honor guard practiced ashore beneath a severe photograph of Queen Empress Victoria draped with a banner for *DYKOMANIA!* PNG LESBIAN ART WEEK.

On the Monday morning after Grainger's *Loco* performance in the green lizard room, the frigate left half her Marines behind for Moresby's tourists and sailed to show the flag to some outer islands — Le Breton's conspicuously not included. The ship's departure meant that his Tiger Stripe tango with Holly might not make the bush telegraph after all.

On Tuesday, while she slept in, he came down for an early breakfast, feeling as chipper as the Throttled Sepik Lark singing outside the Nelli's dining room window. He shared the meal with Nelli's permanent guest centipedes and cockroaches. After breakfast, following Bowman's new counter-espionage instructions, he went out for the first *sankamap* dawn patrol to double-check that no local plagiarists were chasing *Brio* in pidgin as the sun came up. Ela Beach was deserted except for spiny Black Sea Urchins and an imported half-dingo Aussie mongrel pursuing an oversized, home-grown New Guinea rat to its hole under the Lotohaus rack supporting *Lonely Planet* guides.

"Monin'," said the kiosk operator, kicking the dingo.

"Monin'," said Grainger, picking up a *Moresby Times*.

"Yu im mos PNG bigpela Tango Man niuspepa dan Lord Bum."

A spy's worst fear. His face was headline news.

Not just his face. Or Holly's. Their only saving grace was the lighting. Except for a single 40-watter, all the other Nelli's bulbs had burned out: from their necks down, the two partners were shown in naked silhouette. Miss Montana's half was its usual spectacular. Grainger's was something between an embarrassing bulge and a merciful blur.

"Man yu plenti merri wan Tango now yu bigpela P'zola."

He told himself to keep things in perspective. Astor Piazzolla couldn't be a hot number at this lonely end of the planet: the Lottohaus operator's "plenty tango women" pitch to hype sales wouldn't go far off the beach either. Grainger returned to deliver an espionage All Clear with Lord Bum's brekfast kopi of the *Moresby Times*. At which point in double-time a pair of Walkman headphones, syncopating to Canaro, quick-quick-slowed through Nelli's front door.

A native Tangomaniac.

"Name's Maurie, for Maurice. I do Nelli's books once in a blue moon." The syncopater was the owner of the dingo mongrel: a chubbie half-Australian accountant with a Chaplin moustache on the end of a leash. The rest of the time Maurie studied a scratched videotape of Dance With the Champions from the USA. "Like man, that's what's so bloody fabulous. Until you did a real Gold Medal Grapevine in Nelli's window, I'd only seen half the Molinete."

Grainger tried to bow out. ""If you wait until next week," he advised Maurie, "there's a Gold Director on the Southern Cross. I'm just Bronze,.

"Serve you fucking right dancing for a nosebone rag! Look what the cannibal sods have cooked up for me!"

DEATH STINKS. Lord Bum had found a local review of *Death in the Palace*. After the header, it was not kind

"Ballroom politics," said the dingo's owner. "Don't tell me! Man, if it's good enough for teaching Godfrey Bowman, Old Dirk, you're the answer to our prayers." Maurie handed over a card, *¡Tango Paga! & Certified Accountant*. "We meet for practicas Tuesday nights in the East Baptist basement. That's between St Mary's Cathedral for dogans, and the old Ela United. Look for Steamships, you can't miss. Bottom of Paga Hill."

Steamships was Port Moresby's only department store, Number 11 on the Lonely Planet map. St Mary's Catholic Cathedral was Number 20. Grainger stuck a ballpoint tip halfway between the two landmarks, then, after supper, taking Holly with him for Celebrity cover, boarded a PMV — the locals' abbreviation of Public Motor Vehicle — for *¡Tango Paga!* to join the Certified Accountant's Tuesday Night.

The nude silhouette from the *Moresby Times* was tacked up on the former Baptists' basement door. He followed Holly through it to 78 rpm notes of Pugliese's *Recuerdo* backstopped by more enthusiastic whistles. The Paga milongueros and milongueras were a heterosexed assortment of fourteen local professions and skin colours sharing a love of tango, but not much else. Instead of the stab and thrust exported to the rest of the world from Buenos Aires, the seven Moresby couples moved in constant swoops of poorly mirrored action.

Grainger did his Dance Director bit to get the couples off Pugliese's dramatics, on to rock-steady Di Sarli. "Just walk with the boom-boom. Leaders, Forward Left. Followers, Back Right."

The only move was Maurie pointing at a Karlotta's Trilingual Tango Therapy ad in the local *Times'* Personals, pinned beside the nude silhouette. A vivid red diagonal slash had been drawn across it. Maurie said, "We don't have Leaders. Karlotta says it's macho."

Holly said, "It's nuts."

Grainger tried again, as though he was back with Avar's widow-bonking school of total ignorance at the start of a cruise. Maurie flicked the red slash on the silhouette with a dismissive finger. "Skip Karlotta's Nix sign. Give us the molinete you did in the window."

Adrenaline and testosterone did the rest. Backed by wild clapping of all fourteen hands, Old Dirk was begged to show Karlotta the error of her way with Sacadas. "Sure," he said, "I'll drop by in the morning and have a word with her."

Spy Nanny, a life-long bachelor, might have warned him, but Nanny wasn't there. The first hint of a Tango cold war in Papua New Guinea sailed by like one of the poison-arrows in a brochure for the Moresby Museum, when Maurie added, in parting, after driving them back to Nelli's, "If the PMV bloke acts dumb with the address, just tell the pidgi bugger, 'Karlotta lezlez Kremlin'."

But on Wednesday morning a possible confrontation with Karlotta was averted by God summoning his Entourage to join Nelli's centipedes for a Deep Background breakfast.

"All these bloody islands look the same to a PG rating. Hit the Museum for any cannibal crap on Two Tits while I keep getting us past Vulkan's Knickers."

"That should really help get Parental Guidance for Chasing Brio." Holly's sarcasm went undetected. In their joint capacities as Ghost and Research she and Grainger took another Public Motor Vehicle to the Waigani Government District. The regular stop was fifteen hundred meters from their destination. Because of their niuspepa silhouette reputation the driver took them the extra mile.

"Mi kisim yu National Museum an' Art Gallery. Bibi."

The PMV kissed them bye-bye at the hooked dead end of Independence Drive. A sign said Open 8:30 Monday to Friday 3:30 Close. The

Museum door was locked. Grainger looked at his watch.

"Ten thirty. On a Wednesday."

Holly said, "One thing about Beauty Pageants, you learn patience. This is *manãna* land. Someone will probably show up."

They found a picnic table and snack bar under some gum trees. The seats were comfortable. The snack bar was closed. A poster above it entertained visitors by identifying local flora and fauna. Another pair of Sepik Larks did a courtship number overhead. Two enormous Sapphire Swallowtail butterflies completed the act in a sticky patch of Pepsi on the snack bar. Grainger's mind drifted back to the bedroom —

"This is a PNG Pay Action Day! No Guides available."

With that public address squawck, the Museum door opened. Its air conditioning worked. The staff didn't. Visitors left to their own resources passed a Cowrie Outrigger Canoe and the Arrival of the First Australian Gold miners by Steam. Lots of poison-arrows and Bird of Paradise masks. The Impact of World War Two showed up as straw replicas of downed fighter aircraft next to The Arrival of the Cargo Cult and John Frum. Nothing about Le Breton Island.

Holly switched off her PalmNote research. "It's so goddamn sad. Let's get out of here."

The snack bar was still closed. The Swallowtails were still at it. The PMV stop was a mile walk: fifteen hundred meters further south of the equator and closer to the sun. Exhausted and sweat-drenched, they got back to Nelli's to find Freda exuding an air of Arid deodorant and mythic placidity after her penis gourd migraine. "We all find our separate ways to fly to the dream realm of King Midas," she informed them.

"When are we leaving?" Grainger asked Bowman.

"We aren't. I had a deal with those airport nosebones to fly us into Two Tits. If you can't rely on bribes for a Gents' Agreement in New Guinea, what's the point with fucking Etonians?"

Lord Bum stamped upstairs to flagellate his Chartwell Desk. Flying anywhere was out of sight. The roads were broadly cracked again from another quake before the Big Wan. Taxis had vanished.

Grainger fell into afternoon Tropical Routine and more unforgettable love with Holly. Music drifted from the far side of Paga Hill. Native drums joined the Marines left behind for the tourists when *Dauntless* sailed.

"Elgar again." She lay on her stomach, listening. He traced her perfect backbone, from the nape of her neck to the cleft of her buttocks, transfixed by this female vision who had agreed to be his third wife.

Our third time will *be lucky.* He said, "The Royals are playing Nimrod to close the Ceremony."

More themes and variations of his fractal spy-path. She rolled over for his hand to trace her Tiger Stripe. "At Julliard we used to play the student's game of figuring Elgar's riddle in the Enigma — not the easy surface part, like Nimrod being for his friend Jaeger, which is German for hunter — but the deep stuff underneath."

His hand found it. "And what's Julliard's answer?"

"Something cosmic, like where the music came from. Enough Elgar. Let's play Swallowtails instead."

Her muscles quivered. The Marines' brass finished off Elgar's mighty hunter. Only the drums remained; civilised and cannibals, both beating Retreat. A ship's siren sounded in Walter Bay. The deep-throated resonance of a last Empress; then the rumbling rattle-echo followed by a splash, letting-go her anchor. The *Southern Cross* and her shipload of Animal Crackers had caught up.

His heart belonged to Holly: his soul had been escrowed to Gustav Rufus until Mission Accomplished. The daylight hours of Thursday repeated Wednesday's: Entourage-shared meals with Nelli's cockroaches and centipedes, then chasing PNG Colour; the Royal Papua Yacht Club perched between Stanley Street and Champion Parade. Bowman took the salute of a regatta sailpast in honour of the visiting Top Five Hundred with his usual empathy for losers, but otherwise was still out of sorts from the local reviews.

Freda psycho-babbled to buck everyone up. "Death Stinks recalls Mags and mother. The minnow-critics move in shoals: we now Rest with our Musae. After resting we shall kill two birds. I by a visit to the library. Dirk filling his magic promise to help Karlotta's Molinete."

In the continuing absence of stretched limos, Thursday evening's Entourage downgraded to a ramshackled Datsun pickup PMV: a barely mobile glass-free zone with only half the Public Motor Vehicle's regulation number of wooden benches. Frey and Freya oveflowed the front. Grainger shared a broken one with Holly, thigh-to-thigh. Every time the Datsun lurched over an earthquaked crack in the dirt roads, the sensation was a superheated sacada. Musical accompaniment came from a tin-metalled Anglican church.

Em bilong valiant bee, Nogo disasta,
Emgo im konstancee, Folo im Masa . . .

John Bunyan in Pidgin carried Grainger back to Ember Days as a Boy Soprano. The hymn was prophetic: the Master of World Class fictional disaster was constantly being followed. Openly this time: a gray Land Rover stenciled Pitcairn Proprietary, with a Kangaroo-catcher shielding the radiator, and all its black-tinted armor glass intact, emerged from the shadow of the church. The tint prevented worshippers or Grainger from seeing the Pitcairn driver. Bowman over-stretched his imagination with another world-class nicker, "Call the fucker Fletcher Christian." The windowless Datsun stopped for an apparently unbridgeable chasm. Organ notes drifted across the gap. Freda was stuck in Muse mode. "Clio has myth's power to recall History, and so change our direction."

The Datsun's driver reversed hard-left across the church's planted vegetable patch to dodge the crack. Fletcher Christian's Rover went hard right. The singing changed to single tenor, English Australian:

There's no discouragement, Shall make him once relent
His first avowed intent —

" 'To be a pilgrim'." Grainger's recall lapsed out by itself. The Datsun lurched clear of some squashed cabbages. Holly's hip rubbed against him.

"This really is familiar territory for you," she said.

Lapsing on a Mission had no part in it. He blamed love, and told her a scrap of honest truth not recalled since his Spy Nanny Board.

"I passed the hymn-singing for St Paul's — the cathedral's choir school — but flunked math. There were only two questions: one about a train, the other about a parrot."

A flock of Greens flew over the church. The Datsun jammed in a yam patch. Bowman said, "Fuck it. I'm walking back to the Yacht Club. Just tell me when Queen Victoria got laid." He stepped down and stuck a lordly thumb at Pitcairn's Rover. The invisible Fletcher Christian driving it ignored him. The Datsun roared backwards into a heap of treadless tires in front of a combined Medical Clinic & Mission Library with car wrecks piled up around it for spare parts, and a notice under a sagging Michelin Man:

BAM BAM BILONG MERI NO GO PNG!

WIFE BEATING IS ILLEGAL

IN PAPUA NEW GUINEA!

Karlotta's sign was at the bottom of the heap.

¡Take the Macho out of Tango!
Only 2 Days More For Dykomania!

The Datsun's operator slammed a pink palm with a clenched black fist and said, "Lezlez Kremlin meri bam bam!"

Freda maneuvered her bulk between the wrecks and entered the library. Grainger kicked the tires until Bowman was safely collected by a southbound PMV. Pitcairn's Rover circled the pile and headed north. He still couldn't see the face behind the tinted glass — but nor did the invisible driver seem to care about seeing him. If he was regarded as a threat, the tail would stick. Satisfied again at the professional level, on the personal he followed Holly down dog-stained concrete stairs to the Lezlez Kremlin.

"Practica 9pm Thursdays: K5 or 5U$" had been added to a Dykomania poster. The kina was under par with American dollars;, which meant that Karlotta's trilingual therapy was currency-trading at a profit of ten percent. Dance groups weren't usually that shrewd. Most tango clubs started broke and then lost money.

Karlotta herself was cheerleading her troop in an accent blending three languages. "I only vant remind you: greatest compliment I ever in all my life receive is from Marta my partner. 'Lotta you take Macho out of Tango Balls.' Vich is vy ve don't have no time for Follower's molinete — even zo she is such dishy peach."

The troop's cropped heads followed their leader's to take in Miss Peach's dishy blonde shoulder-length as Holly walked through the door. The welcome cooled for Good Old Dirk: a group hiss, led by Marta, the No Balls sidekick of Lesbian Art Week. Marta wore a flirty, floral-patterned miniskirt and diamond-mesh red stockings, with matching lipstick. Karlotta's butch costume was buttoned-fly jeans and waistcoat-vest, both black, and no makeup. Faced with an uncastrated male her tactic was to go for the femoral by freezing him out. She smiled sweetly at Holly and kept her back to Grainger. He prayed she would continue.

If she turned around she could blow all his covers.

The last time he saw her was in Prague, as a hostess in a ball gown arranging placement cards for a supper dance to celebrate *perestroika*. She had a wedding ring on her finger and a Red Army husband on her arm. Moscow's Chief of Staff. She was Spy Nanny's hottest Cold War exhibit.

"The Venus Fly-Trap, Chanel Five-at-a-Time — you must have heard her nickers?"

The Intelligence Community on both sides of the Wall climbed into her Honey Pot. Grainger had only been spared by missing a Wenceslas

Square bus to her apartment. There was no hint of that fatal Soviet attraction in this New Guinea Kremlin basement: Karlotta had traded Chanel and Champagne for the smells of marijuana and stale beer.

"You are too bee-utiful to be Displaced by man," she informed Holly, pointing to the ubiquitous silhouette from the *Moresby Times*. "Dump molinete sacadas. Come mirror back ochos viz me."

The niusppepa couple had been cut with scissors down its red diagonal fault line to remove the offending male bulge. Marta put on a neutered tape version of Canaro playing Arolas from which Gardel's quintessential Latin Lover voice had been electronically severed. Even Dykomania couldn't erase memory of the lyrics.

To feel that life is but a breath,
That twenty years are as nothing . . .

Arolas died at the hero's age of thirty-two, like Alexander the Great. Dead of TB or stabbed by a pimp, choose your myth. Karlotta's breath had soured since Prague. Bile and pot wafted over Grainger as she closed an ocho cortado right in front of him. He turned away to find his escape blocked by miniskirted Marta.

"Milonga," she ordered, in an Aussie twang. "And don't get any wrong ideas from Tango Pago. Down here, skirts lead. Pants follow."

Milonga marched. The music ripped into the rat-a-tat rhythm of *De Mis Amores*, a classic of Contursi's from fascist 1937. Marta had picked the fastest goosestep challenge, where the Leader got to choose. As follower, Grainger was forced to second-guess how they left the starting box.

She went straight into a sideways triple on tip-toes — but decoupled, so that he wouldn't copy her syncopation. Impossible at this speed. His male reflexes started on their own. He managed to rein them in for two slow steps to her three, and with a spy-dancer's sixth sense knew that Karlotta's Kremlin eyes were watching the back of his head. He synchronised a straight-line grapevine — then lost it when Marta presented a parada that stopped him dead: sandwiched where he started, in front of her lover.

Karlotta rendered her gender-neutral verdict in the plural. "*They* vood dance milonga much better if they learned how to follow," she advised Holly. "You should leave Lord Bum's boy. At qvestions of timing, thees vun vas never any good."

"I like him fine the way he is." But going back up the dog-stained stairs she said, "What a bitch. Your milonga was great."

Grainger hugged her shoulder. Karlotta had tagged him from the past as one of Nanny's boys. The only thing that mattered for the future of the Mission was that she hadn't queered his pitch by linking him to Rufus in the present.

Outside the library, Freda stood like a Michelin Woman among the tire piles, clutching a book to her Triple D bosom.

> *A Century of Devotion:*
> *The Kings & Queens of England,*
> *to their loyal Subjects.*
> *1837 — 1937*

"The first date is all we require to put my Frey-God's mind at rest about Queen Victoria's virginity." She pronounced this oracle as a midnight tremor toppled worn-out Goodyears around her. The quake was the last straw for finding a passing PMV. A ballsy Dykomaniac with an instant crush on Holly offered them a tight squeeze back to Nelli's in a tiny Peugeot. Halfway along the Moresby Road they almost ran over Bowman. Grainger got out to make room for his Lordship in the back seat which put Freda in maximum Muse Mode.

"Clio has solved our history problem, Frey darling. Let your Freya show you, using Magic Dirk's arithmetic. 'If the train with Mummy and the parrot leaves the station —' "

"Don't treat me like a fucking idiot. I chaired the Lords' Science Committee on Cold Fusion!"

The Peugeot drove off with Holly and its overheated load of nuts. Grainger trudged alone through the velvet blackness of a New Guinea night. Under Moresby's only working streetlight — at the corner where Champion Parade met Stanley — the Lost Empire caught up with him.

Two code-figures from the world of Queen Victoria, Sir Don Quixote, 5th Generation Bandleader, and the black-bat Vicar of Animal Crackers, were wrestling for a lost soul: the ginger-furred pig Grainger had seen on his airport arrival, snuffling at the Cessna wreck, was about to be sacrificed for profit by its owner, the Brio middleman from the Ela Beach Lotohaus.

The priest whinnied, "I adjure thee in the name of —"

"Bollocks!" roared the Don. "I represent Her Majesty's SPCA even in New Guinea. This poor brute gets slaughtered over my dead body!"

"Den im i cost faivpela ten kina," said the Loto slaughterer.

The $50 argument seemed ludicrous — except for the pig — until

Grainger saw Pitcairn's armored Land Rover cruise like a corporate shark from the shadows. Karlotta must have tipped off the Fletcher Christian driver on the local drums.

His Cold War tango heated up.

Headlights caught him in their high beam. Quicksilver said, "Good God!" The Rover roared straight forward. The pig squealed in terror. The priest's fingers clawed Grainger's arm. He threw the old man to one side, knowing, *This is it for me —!*

The Rover veered a fraction. At what should have been his last moment, the shark's-tooth kangaroo-guard splatted the black-bat figure instead. The headlights swung a circle before returning to the darkness.

The dying face of a High Anglican lunatic stared back at him from the brink of Niugini's spirit world. Thin lips like his own mouthed two last words before the Lotohaus pig's altar.

"Teddy's boy . . . ?"

He had no answer to a senseless question. The eyes of a fanatic that had seemed fixed on his face were already looking past it to the Southern Constellations of eternity.

Con Brio

Twelve

PAPUA'S TANGO OF SEX AND DEATH HAD COME FULL MOLINETE: A New Guinea Saturday Morning where the loss of a nonagenarian missionary by a drunk driver didn't rate more than an inside one-liner in the *Moresby Times* beneath a header in tiny eight-point print:

KRUZE BIZ IM NOT AFFECTED

Mags's arrival was the front page news. Her iconic likeness filled the upper half, morphed by PNG electronic typesetting immediately above the classic bows of the *Southern Cross,* giving the impression that Westminster's former Im Bigpela Iron Meri had been physically welded as a figurehead to the Last White Empress.

Grainger couldn't get the priest's dying words out of his head. "Teddy's Boy" was tangled in one of Arolas's milongas.

The company of studs and broads,
Of dandies, paupers, cops and cons . . .

The cops were Pitcairn security. The victim was killed by one of Pitcairn's vehicles. Pitcairn secured Vulkan on Le Breton. The only connection seemed as out-of-this-world as Freda-babble: Animal Crackers and Brio's Chief Geologist were related.

De Cosmos's current passport name was Louis. The priest's last whisper had been faint. Might he have said, "Looey's boy?"

Pitcairn gave no answers. The company's PR team were spinning their way out of a scandal involving a PNG cabinet minister who kept too much of the cash "Fletcher Christian" was supposed to receive for waging counter-insurgency open warfare with Huey helicopter gun ships among the rebel flowers of Bougainvillea.

A Huey's boy . . . ?

Grainger pondered the priest's last syllables. Lord Bum chucked his bigpela weight around Air Niugini. By Saturday noon, World Class bribes brought God's Entourage and the Churchill Desk back to whimsical Jackson's International Airport just in time to see the travel-worn body of their plane bumping past them on its way to Le Breton Island one hour ahead of Air Niugini's Rescheduled By Earthquake Schedule. In lieu they were offered:

"Im bilong cuppa Missis Pekoe?"

Freda accepted tea. Bowman hit the terminal's last bottle of Aussie champagne. Red-lettered, pidgin Anglo-German warnings of potential disaster covered the entire surface of the departing aircraft's tail.

SAPOS BALUS I BAGGARUP YU MAS

WOKIM DISPELA OL SAMTING

Grainger discarded his Priest-Huey connection: Mercenary chopper pilots with an hour to kill scanned *Hustler's* beaver spread sheets, not mediaeval Animal Prosecution transcripts. Holly used her Local Colour laptop to digitize the Teutonic half of the Locator Signal message stenciled on a parked Twin Otter with one prop missing.

SUPPOSE PLANE HE BUGGERS UP, YOU MUST

WORK HIM THIS FELLOW THING

("Uk Uk gumi"= rubber bung, from the German, rausïm.
this can also be meaning ein Condom!)

She said, "That must be a real help when they find the buggered-up wreckage. I'm going to find some vodka."

"The only way your Lordship's going to hit Le Breton today from here at Moe, you'll have to charter a Special," Air Niugini advised Bowman. "The Otter over there your Mz Gorgeous was just looking at."

"Minus one screw," said Grainger.

"Give me a couple of hours, I can arrange this for three thousand kina — less forty percent in US dollars. Plus a couple of gratis fukfuk rooms at the Gateway with Musac while you wait."

Another small hotel. Another green lizard watching them with unblinking voyeur's eyes from a damp patch on the ceiling. Still no air-conditioning. Grainger loaded more Arolas in the Lotohaus boomboom box to drown out the Gateway's fukfuk musac.

Tango you made me suffer, but I love you
Oh Tango, in whose fatal shelter my heart swells . . .

This time they hung a sheet across the window before Displacing in the nude. Arolas's misery changed to *la Cara de la Luna*, Campoamor's upbeat milonguero.

Like a dream on the face of the moon . . .

She made the transition seamlessly, her chest against his for minimum space on a crowded floor; their Tiger-Stripes touched.

She groaned, "This is too erotic."

Random flashes of high voltage as their four legs displaced.
Your absent eyes were empty harbours
A horizon of dreams and the silence of flowers . . .
Arolas's lyrics returned during their lunar eclipse from the climax of passion. "I don't have words," he said. "I've never felt this with anyone in my life."

"I've never danced this." She kissed her way down to his point of exhaustion. Her eyes looked up at him. "But like they say in Big Sky country: Can I trust you to be there when we get out of jail?"

Trust. Another quake rumbled through the Gateway.

"Godamn France," she said. "More of their nuke shit under Mororea."

He said, "Play your oboe for real. No karaoke."

She sat on the edge of the bed. He lay beside her and looked up at the lizard. Her purity of Piazzolla's *Tanti Anni Prima* melted the last frost of his soul. The lapsed Anglican prayer for marriage came back to him. *Flesh of my flesh . . .* and this third silent time of asking, *Do you take this woman . . . ?*, for the rest of his life, responding to himself, *I do*, he meant it.

"Let me cut loose from Bowman's bullshit," he said when her final note faded, "after this gig you can trust me with anything."

She put down the oboe and lifted the velvet lining of its case lid. "What if I told you Miss Montana isn't what she seems — would you turn me in?"

He tried to think of a crime she could possibly be guilty of, an action so terrible, that even though he knew it, he wouldn't surrender himself to Stockholm Syndrome. The hostage falling for the hostage taker.

"No," he said. "Tell me anything."

"I'm not really Mz Research for Bowman."

"That's it?" He had braced himself for murder. She produced an ID membership card hidden behind the oboe's velvet. "I'm here for Friends of the Earth. To expose Vulkan."

He knew it was the honest truth. "Custer's last Green stand," he said.

"Or Bunyan's pilgrim. You feel it too." She put the Friends card back in its hiding place. "I know you do. There were tears in your eyes outside that tin church. That's why I'll marry you."

V-for . . .

"Get your Cha Cha arth out here in double time." Bowman's lisp carried God's frustration through the door. "Chrithtian thez therth a thpy in my luggage and Magth ith meeting Freda in the lobby. Go down and head them off."

A spy in the luggage. Vulkan Security must have been alerted but the level didn't have to be as deep as Rufus. The trigger could just be Holly turning Green. But first there was more insanity with Freda meeting Mags.

"I don't know what madness His Bumship expects me to avert," he told Holly, "but I guess I have to go down there."

"Enjoy." She put her arms around his neck and kissed him. "I'll still be here. Rewind the Arolas to that 'horizon of dreams' bit."

And the silence of flowers . . .

Bedlam in the lobby. A stately ex-cannibal, stark naked except for his penis gourd, stood in front of the Gateway's magazine rack, gravely studying the headline in USA Today.

BREAKING THE MALE FULL FRONTAL BARRIER !

HOLLYWOOD SEES BIG $TUDIO BUCK$!

Freda was wearing her moo moo for haggling. She saw Grainger. "Magic Dirk, you must translate 'looksi'. I am saying I wish for a client to study the mythic lingam at close hand."

The ex-cannibal responded to Freda's look-see urge with a Primitive's natural courtesy. "Doc-doc em i hamas fity dola imgo Gateway fuk-fuk?"

Grainger translated, "The asking price is fifty American if Doc-Doc wants to get laid like the other White Women who stay at the motel."

"Thank him for the honor. How much for the gourd?"

"Nogat lusim, yewess tirty. Nogat nogat lusim aduarit, tak-tak two hand."

"He says if you don't-don't want to touch it — meaning most ladies do — U.S. thirty. For the gourd by itself, he'll knock it down ten."

Freda took a twenty from her handbag. The Primitive untied a Nike shoelace around his waist and slid the gourd off in time to attract a busload of Middle-American-For-Jesus Ladies en route to a Bible Convention in Cairns, Australia. Accompanied by their luncheon Guest Speaker on Christian Family Values in a Bull Market.

"Quite *extraordinary*. How *does* it stay up?"

Not a brazen hair out of place. Voice so familiar from its clay-cartoon Spitting Image that it was a parody of itself. Grainger was toe-to-toe again with a Westminster Icon's foot (sticking through beneath the news rack) from his backstairs MI5 days at Whitehall.

The ankle had thickened a little with age but the toe was just as ready to boot a "wet" up the arse. The Icon's head was turned away from him. Iron Meri's steel gaze had locked on to a Primitive lingam. As long as it stayed there, the Ex Prime Minister of Great Britain and Northern Ireland wouldn't see what she once italicized in capital letters — as he had stepped like any other honest-builder, nothing-venture capitalist into 10 Downing Street for fund-raising drinks with the Legend: "*Who invited A Blindingly **Obvious** Absolute MI **Wet** like* HIM . . . !"

"All Jesus meri special yewess twenti."

A rush of lingam orders from the Jesus Ladies blocked him from Mags's line of sight. Air Niugini came through with an offer that could complete his escape.

"Vulkan have stopped all scheduled flights with a Volcano Alert, but you can still make it with our Chartered Otter if you leave now. Only one other small glitch. Just three passengers. His Lordship will have to chuck a body out of the lifeboat if he wants to take the Desk."

The "glitch" wasn't small. It was Spy Nanny's Final Exam killer question:

"Adam and Eve and Punch Me, go down to the river to bathe. Adam and Eve get drowned by the KGB. If we make the river the Moskva, who do you think we save? And the answer isn't Punch-me-Not."

Grainger could see the answer coming.

"There's no question about Winnie's bloody desk," Bowman declared, in a cracked-airport-lounge council of war. "It fought the Kraut bastards on the beaches. I can't get rid of Willie's Knickers without Freda, and we need Miss Gorgeous to keep the Diggers happy. But a Cha Cha merchant is as much use on Two Tits — "

Cutting a potboiler down to the short strokes: So long Magic Dirk.

Con Brio
Thirteen

FATE BROKE HOLLY'S ANKLE. GRAINGER BLAMED HIMSELF. TRYING to make light of Bowman bumping him from the Mission, wanting every final moment with her, he used their downtime to dance some high-heeled Canaro in their standby fukfuk room.

"Of course it isn't your fault," she said through clenched teeth, as they waited for Niugini to provide a paramedic. "I was the one who insisted on wearing nothing but a smile and the godamn tango heels. And I'm sure it's only a sprain."

X-rays and a doctor from the car-parts Clinic beside Karlotta's Kremlin diagnosed a hairline fracture. "You'll have to wear a cast and use a chair, at least for a couple of days." She emerged from the Clinic's bed of pain to cope with Bowman's World Class empathy without a local anesthetic.

"A wheelchair's the last bloody straw. The Niu Gini Charter sods are already moaning about the Desk."

"Don't sweat it, Godfrey. Just get the sods to carry me up the Otter steps. When we have to outrun a dead volcano I'll use crutches."

"Can't do that either. Now the bloody plane has a flat from a thumbtack on the runway. But if we're stuck here anyway," he said to Grainger, "Big Tit's stone cold — the quake reports are just scare tactics to keep us away from the Assays — and we need more What-If Ultimate Disaster crap for Hollywood. You can get it by pouring a few Fosters into a nosebone geologist at Nelli's."

The six-inch spike in a tire which had stalled the chartered Otter was no thumbtack. Grainger assigned it to Pitcairn dirty tricks. His offer of free Fosters drew a blank because there were no geologists in Nelli's Bar. He flagged another rusting Toyota PMV and after only one burst radiator finally tracked down a Brit vulcanologist at the National Mapping Bureau. The expert was feeding pidgin-lettered epicentres of Port Moresby's shakes to a computer getting ready for something labelled: Big Wan on imgo Rim of Fire.

"They all seem to start beneath Le Breton," said the Brit, "but I can't say that means an imminent eruption. You never can with a plugged vent. The tectonic picture isn't being helped by French H-bombs under Mororea. The thing to watch for in a dodgy volcano is the gas being turned off — that's what leads to Krakatoa. Living on a speck of cosmic dust with a molten core it's always a question of When, not If."

Grainger returned to the Gateway with enough Ultimate Disaster to satisfy Bowman and Hollywood. "The flat's fixed," a phone call from Air Niugini told him. "We load cripples first so get your girl here soonest. All bags have to go through Vulkan's Special Security Wallaby-bangers in case she's hiding a Tree Hugger in her purse."

In his girl's room, unfolding the wheelchair, he remembered the Friends of the Earth ID behind the velvet lid of her oboe case.

"Nobody but you knows about that," she said, "and it won't show up on X-rays or a sniffer. I'm still going."

He couldn't dump the Desk: it was already strapped on board. Frey-and-Freya were on standby rest in fuk-fuk Valhalla. *Adam and Eve were drowned. Holly gets saved.* He pointed at her crutches. "Be practical. The chance of an eruption may be slight, but if the Le Breton bomb goes off, you've only got one foot to touch the ground."

"And my knickers are labeled Research." She updated her Palm screen. "The world's largest aircraft carrier is steaming to the rescue as part of Mags's book tour. USS Franklin D. Roosevelt, one hundred thousand tons — that's three times bigger than the So Cross — Captain Robert Falcon Scott Junior, from Tucson Arizona, in Command — but it's beside the point. Saint Helen's kept people guessing for weeks."

He had no time to argue. At Checkpoint-Charlie moments like this, recalled on the way downhill from *Endymion* at Honest Spies Reunion dinners, Nanny fell back on nonsense rhymes of Edward Lear, nightcapped with Snottie-Nursed Gunroom limericks.

There was a young woman called Holly,
Who had one leg up on a trolley —

While her wheelchair was being eased out of Nelli's lobby by a medic, Grainger's tiny talent betrayed his last Big Love. For his girl's own good, he removed the ID card from its velvet hiding place and put it in her shoulder bag at the front of the Otter's luggage line for Vulkan's Wallaby-bangers to find.

Another identical Pitcairn tinted Rover waited in the wings. Vulkan's Special Advance Security opened the shoulder bag as its crippled owner and the rest of God's Entourage arrived.

"Friend of the Earth membership card!" the senior Wallaby-banger yahoo'd via cell phone to a still-invisible Fletcher Christian. "One of those Green fucks trying to shaft Brio when she isn't shaving her bikini line!"

The victim looked at Grainger with her green eyes replaying Paul Muni's Dreyfus's *J'Accuse: You're the only one who knew!* . . . while her perfect lips protested, "It isn't possible. Not in my shoulder bag."

"The Freudian Lover's Letter in the pocket," Freda psychologised. "This is so shallow it must be Kleinian."

"If it's a plant to keep us out, it has to be the salted Assays!" Bowman empathised. "Switch seats and toss your Two Tits Colour shit to Dirk."

Vulkan's Inquisition carried their pale witch past him. He looked into her eyes with all the honesty his blue ones could muster from half a lifetime of re-running Spy Nanny's Casablanca.

Play it again: Flesh of my flesh from this day forward . . .

"I'll be there," he promised. "When we get out of jail."

"You said I could trust you. Don't bother."

She flung her PalmNote Research at him. With his spy's reflex for second-things-first he made the catch — and didn't even get to kiss her goodbye before the Wallaby-bangers completed his Gunroom Obscenity chapter in verse.

"Her shaved cunt was so Green, that it had to be seen

Fucked off by a prick on a broomstick."

Otherwise known as a small-t malevo on a Mission, who killed Forever Tango for nothing but Big Money.

Con Brio
Fourteen

HEIR CHARTERED NIU GINI OTTER GOT AIRBORNED THIRD-time-luki in the Flight Log. The flat tire got listed as Natural Causes. "Only fifty white-knuckle landings over Safety Limit she's dinky-die," the aircraft's Aussie pilot reassured God's reduced Entourage. A six-inch spike in the works hadn't been mentioned as one of the causes; Grainger added it under P-for-Pitcairn in Holly's researched PalmNotes.

Loco, loco, loco . . .

He was crazy to let her go. Now that it was too late, he had a thousand even crazier second-thoughts on How to get her back? Wedged between the Otter's fuselage and mock Churchill Desk, he almost convinced himself that there was still room for Love Regained after this Last Mission: that if he bared his soul to Level Five, Holly would forgive his Unexpected trespass against her. All he had to do was double Ghost with Palm-held Research and keep the Bum names straight as Bowman locked another barn door with crypto bullshit behind the pilot's head.

"From here, we double-up codenames as well as Research. Starting with that Fair Dinkum Dinkie-Dieing his joystick in the cockpit."

The volcano took Grainger by surprise: a sacada from nowhere beneath the South Pacific. No clouds, the cone-breast was perfect. No wisp of steam either. After all these weeks of tortoise-racing against possible eruption, Le Breton's time-bomb looked as dormant as everybody said. The Fair Dinkum pilot provided more Dinky Die cheer on the blower.

"Vulkan have only sliced the Left Tit halfway so far. The buzz is they hit the main core lode last week — from here on the motherfuck's solid gold. Excuse the Outback lingo, Doc." Freda was preoccupied with laptop-babble Musing. There was no river for Adam and Eve to bathe in: the remnant of a stream which previously supported typical New Guinea patchwork gardens in Holly's notes now divided a yellow-brown shit-sludge slurping one-third of the volcano's flank. A hard-packed runway skirted its northern edge. "Vulkan couldn't come up

417

from the bottom," the pilot continued the Company tour: "They had to take the hard way, landing the chewing equipment on top. Digger buckets the size of bloody houses! A fleet of Chinook mega choppers from Pentagon Surplus. Waste Disposal — usually the biggest Green headache — on Two Tits, no problemo. The diggers tip the shit into Cyanide Creek. It rises so fast, Civil Engineering has to rebuild the complete godamn strip every night."

The diggers' shitheap rose on command. One hundred tons in a single bucket, released by its mechanised sphincter, defecated beyond the Otter's port wingtip.

"The Nose-Bones have done bloody well out of it. Free use of the Company School, Medical — not the Supermarket, they have to pay for groceries like anyone else that can't grow their own coconuts — plus hard cash for King's Cross weekends in Sidney's fuk-fuk district, and re-settlement on the Atoll of their choice for the twenty odd years Vulkan reckons it'll take to do the Enviro rehab at the end. If anyone's left who wants to come back. There were only a handful of Bones here eating each other to begin with. The Headman's a twenty-karat Abo Golden Oldie in a penis gourd called Olie."

Fair Dinkum banked the Otter into a final white-knuckle circuit before landing. "A word or few about Vulkan Security — those three dots on the strip, next to the Air Ops shed. Pitcairn's crowd of SAS mercs are pretty decent except to Tab Shits, but everybody's a bit edgy since the buckets struck Big Time pay dirt, which is why Boss-man Williams is here himself." Dinky-Die touched the Otter down with a three-point bounce matching the one from Freda's moo moo. "Don't argue with his Torture Team about the price of Coke in China — they're death on drugs getting in for the digger drivers."

Torrential tropic rain. Grainger splashed across the mud runway to find Mags waiting for him outside the shed. At this end of the earth, next to *XXX VICTOR-VICTORIA SHE-MALE CLASSIXXX!* for the locals' beer hall entertainment, some wag had pinned her book jacket Boadicea hairdo under Cuming Attractions.

"Lady Luck and Lord Bum with the Palace arsewipe." A bullhorn crudeness stopped their sodden tracks. The figure climbing out of a familiar logo'd gray Rover with black-tinted windows, looked just like it. In the way that dogs resembled their owners (Grainger with his Afghan's nose), Special Interrogators took on the physical identity of their weapon for intimidation. (Gustav Rufus and a Junta tank.) The butcher's boy heading Pitcairn's ex-para Security brigade was a slab-sided cube, six-feet tall, one-ton on the weigh-scales, wearing bulletproof gray, and hidden behind Ray-Ban sunshades. He put down the bullhorn and said in Sixth Form Etonian anti-climax, "My name's Wallers."

Bowman said, "Lord Bowman of Bridport. It isn't often I chuck my weight around outside Beverly Hills but a title should mean something even on a dung heap of an atoll —!"

"Not on Vulkan private property, and my old man's a Marquis. Lord and Lady Arsewipe can get your Archetypes inside the Ops shed."

Wallers' bulk blocked escape with a monolithic brusqueness in his body language backing up a verbal greeting to a Peer of the Realm that clearly didn't give a Jungian shit if his truncheon-toting animus was grossly out of whack. Hiding as an Old Sherbournian, Grainger took an overlooked chameleon's clay path of least resistance through the shed door. Freda insisted on playing her Muse of Mona Lisa. It didn't amuse Wallers.

"Your Ladyship can wipe that fucking smile. Sit down."

"As a Küsnacht Mender of Minds I prefer to stand."

"Head games won't tear strips off anyone's dick around here. Lord Bum can suit himself. Sit, stand, or disappear with a Pani-bird's screech up his own rectum. It'll do as much good as trying to buy my man in Moresby with shithouse reading material." A fist from a Mapplethorpe study chucked a dog-eared paperback in its Titled Author's direction, then slammed an Interpol dossier on the shed desk in front of Freda. "Forget the Küsnacht crap. I'm the minder. Is this you?"

"I'll have your guts for garters!" Bowman bellowed. "I not only own a hundred million in Brio stock, Palace is my best bloody book! I demand to see —"

"Lord Fukfuk. First you try and con your way in here with a Green cunt splitting her Research for Friends of the Earth. Now it's a cowpat in a moo-moo who's never been closer to a Swiss chocolate factory than six months in Hamburg Korrectional für Damen." Wallers flipped the dossier open. "Elfreda, aka Edwina White, native of Cleveland, Ohio. Seven counts of blackmail from playing Psychic to the Stars and Gustav Rufus, aka Ruffles. She's a quick learner. All five Most Recent charges of Extortion got dropped."

Bowman sat down, speechless. Grainger wondered why Rufus hadn't told him about Freda — who pushed away the dossier, and asked in a voice as flat as Ohio, "So what do you intend to do?"

"Hand over the keys to the Veep Suite in the Company Guest House. The CEO invites His Lordship for Sunday lunch tomorrow, before church. No dancing in the streets tonight, only the usual Mini-Rave at the Rec Centre. I'll leave free tickets at the door."

In a classic Bad Cop / Good Cop switch, the head of Vulkan's Torture Team alchemized into a suburban Welcome Wagon Person, ushering the Entourage from the Air Ops hut to place a bullet-proof Rover coach at their disposal.

"That doesn't mean you, chum."

Back to Bad Cop. Wallers' Mapplethorpe fist gripped Grainger's arm. *¡Resolucion!, he thought. Game over for chameleons.* Pitcairn Proprietary slammed the shed door on the Playing Fields of Eton.

"Mr. Jolly Jack of all trades from Sherbourne. Let's talk about those fancy-dancer Van-Fair emails to New York."

An earthquake, followed by thunder, rolled away. The minder of Vulkan's dirty washing let him hang there . . .

"I didn't like the fishy smell until my man on the Cross found from Dawson-Harris that you were serious ex-Navy. Which explained you playing both ends against the middle in the moonlight with Doctor Salsa's Privates and Bowman's Palace wipe for Pam. None of us can jump far these days on just a Golden Handshake — and what bloke could resist bailing into Miss Montana? Sorry we had to ground her, Dirk. Let's have a beer."

Good Cop Wallers produced a case of Fosters from a Company fridge in a corner of the shed. Grainger hoisted an honest one back and let a butcher's youngest son of a marquis expand on the technical defects in best-selling Death.

"Cross a coronet and a jockstrap! My great-great grandfather rustled cattle in Argentina to buy his ermine. I wouldn't mind Lord Arsewipe's Smelly Knickers names getting Bowman a Life peerage if the books weren't total shit on the professional level. Take one turd from his Palace." Wallers opened the paperback and ripped out an underlined page. "FN rifles have 7.62 millimetre bores. Nine mill is Browning pistols. Well having you aboard should spare him research cockups like that, this time around. The burning pisser is, my Wee Willie has to move mountains for a living. Your Lord Bum makes his millions from stunned mistakes. Maybe there's something from fucking a fortune teller after all. "

Grainger said, "You mean Freda?"

"Three husbands, one Psych Hospital for bashing Number Two with a brick. Freya and her eight Multiple Muses were released into their own recognizance under Prozac. Hubby Three was deep in the heart of Texas. A property developer, specialising in Bulgarian Blackjack."

Gus Rufus. Wallers flipped Freda's dossier into a drawer. Grainger took a second beer and said, "Why don't you turn her over to Interpol?"

"Freda's crazy but she isn't Green. My job here is keeping Vulkan bulletproof from the Tabs. If they want to headline Bowman being taken to the cleaners by his Jungian family jewels, I might tip a wink to a blind eye on Fleet Street. Not InterPol. Besides, what's one more nutter when a whole boatload's due to arrive?"

They finished the Fosters. Another quake rattled the empties. Outside the shed, Vulkan's Head of Security crossed his fingers — "Olie's Hex on the Mountain. Can't blame the old Cannibal sod," — then gutted the flyer of Mags's Cuming Attraction with a Commando knife. "You can have the run of the place for Bum's Research, except the Assay Sheds marked Keep Out."

What Bowman protested as "house arrest" turned into his usual clash of empathy with fact. The Veep bungalow had separate suites with twin baths back-to-back. Vulkan's accommodation was palatial by Nelli's standards — all the air conditioners worked — but His Lordship's fingerprints got taken to operate the Veep Suite's automated front door lock, and one of Wallers' Wallaby-bangers stood guard outside it with an Uzi to stop any unauthorised sleep-walking into an Assay Shed by one of the guests.

Grainger couldn't sleep. Trying to dodge the mute reproach contained under "Le Breton Purple Moths, Extinct" in Holly's PalmNotes for the Island, he made the infinitely worse mistake of listening to her oboe playing Tanti Anni Prima on his Sony headset, and got hammered by the doomed repeat lyrics of Arolas.

Your absent eyes were empty harbours,
A horizon of dreams and the silence of flowers . . .

When he took off the headphones he had to listen instead to Bowman transmuting the Elfreda White Dossier into a Smelly Knickers Plot to keep World Class writing from chasing Brio — before the sounds of Lord & Lady Arsewipe taking a shower to Valhalla in the suite next door. A helium glare showed hell in what was paradise only yesterday outside the bedroom window.

Yesterday, paradise was Locoing to Piazzolla with Holly in the nude....

In Le Breton Island's silent spring there were no flowers. One in a bonker's dozen of thirteen Company prefabs downhill from the Guests' House might hold the information Gustav Rufus needed to double an already unimaginable amassing of wealth. Still going through the motions of trying to keep his shattered spy levels straight Grainger slashed to Pam: `//Mags & So Cross just dropped anchor at Dow 9750. Peace & Quiet won't last long.` Then he got off the bed and went looking for hard evidence to support madness as a Mission.

Waiting for the Dow in Williamstown . . . he walked with Holly's palm-held research along Williams Boulevard and saw it through her green eyes: a Company Town which wasn't the size of a New England hamlet and a road that was no Boulevard. *There aren't any trees in a cyanide forest* her Chasing Colour Notes said. *For the banished Them who once lived here, Le Breton Island really is a Custer's Last Stand.*

Rufus wasn't paying for Love of the Earth. A third minor quake rumbled beneath Grainger's feet, then faded. He didn't blame an old cannibal for trying a last-gasp hex on the mountain to get rid of its invaders. With the valley now a solidifying swamp of mine-waste sewage, and the half-chopped limestone peak denuded to its core, the civic base of Vulkan's operations named for its corporate chief had to be carved halfway up the barren side of the volcano. The huge, helium overhead bulbs left no room for shadows of the island's former life.

He found the first of Holly's *banished Them* in a disco-strobed corner of the Company Recreation Centre. A nude tribal male sat below an otherwise unwatched giant screen showing the latest incarnation of James Bond re-working Goldfinger for the Y2K Millennium above a ticker of Brio's top place on the Dow.

The Aboriginal wasn't old. He was Ancient. Wrinkles corrugated his naked chest and stomach. His legs were pipe stems, but still muscled. Grainger couldn't see his face because of a white clay mask: any emotions behind it remained hidden. The eyes stared without a flicker at Digger Drivers doing a crude Chicken Walk in front of him, clucking adolescent obscenities. "Give us Good Head, man! Olie-Olie!"

The eyes behind the mask saw Grainger —

A fourth quake rumbled.

Bigger than the previous three put together. Enough to stop the jerk-off Chicken Walkers in their tracks. Some agro-conglomerate groceries fell off the Commissary shelves behind James Bond.

"Evnin."

The Headman had a deeper voice than his frail frame indicated. He wore only a shabby penis gourd, but what was an erotic tourist joke for Jesus Ladies in Port Moresby lost its giggle in Williamstown.

"Evnin, Olie." Grainger returned the greeting.

"Yu bilong meri Tee Dee?"

The old man's breath wheezed between each word. Behind him, the reincarnated Agent 007 jet-packed over a division of Chinese Red Army tanks. Grainger shook his head. "Mi no bilong any Teddy." The brown eyes behind the clay mask blinked once. A single tear slipped down its white left cheek, irritation from the disco lights.

"Cum lak T'd'i Frum. Boneeya! Misis merka Nor's'v'lt!" Now the tears poured, carving deep furrows through the clay. The ancient skin beneath had never been exposed to the tropic sun. It was jet black, with an infant smoothness. The Headman grasped his hand with one of dry leather. "Boneeya Nor's'v'lt! Boneeya T'd'i! Tumara yumi bilong golong T'rki."

The digger Chicken Walkers did a juvenile "Bone Ya!" with jerkoff pubic thrusts. Grainger's pidgin was hopelessly lost. Visiting Teddy seemed to be a turkey sacrifice to Eleanor Roosevelt. In Graham Greene's Haiti they used poultry ju ju for Papa Doc. Wallers had given an open blessing to roam freely on Le Breton, but as Spy Nanny always said about *Our Man in Havana*, "Inside the inner circle of chicken feathers is the last place for Alec Guinness to let down the Old Guard."

Partly at the Dirk-politeness level, mostly for Rufus's, he tentatively agreed to the Headman's "tumara golong" Turkey trot as Brio Research. He had searched for Mission madness, now he'd got it: the expression in the aboriginal eyes staring at his own, matched the lunatic glimmer of recognition in the dying priest's at Port Moresby.

Con Brio
Fifteen

U NDER THE LEVEL PRETEXT OF HALLUCINATION — COMING clay face-to-face with Olie — as the possible start of malaria, Grainger checked into Vulkan's field hospital at 04:30. Friday morning arrived early in Williamstown. The Company's Australian medic gave him fresh coffee and a physical OK.

"It's up here." The medic tapped the side of his skull. *"Aduarit.* Spirits of the head hunters get under people's skins when they meet a real Nose-Bone — or hang around them too long, look at Louis. You aren't the first to feel funny on Two Tits. Maybe the last. Old Olie's the end of the line. Take an aspirin."

He was so brainwashed by Bum nicknames that it needed the aspirin to make him realise whose true identity the medic had said felt funny about Olie: it was Brio's chief prospector, Louis, disguised in the novel as De Cosmos. He returned the recycled-paper cup with a casual, "Louis has a head problem?"

"Who wouldn't with five wives!"

"I heard it was four."

"Until last month. He picked the new one up in Borneo. Sweet Sixteen village girl swapped for a pouch of river gold."

Alluvial. Grainger filed "river gold" mentally under Salt and said, "I'm researching local colour for Lord Bowman's new thriller. Louis sounds a real character. Does he give interviews?"

"He tells whoppers. Like the time he played J.C. among the cannibals." The medic checked the clock on the clinic wall and entered Dirk/Research 04:35 in the Patient Treatment log. "The Jesus con got started in the forties, after the War. A Mormon was doing the head-hunter villages, bringing the Word in exchange for a tithe on the Same-time-next-year basis. Louis, or whatever he was going by then, hears about it, rigs himself out in a white robe and sandals with some Devil Thorns around his head, and when the Cannibals ask Where's the Mormon? he tells them Having a Last Pig Feast with my Father in Heaven. The Abos take one look at the bleeding thorns, fall on their knees and fork over. When the Mormon eventually shows up in an outrigger and asks for his tithe they strap him to the Pot for cheating. 'Jesus was here last week,' the Chief says. 'We already paid Him.' "

Dirk/Research laughed on cue. "A con made in heaven."

"Not long for this world, like old Olie. Two of a kind. When I treated Louis for his latest DTs, he swore someone was trying to kill him. I said, 'It's those Borneo boyfriends. You're going to have to quit pinching their meri pussies.' He said it was Wallers." The medic tapped his head again. "*Aduarit.* Shows what eighty years of gin does in the tropics."

"And where is Louis now?"

"Your guess is as good as mine. Probably being dried out again backstage before they bring him in front of the shareholders."

Grainger returned to his half of the Veep Suite in time for the wake-up call from Valhalla next door. The Dow cracked 9800 for breakfast. Bowman matched it with a wolfed-down boiled egg. Promptly at 09:00, the other animals were let out of the Ark. God's Entourage joined the first wave trooping down the gangplank from the *Southern Cross,* then past the Uzi barrels of Security to See The Gold.

Prefab Building 12. Core drillings laid out like pig's intestines. Minute samples of glitter beside each Assay sausage showed how many ounces per ton of stuffing.

"The highest now is up to Seven." A workaday Company geologist generated enough glitz to hustle the stock to $100, making Bowman half a paper billionaire by the end of lunch.

"The question is What else are we waiting to drop? I put it to Wee Willie after I tackled him on Knickers's bloody rudeness when we landed. If Vulkan has nothing to hide, I said, why can't I see De Cosmos? I've been around Westminster long enough to know that taking No comment for an answer *is* the answer. *Ten ounces minimum.* When I dropped that magic Assay number in the soup — Yam and Ginger, make a note of it for Chasing — you should have seen him blink! The reason was right there in front of me beside the dish. *Salt.* I know it isn't possible with the real Brio here on Two Tits — I've seen those core bangers glittering with my own eyes — but we're talking artistic license, not the Life of *Christ that's a big one!*"

Bowman's babble got cut short by another Richter roll. It didn't stop the Diggers' dynamite. Nor Weekend Sight-Seeing on a time-bomb. The visiting blue-ribbon Five Hundred from the So Cross regarded

the volcano with the fascination of mice for a dead snake: a vaguely
morbid curiosity — but no belief that the bomb would go off before
they sailed away with their Gilt-edged share certificates. Part of their
Saturday complacency was due to Vulkan's construction technique. All
the prefab structures were quake-proofed, on sliding-feet foundations,
with everything except the groceries nailed down. The heaving earth
got spun off by Company PR as "lateral wave motion from the French
tests on Mororea. Harmless tremulettes."

Their harmlessness was rising in a Richter Scale dead heat with the
Dow. To add to Grainger's problem of hiding in a reduced Entourage,
Freda fell off her Prozac on the way to Sunday church.

In the confusion of another French tremulette vigorous enough
to knock the Foreign Kinks rack for a loop, she shop-lifted a video of
SheMale ClassiXXX from the Company Store. Bowman bribed the
clerk with ten shares as excuses. "We're a long way from Claridges, "
he informed Grainger. "The inhibitions drop with the knickers in the
Frangipani flowers. I've just heard a buzz that Brio's going to open at
$170 on the Fiji Exchange tomorrow morning."

A trio of last night's Chicken Walkers placed a share order on-line,
then parked their Caterpillar diggers on the stump of the amputated
tit and straggled into the Rave Centre, doubling today as the Company
Chapel. Pitcairn's security bullhorn blared after them,

"Vulkan Family service, two minutes. Heel, you bloody Popsie!"

The latest Brio nicker was a dog: a shaved white poodle bitch with
a pink bow gracing her curly little head. Holding her leash, Wallers
looked like a Para undergoing the Death of a Thousand Cuts. In the
harsh helium light replacing darkness even at noon on treeless Williams
Boulevard there was no room for Grainger to hide under an Anglican
cloak of Lapsed Cynic. Acrid fumes drifted down from smelting
operations above the Company lights to sting his nose-and-throat.

Inside the Rave-Church, in exchange for a signed copy of *Death
in the Palace*, Lord Bum passed on stale dirt obtained from a Digger
driver. "De Cosmos isn't Louis. He's whacked off more names than
wives and twice that in careers. Everything from cornering the Copra
market to running guns for Jesus. I wouldn't put hiding fifteen ounces
past him."

Lady Bowman looked in her purse and said in Elfreda White's
flat Cleveland voice, during a moment of otherwise completely silent
prayer, "Fuck Jesus! My Prozac's run out."

"*Worship the King, All glorious above;*

O gratefully sing, His Power and his Love . . . "

The standing congregation turned their heads in unison from Freda's Prozac to a Company pew at the front, brass-plaqued:

ONLY FOR C.E.O.

"Our Shield and Defender, The Ancient of Days,
Pavillioned in Splendour and girdled with Praise. . . ."

Pitcairn's Security shielded him. All Grainger saw of Vulkan's CEO was a crew haircut, and two corporate arms reaching out for the poodle. Wallers tugged its leash. The dog yelped louder than the singing.

"His Chariots of Wrath the deep thunder-clouds form,
And Dark is his Path on the Wings of the Storm. . . ."

A crimson flush of anger suffused Wee Willie's bull neck. The Company congregation followed their leader in heightened devotion. Grainger used the Level One honesty of boredom in church to check the audience.

"The Earth, with its store of Wonders untold,
Almighty, thy Power hath founded of old . . . "

Widowed faces from his Dance Hosting — dominated by Mags' Hair (back view only: once again she didn't see him), led an Unexpected VIP handful of Episcopal investors from the So Cross. Dawson-Harris commanded the second pew. Quicksilver's RAF blazer represented Empire values as guest organist. The Vulkan Family dressed in Tilley tropical Sunday best. Olie's white clay face and antique penis gourd stood out of the back row (credit Bowman's quote) "like a foreskin at Sid's wedding." No other face in the audience had leathered enough in the tropics to be De Cosmos, slash Louis.

"Frail children of dust, and feeble as frail,
In Thee do we trust nor find Thee to fail . . . "

One minor surprise. According to the medic's Aduarit yarn during Grainger's early morning malaria check, the Headman was supposed to be last of his Nose-Bone line on Two Tits, but seated next to him was a small, jet-black boy in immaculate white shirt, shorts, and knee socks. The bottoms of the socks had been cut off so that he could walk like his ancestors in a four-year-old's bare feet. Grainger let his boredom look past the kid, through a prefab chapel window at the other Le Breton Island remains. Looking for Holly.

Your absent eyes were empty harbours,
A horizon of dreams and the silence of flowers . . .

Arolas's lyrics mixed with the hymn and left-over Coleridge from School. The *Southern Cross* was a toy ship below black lava cliffs, their reflection floating on a painted ocean.

"Hath stablished it fast by a changeless Decree,
And round it hath cast, like a Mantle, the sea. . . . "

A Bull with Golden Horns fluttered at the liner's masthead. Freda's Prozac-inspired design for a House flag of Mythras. "Her history muse dreamed it up at Saint Helena," Bowman said. "We can tie it into Napoleon's cape for the arsenic bit in Brio Two." The sea was visible, and changeless; emerald-sapphire South Pacific, mantling yellow-brown cyanide sewage. The Decree was posted on the chapel wall:

ANY PERSON REMOVING OR DEFACING
COMPANY PROPERTY OF VULKAN EXTRACTION INC.,
WILL HAVE COST OF SAME DEDUCTED FROM THEIR PAY
AND IMMEDIATELY BE TERMINATED.

"Thy bountiful Care what tongue can recite?
It breathes in the Air, it shines in the Light . . . "

Ancient Olie chanted pidgin. The four-year-old stayed mute. The poodle howled. Grainger looked at Wallers fingering his Uzi while glowering the word "Bitch!" and wondered whether Louis slash De Cosmos could have been terminated with CIA-styled prejudice?

"It streams from the Hills, it descends to the Plain,
And sweetly distills in the Dew and the Rain. . . . "

Anything was possible in this atmosphere. Outside the window the blazing light of tropic noon baked Vulkan's sewage-sludge to Sodom's crust; and the smelted air the congregation breathed had a sulphur-whiff of hell.

"Thy Mercies how tender, how firm to the End,
Our Maker, Defender, Redeemer, and Friend. . . ."

"Be seated for Collection. Captain Dawson-Harris will read the lesson."

Wallers' barked the order of service. Two Pitcairn mercenaries passed a plate on the Company's behalf. The Torture Team leader sacrificed a crisp Australian twenty for Wee Willie and Popsie. The barefoot boy dropped fifty PNG toya of pocket money in the plate. Olie ignored it, lost somewhere between his smoked ancestors and a study of Grainger's face. ONLY C.E.O. Williams followed John the Divine with a closing corporate prayer.

"To retrieve the concentrate more cost-effectively so that all His children in the Vulkan Family may return home to worship in the bosom of our Loved Ones and return the Site to thine inhabitants in whose Holy Name we hold it in trust, the better-rehabbed than when thy faithful servants found it. And now in its entirety let us sing —"

From many an ancient River, from many a palmy Plain, They call us to deliver their land from Error's chain . . .

"The Missionary Hymn, regardless of theological position," Spy Nanny used to dead-pan in silly-pipe reminiscing about Greene.

Can we, whose souls are lighted with Wisdom from on high, Can we to men benighted the Lamp of Life deny? Salvation! O Salvation! The joyful Sound proclaim, Till each Remotest Nation has learned Messiah's Name . . .

Grainger's benighted objective was to smoke out De Cosmos.

Waft, waft, ye winds, His story, and you, ye waters, roll, Till, like a Sea of Glory, it spreads from Pole to Pole; Till o'er our ransomed Nature the Lamb for sinners slain, Redeemer, King, Creator, in Bliss returns to reign.

The rehab service ended.

"I have *absolutely* no time for bliss, but I *do* like a *short* sermon," Mags proclaimed, shaking Chief Executive hands at the Company church door. "Good morning, Freda, Godfrey, and — " in a historic non-plus for words, caused by looking at Olie's gourd, before she looked at Grainger; conjuring an invisible Ghost of Wetness in Whitehall, brought finally face-to-face — "*Um.*"

For even her monosyllable, the ground shook . . . as Westminster used to, when Spy Nanny's backstairs world received a direct hit from an Iron Meri rocket. Grainger took advantage of an automated Earthquake Survival Drill Siren to beat one more safe retreat before the Rusting Widow's Question Period.

She didn't have one. The Iconic eyes staring directly at him were a complete blank. And there was something about them, the arching of the eyebrows wasn't as he remembered . . . from nearly two decades ago. He put the Iconic eyebrows alteration in the mental column for Plastic Surgery, and her life-saving lack of recognition down to Age.

Con Brio

Sixteen

TEN LITTLE INDIANS CROSS THE NEVA TO TURN LENINGRAD BACK INTO *St Petersburg: Who do we save?* Spy Nanny's nursery exercise was reality. With Mz Research on crutches and Lady Luck off Prozac, God's Entourage was already down to only two Mission levels of cover for Grainger. When Mags declaimed a characteristically Unexpected last-minute edict — that she would stay overnight and Damn the Survival Alert — the level came down to 1.

And then there were none.

For the first time in the coded life he could remember, Grainger felt that he was down to nothing but himself. When he volunteered to refill Freda's Prozac, to escape Mags — her classic "Damn the Survival" Iron Lady performance banished his doubts raised at Church about her eyebrows — Wallers gave him a lift via one of Pitcairn's armored Rovers. The Company provided a generic stand-in for the Prozac prescription, but the medic dispensing it had no guarantees. "Same as old Louis in his DT's last week screaming he was the Archbishop of Canterbury's brother before the snakes arrived! Every neuron's different. She may stay as she is, or become Lady Macbeth and the Queen of Sheba."

"Fucking them both with a dildo," Wallers added. "She grabbed a double-header plus batteries when she swiped the porn video. We've removed the Veep Suite carving knives. If she turns into Cleopatra, Lord Bobbit can check his own asps in the bed. The last thing we need is Mad Cow. My advice, Drop a double dose of pills in her Pekoe and waltz her back on the Cross." Wallers dodged a cubic yard of fallen rock tossed into the road from the last quake, and said, "This isn't the ideal time to add to your baby-sitting problems, but since we're getting close to an every man for himself situation, as one Old School Tie to another, before you stick your neck out to save His Lordship's, you ought to know the fingerprints we took for the Veep Suite lock came back this morning, and Bowman isn't Bowman."

The Rover's kangaroo-catcher ploughed between two more wheel-high boulders. Grainger's initial surprise about the fingerprints was mixed with a nagging chagrin that spy talent with a Big T wouldn't

431

have been fooled by lordly bullshit for so long, but at least he could totally ignore it from now on.

"If you're worrying about your paycheck," Wallers said, "you don't have to. The real Bowman's still paying his bills, just staying out of circulation in Buenos Aires while he gets over plastic surgery. I guess it's what the Book Biz means by Vanity Publishing. The guy you've been nurse-maiding is a hired double who used to do Pre-owned Jag commercials."

The Rover let him off at the Veep Suite's door. Grainger looked at the Pitcairn pharmacy label on Freda's prescription and wondered if Wallers' Old School helping hand had also terminated the geologist Louis / De Cosmos down a Borneo rat hole where there really were poisonous snakes at the bottom?

In the here and now moment of entering the Suite, there was the immediate question of how to handle his fraudulent employer. As though nothing had changed: a decision made trivially simple by the non-Bowman announcing, "We can forget these Frog Tests in Mororea. Vulkan's Number Two in Volcanoes showed me their computer model which has Big Tit staying dormant for the Third Millennium. Getting the ore out only takes a couple of years at the rate the diggers are chucking shit in Cyanide Alley, and the fabulous news for a Sequel — a chain of gold Tits runs right down the guts of New Guinea!"

"What about Freda's prescription?" Grainger asked.

Non-Bowman shrugged. "You can't tell with designer drugs. I found that writing Palace. Do what Knickers says. Trot her back on board to lap dance Doctor Salsa. I'm picking up more Fijian Brio while we finish Chasing for the Booker."

Grainger expected a firestorm from Freya for being forcibly shipped out of Vulkan's Valhalla, but Lady Luck mused quietly on the Company's generic and let him return her to the quarterdeck awning of the last White Empress as a pale shade of the Queen of Sheba.

A sulphorous breeze fluttered the Golden Bull's Horns just below the *Southern Cross's* masthead. The final ten ladder rungs had been marked off like a thermometer to represent the last hundred points of ascent by the Dow. Its lower five were painted red; the upper rungs, still white: only 50 from the Pole!

He deposited Freda into the care of the ship's medical staff, on loan from the Mayo Clinic for the Ten Thousand voyage. In the Antares Lounge beneath Orion's Belt, Quicksilver was first up to the bar.

"This one's on me for losing your gel. Tried to buy you a second chance with her, didn't we Tail Gunner, before our run-in with the Mad Prospector? Even booked her a spot at the Captain's Table in exchange for No Shore Leave while we were at this benighted slag heap, but no joy. Your ladybird flew away home on Qantas for Sydney and points north. Truly sorry Old Boy."

Loco, loco, loco . . .

He would never be free of the madness in letting her go. His argument that it was for her own good would never hold water, even though it was true. He accepted Quicksilver's sympathy with Tanqueray, bought the obligatory return round for the drummer, then asked, "This Mad Prospector run-in — you mean you met Louis at Moresby?"

The bandleader shook some Schweppes bubbles off his RAF moustache. "Here on the slagheap. Having a chin-chin with the Last of the Cannibals before your Fletcher Christian's crowd clapped him in irons after church."

The company of studs and broads,
Of dandies, cops and cons . . .

Tango's language was straightforward. Betrayal, sex and death: the facts of life. He was sick of the never-ending Old Boys' oblique backhanders, of Spy Nanny's understated Adam-and-Eve catastrophes with hidden numbers, of a phony Lord Bum's openly arsewiped names — coarsely nickered references to people and places which required a lifetime of deception to decode. And even then, even now, when a man's heart was broken, kept him still playing along to the same old spy tune of Elgar's forlorn hope for misplaced glory.

He said casually to the drummer, as though it was the last thing on his mind, "Tell me more about Louis and Olie getting arrested."

"More like Laurel and Hardy at the Old Folks Home. Some pidgin hassle about Big Tit bilong Gold Mountain. All Greek to me, man. Then Chief Heavy Bugger Wallers breaks it up with his Uzi. Last I see is Methusalah's beard flapping out of the rear turret of a Pitcairn paddy wagon as we hit the Assay Shed."

Whose latest rumour of the ore's purity raised Brio fever to a high enough temperature for a Gold Diggers' Dance that evening aboard the *Southern Cross*. This ball's costume theme was Mythras. Doctor Salsa, half-dressed as the Sun God, cited broken contracts to get Grainger to attend.

"You'll never Host again out of Miami if you don't," Avar threatened in the broken-kneecap accent of New Jersey. "And no Miami means no Love Boats. Think about that."

Dawson-Harris had deeper worries. "These rumours about the volcano's signs of life? Blame it on being gun shy after our pummice brush with Montserrat — but I have five hundred lives to think of and it takes time for the old girl to raise steam. I'd be grateful for any Company hard word of early warning."

In Wallers' world a Captain's gratitude still carried the force of Old Boy law: and despite a world of deception on every human level, Grainger still had Pam and *Vanity Fair* as a layer of cover. He turned his attention to the Tail Gunner's story of Methusalah's Beard and thought about Olie's *tumara golong* invitation to a turkey shoot.

The day before tumara, the Dow ticked in a Holding Pattern, counting out the chicken-hearted beneath the flag of Mythras. As the Company and US Geological Survey computers predicted, Mount Le Breton didn't erupt, but a first faint wisp appeared at its summit. Non-Bowman stood at his mock Battle of Britain Desk in the Veep Suite, pretending to fight the forces of darkness under the steam plume, and a Churchillian black cloud about De Cosmos and the Assays.

"Even shagging five wives at eighty, the old fucker can't need two days sleep. Knickers is deliberately keeping him out of sight down a Portapotty. You stay ashore and dig. I'm moving the Desk to the boat to be on the safe side — for historical value."

Grainger had spy-leveled his way through every quake-proofed prefab on the island, wondering about Wallers dropping De Cosmos down deep dark holes: he hadn't leveled the Diggers' latrines.

Primitives had their own obsessions. Like Mary's little lamb, Olie and Great-Grandson followed him from the Company Kindergarten's toilet (pissing it up with Wallers at the Rec Centre) to the Company Store's, and wherever else he tried to answer calls of nature unobserved. Pitcairn's black-tinted Rovers couldn't care less, but every time he stopped to pee Those Eyes fixed on him through the clay. When he shook off the last drop of Fosters all he got from Olie was more, "Plis T'd'i." He said in blunt English, "I'm not —"

"Plis T'd'i."

He took another aspirin to combat Aduarit made worse by a Richter 7, then slashed to Pam. *Waiting for the Big Tsunami just became an academic question, standby for Great Escape logistics: Yours seriously unrattled.* To want his hand held on-line was understandable but irrational. Manhattan could do nothing to help Le Breton Island except keep up his pretence of cover for which nobody else gave a damn.

"Tsunami low risk" was the Pacific Warning Centre's educated guess. Escape logistics were simple arithmetic: the So Cross already had a complement of 500 drop-ins from Contentment, plus Lord False God and the re-embarked phony Churchill Desk to be saved for mock-history. The closest Chinook chopper on the Big Island could carry fifty at a time. In compliance with Murphy's Law, its main rotor was fried. Even repaired, there were a thousand in the Digging crew, plus a handful of Them. The round trip took five hours. If Big Tit roared . . .

Vulkanology still insisted, "Never happen!" and pointed to gentle Richter readings from the peak.

Dawson-Harris kept his head firmly at sea level. "We might ride out large tidal waves beyond the thousand-fathom line. Inshore, a giant tsunami would drive my vessel against the cliffs and crack her like an egg. Passengers' complacency never ceases to amaze. None of the rats like His Lordship are in a rush to leave a ship anchored fore and aft to a mountain of gold. I only spill this down the hawse because you're Ex-Silent Service. For God's sake don't quote me."

"Fact," said Lord-still-a-Rat, from the riveted safety of his Larry & Viv Suite, with the lovers' signed Hollywood glossies on its mahogany door: "A couple of stray farts from Withering Heights means fuck all making Gone with the Wind. Do you really think a company the size of Vulkan is going to sink its Caterpillar teeth up to their anuses in piles of limestone rubbish? Every deep breath we take, the diggers strip ten tons of overburden. More important, De Cosmos is awake. According to Freda's sickbay attendant, Knickers tipped the old shit out of his Portapotty long enough for an enema, which must mean twenty ounces added to the Assays. Hop ashore and keep looking."

Grainger hopped back to Spy Nanny's Field Rules for Who do we save in a Cuban Missile Crisis? and went after the stray warheads one fart at a time.

"It's rare in the extreme to find super-rich ore in a pyroplastic cone like Le Breton's," Vulkan's Geology Number Two told him. "But not out of the question. Now let me ask you one: are we talking Real Life, or just for Lord Bum's novel?"

Wall Street also had the jitters. Mythras battling the Bears produced up-and-down scales on the ship's bullhorn.

When do we burst the Bubble?

Wallers had gone mum. Pitcairn's black Security choppers took off around the clock, stuffed with Geiger counters and seismometers. If De Cosmos was out of his PortaPotty he was still Para incommunicado. The dark side of Big Tit's nipple had to be the last remaining spot for Pitcairn Gestapo to keep him hidden from the visiting shareholders. And the bottom two-thirds of the dark side was also submerged in shit-sludge. Crazy as Grainger's process of elimination seemed, the only place left for Louis on Le Breton was the top of the slag heap.

Which meant a Smoked Tumara trip with Olie to the crater.

// APPOCALYPSE NOW AROUND THE CORNER! He slashed the rest of his ThinkPadded getaway plans to Pam in the laid-back-level language that Cheltenham's spy-finishing school taught:

> **From: // punch me not @ williamstown**
> Being of sound mind — A testament to My
> Fair Sony capability. It's solid-state,
> not tape. If for show business beyond our
> control I can't slash "live," play any
> multimedia bits remaining through your
> ThinkPad and it'll nametag the voices **
> in **TEXT boldly.** Mine first. eg:
> **ME:** Vanity of vanities ...
> Rumbling volcanoes bring out the
> Ecclesiastes in even a vocal-simulation of
> the ghost behind the man.
>
> ** Most of **BUM's //cast** are in there.
> Sometimes he's tagged **GOD,** depending how
> sensitive the machine is feeling; **DAWKERS**
> is Captain of the So Cross — sometimes
> it adds **HARRIS,** and **KNICKERS** is Wallers.
> **QUICKSILVER** is usually himself but also
> **DON QUIXOTE.** If Sony doesn't know the
> voice it uses *NK.* In moments of hi-tek

```
confusion — like mine, yesterday when I
actually thought for a moment that MAGS
might be an imposter! — when text goes to
pot it cuts out the hash[###].***
***Tag this:
```
AN AMUSING AFTERTHOUGHT
```
If it senses a quote or hysterical
laughter in moments of extremis it should
add [+itals] !
```

Only something as crass as Public Relations would spin the Quicksilver Quartet ashore to cheer up Vulkan's landlocked troops while their Chief Executive and his close-shaved Popsie fled the quarterdeck in the last getaway flight by Otter before an earth-shattering Richter 8.1 wiped out the takeoff strip that Sunday night.

Only a biblical God of vengeance could arrange to have Randy Karaoke rehearsing next door in the Veep Suite, where a traitor-lover — Grainger — trying to find comfort in Arolas's bleak Street of Farewells, was force-fed Jerome Kern's and Oscar Hammerstein's over-ripened Tin Pan Alley version of Could I Forget You?

. . . Or will my heart remind me,
That once, we walked in a moonlit dream . . . ?

The South Pacific moon was there, outside his quake-proof window, but Holly wasn't. And from that look in her green eyes after their last crippled tango on the tarmac in Port Moresby, she never would be, even if Spy Nanny's dice miraculously rolled him out of this Black Hole in the corner of the Rim of Fire.

. . . Or will my heart remind me,
How sweet you made the moonlight seem . . . ?

The Roulette chambers of his heart were overloaded by a lip-synching micro-spy who only knew the pony-tailed key of F-for-fukfuk-foxtrot in a nasal tenor. It reminded him of that milonguero moment of *la Cara de la Luna,* when Holly trusted him enough to offer herself like a dream on the face of the moon, the private perfection of her body ogled by a lizard.

. . . Will the glory of your nearness fade
As moonlight fades in a veil of rain . . . ?

The moon didn't fade. It blacked out in a cloudburst. He walked through it anyway. And still the words pursued him: because of the

Karaoke echo between the raped Tits he was haunted.

> *. . . When every night reminds me,*
> *How much I want you back again.*

The clouds parted in a swirling figure-eight pattern to torture him with the *Tanti Anni Prima* Piazzolla ochos he had lost. The stars of heaven's Southern Cross shone with the crystal purity of Holly's oboe. The mountain slept like the Chicken Walkers in the Rec Centre after the Rave blast of disco and six-packs of Fosters drove the Diggers, and a passing Judas-spy, out of their skulls to find nirvana in a slag heap.

Con Brio

Seventeen

Halfway up a plugged volcano . . . Mida's golden line across the valley was almost at Grainger's eye height. Another five hundred feet of limestone precipice had been leveled by the Caterpillar diggers since Lord Not-God's arrival by Otter on the Island. The roar of Diesels echoed non-stop between the twinned cliffs. A former plateau lay bleeding from solutions of tropic rain with enough arsenical waste to kill Napoleon's Grand Army. On the volcano's flank the last fringe of Casuarina trees wouldn't stand much longer. "*The waste engulfs them from below,*" Holly had italicised in her green PalmNotes. "*Each Typhoon tears the upper ones away. The Archetypal Trunks get left behind like Easter Island giants waiting for their last storm.*"

It could be a description of his guide. The Headman still wore only his penis gourd for the climb. His great grandson had on the no-longer white shorts from church, and shirt (minus the feetless socks), and carried a small leather satchel over his shoulder. Already the altitude above the trees affected breathing but, as the group pace was determined by a four-year-old, Grainger didn't find their ascent difficult. Olie had the hardest going; arthritis, not temperature, freeze-locked his ancient joints and bones. He gave no hint of pain, or any other emotion, when he said at a tight corner,

"Rot bilong T'r'ki, emgo showim misis Nor's'vlt."

Language was a barrier, not a survival aid. When Grainger asked, "Tok isi, Olie. Eleanor Roosevelt okay. Wanem Turkey exactly?" he received a rheumatic wave reminiscent of the Animal Crackers priest in the Jamestown graveyard on Saint Helena.

"Lak Looi!"

Like Louis. Could the geologist truly be the dead priest's brother? Olie's eyes, fixed on him as usual, provided no rational answer. He wanted to ask the child a practical question — did he have a water bottle in his satchel? — but couldn't. First, the little boy was mute: he hadn't sung a note in church. Second, Grainger didn't know the great grandson's name and a Headman wouldn't reveal it without the right magic. The Moresby Museum Diorama associated S-for-Silence in Holly's PalmNote italics with "*Stealing the pre-puberty Spirits of Our*

Side before they're old enough to protect themselves from the Other Side's Spells." That didn't quench his thirst. He asked Olie directly, "Mebbe drink?" All he got to satisfy it was a hand-wave hint of once-regal impatience.

At least the air was pleasant. With the land at full afternoon heat, a breeze from the ravaged plain swept upwards over the volcano's cone to be cooled by convection to the temperature of an English spring. Ten thousand feet by rough estimate, and they had to get back before dark.

"Olie, ples i liklik o longwe yet?"

"Ples i liklik klostu."

There was no "place" except an old lava flow "close-to." The anchored *Southern Cross* was a longwe-off white dot. Through binoculars, the golden flag of Mythras was only four red rungs short of the Dow's Y2K advance towards the Pole.

"Boneeya!"

The shadow of a vulture swept overhead. Olie grasped his great grandson's shoulder. In Holly's PalmNotes under V, "Le Breton Vultures (see, Raptors = Represent the coming of a god) supposed to be extinct." With no italics.

The mountain moved.

Olie ignored it. His four-year-old descendant hitched up his school satchel and kept learning to follow a Smoked Man's spirit path the hard way, in silence. Grainger tried to block Spy Nanny's Aduarit drawl in his head. "Adam-and-Eve and Philby find a live Hydrogen Bomb on Christmas Island: Who do we save?" . . . but the blocking attempt brought no success. The dead bomb beneath them all kept ticking.

At twelve thousand arthritic feet — four thousand meters, judging from the melt line — Vulkan's empire was Lilliput: Dinky Toy Diggers and Matchbox Company Stores for adults to play havoc with while five-hundred others gambled on a toy boat with no safe harbour. The kid still didn't say a word, or seem scared by the height.

"Lukatim gut!" Olie warned.

A good look showed the first ice. Only in patches, but four bare feet were going to be frozen unless the old man knew how to reverse the Fijian Fire Walkers' trick. It was near enough to the top to see the crater's lip. Yellow-crusted from sulphur, which meant a hell of a lot more gas escaping than Vulkan's spin doctors of geology let on.

More movement.

Nothing compared with the last — but comparison got odious when fissures opened to release snake-hissing jets of scalding sulphur dioxide between a child's toes.

Thirteen-thousand feet: the great-grandson pointed soundlessly. Wisps of white steam issued from the toy ship's funnel. In Spy Nanny's library it would have been a Boy's Own Adventure signal for Pompeii or Dunkirk. Escape by sea! *Adam and Eve and Pliny plus half the British Army. Who do we save?*

Grainger said, "New Year's countdown in Times Square," to the Sony, for Pam's jaded consumers of up-market eye-liner and wrist-Swatches. "The Dow's about to make ten thou. The sound won't reach us for five seconds —" *Four, three, two* . . . Carried on the upward wind, the siren notes of Wall Street madness arrived.

"Huh huh."

A sound more cough than laugh issued from Olie's gut in harmony with the siren. Which stopped. Through binoculars, the gilt-horned bull retreated down the masthead ladder. Mythras hadn't made it after all.

"Hee hee."

Olie was definitely laughing. An emotion not supposed to happen with an uncrackable clay face. Afraid that the joke was altitude sickness, Grainger asked the old man: "Im go haha. Wot is?"

Olie clutched his great-grandson as he had when a supposedly extinct vulture cast a shadow, and pointed a black-purple index finger at the diggers' devastation across Cyanide Valley. "Im no gol."

The child nodded solemnly.

Grainger still tried for rationality in a world where everyone Chasing Brio was nuts.

"No gold yet, Olie. Digger imgo deeper."

"Nogol evah, T'd'i!"

The toy Caterpillars were halfway to the Island's bowels.

"Im tru, T'd'i. Digger im rong Tit."

Nothing could be true or go right for a Last Nose Bone's Aduarit. Even if the Assays had been inflated five-hundred percent by an invisible Louis De Cosmos, for as little as three ounces per ton Vulkan would dig to the dark side of the moon. He switched off his Sony link to New York and snapped at Olie. "Fo lastime getit! Mino goddamn Teddy!"

The mountain shrugged its head and shoulders . . . dismissing Vulkan and the Dow like the Bull of Mythras with a gnat.

Con Brio
Eighteen

INDING HIMSELF AND THE SONY STILL ALIVE RESTORED GRAINGER'S faith in technology: the digital wafer was as much a talisman as the resurrected vulture. For his last mile of Mount Le Breton, talking to Pam in New York, even at satellite-remote second-hand, let him believe in faint hope.

Getting Holly back.

Loco loco loco . . . The volcano had stopped shrugging but sulphur jets hissed everywhere. Truck-load chunks of frozen lava liberated by steam tumbled from the summit. The child's bare feet would have been crushed or scalded twice, if he hadn't lifted the boy clear.

"Clay-faced Great Granddad seems oblivious, doing his Trance of the Fire Walkers snail crawl to God knows where." he told Pam. "Things are heating up too much for a kid. I'll stick with Olie as far as the ledge below the lip, then leave the boy and go the last bit alone."

"Nagat pik'nini! Wil'm imgo T'rk'i lak cum Boneeya Tee Dee!"

A pumice tumbler the size of a Volkswagen Beetle almost blocked out the mute descendant — suddenly allowed a public name.

"Howcum pikinini nom William?" he asked the old man.

"Pikini Wil'm lak be Boss Vulkan."

Holly's Palm-reading from the Museum verified the fact, "It was common practice to take the names of White Kings and Queens for role-model protection to replace the ancestors when the old Aduarit magic faded."

"Turkey."

Another Aduarit conjuring trick: Olie's grandson wasn't mute; he spoke English, the Museum's "lingua franca of the Cargo Cult invaders." And then the hat trick: a miracle-monument to Nose-Bone faith. In the face of utter destruction down below, a hundred feet above Grainger's head, wing by wing, strut by strut, the T-for-Turkey wreckage of a Grumman Avenger had been re-assembled where it once crash-landed. "A kid's model-building act that must have taken a platoon of men," he told Pam.

"Mi do im." Olie said.

One antique arthritic? Grainger couldn't buy it. The airframe's restitution was even more complete than the original. SAPOS BALUS I BAGGARUP Black Box Disaster instructions had been painstakingly hand-lettered in red, yellow, and white clay on the buggered-up Turkey's tail. "Smoked Magic offers a moment of Shared Wonder for our Western hearts and minds to Learn and Heal," Moresby's Museum lectured Lonely Planet visitors: "On no account break the Shaman's spell."

Grainger saw him.

A hunched figure, shivering with cold and chained with stainless-steel handcuffs to a ringbolt in the Avenger's reassembled bomb-bay door. A prisoner with an Anglo-refined face as old as the rice-papered Vicar of Animal Crackers who died in Grainger's arms — with the same features above a Methuselah beard, but leathered by gin-tanned decades of tropic sun.

"*Boneeya Tee Dee.*" Olie touched his clay head to the rock; a universal gesture of worship in the presence of a ghost. *Teddy God Louis De Cosmos. Finder or Salter of Brio's gold?*

Wallers chose that moment of shared wonder to come around the mountain. A helicopter's throbbing roar of rotors smashed the shaman's spell.

"Lie flat! It's going into hover!"

Grainger grabbed the child. The chained figure cowered under the Turkey's fuselage. Olie sat cross-legged, phlegmatic on a Fire Walker's bed of fuming lava.

Pitcairn's black-tinted helo had armed with rapid-fire cannons. Its hatch slid open. Wallers jumped down and shouted some query at the prisoner. The prospector shook his head, and got an Uzi butt between his ears. Louis's semi-conscious body was uncuffed and tossed into the chopper. Wallers and Pitcairn's cannons lifted off again.

Staring after that tortured Anglo face, for no reason he could fathom except giddiness from altitude or gas, the fracture in Grainger's heart caused by losing Holly spread to his mind. He just lay there on the rocks: one half of him holding the boy, the other watching Olie. An insane old man preparing to ascend the last nearly-precipitous incline using already-positioned ropes.

Enough for a spy to hang himself?

"Nylon parachute harness," he said to the Sony. "More Avenger relics. The harness still has the packer's tag from Pensacola — fifty years!

It looks sound enough to take us our last mile. Only thirty meters, but on this north side the lava wall is permanent sheet-ice." He switched from New York to tell the child, "William first," then took the boy's hand.

Rumble . . .

Bulging, like Mount St Helen's in Holly's entry under V-for-volcano. No one is saved. This is the way Spy Nanny's world ends.

It didn't. The monster fell back in its lair. Third-time-luki, he and the boy were on the ledge. The Avenger loomed over them. From below, it had seemed another toy. Close-up, from ledge to cockpit, Grumman's restored killing machine was twice Grainger's height. Almost three of Olie's. "Le Breton's equivalent of Mount Rushmore. He's propped the underbelly with wood — every stick carried up this slope! — so its wheels once again have a Turkey's scrawny legs."

The prop blades had been hammered with a stone club, now lying below the nose, into a semblance of straight. To reach the cockpit a crude ladder of Casuarina strapped with vines leaned against the reattached right wing. Grainger still couldn't believe one old Bone flew the wings up here single-handed with a penis gourd.

"Olie," he said, "yu T'rk'i kago im bilong hevi ten-ten man!"

"Tenkyu."

Geology trumped primitive modesty. The steam at the summit plumed into a rolling black cloud obscuring the last hundred meters. A steady shower of unseen pebbles rattled machinegun fire against the crater's inner rim.

"Wil'm yu mas givim Ol'i kago plis."

"The boy's taken off the cargo school satchel and given it to his great grandfather," Grainger advised Pam. "I'm looking for some quick way down but running on a sheet-iced pitch of one-in-two means vertical free-fall."

Olie removed the satchel's contents. Papers. A small bottle.

"And a video cam?" Grainger said. "Whyfor?"

"Misis Nor'svlt yu tak em plis."

Olie handed him the bottle; an in-flight miniature of Mumm's Champagne labeled, "Courtesi AirNiuGini."

"Yumi drinkim?" Grainger asked.

"Nagat dringim. Misis Nor'svlt bangim bot'l lakam poto." Olie passed him the papers.

Grumman Avenger Year 1944 Serial No. 10,000

A flight log. Its front page registered the aircraft, and acknowledged receipt from the manufacturer. A cracked, assembly-line photo below registration explained re-incarnation.

The First Lady, Mrs. Eleanor Roosevelt,
commissioning "Turkey" 10,000!

"Mumms the word." He sent that bad pun to Pam to ward off the next extremis moment from the mountain, and prepared to crack Air Niugini's mini-magnum over the reassembled Turkey's nose.

"Nogat!" Olie shook his clay mask. "Nogat mi go kokpit lakem Tee Dee." The Headman placed a final piece of paper in his great-grandson's hand, then asked Grainger to interpret. "Yu rid fo Anglis plis?"

"This document is a copy of the original grant for mineral rights to Vulkan on Le Breton Island."

"Em i hamas tamaras, plis?"

"How many tomorrows is it good for? The original term says ninety-nine years —"

"Nanty-nan, yes. Lakam Duk Dev'n'sha."

"Mi nosee the Duke of Devonshire, Olie, but em mortage im bilong gudfo — what's eighty?"

"Etpela ten yars." The old man nodded in apparent satisfaction and turned again to his great-grandson. "Wil'm yugo bilong man, bilong meri, bilong pikinin, bilong man, bilong meri, bilong pikinini all call im T'd'i Wil'm."

The boy's eyes widened but the prize was hollow. "Olie's just passed the mineral rights from generation to generation until Vulkan's term expires," Grainger relayed to Pam. "A mountain of sweet fuck all for a vanished island of descendants."

"Nogat gold imgo Vulkan. Im bilong Bon'y'a'T'd'i Wil'm!"

"I don't get this one, Olie. An hour ago you said there was No Gold."

Pitcairn's death chopper appeared again around the mountain. Primitive faith in the *Aduarit* spirit gods of the ancestors was no match against the Twenty-First Century machine force Vulkan massed above and below them.

"Hee hee. Small Tit false. Im gold real here."

Olie gave another coughing last-laugh, pointed at the cyanide carnage from the limestone stump across the valley, stamped twice on the mountain's cone-breast beneath his bare feet, placed a hand on his great-grandson's head in a wordless blessing, then, using the Casuarina ladder, climbed the last few arthritic steps required to place him in the Avenger's cockpit.

"Bon'y'a T'd'i bok plis."

Grainger put it in the old man's hand. The Grumman Flight Log returned to its final resting place. Seeing a naked figure with its white-clay mask staring at infinity through emptiness — even Smoked Magic couldn't restore vanished Plexiglas — Grainger felt inexpressible sadness for something so hopelessly pathetic.

"Kikim bloks."

He kicked away two chunks of Casuarina from the perished tires. What he saw beneath them knocked aside his mental last spy level.

Two gold streaks glittered in the lava under the Turkey's wheels. Judged against the pig's intestines cores laid out in the Assay Shed, he estimated ten ounces of unsalted white-veined quartz to each flat tire. Making twenty overall! A gleam of infinite triumph flashed in a great grandfather's eye.

"Wil'm takim poto."

The child pointed the minicam waveringly at the resurrected aircraft on its newfound golden altar.

"Now T'd'i bangim misis Nor's'vlt Mumms plis."

Grainger stopped fighting the Names War. He raised the bottle.

"Fuck out of the way. We're coming in!"

More bullhorn obscenity from Wallers. Pitcairn's death-hover sequence repeated. Guns and dust. Anglo-Empire faces in the hatch. The agonised one was Louis.

"Tell us you lying old shit! Is the gold here on Big Tit or do we shoot your sonny boy in the balls?"

He didn't mean the child. Or Olie. Neither of them were hostages to Fortune. Wallers held a tight-rolled copy of the magazine. In a practice borrowed from SAS soft torture for the Hard Men of Northern Ireland, pressed across the back of a captive's neck to arch the spine, it forced the prospector's face into the dust thrown up by the rotors. The ashen face of an aristocrat, not a phony Bowman's half-life peerage, stared point-blank at Grainger. So did the chopper's twenty-millimeter barrels.

"Boneeya." Olie bowed from the cockpit. First to Wallers' victim. Then to Grainger, "Nu T'd'i. Im tru."

New or old, in that instant it *was* true. In the agonized features of Louis, nickered by Bowman as De Cosmos, he saw his own origins from the Big Lie.

I, Stuart Grainger, am Looi-Tedi's sonny boy.

Wallers arched the victim's backbone into the shape of a Stone Age bow in the Moresby Museum. "For the second-last time of asking! Who goes first: Father, Son, or Holy Ghost —?"

SAS paras never play Blind Man's Bluff. Grainger realised another starkly simple truth: Wallers had let him wander up here to the lunatic asylum because he was the hostage who would lead Pitcairn to the gold. Human decency said he should tell them, *It's hidden under the Turkey,* in exchange for the old man's life. Mission duty said, Only tell Rufus, in Dallas. Cannon bursts shattered the rock beside his left hip. Then his right. Pumice shrapnel slashed his honest-tourist Tilley shorts and hat. One arm and leg were bleeding. It didn't hurt, yet. But it would.

"This is your final —!"

The prospector's spine was going to snap. And now the physical pain came for Grainger. The mental was worse. He tried not to show either. Not well enough. The tortured face in the hatch relieved him of the burden. Trapped between Saving and Losing the Treasure . . . just like all Nanny's bedtime spy stories of Adams-and-Eves . . . De Cosmos, or Louis, or latter-day Jesus Christ who conned the Mormons, made his decision who to save.

His thin lips mouthed first, "Gold" then, "here." The cannon-fire stopped. Pitcairn's chopper lifted off in triumph for Wallers the butcher's boy to proclaim the Real Mother Lode. Dirk-the-tango-traitor had served his malevo purpose as an Anglican Judas goat.

This is my blood I shed for thee . . .

Not knowing what he was doing . . . *Those things we have done we ought not to have done* . . . he smashed the mini-bottle of Mumms as a Black Sabbath atonement for his betrayal that saved Holly.

Bubbles foamed on Turkey 10,000's nose, then dripped to the ice. He put his good arm around the child, and called to the ancient figure waiting in the cockpit for some *Aduarit* spirit destiny unfathomable:

"Stap gut, Boneeya Olie. Go well to Teddy Frum."

A butcher-boy bellowed above him, "Crooked old fucker — your number's up anyway!" A bearded human figure plummeted from the chopper.

Our Father which art in Hell. A fucker with my face!

The face behind a mother's lie so tiny that it no longer mattered. The body and blood of De Cosmos vanished into the reborn molten maw of the volcano. Whether it truly hid the paternal DNA that all a son's spy levels sprang from . . . ?

The only honest answer was the rattle of pebbles in the crater. And still no further rumble from the mountain. Instead, beneath Grainger's feet as he descended, he felt a continuing, tremulous, lightly-orgasmic, shivering. It was so slight, yet all-encompassing, that it raised every hair on his neck. The child's beating heart fluttered against his wounded arm like a fledgling sparrow kicked out of the nest.

Animals know when the Big One's coming.

The sulphur jets switched off. Which was good — until he remembered the Rim-of-Fire expert saying in Port Moresby, "the gas stopping leads to Krakatoa." But offsetting the Experts, Holly had told him, "Mount St Helen's took weeks — "

He and the boy were back at the ledge with the nylon parachute harness-lines for the steepest part of the descent. In the hour that had passed, the tropical glacier had crept down again even faster to cover Olie's gold. Grainger was eye-level once more with the truncated-limestone pillar of worthless salt across Cyanide Valley.

If this happens to Global Warming at the equator, he thought, to block out the Big Question Mark behind him, *what price Gus Rufus and Dow Jones avoiding the next Ice Age?*

Loco queries. His Level Four client only paid him a small-t's wages to burst Tumara's Market bubble. The bleeding from his arm and leg had stopped. Even if the pain hadn't, Spy Nanny's motto for Punch-me-Not's survival was No Second Thought after Mission Accomplished.

Save the child and win Holly.

It came to him without thinking. He just knew that if he salvaged this last one of Holly's banished *Them*, she would come back. "I'll go first," he said to the boy. "When I'm steady with the line, put your arms around my neck." He slung the video cam, with its proof of Louis's murder and Le Breton Island's real Brio, over his free shoulder. "We've made the rough part," he advised Pam in Manhattan, through Sony. "The rest of the way it's plain sailing, slash . . . "

/////

/////

/////

/////

/////

/////

/////

/////

ME:

[###+itals] *E is for Epilogue to an Enigma* [###]
getting stitched up while [###] extracting
moments of lucidity from stark panic [###]
Choking on fumes [###] from Ring of Fire
Web sites [###]

NK:[Not Known]

Here at News Central in Atlanta [###]
Experts now predict [###] almost certainly
[###] catastrophic [###] possibly imminent
[###] than Krakatoa [###] drop in the Dow
[###] no relation to Brio rumor biggest-
ever mining scam [###]

ME:

Computer charts confirm worst case [###]
Franklin D. Roosevelt carrier still a
day's steaming to salvage Mags' book tour
[###]

DAWKERS:

Can't hazard my own vessel any longer.
We've already embarked an extra three
hundred [###] exceeding the life boats'
capacity could cost [###]

MAGS:

Utter drivel [###] to introduce myself except

to say the Lady's obviously **not** for
Burning **[###]** until my book tour **[###]**
Island Story **[###]** can't be over **[###]**
a Tsunami's no *excuse* **[###]** Whoever's
responsible for this *travesty* **[###]**

ME:

I knew when she looked at the penis gourd
[###]

MAGS:

Man's a complete **Wet!**[###+itals]

VOICE PRINT MAGS = FALSE ID

DAWKERS-HARRIS:

Madam, whatever your name is**[###]** consider
yourself under arrest **[###]** Quartermaster,
place this Lady in irons **[###]**

NK:

Shareholders deserve to be told **[###]**
trying to round up every helicopter in
the South Pacific in time for the Quarterly
[###]

ME:

Tail-spinning bullshit from Vulkan **[###]**
the rotor on the nearest Chinook at the
Grasberg mine in Iryan Jaya is still fried
and **[###]** the So Cross left minus Yours
Sincerely under the operating table **[###]**
with flag of Mythras still flustered at
half mast as corks popped to drown the Dow
[###]sole bright spot in this darkness at
[###] Nanny's favourite High Noon **[###]**
Nitrous Oxide **[###]** Laughing gas Coral-
stranded with Olie's kid and last Loony
Tune of Empire to have missed the boat
[###]

DON QUIXOTE:

Not too up on nautical numbers except
Pinafore but brought along the mouth
box **[###]** bit late for Polishing the
Handle **[###]** a few bars of the Light
Fantastic**[###]**

NK:

Quote, Thermal Inactivity was always reported by Company as quote Relative **[###]**

ME:

Spin-doctoring accompanied by now-constant
tympanic rumble from the patient's guts
[###+itals] *The Volcano knows* **[###]** so did
Olie. Moment of Fact, Pam: On Bligh
Island, fifty miles away, while digging
for calcite, layers of volcanic ash now
show Mount Le Breton has a three-thousand-
year Off, eighty-year On cycle — plus or
minus ten per cent. If the terror factor
had gone Plus, instead of **[###+itals]** *Ifs
and Ands* **[###]** Olie's know-how of Big Tit's
feminine cycle is lost forever in the
mists of Our Side **[###]** traditions swept
away like Boundary Road and the dancing
Kree **[###]** by Darwin's ruthless **[###]**
Blitzkrieg of history doesn't matter **[###]**
if magma pressure eases and the lava stops
for another three millennia **[###]** the real
gold will still be there when the mortgage
has run out **[###]** a Primitive beats Vulkan
at the Duke's game of monopoly **[###+itals]**
Gaia just shrugged her shoulders **[###]**
Goddess Mother of the Planet ain't amused
but for someone raised from Chaos, the
old bitch **[###]** Freda got charged with
attempted murder **[###]** stabbing Bum with
his own penis gourd **[###]** as accessory to
Wallers killing Teddy De Cosmos **[###]** the
whole island just lifted! **[###]** a Monster
Explosion
[######################+itals]

/////

/////

/////

But around it is cast like a mantle [###] rock of
ages past [###] no hope for us on dry
land [###] moving by instinct common to
Leatherneck Turtles and Flying Dutchman's
[###] grandson in my arms [###] plus
his minicam and Vulkan flashlight [###]
last blind run at a stab in the dark
[###+itals] *Mother of the Free* [###] sound bytes
of Elgar [###]

QUICKSILVER:

Lost my Tail Gunner. Mind if I hum along?
[###] Run Rabbit Run seems apropos [###]

ME:

We always came last in the Three Legged
race with Panda [###] wearing our Bunny
Suit [###] Rabbit lost the Egg and Spoon
[###] Laughing Gas worse than going to the
dentist [###] P and R joining this Mad
Hatter marathon [###]

QUICKSILVER:

How about the Picnic Party [###]

ME:

Putting it on the record [###] Big Tit
had the last laugh. The crater explosion
sent Olie and Avenger into orbit with the
gold [###+itals] *Christ that was only the warm-up*
[###] whole mountain is bulging like [###]
the distance to cliff-edge measured in
yards [###] running over solidified sludge
which turns to jelly [###] for one last
look back [###] Hiroshima rising out of
the crater. Olie is a Smoked Man beyond
his [###] great-grandson once more struck
mute [###+itals] *Jesus she must blow soon* [###]
still bulging. No Bang yet [###] following
instinct through gorge of million butterfly
[###] Vulkan tailings like liquid lemming-
shit over the cliff [###] steps carved
by [###] Other Side's hands [###] down to
nothing more certain than [###] cruising
shadows [###] of Great Hammerheads
[###+itals] *I love you Holly* [###]

QUICKSILVER:
 Bit early for White Christmas **[###]** After
 the Ball is Over? **[###]**

ME:
 Try Knees up Mother Brown **[###]** from
 Graham Greeneland's icy mountain **[###]** the
 coral strand shimmies **[###]**

QUICKSILVER:
 Got it! Like my sister Kate **[###]**

ME:
 Aunt Doodlie had Swiss Family **[###]**
 Robinson Crusoe had a raft **[###]** No
 footprints this damn Friday **[###+itals]** *'Ere!*
 'Ow do we get 'ome? **[###]** End of the World **[###]**
 exit giggling Beyond the Fringe **[###]**
 All Hope abandon. Thank you, Dorothea
 [###+itals] *A little child shall lead them* **[###]** Olie's
 Wil'm pointing **[###]** scrap of faded yellow
 rubber **[###]** hole in cliff wall **[###]**
 Anyone Finding This Life Raft report at
 once to nearest U.S. Navy **[###]**

QUICKSILVER:
 Port in a storm dated Perishable 1947
 [###] One Man Only sounds a bit dodgy
 [###] after you, old son **[###]** All aboard
 [###] isn't quite enough room **[###]** Under
 the apple tree for anyone else but **[###]**

ME:
 I'm a strong swimmer. You hold the boy
 [###] in the raft **[###]** I'll hang on the
 side of **[###]** my Half-Arsed Life **[###]** not
 in Apple-Pie order

 **[##
 #########]**

 the Motherfucker of all Big Bangs

 **[##########+itals###+itals###+###+itals##
 #+itals+??]**

Rumble, Rumble, Rumble I don't want to leave the jungle. Turn
off the wireless *I'm so happy in the jungle* and close
the door if everyone's in the cellar! *Run
Rabbit* — That's another bloody Heinkle. *Run
Rab* — Not down, **off!** No it isn't, not a
Heinkle, that's a bloody Messerschmidt.
What on earth does it matter what's going
over as long as — ? Who's got William? Is
that next door? Charlotte has. No, the
other side, Number 25, thank God. We've
lost the lights. Who's got the candles?
Charlotte hasn't. What are they doing in
Hampstead anyway. I've found him. The
Heath's no use to Jerry they should be
doing the bloody docks. Shine the torch
he's under the stairs! The Germans are
such absolute fools. Please, James,
where's Mummy? I refuse to sing any more
lieder for the Duration. And I can't find
Panda. Not James I'm your father call me
Daddy now you're not William any longer.
I think that's the All Clear. Or Rabbit.
**Christ, that is the other side too. Three
families.** If 21's gone as well we're
left in the middle they're simply bound
to — Where the hell is Charlotte? Out
in the garden with the sand pails, Jim.
Has anyone seen the Colonel? he didn't
have his tin bowler. Someone has to do
the pails for the damn incendiaries, when
you're driving the ambulance, but if
you're going to be hysterical give Willum
to me James. I'm his father I fell in love
and his name isn't — Stupid man, give me
the boy. Come here to Aunt Joan, David,
and we'll sing Brahms **Lullaby and** — That's
across the road! — **goodnight.** Worst bloody
show we've had yet! I don't know about
Jerry Leaders except Adolf Guttersnipe
but Brahms sounds damn Hunnish Mrs.
Cross if you ask — All right everyone,
the Colonel's — Please, has anybody seen

Black Cat? **The whole of bloody Boundary Road — !** *It's all right darling, Black Cat can see in the dark like Panda and Rabbit. Not like us! What the hell possessed 'em to bring a kid back to the trenches at a time like — Oh, are you here Gauer? I'm not David properly, Aunt Joan, I think I'm just a Snod. Where's Mummy? Never mind, precious, we all have our stage names, they're more fun than* **[###+itals]** *Loco loco loco* **[###]**

DON QUIXOTE:
You've finally come round, old chap. Just hang on a minute longer. Mouthbox got waterlogged or I'd give us a **[###]** nasty thump on your noggin **[###]** too much for the So Cross, I'm afraid the tsunami **[###]** another Dunkirk Miracle, our cockleshell surviving **[###]** Panda and Rabbit yarns really kept our peckers up **[###]** Franklin Roosevelt's hove-to as they say **[###]**

NK:
Rescue Team stand by your **[###+itals?]**

ME:
Time gentlemen **[###]** ran out **[###]** and P&R can't change spots **[###]** someone look after my Pair **[###]** He can't let us go now we've **[###]** Prepared one too many Teddy faces **[###]** no question Olie's real **[###]** Max love **[###]** *Last tango with Miss Montana's perfect* **[###]**

NK:
Body to Temporary Morgue in Lower Hangar **[###]**

NK:
Captain Scott speaking **[###]** Media Relations will interface in the Sickbay for Survivors' photo-op at 02:00 **[###]**

NK:

My name is Wil'm, age four. My great grandfather said when I grow up I will be Le Breton Head Chief. Now I am only a small god. Thank you **[###]**

DON QUIXOTE QUICKSILVER:

For a grace note? **[###]** Always spot one of Nanny's **[###]** Fellow flew straight and level **[###]** brought us through **[###]** Good day's work from Old Dirk **[###]** Nice cup of tea **[###]** piece of toast would go down well **[###]** What the Empire was all about, actually **[###]** Keep on to the end of the road. Right tune for the occasion **[###]** like the Century **[###]** and Y2K **[###]** A bunch of twaddle now it's over **[###+itals?]**

/////

/////

/////

/////

Dal Segno

al Coda

A S IT WAS IN THE BEGINNING . . . NO HALF LIFE ADVENTURE TURNS out to be Yours Truly all our own. The line between virtual and actual is blurred by history and technology even as we write. Dearest David's tidal wave of make-believe is no sooner processed on the page than a monster tsunami scythes the Pacific and Indian Oceans to be screened around the world. A scam called Bre-X gives mining a bad name after Darling Willum's first draft of G is for Gold has already aborted -- but which Dear Text Reader is going to fall for that?

One in Australia: out of the wild blue random chaos of the Internet comes black-and-white confirmation of our Brisbane-Le Breton connection. Also, proof that Monsieur Laurillard's friend Freud still hits the nail on the windowsill. Charlie's soured "Old Admiral," the possible Grandfather who refused to allow his son of less than legal age to marry a woman bearing a child out of wedlock ... turns out to have had a dubious first marriage himself! Not recorded in *Tatler*, nor on film for a Wardroom Wedding Album complete with Crossed Swords, which seems evidence enough for a Court Martial that a junior naval officer got a Portsmouth chippy up the stump and didn't want to see Le Breton family history repeated.

And adding financial injury to the physical insult of bastardy, the same Internet source from Down Under is delighted to advise that the Estate of our late Uncle Edward ("Tony" Brisbane Le-B, who denied us our twelve shillings and sixpence after Teddy was shot), was found to include the flag carried by Lawrence of Arabia before he became Peter O'Toole, and that said Flag (somehow acquired by Grandfather as he stood on the sloping deck in that torn photograph circa 1919) has just been peddled at auction by Sotheby's for two hundred thousand pounds Sterling. SOLD to a Royal House of Bedouins to be stuffed in a Palace Toy Cupboard somewhere in the desert.

Panda: *(Worriedly re-incarnated to express habitual Concern)*
"Does that mean He's going to sell
Us as well?"

Rabbit: *(Dourly returned to expect the lop-eared Worst)*
"Who's going to buy one eye and no
fur?"

Owner: *(Finally resigned to Toy quibbles without End)*
"One eye was good enough for
Nelson. We'll dodge Sotheby's and
try on-line with eBay."

Manners maketh man. It doesn't need Aunt Dorothea's Victorian reminder to make us take back a bad joke, in poor taste. A welter of second thoughts in first person plural had already been brought to the surface by that trip down our boyhood's D-Day Memory Lane which kicked off this adult story.

What are yew sinking?

Even Abe's South African sibilant query no longer annoys us when it turns up as one of the ghosts from analysis Couched in our head. We're *thinking* now that the Boy's Own yarn in Victoria's Times-Colonist, was itself triggered by a real journey. Those Beaches in Normandy were the end of an arc which began at Capo Passero, on the south-eastern tip of Sicily. Only one small plaque marks the spot where Operation Husky touched ashore, yet, at its H-Hour, on July 10th, 1943, the assembled Liberating fleets and armies massed for Invasion were larger than those which crossed the English Channel one year later. After June 6th, 1944, the Italian Campaign became the Forgotten Army, or more derisively (by people not worthy to lace up an Infantry boot), the D-Day Dodgers.

In a glorious Italian spring of 2009, starting on Liberation Day, I followed the Dodgers' trail, marked by War Cemeteries across Sicily, through Tuscany, and finally, twenty years after I received its photograph — thanks to the kindness of (Miss) Marjorie Smyte at the Commonwealth War Graves Commission (Enquiries) — to Forli.

Plot 6, Row D, Grave 9.

Miss Smyte's kindness was real, but no photo can prepare you for the reality of Battlefield death. Forli is a small cemetery. A bronze engraving at its entrance states that it contains only *738 burials, of which four are unidentified by name, and by countries they comprise: United Kingdom 526. Canada 7. New Zealand 165. South Africa 30.*

India 8, Pioneer Corps of Southern Africa 1. Seychelles 1.

One of those India (8) was a member of a truly Boy's Own regiment: *Queen Victoria's Own Madras Sappers & Miners.* One of the Canada (7) was from the West Nova Scotia Regiment. *A Soldier of the 1939- 1945 War, Known unto God.*

The Canadian white stones are each marked with a maple leaf. Here and there the stones are capped by a Jewish Star of David. The bases of all the stones rest in flower beds reminiscent of Nan's Cottage English garden: Roses and Catnip (Nan would have called it *Nepeta cataria*) luxuriate in the sunshine of Italian spring. The Catnip was so exuberant that its fronds of purple flowers had hidden an inscription from the lens that took Miss Smyte's photograph of Teddy's grave. The Catnip almost hid it from me.

Only as I dropped to one knee — to place a handful of Tuscan wildflowers among their domesticated cousins — I saw the tops of some extra letters carved beneath the conventional formality of a Military Death. The Rank, the Name, the Regiment, the Date, the Cross.

DEAR SECOND SON

I pulled aside more Catnip … revealing the grief of a parent thought of until this moment as harshly selfish … CAPTAIN H.B. BRISBANE-LE BRETON RN … and his second wife, the mother of Teddy … and finally, so deep in the flower bed that leaves of English Violets which had ceased blooming completely obscured it:

ONE OF THE BEST

I had no way of telling if any other eyes than mine had read the words since the time of their inscription. And so I left him where at last I found him — without DNA testing still none the wiser about the absolute truth of my paternity — but for some intangible reason feeling fairly certain. And on my way to Normandy made another small pilgrimage: first to Antibes (to find for myself *La Residence des Fleurs,* the address that Greene's one-liner had embossed at its letterhead) and then to Hyères to watch the modern high speed launches take school children on ecology outings across to Porquerolles, where Charlie and Nan played beneath the fortress guns.

Pair: (*For once In-Unison*)
  "So it was all true!"
Owner: (*For once inclined to accept Most of It*)
  "Perhaps."

At least, now that our Nursery friends of a lifetime have once more found their voice, they can stay where they belong, next door to Greene's *Ways of Escape*, resting safely between *Pilgrim's Progress* and *The Good Companions* on our bookshelf of the mind.